His Most Exquisite Conquest

ELIZABETH POWER
CATHY WILLIAMS
ROBYN DONALD

D1434109

MILLS

First Published in Great Britain 2016
By Mills & Boon, an imprint of HarperCollins*Publishers*
1 London Bridge Street, London, SE1 9GF

HIS MOST EXQUISITE CONQUEST © 2016 Harlequin Books S. A.

A Delicious Deception, *The Girl He'd Overlooked* and *Stepping out of the Shadows* were first published in Great Britain by Harlequin (UK) Limited.

A Delicious Deception © 2012 Elizabeth Power
The Girl He'd Overlooked © 2012 Cathy Williams
Stepping out of the Shadows © 2012 Robyn Donald Kingston

ISBN: 978-0-263-92063-5

05-0516

Our policy is to use papers that are natural, renewable and recyclable products and made from wood grown in sustainable forests.The logging and manufacturing processes conform to the legal environmental regulations of the country of origin.

Printed and bound in Spain
by CPI, Barcelona

A DELICIOUS DECEPTION

BY
ELIZABETH POWER

Elizabeth Power wanted to be a writer from a very early age, but it wasn't until she was nearly thirty that she took to writing seriously. Writing is now her life. Travelling ranks very highly among her pleasures, and so many places she has visited have been recreated in her books. Living in England's West Country, Elizabeth likes nothing better than taking walks with her husband along the coast or in the adjoining woods and enjoying all the wonders that nature has to offer.

For Alan—
with love and fond memories of Monaco.

CHAPTER ONE

THE tread of confident footsteps echoed across the sun-warmed tiles of the terrace—the tread of a man whose presence spelled danger.

Even without turning around, Rayne guessed who he was and could sense a desire in him to unnerve her.

No, it was more of a determination, she decided, with every cell alert, tensing from the fear of being recognised—an assurance that whatever this man wanted, this man got.

'So you're the little waif my father plucked off the street, who's showing her gratitude by deigning to drive him around.'

She had been looking, from her vantage point through the balconied archway, out over coral-coloured blocks of high-rise apartments, some with roof gardens, others with pools that seemed to throw back fire from the setting sun. But now she ignored the glittering sea, the palace on The Rock and the sun-streaked cliffs that were a feature of this coast—but particularly of this rich man's playground that was Monte Carlo—swinging round instead with her blazing hair falling heavily over one shoulder and her body stiffening from the derisory undertones of the deep English voice.

His clothes were tailored to perfection. And expensive, Rayne decided grudgingly. From his pristine white shirt and dark designer suit, to the very tip of his shiny black shoes. A man whose cool, sophisticated image masked a deceptively ruthless nature and a tongue that could cut with the deftness of a scythe.

For a moment she couldn't speak, stunned by how the years had given him such a powerful presence. Recent newspaper photographs, she realised, had failed to capture the striking quality about him that owed less to his stunning classic features and thick black hair that had a tendency to fall across his forehead than to that breath-catching aura that seemed to surround his tall, muscular frame.

'For your information, I'm twenty-five.'

Why had she told him that? Because of the condescending way in which he had referred to her? Or to assure him that she was a woman now and not the shrieking eighteen-year-old he had had to deal with that last time they had met.

The cock of a deprecating eyebrow told her he had taken her response in the way that his calculating brain evidently wanted to. That she was more than eligible to bed his father, and that she was probably planning to do so—if she hadn't already—with purely mercenary motives in mind. But there wasn't a glimmer of recognition in those steel-blue eyes...

'And he didn't pluck me off the street,' she corrected him, allowing herself to relax a little. 'We were both victims of a spiteful ploy to relieve me of my possessions. I came to France—and then Monaco—for a break, and I was left with no credit cards, no money and nowhere to stay.' Why did she feel she had to justify herself to him? she thought with her jaw clenching. Because she hadn't been sitting in that pavement café just by coincidence? Because as an experienced journalist who had researched her subject thoroughly beforehand, she knew exactly where Mitchell Clayborne would be? 'Your father very kindly offered me a roof over my head until I could get things sorted out.'

That wide masculine mouth she had always thought of as passionate compressed in a rather judgemental fashion. 'A bit remiss of you not to have booked ahead.'

Why did every word he uttered sound like an accusation? Or was it just guilt making her imagine things? The dread of being found out?

'My mother's been ill for the past year or so. Now her condition's stabilised she took up her friend's offer to go away for three weeks, and so I decided to just take off.' It had seemed like a good idea from the security of the little rented Victorian house she still shared with her mother in London, although she knew that Cynthia Hardwicke would have thrown up her hands in horror if she knew the real reason her daughter was taking this trip. 'I had somewhere to stay until that morning.' She shrugged and didn't think it worth bothering to tell him that her friend, Joanne, who now lived in the South of France with her husband, and whom she'd been planning to spend some time with, had been unexpectedly descended upon by her sister and her three young nieces, so that Rayne had had to politely offer to move on before she was asked. 'With the holiday season barely started, I didn't envisage too much problem checking in somewhere.' Except that she hadn't reckoned on being robbed before she'd got the chance. 'I'd hired a car for the day, stopped for a coffee and…well… you obviously know the rest.'

He knew what his father had told him, but Mitch was clearly biased, King thought, and he could see why. Despite referring to her as 'little' just now, this woman was—what? Five feet six? Five seven?—with a good figure. And quite striking, too, with that Titian red hair. Or did they call that auburn? Her skin was creamy, complementing big eyes set just wide enough apart for his liking and a particularly full mouth a man could easily get carried away by. And there was certainly nothing waiflike about that air of confidence about her which, being as shrewd a judge of people as he was, did seem rather too assertive for a woman without an agenda. He wondered what that agenda could be, as he recalled how Mitch had said he'd picked her up.

Apparently his father had been leaving his usual lunch venue last Wednesday, alone because, as cantankerous as ever, Mitch had that morning had a barney with the latest chauffeur King had engaged for him and sent the man packing.

Rigid to routine, it was typical of Mitch that he'd refused to change his plans or wait for another member of staff to drive him into town, and had taken the old Bentley—which had been modified for him to use—himself. Not that he thought his father wasn't capable. But it was inadvisable for a sixty-seven-year-old man of Mitch's prominence to be out without proper security, even for one who wasn't so physically challenged. After transferring himself into the car—always a struggle for him—outside the café and folding up his wheelchair, the wheel he'd taken off was snatched from under his nose in broad daylight. It just went to show how susceptible he was. It also proved how easily his stubborn independence could be taken from him, and would have been if this supposedly ministering angel King saw before him hadn't leapt up and given chase.

He affected an air of effortless charm. 'It seems I should be thanking you for looking out for my father, Miss…'

'Carpenter. Rayne Carpenter.'

It wasn't her real name. Well, not entirely. It was her mother's maiden name and the name Rayne had used in the small provincial newspaper she used to write for. But then introducing herself as Lorrayne Hardwicke would only have earned her a one-way ticket out of there, she thought with a little shiver, even though she had been planning to tell his father exactly who she was in the beginning. At first…before those thieves had intervened and thrown all her well-laid plans awry.

'You're the best reporter I have, but you've got to come up with a story!' her editor had told her six months ago, before he'd been forced to let her go when her mother's worrying illness and inevitable operation had forced her to take too much time off.

Well, she could come up with a story! she thought now, with her teeth clamped almost painfully together. It was one exposé she wanted, and one everyone would want to read. Except that this one was personal...

She saw a muscle twitch in the man's hard angular jaw as he came closer—close enough for her to catch the scent of his cologne—as fresh as the pines that clothed the steeply rising hillside.

'I'm Kingsley Clayborne. But everyone calls me King,' he told her, holding out a hand.

I know who you are!

Her confidence wavered. She didn't want to touch him. But fear of his checking up on her if she showed any sign of unease or aversion to him forced her to plaster on a bright smile. Taking the hand he was offering, she found herself responding before she could stop herself, 'I'll bet they do!'

Feeling her slender hand tremble in his, King let his fingers find a subtle path across the blue vein pulsing in her wrist. He noted the way it was throbbing in double-quick tempo. There was something about her eyes too. Deep hazel eyes flecked with green, which were darkly guarded as they fixed on his. But fix on them they did, with a contention that was as challenging as it was wary, and which mirrored the superficial smile on her beautiful bronze-tinted mouth.

He knew his father could take care of himself. He was a man of the world, for heaven's sake! But Mitch was also vulnerable to a pretty face, and therefore to unscrupulous gold-diggers—and this Rayne Carpenter was one hell of a cagey lady.

Even so, he wasn't blind to the long, elegant line of her pale, translucent throat, or the way it contracted nervously beneath his blatant regard. Any more than he could fail to notice that her breasts—the cleft of which was just tantalisingly visible above the neckline of her chic but simple black dress—were high and generously proportioned. Quite a handful, in fact.

Hell! He was surprised by how acutely his body responded to the femininity she seemed to flaunt without any conscious effort, especially when his keen mind was telling him that Miss Rayne Carpenter was definitely one to watch. But there was something about her...

Some memory tugged at his subconscious like the fragment of a dream, too elusive to grasp, but still powerful enough to deepen the crease between his thick, winged brows, compelling him to enquire, 'Have we met before?'

Beads of perspiration broke out over Rayne's body, as tangible as that strong hand that was clasping hers, prickling above her top lip and along the deep V between her breasts.

She gave a nervous little laugh and said, 'I hardly think so.'

She wasn't sure whether he had let her go or whether she had been the one to break the contact, but as her hand slipped out of his she realised that she was desperate to take a breath.

Deep inside her something stirred. Resentment? Dislike? What else could have produced this overwhelming reaction to him that had her blood surging, not just from his question, but from the unwelcome and disturbing touch of his hand? After all, anything she might have felt for him he had killed off a long time ago, she assured herself caustically. But it had been more than a touch, she reasoned, despising him—as well as herself—for the way he was making her feel.

With one simple handshake she felt as though she'd been assessed, undressed and bedded by him, because behind that probing scrutiny that had trapped the breath in her lungs there had been a fundamental appreciation of a man for a woman. Yet there was still no sign of recognition...

Her breath, marked with trembling relief, shivered shallowly through her when he accepted her denial of having met him before. But then everyone she met nowadays who hadn't

seen her since she was a teenager remarked on how much she
had changed. Seven years ago she had had no real curves and
her hair had been short and spiky, as well as a different colour. And back then, of course, she would simply have been
known as Lorri…

'Those thieves must have reckoned on your being a definite pushover, don't you think?' he remarked smoothly. 'For
the three of them to have targeted you so precisely?'

She took a step back, finding his dominating presence
much too stifling, his question baffling her even as it warned
her to be on her guard. 'I'm sorry…?'

'I mean that they must have noticed you taking more than
a passing interest in my father to be so certain you'd rise to
their bait when they took that wheel and rush off and help
him as you did.'

Could he hear her heart hammering away inside her?

'I don't like seeing anyone taken advantage of,' she said
pointedly, and then, with barely concealed venom, 'for any
reason.' Now, with her head cocked to one side, she demanded, 'What exactly are you insinuating, Mr—'

'King.'

Perhaps 'Your Majesty' would please you more!

She had to bite her lower lip to stop from crying it aloud.
He was rich and powerful now. As well as ruthless, she decided bitterly.

Even then, all those years ago, when she'd crashed in on
the ugly scene between him and her father, she had seen a
side to him she hadn't realised he'd possessed. A steel edge
to his personality, coupled with a determined lack of scru-
ples for a young man who, while still only twenty-three, had
been forced, through his father's accident, to learn the ropes
quickly so that he could pick up the reins of a company about
to explode on the world.

'I couldn't help but take an interest in him—or in what he
was doing, certainly!' she breathed now, hating him for the

part he had played in destroying her father, while warning herself that nothing would escape this man's notice or bypass the keen circuits of his cold, intellectual mind. 'I was struck by the way he'd overcome his obvious difficulties to be able to drive himself around like that. I wasn't aware that admiring someone's capabilities actually constituted a crime.'

'It doesn't.' His smile seemed to light his face like the evening sun lit the rooftops of Monte Carlo, leaving her struck by its transformation from a dark enigma to one of pure blinding charm.

Rayne's throat worked nervously. Was he backing off?

'As you've probably been told, my father's chauffeur left… rather suddenly. Hence the reason he was without a driver, although, I should say, thanks to you, that that breach has been miraculously filled.'

She nodded, ignoring the sarcasm lacing his words.

Her heavy hair moved softly around her shoulders, King noticed, the warmth of the evening light turning it to flame.

His thick black eyelashes came down as he followed the rivers of fire to where they ended just above her contrastingly pale breasts. 'I gather you didn't lose everything at the hands of those criminals.' A toss of his chin indicated the clothes she was wearing, but the way those appraising blue eyes slid down her quivering body invested even that innocuous statement with disturbing sensuality.

'My clothes were in my car.'

'And they didn't take your keys?'

'No. They were in my jeans pocket.' With her cellphone, she thought—mercifully!—although she didn't tell King that. She had taken it out of her bag to text her mother just minutes before Mitchell Clayborne had emerged from the hotel restaurant next to the café the other day, and she had been immensely relieved that she had. It meant that she had been able to cancel her credit and debit cards and report the crime to the police in the privacy of the hired car, while leaving her cellphone number with them in case of any developments—so nobody would be ringing and asking for Lorrayne Hardwicke on her host's landline.

Tilting her head, she viewed the formidably attractive heir of Clayborne International with her throat dry from a raw sexual awareness and enquired, 'Do you interrogate all your father's house guests like this?'

His mouth tugged on one side as he moved over to the granite-topped table on the terrace and poured himself some coffee from the silver pot a manservant had brought out a little while ago. A masculine hand—long-fingered and tanned—queried whether he should pour some for her.

Rayne shook her head, dragging her gaze from the stark contrast of an immaculate white cuff and dark wrist to note that he added no cream or sugar to his cup.

'But you're not just a house guest, are you?' he remarked wryly. 'You've insisted on working while you're here until you get your affairs straightened out, which makes you an employee of sorts—albeit a rather unconventional one—and my father doesn't engage anyone these days without consulting me.'

And that just showed who was ruling the Clayborne empire now, she thought, resenting the authority he exuded as well as that brooding magnetism and forcefulness of character that lent his features a strength and quality that went way beyond mere handsomeness. 'You must excuse me if you think I'm being overly cautious.' She watched him drink through the steam rising from his cup and then set the fine china down on the table with cool economical movements. 'But, as I'm sure you're aware, my father is a very wealthy man.'

So are you, she supplied silently, remembering how amazed she had been to read that article that reported him as being higher up Britain's Rich List last year even than Mitchell Clayborne. That it was at her father's expense that the Claybornes were in that enviable position was something she refused to dwell on. She was aware, though, of the numerous enterprises King was involved in outside their technological empire, and reluctantly accepted that a man of his drive and determination would succeed at anything he turned his hand to. She looked at him askance and with a confrontational note in her voice queried, 'Meaning?'

He made a careless gesture with his hands. 'A beautiful young woman. An obviously rich but vulnerable older man whose ego needs a bit of boosting. An unlikely prank-turned-robbery in the midst of a crowded café. You must admit it couldn't be a more finely tuned scheme to play on the older man's sympathies and to get you into this house if you'd engineered it yourself.'

The colour already touching her cheeks intensified on a surge of guilt because, of course, she had been waiting at that table specifically for his father's appearance, but not for the reasons his sceptical guard dog of a son was suggesting!

Still trying to deny the heat coursing through her veins from his remark about her being beautiful, she retorted, 'That's preposterous!'

'Is it?' He slipped a hand into his trouser pocket, bringing her attention unwillingly to the hard lean line of his pelvis until, shocked at where she was looking, she dropped her gaze down over his intimidating stance and long, long legs. 'It isn't unheard of.'

'Except for one thing, King.' They both glanced in the direction of the shaky, gravelly voice, accompanied now by the unmistakable squeak of the wheelchair approaching. 'She didn't want to come.'

It was true. She hadn't at first. When those thieves had left her with nothing but a car with a virtually empty fuel tank, no money or credit and no place to stay, she had been uncomfortable enough with Mitchell Clayborne's gratitude for returning his property without his offer of assistance when he realised the loss and inconvenience that helping him had caused her. After all, she'd been lying in wait for him solely for one reason: to confront him with who she was and to threaten him if necessary with exposure in the papers if he didn't come clean and admit the wrong that both he and King had done to her father. To try and prick his conscience—if he had one!—where Grant Hardwicke had failed, because Mitch Clayborne and his son had taken something more precious from her family than a simple wheel! But he'd seemed so shaken up by those morons running off with it that it hadn't been the time or the place. Besides, she'd only been waiting at that café because she knew she would never have got past this villa's impregnable security if she had tried to see him here, so, after her initial hesitation, she'd decided to grab the opportunity she was being offered with both hands.

After all, the Claybornes owed her family big time, she'd decided, and all she had to do was bide her time until she had got her credit cards sorted out, enjoy a bit of luxury for a night or two and then, when her host was feeling better, she'd come clean and tell him who she really was. But it hadn't worked out like that.

'Hear that, King?' Mitchell Clayborne brought his chair out into the scented dusky air, warm still even though the light was fading. His iron-grey hair, combed straight back, was still thick like his son's, but his face was more harshly etched as his lined blue eyes clashed with the brooding intensity of the younger man's. 'I said she didn't want to come.'

Despite the gathering shadows around the pale stonework of the house, Rayne saw a fragment of a smile pull at King's sensual mouth.

'Your discretion becomes you,' he remarked quietly. His eyes said something quite different, though, she was sure, as they swept over her tight, tense features—as did the scarcely concealed scepticism with which he spoke.

Did he know? she wondered with her heart banging against her ribs. Had he guessed who she was and was just playing with her? Or did his only beef about her stem from the fact that she hadn't come through his stringent security system? Been passed to him first for his cold and calculating assessment?

'Leave her alone, King.' Mitchell was pushing himself over to the table as King reached for the cut glass decanter beside the coffee pot and poured some of its golden contents into a matching tumbler. 'Can't I enjoy a bit of female company without you vetting her like she was some filly with a dubious pedigree?' Mitch took the glass from the man who was more than thirty-five years his junior, and yet whose influence and power in the corporate world was more respected and deferred to even than the older man's these days.

King's shoulder lifted and a sudden last shaft of sunlight, piercing through the trees that decked the hillsides, splintered colour from the crystal decanter in his hand. 'Of course.' Replacing its stopper, he put the decanter back on the table with a dull thud. 'But be it on your own head, Mitch. I'm not going to be riding this one.'

Rayne's back stiffened from the double entendre as she watched him walk away, looking every bit as proud as the man in the wheelchair, but exuding an air of such uncompromising autonomy that lesser men, including his own father, could only hope to aspire to.

'He doesn't like me,' Rayne observed dryly, her confident manner concealing how uncomfortably sticky he'd made her feel beneath her light clothes. Had he picked up on the fact that she was hiding something from them? Or was her guilty secret letting her imagination run away with her?

'You'll have to excuse my son. He suspects every woman who happens to give me the time of day,' Mitch told her. 'Especially if she's young and pretty. Usually he manages to frighten them off before the dust has time to settle under their feet.'

'That's pretty selfish of him.' Rayne's eyes lingered in

the direction the other man had gone, her jaw tightening in rebellion.

'He has no reason to be. With a physical and intellectual package like that, they all wind up wanting King anyway.' He gave a harsh bark of laughter. 'Well, who would want an old fossil like me?' He started to cough, the contents of his glass threatening to slop over the side. As Rayne moved forward to take it from him, he waved her impatiently aside. 'But what's a man to do?' The terrace lights had come on, taking over from the sun that had dipped behind the mountains and glinting on the crystal he lifted to his mouth, draining it in one swift gulp. 'He calls it protecting my interests. Here—' he thrust the empty glass in her direction '—pour me another one, will you?'

Rayne looked at him dubiously. He was already looking rather florid. She'd also learned from his late-middle-aged and amiable Swiss housekeeper while she'd been there that Mitchell Clayborne had high blood pressure as well as a heart condition, which was why Rayne had been hesitant to tell him who she was and why she was there. 'Do you think you should?'

'For heaven's sake, girl! You have the audacity to question my actions while you're a guest in my house?'

'I didn't mean to.' Nor did she want to find herself worrying over someone who had treated her father so abominably. It felt like a betrayal, somehow. But her father's ex-colleague and business partner seemed world-weary and surprisingly bitter, she had decided over the past few days, guessing that it was probably because of his disability, although having an heir as forceful and dynamic as King couldn't help. But she was getting used to her host's outbursts, startling though they were, and so she took the glass he was handing her and poured him another drink.

'You're behaving just like King,' he persisted. 'And while

he's excused through blood, I won't take it from anyone who isn't. D'you understand?'

'Perfectly,' she breathed with mock deference as she handed him his refill, and caught a surprising glint of warmth in his watery blue eyes. 'If you don't need anything else,' she tagged on, uncomfortable even with fraternizing with him because of what he had done in the past, 'I think I'll get an early night.'

He smiled, gesturing her away with his glass, his angry mood dispelled. 'Good idea. Oh, Rayne…' Stopping before the open door that separated the luxurious living quarters from the terrace, she turned round with the scent of a potted gardenia trespassing on her senses. 'About King… Did you do something to antagonise him before I came out?'

Her heart skipped a nervous little beat. 'No. Why?'

'I haven't seen him quite so…intense before.'

She shrugged, trying to shake off the feeling of exposure she had sensed under those steely-blue eyes, trying not to remember how she had felt in the past. 'Perhaps he had a hard day.'

'Nonsense. He thrives on hard work and pressure where lesser mortals crack up and fall by the wayside.'

'He sounds like a dynamo.'

'He is.'

'Even dynamos can break down.'

'If you think that, then you don't know King.'

Don't I? she thought bitterly, but said, 'Obviously not.'

'But you will,' he said, seemingly with some relish. 'He's going to be around for a while.'

'That's nice.' She was finding it difficult keeping her voice light, making out that she didn't care one way or the other, while her insides were screaming with guilt and resentment and a whole heap of worrying doubts over what she was getting herself into.

'And Rayne…' About to step inside, keen to escape to her

room, Rayne glanced reluctantly over her shoulder as Mitch called to her again. 'Be nice to him,' he advised with just a hint of caution. 'For both our sakes.'

I'll fall at his feet, shall I? she suggested silently. *Like I'm sure every nubile woman he meets probably does!*

Her face ached from her forced smile as she got out, 'Of course,' aware that she was suddenly in danger of finding herself in way over her head, even as she told herself that she refused to be intimidated by King's arrival. He might look like the stuff of every woman's dreams, she accepted grudgingly, as the spacious interior of his father's summer retreat, which had astounded her with its elegance and luxury ever since she'd been there, now felt as though it was swallowing her up. And if just a compliment from him or the most casual of physical contact—like shaking hands with him, for goodness' sake!—made her pulse quicken a bit…well…it was only her hormones working, wasn't it? She was only human, after all! But she'd come to Monaco to try to right the wrong that had been done to her father and she had no intention of letting a man like King—or her uncontrollable hormones—stand in her way!

CHAPTER TWO

THE shapes and tones and hues of Monte Carlo took her breath away, as they had been doing every time she'd looked down on them from her bedroom balcony over the past few days. But this morning, with the sun still low enough to have turned the sea to gold and wrapped the distant mountains in a haze of heat, this wakening resort seemed, like her, to be holding its breath, before offering up its vibrant heart to another day of wealth and glamour and total luxury.

Rayne grimaced at the comparison because she hadn't come to Monaco to indulge herself. But while she was here, she thought, noticing how the trees on the steep ascent of the hillside above the house were touched with the same flame gold as the water in the harbour, then at least she could appreciate the scenery.

The only blot on her immediate horizon, she decided, was King.

She'd been careful before she'd embarked on this trip to do a little research into where he would be, and right now he should have been attending some week-long charity function in New York. After all, King didn't live here. He had some luxurious pad in London, and she'd heard that he and his father didn't always see eye to eye.

What he was doing here, she didn't know, only that it was going to be difficult enough confronting Mitch with who she was and why she was there, but with that six-foot-something of potent manhood thrown into the mix, the prospect was no less than unnerving.

He was hard, ruthless and clever. He was also suspicious, which left her feeling as though every secret she harboured was under threat of being exposed to him, while every feminine cell in her body reacted to his raw sexuality with a strength that left her shocked and ashamed.

She'd thought such wild reactions were the predilection of teenage girls. Because he had affected her then—seven years ago—although he'd scarcely spared more than a passing glance her way. A wheat-blonde, spiky-haired teenager with purple-shadowed eyes and lipstick. An experimental and pathetic Lorri Hardwicke, whose nevertheless deeply buried secret had been an excruciating crush on the firm's youngest and most dynamic recruit who, not long out of university, was already being primed for directorship.

She had wanted him from the first instant she had nearly collided with him as he was coming out of the office one day when she had been meeting her father for lunch, and from that moment she had woven all sorts of wild fantasies around him.

Young and guileless and between jobs, introduced to him only briefly, she'd jumped at the chance to help out in the office for a couple of weeks when one of the typists was on leave. It had offered her a chance to be near King, after all. But he'd scarcely spoken to her and, like Mitch, he had spent a lot of time out of the office. And when he was there she'd watched him from a painful distance behind her frosted glass partition, imagining a golden future when he would suddenly realise she was there, waiting in the wings for him to notice her, ask her out and initiate her into the sophisticated art of making love. Because with a man like him, she had decided, without any doubt in her fixated young mind, lovemaking would be no less than an art.

Even after she'd left, she still kept hoping. That was until the evening he had come round to the house and shattered all her dreams. Made her hate him with an emotion all the more intense because of what it had replaced.

Bitterly her thoughts drifted back to that night seven years ago. It was just a few weeks after her father had had a row with Mitchell Clayborne and walked away from their partnership—with devastating repercussions.

She had been to the gym and had cycled home in the rain, coming in to hear raised voices, her father's thin and defensive, King's deep and inexorable.

'You're the thief, Grant Hardwicke! Not my father! Stay away from him. Do I make myself clear? Leave him alone or you'll have me to deal with!' It still made her shudder to remember his cruel, icy threat. 'Believe me, after this you won't know what hit you if you ever dare show your face at our house or at the office again!'

Towering over Grant Hardwicke, King had been standing in the hallway of the modern detached home her mother had so prized, while her father had seemed to visibly diminish before Rayne's eyes. His features blanched and strained, she had seen Grant grab the doorframe as though it was too much of an effort to support himself under the weight of the younger man's hostile and verbal attack.

Soaked to the skin, hair flattened by the rain, she'd flown at King like a drenched sparrow as he'd come striding back across the hall.

'Don't you dare hurt my father!' she'd sobbed, lashing out at him, her flailing fists ineffectual against the impenetrable wall of his body. 'I'll kill you first! I will! I'll kill you!'

'Calm down, Lorri...' He had referred to her by name. It was the first time she could remember him using it, much less showing her any attention, but then it had been only to catch her flying wrists and thrust her aside as if she were an unwanted toy. 'Don't waste your hysterics and your childish little threats on me,' he'd warned with particular brutality to her teenage pride. 'Save them for someone who deserves them,' he'd snarled savagely. 'Like your father!' He had slammed out of the door with his hurtful and puzzling words burning in her ears.

'It's about that software, love,' Grant Hardwicke had breathed brokenly when she had rushed over to him. He'd looked drained and exhausted as she'd helped him onto an easy chair. 'Mitchell's saying it's company property and King's backing him up. I'm afraid they're determined to keep it. I've lost everything, Lorri. *Everything*.' She had never forgotten the desperation in her father's voice.

'But it's yours, Dad. You wrote it!' Rayne remembered stressing, as though that had counted for anything where the Clayborne men were concerned. It was software he had written especially for the medical profession. One he had said would benefit a lot of people—because her father was like that—caring and generous. It was something he had produced for the common good. It was his baby. His brainchild, which he'd conceived and worked on and slaved over in his own time before he had ever joined forces with Mitchell Clayborne. But Mitchell Clayborne had stolen the credit for it, launching it under his own company flag with the full knowledge and support of his equally unscrupulous and ambitious son and heir.

Her mother had been out at a line-dancing class that night and Rayne was glad she had because it was the first and only time in her life she had seen her father cry. Her strong and devoted father, who had always been her rock and the backbone of his family, reduced to tears in losing all he'd worked for. But he had no proof of his copyright for that software he had written, and the Claybornes had gone on to prosper unbelievably because of it, while Grant Hardwicke's troubles had only increased.

Because of his age, he had found it impossible to get another position. He'd started drinking, which made him ill, and then he was made bankrupt, which in turn meant her mother having to lose her lovely home.

Rayne was certain that all her father's problems had started that night she had walked in on King's unmitigated venom. A venom that had had a poisoning effect on her family, virtually destroying everything that had been good about it, everything she'd loved.

What she had felt for him had been unreal, Rayne thought bitterly, mocking herself now. A teenage fancy, as insubstantial as mist, killed off by his pulsing anger and his verbal brutality towards her father, even before she'd realised how unscrupulous he was. As well as defending Grant, she knew now that in striking King that night she had been giving vent to the loss of all her young dreams. But long after the anguish of that night had receded, it was the physical power of him and those firm hands on her body as he'd put her from him that had lingered in her memory…

She came downstairs now with half a hope that, in spite of what Mitch had said, perhaps his son's visit might have been a flying one and that he might have been called away on some vital company business during the night.

That was until she saw him striding in through the front door in a short-sleeved white shirt that exposed his tanned, muscular arms and dark suit trousers hugging his powerful hips and her heart seemed to stand still before vaulting into a double-quick rhythm.

'Good morning, Rayne.' He was tie-less, she realised, with her gaze instantly drawn to the bronze skin beneath his corded throat. The white T-shirt she had teamed with her jeans suddenly felt too snug for her breasts as that steely gaze burned over her. 'I trust you slept well.'

She hadn't, but she said in a tight little voice, 'Very, thank you.' In fact she had been waking up all night, going over that scenario with him on the terrace, aware that it was absolutely imperative that she confront his father about that software before King had a chance to work out who she was.

Consequently, the bruised-eyed-looking creature who had

stared back at her from the mirror this morning as she'd swept her hair up into a loose knot left her feeling quite bedraggled in contrast to King, who looked as fresh and energized as the morning and ready to take the world on those wide, powerful shoulders.

'You'll be pleased to know you won't have to drive my father into town as you were planning to do this morning,' he said smoothly, those keen eyes seeming to assess her every reaction. 'He decided to leave early and, as I was up, I drove him in myself.'

The front door was open and she could see the huge bulk of the Bentley parked there on the drive. A short distance away, the sleeker, more powerful beast of a black Lamborghini stood gleaming in the bright morning sun.

'You didn't need to do that. I mean...' her eyes strayed towards the carved wooden door concealing the lift that would have borne Mitch down in his wheelchair. '...he should have called me.'

'Oh, I think I did.'

Meaning what? Rayne's throat contracted nervously from the way he was looking at her. That he was protecting his father from her supposedly mercenary clutches? Or was his sole intention to get her alone? And, if so, why? To interrogate her further?

Mentally, she pulled back her shoulders, telling herself that he was just trying to unsettle her. That he'd hardly be likely to discover the truth about her just so long as she kept her head.

'In that case...' she flashed him what she considered would look like a grateful smile '...I'll go and get some breakfast.'

'I think you might be disappointed there.'

Stopping in her tracks, she glanced up at him with her brow furrowing. 'Excuse me?'

'I instructed Hélène not to bother. I've given her the morning off.'

A cloud of wariness darkened the green flecks in her eyes.

Why had he done that? Had he realised who she was and was planning on giving her marching orders while his father was out of the way?

A smile illuminated his strong features like the sun burning through the haze of the mountains she'd been admiring earlier, making her pulse quicken in infuriating response. 'As it was such a lovely morning I thought I'd have breakfast out. I also thought you might care to join me.'

Oh, did he?

'No, really. That's very nice of you,' she blurted out, even though 'nice' was definitely not a word she would have applied to Kingsley Clayborne, 'but…'

But what, exactly? She couldn't claim she never ate breakfast after what she had just told him. Nor could she inform him that she didn't like him, and that if she had to choose between sharing breakfast with him or with a pride of lions, she'd take the pride of lions.

'I…I need to stay here for when your father needs to be picked up,' she hedged, wishing she didn't sound so defensive.

'He won't. Not until later. If you haven't discovered it yet, you'll soon learn that my father is a creature of unwavering habit. Always reliable, but sometimes tiresomely predictable.' Which was how she had managed to meet him that day outside that café. 'He's doing some business and then playing chess with a friend and won't be ready to come home until mid-afternoon. Any change in those plans and he'll ring me. That's settled then,' he declared when she procrastinated too long, having run out of reasonable excuses. 'And I can assure you…' his tone had changed in a way that sent a cautioning little shiver through her '…I'm not trying to be nice.'

'I'm glad you told me.' She sent another forced smile over her shoulder as she obeyed his gesture for her to precede him through the front door.

'No,' he called out as she moved towards the Bentley, 'we'll take mine.'

A skein of unease uncoiled in Rayne's stomach after she'd crossed the tarmac and pulled the door of the Lamborghini closed behind her.

This sleek and powerful machine with its cream leather-scented interior represented major success. Arrival. It was also Kingsley Clayborne's territory. With its smooth engineering wrapped around her and the cushioning curves of the passenger seat seeming to suck her in, she felt uncomfortably under his influence, as though her own power and control had suddenly been considerably reduced.

'Relax,' he advised, sensing her tension, obviously thinking it stemmed from something else altogether, she realised, when he tagged on, 'I might be renowned for my love of power, but I'm not altogether insensitive to those riding alongside me.'

Was that what he thought? That she was afraid of how fast he might drive this thing? Or was he talking about a different kind of power altogether? Because she didn't doubt that he enjoyed being in command. Of himself. Of others. And of his multi-billion, multi-national company. Because, where the Clayborne empire was concerned, it was common knowledge that he had been the one taking all the major decisions for some years now.

'I'm pleased to hear it,' she said, her voice overly bright, and kept her eyes trained on the panoramic views from the window on her side so that they wouldn't stray to the movement of muscle beneath the dark cloth spanning his thigh, or be pulled by the flash of gold from the slim watch on his wrist as he changed gear with that masculine hand.

'It's stunning, isn't it?' he remarked, aware, as her eyes drank in the scenery from the awe-inspiring sweep of the road. A road that ran all the way along the French Riviera to the Italian coast, she remembered reading from a travel brochure before she'd left England. Someone had called it the most romantic road in the world.

Feeling as though the Lamborghini were a bird and that they were travelling on its wings, they soared above terracotta-roofed houses dotted amongst tree-smothered cliffs, above church spires and tumbling hillsides that plunged down to the rugged coastline and the sea.

Above them the Alps presided, white-capped and as age-less as time. And just a little bit unnerving, Rayne decided, although not as unnerving as when King suddenly pulled into a surprisingly deserted lay-by. Her mind raced with the instinctive knowledge that Kingsley Clayborne would never do anything without a reason, and that that reason wasn't just to enjoy the view.

'What are you imagining?' he enquired mockingly, wise to the half-wary, half-questioning look she shot him. 'That I brought you up here to seduce you?'

She gave a tight little laugh. 'No. Why? Did you?'

Dear heaven! Had she actually said that? Obviously her nerves were getting the better of her, she thought, in letting her tongue run away with her.

He laughed. 'No.' The engine died under the portentous turn of the ignition key. 'Of course, if you were hoping I was...'

Every nerve in her body seemed to pull like overstretched rubber bands. There was a time, she thought, when she was young and blinded by his looks and his devastating persona, that her heart would have leapt in wild anticipation of what he might be planning, not thumping in screaming rejection as it was doing now. Or was it? she startled herself by won-dering suddenly, deciding not to go there.

Turning to him with her cheeks scorched scarlet, she said pointedly, 'Are you always so sure of yourself?'

He laughed again, under his breath this time. 'Are you?'

Her own question, lobbed back at her, left her speechless for a moment.

With his bent elbow on the steering wheel, a thumb and

forefinger supporting his chin, his thick lashes were drawn down as he studied her reflectively, giving her every ounce of his attention. Dear heaven! What she wouldn't have given for this much attention from him seven years ago!

Berating herself for even thinking along those lines, unable to meet his eyes, she still couldn't stop herself appreciating his classic and magnificent bone structure, the chiselled sweep of his forehead and cheekbones, that proud flaring nose, that tantalising dent in his chin...

'I'm just finding it hard,' he expressed, shocking her back to her senses, 'determining why any woman would accept a strange man's hospitality—even if he is driving a Bentley—unless she's either very foolish or hoping to gain something out of it.'

Of course. Rayne bit the inside of her cheek.

'I suppose in normal circumstances I wouldn't even have considered it,' she told him, finding her tongue. 'But in view of his age and the fact that he said he had a house full of staff to look after me, I thought I'd be perfectly safe.'

'And were you aware of who he was?' he enquired. 'Before he brought you home with him?'

Rayne's heartbeat increased. Be careful, she warned herself. He doesn't know who you are. Just breathe normally. Keep your cool.

'I knew the name, certainly...as soon as he said it.' She gave a nonchalant little shrug. 'Who wouldn't? Who doesn't know the name of the man who gave MiracleMed to a grateful medical profession?' It was an effort to smile. To pretend to believe what everyone else believed about Mitchell Clayborne. 'He's a very clever man.'

That firm mouth twisted contemplatively. Such a cruel yet sensual mouth, she decided, in spite of her dislike of its owner. Crazily, she wondered how many women had felt the pressure of it, known the power of this man's unrestrained passion.

'Yes,' he breathed, 'but I meant before those delinquents sidetracked you into chasing after them.'

Rayne gave herself a mental shake. What the hell was she thinking about? she berated herself.

Unconsciously now, she brought her tongue across her top lip. She hated lying, even on her father's account. 'Are you still suggesting I planned for someone to rob me so I could play on your father's sympathies and wheedle my way into his house for some financial benefit?' she queried, her voice cracking slightly because she wasn't being straight with him, even if it was for reasons other than he was implying. 'If you think I'm interested in your father's money, then all I can say is you've got a very overstretched imagination!'

He laughed softly, unperturbed by the rising note in her voice.

'And I could suggest that the reason you don't like women taking an interest in your father,' she went on heatedly, with a sudden surge of pity for Mitchell Clayborne that surprised her, 'is because you might lose all *you* stand to gain if he reciprocates!'

'Hardly,' he said with a tug of that sensuous mouth.

Because he was involved in so many other enterprises besides the company his father had founded and in which her own father had played such a major part, a man of King's calibre, determination and unwavering command, she accepted rather grudgingly, didn't need to rely on anyone or anything, least of all the prospect of inherited wealth.

'Let's eat,' he said, restarting the engine, the cutting edge of his gaze picking up on the way her lovely breasts rose and fell.

But with what? he wondered. Relief?

As his success depended on his keen ability to sense any subtle changes in mood or behaviour—both in his business rivals and in his own workforce—his experience had served him well, and it didn't let him down now.

Rayne Carpenter portrayed all the characteristics of a woman who wasn't being entirely honest, he decided, pulling away. And yet what could she be hiding if it wasn't a very determined plan of action to ensnare Mitch? He had seen his father preyed upon before—several times—but once in particular, and with disastrous consequences, and he'd be hanged if he'd stand by and let Mitch bring such devastation down on himself again.

No, he decided, with sudden inexorable purpose. The thing he had to do was to keep her away from his father—at least until he could check her out. And the best way to do that was to claim all this dubious young woman's time for himself.

He had some time on his hands as his second-in-command had taken over his commitments in the States, and he had already promised himself a short break when it was over. He had never had any difficulty seducing any woman he put his mind to seducing, and with this one, he decided grimly, conscience didn't even come into it. If she was the sort of woman who was out just to prey on Mitch, then the prospect of even richer pickings with him should get her opportunistic juices flowing nicely.

It was an unfortunate choice of words, and one which was making his mind work overtime as he imagined her hot and compliant, moist with the honeyed heat of desire. He felt his body's hard response as he imagined freeing those beautiful breasts from their restricting cups and moulding them to his hands, feeling each sensitive tip blossom as he took it into his mouth.

He shook away his errant fantasies, trying to pull himself together. It was probably because he hadn't had a woman in his bed for some months, he decided, that his body was behaving like a rampant adolescent's now. Still, he couldn't deny that the prospect of stripping this unsuspecting little gold-digger bare—and in more ways than one—excited him immensely.

The café to which he took her was situated in a pedestrian thoroughfare, paved in the same peach and cream tones as the buildings which flanked it. Baskets of flowers — red and purple and pink — decorated ornamental street lamps, while luxuriant foliage grew in abundance outside the shops and cafés. There were orange trees, Rayne recognised, growing beneath the artistically wrought balconies of the buildings, whose pastel-coloured shutters and breath-catching architecture were a testament to human creativity, in contrast to the awesome cliffs that formed a mighty backdrop behind the buildings that stood at the head of the elegant avenue.

'Here we are,' King invited, pulling out a chair for her, the smile he gave her appreciative of her wonderment in spite of what he had been thinking about her earlier.

A little later, drinking coffee with home-baked rolls spread thickly with locally made jam, Rayne was relieved when King's conversation touched only on things like the area and the recent airways strike. Safe, casual topics, she decided gratefully, until he suddenly enquired, 'Do you usually take your holidays alone?'

Instantly she tensed up. That almost criticising note was back in his voice and now that he'd brought the conversation back to a personal level, she had to remind herself to be on her guard.

She thought of Matt Cotton, whom she'd been seeing on a purely platonic level for a year or so before they had parted six months ago. He'd been the only man she had ever considered getting serious with—serious enough to go on holiday with, at any rate. But after their relationship had moved up a notch, the first weekend she had slept with him when they had gone away together, she'd been so disillusioned by his suggestion that they move in together 'to see how it goes' that it had come as quite a shock to her to realise that she wanted more than Matt was offering. What she wanted was the sort of relationship that her parents had enjoyed. A lifelong commit-

ment inspired by love and trust and respect for each other—
and she intended to settle for nothing less.

Considering King's question now about taking her holidays alone, and feeling that she was still on the end of a subtle line of interrogation, she enquired pointedly, 'Would you
have asked me that if I were a man?'

The arching of an eyebrow as those compellingly blue
eyes tugged over her assured her that she was anything but.

'If you were my woman, I wouldn't be happy with you
roaming around a strange country on your own.'

'But I'm not your woman, am I?' Bright emeralds fastened
on steel as she met his gaze, reminded by the raw sensuality with which he was looking at her of how much she had
once longed to be just that. The woman he drove home, undressed and adored in long, exotic nights of pleasure, while
she writhed on his bed, allowing his lips and hands licence
to every hidden treasure of her body.

Shockingly her breasts burgeoned into life without any
warning, their weight heavy and aching, their tips excruciatingly tender against the full cups of her bra.

Surely she didn't still want him in that way? Not now. Not
after the way he had supported Mitch in treating her father
as he had, when all he had been trying to do was claim what
was rightfully his.

'That's right—you're not,' he stated, causing her to flinch
from the way he managed to make it sound as though she was
the last person he'd ever consider taking to bed. Which was
ludicrous! When she would have rejected any overtures from
him with every fighting cell in her body! 'And you haven't
answered my question—which wasn't intended with any lack
of political correctness or offence to your femininity. Do you
usually take your holidays alone?'

Fighting off a barrage of conflicting emotions, she
shrugged and answered, 'No, not usually. But as I told you
last night, my mother's been ill.' Very ill, she appended si-

lently, thinking of the operation and the treatment that Cynthia Hardwicke had had to go through during the past year. 'There hasn't been much time for holidays. But when her old school-friend invited her over to her villa, I realised I was on my knees from all the months of worry and that I was desperate for a holiday too. I'm ashamed to say it, but I think it hit me even harder than it hit Mum,' she found herself admitting to him. 'You can't possibly imagine the unbelievable strain it can put you under when something like that happens to someone you love.'

A dark shadow seemed to cross his features. 'Oh, believe me, I can,' he assured her grimly.

She frowned, and then almost immediately realised. Of course. He was talking about his father.

'What happened to Mitch?' she enquired unnecessarily, because she remembered her parents telling her in the past. But a stranger wouldn't know, would she? Rayne reminded herself. And that was what she was as far as King Clayborne was concerned. A stranger.

'A road accident,' he said, and his words were hard and clipped. 'It deprived him of his mobility—and of his wife.' *Your stepmother,* she nearly said, but didn't. She wasn't supposed to know, was she?

'That's dreadful,' she empathised, because hearing it again—and so many years on—didn't make it any less tragic. She couldn't understand though why he sounded quite so... what? Bitter, she decided.

'What about you?' Putting down his cup, the inscrutable mask was firmly back in place again. 'Have you any brothers or sisters?'

Rayne shook her head.

'And your father?'

'What about him?' she enquired, sounding unintentionally defensive.

'You haven't mentioned him.' The glance he shot her was a little too keen.

Rayne felt tension creep into her jaw. 'He died—just over a year ago.'

'I'm sorry.'

No, you're not, she thought acridly. *But you will be! You and your father! I can promise you that!*

Because she was certain that it was her parents' financial difficulties following her father's bankruptcy, and then the shock of his unexpected death from a heart attack that had made her mother ill. That was when she had vowed to right the wrong that the Claybornes had done to her family. After all Cynthia Hardwicke had been through, though, Rayne didn't want to do anything to worry her. But with her mother having been persuaded to go off to Majorca, Rayne had been able to come away without too many awkward questions being asked.

'So what do you do when you aren't running around this country picking up strange men?'

She ignored the deliberate snipe. 'I type a little.'

'You type?'

'Well, a lot, actually.' Well, she did, didn't she?

'Are you saying you're a PA?'

She chewed on the inside of her mouth, trying not to compound the lies. 'No. I'm freelance.'

'You work for an agency?'

She shook her head. 'For myself.'

'Typing.'

She didn't know why he sounded so disparaging. 'That takes up a fair proportion of my work.' Which was true, she thought. It did. 'What's so strange about that?'

'Only that you strike me as a woman who would have carved out a more determined career path for herself.'

Rayne was glad he couldn't detect how her deception made her heart skip a beat. 'I have.' She saw the question in the heart-stopping clarity of his steel-blue eyes and letting her own slide away, told him trenchantly, 'Seducing rich elderly men!'

His mouth twitched at the corners as though he were trying to assess the authenticity of her remark.

'I think it's time we left,' he stated blandly.

The journey back was an uncomfortable one, not because of King's driving, because he handled the Lamborghini like a dream. But since leaving the café he had barely said two words to her and now, motivated by the view from the ribbon of road that displayed the whole sweep of Monaco below them, Rayne tried to lighten the mood a little by remarking, 'This scenery's unbelievable. So is this weather! Was it as lovely as this in New York?'

'Who said I was in New York?'

Mistake! Rayne admonished herself, feeling those perspicacious eyes roving over her like a hawk's, waiting for her to show any weakness; waiting to pounce.

She shrugged and said as nonchalantly as she could, 'Mitch.' She could hardly tell King that she'd run a check on him before she'd been stupid enough to come here. Because that was how she was beginning to feel, she realised, despairing at herself. Utterly, utterly stupid!

Consoling herself with the thought that she was worrying unnecessarily and that it was only her jumpiness and her overreacting that was creating suspicion in his mind, she ventured to say carelessly, even though it was a lie, 'He led me to believe you were over there on some business or other.'

'Did he now?'

She saw his hands tighten on the wheel, the knuckles whitening above those long dark fingers. But surely Mitch would have known where he was, wouldn't he? She swallowed, her throat suddenly feeling dry.

'Do you come and see him often?'

'Not as often as I should. And I wouldn't be here now if

Hélène hadn't contacted me to tell me Mitch wasn't feeling his best, and also happened to mention the attractive young chauffeuse who had very surprisingly stepped in and taken Talbot's place. I got here as soon as I could, and I'm glad I did.'

'Why? Because you don't trust me?'

'Men in our position can't afford to trust anyone.'

'That's pretty cynical. Is that what money does for you?'

'Unfortunately, yes.'

'So why flaunt it? I mean this car. The Bentley. All those houses you probably own. If you don't want to attract the wrong sort of people you could always drive a Mini.'

'But then I wouldn't be enjoying the benefits of all I worked for.'

All my father worked for! she wanted to scream, and had to bite her tongue to stop the words from tumbling out.

'And is that all you work for?' She couldn't keep the disdain out of her voice as she added pointedly, 'Lamborghinis? Homes in England, Switzerland and who knows where else? Relaxation aboard exclusive yachts?'

'You've really done your homework, haven't you?' He was frowning as he directed a sidelong glance her way, making her realise she had said too much.

'I only know what I read. What everyone reads,' she tagged on quickly, not wanting him to guess how avidly she soaked up any information about him—and always had.

'It isn't just my money that's bothering you, is it, Rayne— if Rayne's even your real name,' he speculated, causing a little shiver to run through her as he operated the remote control switch and opened the gates because they had reached the house. 'It's something much more fundamental than that.'

'Don't be ridiculous! I don't even know you,' she prevaricated with colour suffusing her cheeks as the car growled through the gates towards the exclusive villa standing in its prominent position, high in the hills.

'Maybe not,' he agreed, pulling up outside and cutting the engine, then making every nerve in her body zing as he threw his door open and added with nerve-racking purpose, 'But I think the time has come to change all that.'

CHAPTER THREE

'YOU'VE got it all wrong!' Rayne threw over her shoulder, flying ahead of him into the villa. Her blood was pounding in her ears, her racing heart making her sound as though she'd just run five miles.

'Have I?' King demanded grimly, the strength of his own hormones putting a flush across his high cheekbones. 'I'm not a callow youth, Rayne, and if your story holds any water—as I'd like to believe it does—I can't think of any other reason why you constantly feel the need to antagonise me.'

Oh, dear heaven...! She stopped dead, breathing hard, her lashes coming down over her eyes, because he could see it, even though she was refusing to. But how could it be this strong, she wondered hopelessly, when she despised him as much as she despised Mitchell Clayborne? It was as if all of her pent-up teenage frustrations about him had rushed back and were screaming to be dealt with. But how could he be so astute? How could he tell?

Dry-mouthed, she touched her tongue to her top lip as he turned her round to face him.

'You terrify me,' she said, startling herself, because surely that was Lorri speaking. The hapless kid who had adored him from a distance, and who would have died for him, given half the chance. Not the mature twenty-five-year-old who knew him for what he was and hated him with every trembling bone in her body.

'I know,' he acknowledged sagaciously. 'But it's yourself you're afraid of, Rayne. The fear of an involvement that wasn't in your plans. Well, believe me, my beautiful girl, the thought of what you've been doing to me since I got here—and what you can still do to me—terrifies me, too.'

She laughed, but her throat felt clogged. 'You? Terrified?'

'Does that seem so strange?'

'No, just inconceivable,' she responded, wishing her credit cards were sorted so she could tell him where to go and just get the hell out of there. As it was, she felt like a butterfly caught in a fly-trap whose promise of the sweetest pleasure only hid danger beneath. Her head was spinning and her legs felt weak, while every organ in between was throbbing with the almost uncontrollable need to reach for him, pull him down to her and drown beneath the pleasure of his ravaging mouth, breathe in his heady, far too tantalizing cologne.

'Why? Because I'm a man? And obviously a very experienced one at that?'

'Something like that.' She didn't know what she was saying any more. Couldn't seem to tell him where to go, or drag herself away from him—even if she'd wanted to. Because that was just it, she realised suddenly. She didn't.

'I might be a man of the world, but I'm willing to bet you could give me a run for my money.'

Was that what he thought? Rayne swallowed, guessing that he would probably laugh if she told him how few sexual encounters she had had in her lifetime.

'And that's your experience speaking, of course.'

'Of course.'

Well, that's where you're wrong! she wanted to fling at him, wishing she had the nerve to play along with him and do what some other women in her position might do. Flatter his ego and enjoy a brief spell of the pleasure he could give her, then watch his anger explode when he found out who she really was and realised she'd made a fool of him. Oh, to hurt him as he'd hurt her! Hurt her father when he'd joined Mitch in taking what had never been theirs to take! But common sense warned her that men of King Clayborne's character couldn't be hurt, and that even to entertain such a tempting idea was no less than crazy.

Instead she said, 'Well, dream on, King. I didn't come here to have a fling with you or anybody else, and you're very much mistaken if you think I did!'

'Not intentionally, no.'

Pulling herself out of his disturbing sphere, she viewed him warily from under her lashes. 'And what's that supposed to mean?' she challenged shakily.

'I'm sure you didn't intend to charm your way in here only to find yourself fighting an attraction that is bigger than you are. Bigger than both of us, if I'm honest. But you're giving off pheromones, Rayne, that no man this side of ninety could possibly ignore. And quite simply, darling, I wouldn't dream of insulting you by pretending to ignore them. And if you refuse to accept the effect you're having on me, I'm sure you're way too experienced not to acknowledge this.'

It was inevitable what was going to happen. But even that acknowledgement couldn't have prepared her for the onslaught on her senses when his head dipped and his hard masculine mouth finally covered hers.

It was like two universes colliding. A barrage of riotous emotions and sensations that rocked her to the very core of her femininity, driving everything from her mind but the need to be kissed and stroked and caressed by this man and this man alone—because she still wanted him, much, much more than she had ever wanted him before, and with a hunger that excited and thrilled her even as it appalled.

And he wanted her too...

She didn't have to be experienced to recognise the rock-hard evidence of just how much as his arm tightened around her, locking her to him, and shamelessly she realised that that was what he had been referring to a moment ago, rather than just the inevitable joining of their hungry, ravenous mouths.

With a small murmur, which was half-need, half-despair, she wound her arms around his neck, glorying in the sensations that his six-feet-plus of power-packed masculinity sent coursing through her as she moved convulsively against his hard warmth.

'Can you deny it now, Rayne?' His voice was hoarse, a ragged whisper against the softness of her cheek. 'What is there to lose in admitting that you want me every bit as much as you've made me want you?'

And just how much he hadn't even realised until now. He'd had women in his time who'd given him pleasure and to whom he'd given pleasure in return. But that was all it had been. Pleasure. This girl, however, had a way about her that excited him and made his anatomy harden to such an extent that it hurt.

But why? Why, when to seduce her had been a cold, calculated plan? When he'd intended to remain detached and—if he was honest with himself—to have her begging, virtually down on her knees, for him to take her?

Well, that just showed him, he thought, mocking himself for his lack of immunity, his inability to stay unaffected, when all he wanted to do right now was rip off her clothes and carry her up to the nearest bed and feel her warm softness closing in around him, her body bucking beneath his as he drove into her.

Steady on, King...

He was breathing raggedly as he lifted his head.

'So what's it to be, Rayne? Your bed or mine?' He was amazed at how cool—how indifferent—he managed to sound.

There was nothing cool, though, or indifferent, about the hand that was suddenly making contact with his left cheek, taking him so unawares he nearly overbalanced.

'How dare you!' Rayne found she was trembling so much

she could hardly get her words out, realising that it wasn't just his effrontery that was responsible for her impulsive action. It was also aggravated by the knowledge that she had invited what had happened between them every inch of the way, so that her anger was directed more at herself and her abandoned response to his kiss rather than at him.

'I'm sorry. I could hardly help jumping to what I believed was a very natural conclusion,' King expressed, holding his smarting cheek, deciding that he had rather overstepped the mark. Nevertheless that still didn't stop him from enquiring mockingly, 'Are you usually prone to bursts of violence?'

'You drove me to it!' It was a small wild cry, born of her despair over responding to him in the way she had, and for striking him, which she was thoroughly ashamed of now.

'You drove yourself to it,' he said quietly. 'Firstly by refusing to acknowledge that there's definitely something between us, and then in not doing so, suddenly finding yourself way out of your depth.' His mouth moved in a kind of contemplative half-smile. 'I'll just put it down to frustration, shall I?' he remarked, his eyes skimming over her in a shaming reminder of what had just transpired.

'Put it down to whatever you like!' she breathed, shocked by the passions he could arouse in her and, pivoting away from him, she fled up the stairs, wanting only to crawl into a hole and pretend that none of her shameless behaviour had ever happened.

In the privacy of her room she sank down on the sumptuous bed, dropped her head into her hands and groaned.

Whatever had come over her? Not only to throw herself at him as she had when he had had the audacity to kiss her, but then to slap him like that afterwards as though it had all been his fault. Being quite honest with herself, she was forced to admit that he was right. She *had* wanted him to kiss her. Wanted it like she had never wanted anything. A man who had hurt her father and, with Mitch, had as good as destroyed her family. Was that why she had hit him? Was it all part of the need for retribution? Or was King Clayborne simply always destined to bring out the worst in her?

Angry tears burned her eyes, but they were tears of remorse and scorching shame too. How could she have responded to him so easily, and without so much as a conscience? Without any thought for what the Claybornes had cost her parents. Was she really that weak? She padded over to the en suite bathroom to try and scrub the taste of King Clayborne off her mouth, promising herself, as well as both of her parents, that she would never let it happen again.

And if he did find out that she had been lying to him?

She shuddered, closing her mind against that intimidating scenario. That was something she definitely refused to think about on top of everything else.

The florist at the other end of the line seemed to be taking forever to deal with the order Rayne was trying to telephone through.

'And the name on the card?' she asked mechanically, in heavily accented English.

'I explained to the lady I spoke to first that I haven't got a card, but she said it would be all right if I brought the cash down before you close this afternoon. My name's Lorrayne Hardwicke,' Rayne told her, sending anxious glances towards the closed door.

She had come in here to the study to make a couple of calls and to try and sort out a birthday bouquet to be sent to her mother. She'd wanted to do it from the privacy of her own suite, but the maids were changing the bed and giving the rooms an extra fine clean today, and time was getting scarce if she wanted her mother to receive her flowers in the morning.

'I'm afraid I cannot process the order unless we receive the credit or the money…what is it you say? Upfront,' the woman emphasised, remembering. 'I'm sorry, *mademoiselle*, but those are the conditions.'

'But your manageress distinctly assured me it would be all right,' Rayne despaired. She hadn't missed sending her mother flowers on her birthday since she was eighteen, when things had started really going downhill for her parents. And OK, she couldn't pay with a card, but she had a small amount of cash that she had earned from chauffeuring Mitch around, and the florist *had* said it would be all right.

'My manageress has just left for the afternoon. I will try and get hold of her and ring you back if you will give me your number. What did you say your name was?'

'Lorrayne Hardwicke.'

'Can you spell that, please?'

Rayne darted another glance towards the door as she heard voices on the other side of it.

'I'll call you back,' she said quickly, snapping her cell-phone shut a fraction of a second before the door opened and King walked in.

'What the...?' His smile for whomever he had been talking to outside was wiped away by surprise at seeing her sitting there behind his father's desk.

'My room's being cleaned and I needed to make a couple of calls,' she told him croakily, not sure what was disturbing her most. Nearly being caught red-handed blurting out who she really was, or the visual images of what had happened between them earlier in the day. 'Of course, if I'm intruding...' She was already swivelling back on the studded leather chair.

'I wouldn't say that.'

In fact he was looking at her over what seemed like an acre of polished mahogany as though he was imagining her naked and spreadeagled across it. Or was that just what her own wild imaginings were conjuring up? She slammed the lid down on her errant thoughts before they could manifest themselves on her face. 'I...I didn't hear you come in.'

'Evidently not.' He'd been to pick up Mitch at his own insistence, and had come in here to find his pen to sign some letters his secretary had faxed through while he was gone. 'Otherwise you wouldn't be acting as though I'd just caught you rifling through the silver cabinets.' A distracted smile twisted the sensuous line of his lower lip. 'Perhaps that's it,' he declared airily, pocketing his pen. 'Are you looking for something, Rayne?'

'No.' At least that much was true. If she had been, it would be for the evidence that would prove that MiracleMed was her father's. She knew, though, that she didn't have a cat in hell's chance of finding it here in this luxurious Mediterranean retreat, if in fact any proof existed at all.

'If you must know, I'm just a bit peeved because I was trying to order some flowers for Mum,' she told him, gripping the padded arms of the chair, which she seemed to have become rooted to ever since he had come in, 'but it seems you can't even breathe these days if you haven't got a credit card.'

He nodded. 'Make the call,' he advised. To her stunned surprise, he was taking his wallet from the inside pocket of his jacket. 'Make the call,' he reiterated, taking out a credit card.

'I...I couldn't possibly,' she stammered, blushing to her roots as she realised how her statement must have sounded. As though she was asking him to help her. 'I didn't mean I wanted you to...'

'What's the number?' he asked, ignoring her embarrassment.

Seeing how determined he was, she quoted it from the piece of paper she'd jotted it down on earlier.

'Now what is it you want?'

With a little shrug, feeling indebted, uncertainly she told him. He dealt with it swiftly and effortlessly. And not only that—in fluent French!

'And the recipient?' he enquired, reverting to English to ask her.

Cynthia Hardwicke, she almost said, realising only just in time that that would blow her cover good and proper. 'Address it to "Mum," care of...' Casually she filled him in with the name of the friend her mother was staying with. 'And the message is simply, *Happy Birthday. Love from Rayne.*'

It took him just seconds, it seemed, to supply the florist with his own details, his voice deep and confident, its dark rich timbre sending an unwanted tingle along Rayne's spine.

'Thanks,' she murmured when he had finished, unable to look at him as she came around the desk. 'I really wasn't asking you to do that. I can let you have the cash.'

'There's no hurry,' he said, his tone surprisingly reassuring, the sudden touch of his hand on her shoulder bringing her startled gaze to his.

She looked instantly wary, King thought, noticing the guarded emotion in the green-gold depths of her eyes. They were, quite simply, the most beautiful eyes he had seen on any woman he'd ever met, but there was some other emotion behind the wariness that was defying him to touch her. Sadness, he was startled to recognise. Deep-buried, but not altogether concealed. And he knew in that moment that some-how—somewhere—those eyes had penetrated his conscious-ness before. Last week? Last year? He gave a mental shrug. Perhaps it was only in his dreams.

'We got off to a bad start.' He was surprised at how hoarse his voice sounded. Was it because his hormones had kicked in again, causing him to harden from the warmth of her body through her thin blouse? Or was it the dark and heady mix-ture of her perfume? 'I thought it might be sensible if we were both to try again.' Otherwise she'd get away from him, he was sure, and he'd never lost a woman he'd set his heart on having in his life.

'Try?' she ventured croakily, realising why she had never stood a chance against his potent masculinity as a teenager. He was really quite amazing. With those dynamically dark looks. In the way he spoke. The way he carried himself. As if he owned the world. Which he probably did. Or a fair proportion of it anyway, she thought cynically, resenting him for how rich he was, how influential, and for making her wish that she was spreadeagled over that desk with him…

'To be civil to each other,' she heard him saying. 'I'll accept that your reason for being here is all above board. And you…' He was massaging his lower jaw with his free hand. 'You'll promise to keep your hands to yourself.'

Wings of colour touched her cheeks from his all too shaming reminder of how she had struck him. 'As long as you promise to do the same with yours.'

'If that's what you want.'

Rayne felt her throat constrict. 'What's that supposed to mean?'

He smiled silkily. 'You know very well.'

Yes, she did. The last thing she wanted was for him to spell it out, but it seemed he was going to anyway as he went on.

'Calling a truce, unfortunately, isn't going to put paid to the fact that there's a definite chemistry between us, Rayne, even if you do want to deny it. But a woman doesn't respond to a man the way you responded to me unless she wants that man to make love to her. Even if she is, as I'd very much like to rule out, a woman with some other agenda.'

'I got carried away—that was all,' she said quickly, hating to admit it but desperate to quash any adverse notion in his mind about her reasons for being there. 'So. I find you attractive.' Who wouldn't? 'But we don't always give in to what our baser instincts are telling us to do, do we? I'm sorry I reacted in the way I did.' She was referring to striking him. 'I was just a bit wound up, that's all. Unprepared…'

'For what happened between us?'

She nodded.

'And are you still unprepared?'

No, she wasn't, she realised, because even this conversation with him was turning her on, making her body zing with a host of traitorous impulses.

'I can deal with it,' she said huskily, wishing she could tear herself away from him, but she couldn't seem to do it.

'Can you?' When she didn't respond, too sensually aware to answer, coolly he suggested, 'Let's see.'

As he was speaking he'd positioned himself on the edge of the desk. Now, as his arm snaked around her tiny waist, Rayne lost her balance and shot out a hand to steady herself, gasping as she made unwitting contact with the hard, bunching muscles of his thigh.

The intimacy sent shock waves coursing through her body. She could tell from King's sharply drawn breath that it was having a devastating effect on him too.

'Heaven help me if you weren't sent here just to drive me out of my mind!' he rasped before his mouth came down to plunder the warm, willing cavern of hers.

This time she didn't stop to think because the scent and sound and feel of him were driving her insane for him and suddenly she was utterly lost to the eager and hungry demands of her own body.

When he tugged her blouse open and pulled a lacy cup down over her full, high breast, she arched her back, angling her body in sweet invitation to him to take the hard throbbing tip into his mouth.

Proud of her femininity, she writhed between his thighs, thrilling in his strength as he used them to clamp her to him, while he continued to drive her crazy by suckling harder at her breast.

Unlocking her womb, she thought crazily, as sensations spiralled downwards to the most secret heart of her, making her hot and moist in readiness for the hard penetration of his body.

'Deny it all you like, you're going to be my woman, Rayne. You *are* my woman. Understand?' he breathed raggedly against the sensitised hollow of her ear. 'Otherwise why would you let me do this?' His fingers found her other breast, making her gasp and strain against him as he tormented the sensitive bud. 'Or this?' His other hand slid down her body to clasp her buttock, caressing and moulding, its heat searing through her thin trousers before it moved possessively round to cup her aching femininity. 'Why?' he demanded huskily. 'If you can't accept that, too?'

She wanted to protest. She knew she should. But how could she? she demanded chaotically of herself. When she knew she had been made for this! That she was his and always had been, and that even if her mind recognised the treachery of acknowledging it, her body wouldn't listen.

But she had to make it listen...

He's your enemy. So what does that make you?

Dredging up every ounce of self-discipline that she could muster, she wrenched herself away from him.

'I don't want this!' she choked, dragging the back of her hand across her mouth.

'Really?' Still perched on the edge of the desk, he was breathing as heavily as she was. 'Then you're putting up a darn good show of convincing me otherwise.'

'I don't care what you think.' Which was a joke, she thought distractedly, even as she said it. Because, for some strange reason she still did. 'I don't want to get involved with you.'

'Why not? When it's so patently obvious that we could be good together?' He looked hot and flushed and still so obviously aroused. 'Are you in a relationship with someone else?'

'That's none of your business,' she snapped, straightening her clothes with faltering fingers.

'So you aren't,' he deduced correctly.

Because wouldn't it have been the best way of keeping him at bay, she thought, realising it too late, if she had said she was?

'So what was it, Rayne? A disappointing attachment?'

You could say that! her heart screamed bitterly, because there had been nothing that had shamed or disillusioned her more than her reckless crush on him.

'I just don't go in for casual sleeping around.'

'I'm pleased to hear it,' he responded deeply, his eyes fixing on her with a dark intensity. She looked really quite shaken, he thought, wondering why, when in every other way she seemed so much a woman of the world. 'For what it's worth…it doesn't rank very highly with me, either.'

'Hah!' Despite her brittle little laugh, she couldn't help wondering if he was telling the truth. She wanted to kick herself for hoping that he was.

'You really have a very low opinion of me, don't you?' he remarked, running a long tapered hand through his thick hair. She was surprised to notice that it was trembling slightly.

So even the high-and-mighty Kingsley Clayborne was human!

She wondered why she was even allowing herself to grant him any concessions, and put it down to the fact that she was so affected by him—by what she had allowed him to do to her—that she was still too unsettled by it to feel anything.

'Why should it matter to you what I—' she began as she was smoothing back her hair, but broke off when a stick prodding the door he'd failed to close brought it flying open. Both of them had been too otherwise preoccupied to hear the wheelchair approaching.

'King? Rayne? Oh, there you both are!' Mitchell Clayborne's colour was unusually high as he manoeuvred his chair into the room and Rayne guessed he'd been doing too much, against his doctor's orders.

'King, I wanted you to retrieve the book I dropped down behind the bedside cabinet but, since Rayne's here, she can do it for me and perhaps read a little to me. Have you finished with her?'

King's eyes were speculative as, on his feet now, he regarded her from his superior height, looking totally unfazed by what had just happened between them.

'Yes, I've finished with her,' he told his father.

Reluctantly inhaling his scent, keen to get away, Rayne brushed past him, although she could tell from that slight compression of his devastating mouth that what he was really saying was that where she was concerned he hadn't even begun yet.

CHAPTER FOUR

THE following day Rayne decided to escape from the house for a while, needing some time to decide what she was going to do.

She was uncomfortable associating with the people who had wreaked such devastation on her family, but she couldn't see what else she could do. She didn't want to leave there without the evidence or admission that she was determined to secure for her father's sake.

She had started asking Mitch questions last night while she had been reading to him—very subtly, and supposedly innocently. Like how he had begun in business. And when exactly had he hit upon the idea for the MiracleMed software. How he had felt when it had taken off.

'King must have been very proud of you,' she'd ventured, assessing his reaction, looking for any change in his hard, world-weary features, any note of guilt in his gravelly voice.

He'd seemed all right at first. But then he'd grown more and more agitated, even when their conversation had reverted to more casual topics. As well he should have! Rayne thought bitterly.

He'd looked so unwell, though, and had sounded so breathless that her conscience wouldn't allow her to ask any more leading questions.

'I think you should go to bed,' she had advised worriedly, ringing the bell to summon one of the male members of staff to help him. She was frustrated, though, that yet another day had gone by and she was still no nearer to realising her goal.

Now, this morning, he had sent for her and told her that he didn't need her services today, and so she'd decided to take herself down into the town for a proper look around.

'You'll need some of these,' he'd told her from his bed, pressing a whole wad of banknotes into her hand.

Shocked and embarrassed, she had thrust them back at him. 'I can't,' she'd protested, appalled at taking money from anyone—let alone someone she despised so much.

'Don't be silly. How do you think you're going to get around and buy the odd souvenir?' he'd demanded of her gruffly. 'With those big bright eyes and that naturally winning smile?'

Shrugging off his compliment, she had to accept that he was right. Being robbed hadn't exactly left her in a position to be proud.

'I'll pay you back,' she'd promised resolutely, not only for his benefit, but for her own. She didn't like being in this man's debt any more than she wanted to like him, but he was making it very hard for her not to do either.

Now, coming down into the hall, her heart sank when King appeared, looking dynamic in dark blue corduroys and an ivory-white shirt that left his forearms bare, just as she was asking one of the maids in her somewhat limited French if she could call her a cab.

One fluent instruction from him in the girl's own language had the young maid almost bobbing in compliance before she cast a swift glance at Rayne and darted away.

'What did you say to her?' Rayne enquired, puzzled, because it certainly didn't sound like anything as simple as ordering a taxi.

'I told her I'd take care of it,' he replied succinctly and without any of the mental disturbance that just the sight of him was producing in her.

'I don't need you to rescue me from every difficult sit-uation,' she assured him with a slight tremor marking her words, unintentionally conveying to him how unsettled he was making her feel.

'Nevertheless…you've got me.' There was triumph in the clear blue eyes that drifted lazily over her tie-waisted che-quered blouse and white cut-offs. 'Now, where did you want to go?'

'Nowhere in particular,' she said, being deliberately ob-structive. She wanted his help even less than she wanted his father's, and she certainly didn't welcome how her body was responding just from the way he was looking at her. 'I was just going to do a bit of sightseeing—and without having to worry about the car,' she told him, wishing he'd just take out his phone and order the cab he'd said he'd deal with.

But with a hand at her elbow, sending her thoughts spin-ning into chaos, he said, 'In that case, I'll be more than de-lighted to show you around.'

She wanted to protest. To tell him that she was going out because the strain was proving too much, being in this house with her father's bitterest enemies and not feeling able to tell them who she was. But mainly, she decided, it was because of King himself. Because he disturbed her equilibrium so much and made her feel so ashamed of how he made her feel every time he came near her that she wanted to put as much distance between him and herself as she possibly could.

But with King Clayborne, she was discovering, argument was futile.

Consequently, it was with a raging awareness of him and a mind that was far from relaxed that she allowed him to drive her into town.

She was relieved, though, when he kept the conversa-tion light. Impersonal. Not touching on any awkward top-ics. Like why he made rockets go off inside her every time he touched her. Or why she pretended not to want to go to bed with him, when every betraying cell in her body assured him that she did!

Instead, he acquainted her with the lesser-known facts about Monaco as they drove down through its flower-decked streets which, earlier in the season, formed the circuit for the world-famous motor racing Grand Prix. And he gave her an insight into the country's history and its royalty, making it interesting for her. Making her want to know more as she listened to his deep and sensually caressing voice, remembering how it had warmed and excited her all those years ago.

'Did your mother receive the flowers?' he asked as he finished parking the Lamborghini in a space he had had no difficulty finding.

'Yes, thank you,' Rayne responded succinctly.

'Did she like them?'

'Probably,' she answered minimally again.

She caught the curiosity in his eyes and in the faint smile that touched his hard yet exciting mouth, and she knew she had to explain. He had paid for them, after all.

'When I rang Mum earlier, the friend she's staying with said she was still asleep. She offered to wake her to show them to her, but I thought it best not to disturb her. After what she's been through, she needs to get all the rest and relaxation she can.'

'She must appreciate having such a thoughtful and caring daughter,' he commented, taking the keys out of the ignition.

'She deserves no less,' Rayne expressed, absurdly warmed by what had been no less than a compliment from him. 'She's always been there for me.'

'You've been fortunate in having such a good relationship with your mother.'

'Didn't you with your mother?'

The question slipped out and she didn't know why she had asked it. He could have had seven doting mothers for all it meant to her.

'My parents divorced when I was five. My father got custody. I only saw my mother on a few occasions after that. She preferred rearing horses to rearing children. The last I heard, she was living on a stud farm with her third husband somewhere in Colorado.'

Rayne shrugged. 'That's a pity,' she said, meaning it.

In answer she saw the firm masculine mouth compress. 'Not really. I went to boarding school, which was best for Mitch and for me. I learned how to be self-sufficient—independent—from a very early age, which stood me in good stead, as it turned out.' He wasn't actually spelling it out, but Rayne didn't need to ask to know that he was talking about Mitch's accident. 'I don't know whether I would have been so equipped to handle everything that was thrust on me if I'd had the type of family life that most people take for granted. I think it's true what they say. That what you've never had, you never miss.'

Rayne didn't wholly agree with that. After all, if he had had a bit more maternal love perhaps he wouldn't have been so ruthless and insensitive towards other people. Like her father, she thought achingly, her teeth clamping together as she looked away.

'I was lucky,' she murmured half to herself and in a tone that emphasised the whole poignancy of her loss. 'Dad was always there too and he was quite simply the most caring, understanding and honourable man I've ever met.'

'Quite a happy family, then?' He sounded quite cynical, and Rayne wondered why. Was it because he hadn't known that sort of stability himself? Being packed off to boarding school. Being made to feel abandoned—although he hadn't said so—by both his parents.

She could almost have felt sorry for him, except that King Clayborne wasn't the type of man to inspire pity.

Even so, against all the odds, she was surprised to find herself enjoying his company as he guided her around the

Principality. She even found herself laughing at something he was saying as he brought her across the tree-fringed square that gave onto the wide imposing frontage of the palace.

Pale and majestic with its crenellated towers, it was once the home, Rayne reminded herself, of the beautiful actress of the nineteen-fifties who had been plucked out of Hollywood and brought here by her prince, only to steal the hearts of his people.

In fact there were photographs of her adorning shop windows all over the town, Rayne had noticed, still a lure for the tourists even so many years after her death, a beautiful legend whose name had become synonymous with Monaco.

'It must have been like a fairy tale for her,' Rayne whispered a little later when she saw yet another image of the princess in the latest shop window they were passing. 'To win not only a prince's love—but a whole country's.'

'Even a country that is less than five hundred acres across.'

She pulled a face and smiled, amazed at how small an area Monaco took up, amazed too by King's knowledge of it.

'And you? Do you believe in fairy tales, Rayne?' he asked, his voice suddenly strung with mocking amusement.

'Fairy tales?' She pretended to be considering it as she looked up at him askance.

'Happy ever afters. Two people living side by side and loving each other until death they do part.'

'Well, it's obvious you don't,' she lobbed back, noting the cynicism with which he'd said it. But then, after the way his parents' marriage had broken up, she supposed she could understand why.

'I know what Mum and Dad had,' she murmured almost reverently. 'All right, it wasn't exactly a fairy tale. They had their ups and downs. But they loved each other, and knew they always would.' And they had instilled in their only daughter the importance of the qualities that kept a marriage strong. Love, trust and faithfulness. It was something she strongly believed in and it was something she staunchly refused to allow anyone to dismiss lightly. Even King Clayborne. 'You were just unlucky,' she said, moving away from the window and the image that had sparked off this unwelcome conversation with him in the first place.

The cathedral. The palace. The exotic gardens. They did it all. He even showed her the amazingly palatial building of the famous casino, although they didn't actually go inside.

It wasn't until they got back into the car that Rayne realised she'd switched her phone off before going into the cathedral and had forgotten to switch it back on. She chastened herself for letting everything go out of her mind simply because she was with King.

She started when her phone began to ring almost as soon as she had switched it on.

'Lorrayne?' Cynthia Hardwicke said when Rayne put the phone to her ear.

Immediately Rayne tensed up. King hadn't yet switched the car's engine on. Could he have heard the way her mother had addressed her?

Trying to sound normal, she wished her mother a happy birthday when she had finished enthusing about the bouquet Rayne had sent her.

'I'm glad you like it,' she breathed, relaxing a little, relieved to hear her mother sounding so buoyant. She envisaged Cynthia Hardwicke, with her grey-tinged auburn hair freshly tinted for her holiday, starting to regain the weight she had lost, her skin—usually as pale as her own—beginning to bloom again beneath a welcome Majorcan sun.

'Like them? I can't tell you how much they've brightened my day! But why did you have the message signed "Rayne", love?' She gave a little chuckle. 'Weren't you thinking?'

Catching her breath, Rayne cast a surreptitious glance at King.

He was scanning through various menus on his own phone.

Checking appointments and deleting texts, she decided, her eyes drawn to that strong, steady hand that had driven her nearly mindless for him yesterday.

He still hadn't started the engine, letting her take her call.

Killing time, she suspected, while he waited for her to finish. Nevertheless, she knew that although he was displaying all outward signs of being courteous and respecting her privacy by appearing otherwise engaged, that sharp brain of his was probably attuned to every agitated response she was uttering.

'I couldn't have been. I'm sorry,' she added quickly, because she certainly didn't feel happy being forced to deceive her own mother. 'But you're all right, are you?' she asked uneasily, having sensed a flicker of interest from the man beside her since uttering that apology, even though he still appeared preoccupied with the obvious running of his business.

'Of course I am,' Cynthia Hardwicke assured her, although there was a curious note in the disembodied voice. 'But are you? You don't sound yourself, darling. Is anything the matter?'

'No, of course not.' She laughed to try and convince her parent that everything was as it should be, to try and behave normally.

'Are you with someone?'

Rayne could feel herself growing hot and sticky from her toes upwards.

'Who is it?' Her mother persisted in wanting to know.

Rayne hesitated before replying. 'It's just a friend.' Involuntarily, her gaze strayed to King and his heart-stopping profile. It exhibited forcefulness overlaid with unstinting sensuality. Authority and energy, harnessed with a magnetism that had the drawing power over a woman that the moon had over the tides. But he had obviously picked up the gist of the conversation because his mouth was twitching now in what she could only describe as sensual mockery. He clearly didn't regard her as a friend, any more than she considered him one. Though for plainly different reasons where she was concerned!

'I thought I knew all your friends,' Cynthia pressed. Which was true, Rayne thought. She did. 'You're sounding pretty secretive. That's not like you.'

'It's no one of any significance,' Rayne stressed, already regretting the comment when she saw the way King was looking at her as she wound up the conversation and rang off.

'Why didn't you tell her about us?' he enquired, turning all his attention towards her now.

'There is no "us",' she reminded him tartly, feeling the heat of shame creeping up her neck and into her cheeks when a masculine eyebrow lifted in obvious dispute.

'No? Not when I only have to touch you to send your hormones rocketing through the roof? I'd say that was significant enough to constitute an "us".'

He'd also taken her out to breakfast that first morning. Showed her around Monte Carlo and bought her lunch today. Not to mention making his credit card available to pay for her mother's birthday bouquet!

'I'm sorry about the way I described you,' she felt she had to offer, even if his reasons for helping her might be purely self-motivated. 'But I had to put her off the scent.'

'The scent of what?' he asked smoothly.

'That I'm here.'

'In Monaco? Or with me?'

'Both,' she answered truthfully now. 'She thinks I'm staying with my friend in Nice. If I told her I was in Monte Carlo on my own, she'd worry.'

'And if you said you were with me?'

'Then I'd have to explain how I came to be in Mitch's house in the first place, and she'd worry even more.' No, more than that. She'd have a fit, Rayne thought, shuddering to think what Cynthia Hardwicke would say if she knew that her daughter was hobnobbing with the family who had ruined her husband. Another shiver went down her spine as she thought of how easily she could become involved—especially with King—if she didn't watch her step.

'You don't think she'd approve of you picking up older men?'

'I didn't pick him up,' she reminded him, stressing the point. 'I meant I'd have to tell her how I'd had my belongings stolen. With losing Dad so recently, Mum gets worked up about things and imagines something terrible's going to happen to me. If she thought I needed her in any way, she'd be over here like a shot, and I couldn't risk letting her do that.' Even if the Claybornes hadn't been in the picture. 'She needs her holiday a hundred times more than I need mine. I don't intend doing anything that would spoil it for her.'

'That's very commendable,' he murmured, the sound rumbling deeply from his chest. 'You love her very much, don't you?'

His observation was, like his eyes, so direct and probing that she looked quickly away without answering, ashamed to let such a hard-headed character as he was see the welling emotion she had to fight to control.

King couldn't take his eyes off her tight, tense features—the perfect structure of her forehead, the pert nose with those slightly flaring nostrils, the gentle curve of her cheek.

This girl was a real enigma, he decided, with his face a study in concentration. On the one hand she seemed guarded and extremely defensive, which aroused his natural suspicions, especially since he'd taken her as a gold-digger. Definitely like someone with something to hide. Yet on the other hand she spoke about and behaved towards her mother as though she would give her life for the woman if she had to, which didn't quite tie in with the hard-headed opportunist he was prepared to think she was. He was finding, he realised, that he harboured very conflicting opinions about

Rayne Carpenter, and it wasn't in his nature to be confounded by anyone. And on top of that there was still this strong and nagging feeling of having known her before...

'We all do things according to what our consciences tell us we should do, don't we?' she suggested meaningfully, wishing she could control her tongue and not let her emotions run away with her until she was ready to hit him—and his father—with the truth.

'Should it prick my conscience that every time you come within a yard of me I want to take you to bed?' he said softly, fondling her hair. 'Or that you want me to against your own better judgement?'

The space between them was suddenly charged with so much electricity it was as if someone had lit a whole box-ful of fire-crackers and Rayne's heart started hammering in her chest.

'Can we drop this subject? Please,' she breathed emphatically.

Her breath seemed to stick in her lungs as his arm came across the back of her seat, bringing him closer to her.

'Have you never heard the expression "He who pleads is lost"?' he murmured with his smile predatory, his lashes thick and dark, shielding his eyes as they rested on the fullness of her trembling, slightly parted mouth.

When his lips touched hers it was only to make contact with the outer corner of her mouth, a contact that left her craving the full onslaught of his kiss, made her grasp the seat to stop herself from twining her arms around his warm, muscled torso as he lifted his head.

'What's wrong, Rayne? Can't you accept the consequences of what you've got yourself into?' His voice was quite steady, not ragged with sexual desire as she'd imagined it would be. In fact there was a note of hidden danger in the very choice of his words.

'I wasn't aware I'd got myself into anything,' she uttered

tremulously, knowing he was still suspicious of her, still vigilant, even if she had imagined that softening in him just now, because she had, she realised, telling herself now that she had been a fool to do so.

'Then you obviously need convincing,' he said.

She expected him to demonstrate exactly what he meant, but he didn't. Instead he simply started the powerful car and drove them back to the villa.

So what had he meant by that? she wondered when, once there, he left her to her own devices, abandoning her to deal with some business in the study. Did he intend to keep her on tenterhooks—make her wait until her guard was down before proving his point to her again? That she couldn't resist him. Or had he guessed the secret she was keeping from him and Mitch and was merely luring her into a false sense of security until such time as he disclosed what he had uncovered?

And that was a very unfortunate pun, Rayne decided with a grimace because, if she wasn't careful, she was in danger of him not only guessing who she really was before she was ready to tell him, but also of winding up in his bed! And wouldn't that be a double victory for him? She shivered just from the thought of it, although even self-loathing couldn't temper the excitement that heated her blood every time she considered him being her lover.

'I don't think you should be doing this,' Rayne counselled, watching Mitch manoeuvring his chair along the wooded path where he had insisted she bring him today. 'Getting out so early so as to give everyone the slip is one thing, but persuading me to bring you over such uneven ground as this—'

'Will you shut up?' Mitch said, carrying on ahead of her, his hard mottled hands on the wheels pushing him stubbornly to his goal.

The trees thinned out, making Rayne gasp, not only from the sheer danger of the cliff edge just below them, but at the panorama of nothing but glittering sea and sky that had suddenly opened up in front of them.

'Can you show me anything better than that?' Mitch challenged, waving a hand towards the view. 'I used to come here a lot when I was young. It's where I proposed to my first wife.'

'King's mother,' Rayne said tentatively.

'Did you know she left me?' He gave a harsh bark of laughter. 'Of course you did. Everybody knows it. Everyone knows I'm not the easiest of men to live with.'

Rayne glanced down at him, noting something that sounded remarkably like regret in his voice. Did he still miss the woman who had deserted him and their five-year-old child? Miss her still, even though he'd finally found someone else to take her place?

'As a boy, King blamed himself for his mother leaving us. For leaving him,' Mitch was saying, much to Rayne's surprise. 'It hardened him. Made a cynic of him. Especially where marriage and family is concerned. We never could form the bond we should have formed. He was already a man by the time I met Karen.'

'Your second wife?' A woman half his age, who had died so tragically when their car had come off the road, Rayne reflected, although it was King she was reluctantly thinking of. King, the child who had lost a mother, even though she was still alive. And King the man, who was left scarred by the desertion. Left hard and uncaring. Unable to trust...

Mitch nodded and started to cough. 'Here. Help me with this thing, will you?' he spluttered.

He was having difficulty opening the zip of a leather pouch he'd brought with him. When she gave it back to him, he swore when he looked inside.

'What's wrong?' Rayne asked him anxiously.

'Does anything have to be wrong?' he wheezed, turning his chair with such angry force that it lurched sideways, lodging one wheel in a grassy hollow.

Rayne shot over to grab the handles, trying to pull it free.

'I can't move it!' she gasped, finding the man's bulk and the awkward angle of the chair too much for her inadequate strength. To add to that, Mitch's breathing was beginning to worry her.

'I'm going to ring King,' she said quickly, taking out her phone when her attempts to dislodge the chair proved ineffectual.

'No! We don't need him,' Mitch protested to her dismay.

'I'll have to,' Rayne told him, too frightened by the danger of the situation to be intimidated by him, even if every bone in her body rebelled at having to explain to King.

He answered her call on the second ring, his voice deep and strong, the voice of a man who could take on the world and come out fighting.

'King! It's Mitch! We're...' Quickly she acquainted him with their exact location. 'He's got his chair stuck in a rut and he seems to have come out without his medication. It's for his breathing. I think it's—'

'I know where it is,' he rasped, and that was it. He was on his way before she even had time to cut the call.

Rayne couldn't have been more grateful when she heard the throb of the Lamborghini's engine. Through the trees she saw the car practically skid to a halt and she went weak with relief when King leapt out and raced towards them without bothering to close the door.

'Thank heaven you're here!' she breathed.

It was with immense gratitude that she relinquished the handles of the chair into his stronger and more capable hands.

'Keep clear of this,' he ordered, and with his efficient and determined strength managed to bring the man and his chair back onto even ground.

How effortlessly he had saved the day, Rayne marvelled, with tears of relief biting behind her eyes now that the ordeal was over.

'You should never have brought him out here,' he admonished after he'd overseen Mitch take his medication and was now pushing him back to the car. 'Or at the very least you should have told me where you were going.'

'He didn't want me to,' Rayne argued, refusing to be the whipping boy for two very indomitable males.

'Then you should have refused to drive him. Or at least used your own initiative to let me know where you were going.'

'It wasn't her fault.' Mitch sent a scowling upward glance back over his shoulder at his son. 'And stop talking about me like I wasn't here. That isn't like you, King. Anyway, I wanted some freedom. I get sick and tired of people fussing over me. Rayne doesn't fuss over me,' he expanded surprisingly, without looking at her as she trooped along beside them, still feeling shaken, and now unjustly chastened, by King's flaying tongue.

'I really didn't know he was going to get me to drive him here,' she admitted, trying to placate him, sensing he was still angry with her after he had got his father and his chair back into the Bentley and was now moving back to his own car. 'But I couldn't go against his wishes and tell you he was going out. He's got so much pride, King. Almost as much as you,' she tagged on by way of an accusation, surprising herself by defending Mitch. 'He feels humiliated asking you to do the simplest things he used to do himself,' she uttered with angry tears welling up in her from those frightening moments when she'd been hanging on to that chair, sick with worry over Mitch Clayborne's state of health. 'Have you never felt humiliated by anything?'

She looked like a warring goddess, King thought, seeing her eyes dancing like splintering emeralds and her tousled red hair falling wildly round her shoulders as her beautiful body squared in decisive challenge against him. But those tears were genuine, and the fierceness with which she was standing up for his father touched him in a way he didn't want to be touched.

One stride was all it took and he was reaching for her.

'It's all right,' he reassured her, enfolding her in his arms and feeling her slender body shaken by sobs. 'It's all right. There's no harm done,' he murmured into her perfumed hair.

It seemed so right to cling to him, Rayne thought, steadied by his hard warmth. He seemed so dependable and strong. So much so that she wanted to stay there with her head resting against his shoulder while she breathed in his very masculine scent and felt the heavy beat of his heart drumming against hers.

But that was just a flight of fancy because of all she'd been through this morning, she told herself. Because she needed someone and he just happened to be here.

'I've got to get Mitch home,' she said huskily, pulling herself free, and tripped across to the Bentley without a glance back.

In her room the following evening, Rayne paced the tastefully patterned tiles, reflecting on the previous day's events.

That episode with Mitch had been scary, but so had those traitorous feelings she'd experienced during those few crazy moments in King's arms.

Sexual attraction was one thing. You didn't have to know or even like someone very much to feel its unmistakable and often dangerous tug. But what she had felt when King had shown that tender and more understanding side of his nature yesterday had been thoroughly more bewildering and complicated.

She was there to get an admission—and through the tabloids if Mitch refused to comply with what she wanted—and getting emotionally involved with King Clayborne wasn't on her agenda. Even if Mitchell Clayborne thought it should be!

'Is there something you're not telling me, Rayne?' he had

asked her after she'd pulled out of King's arms and climbed into the Bentley yesterday.

'No, I don't think so,' she'd refuted, knowing full well he was referring to the embrace he had just witnessed between them.

'Pity,' he'd expressed, although that unusual glint in his watery blue eyes had assured her he didn't believe her. 'You'd be a good match for him. He needs someone who'll stand up to him once in a while, and I must admit it would be no hardship to me if you were to stick around.'

Which she definitely wasn't going to! Rayne thought now, with the same stab of guilt she'd felt yesterday in realising that she was unintentionally getting herself caught up in Mitch's affections.

She was getting far too involved with both men, and she had never intended that, she thought despairingly. The longer she stayed, the more she was becoming embroiled in their everyday lives, their worries, their concerns and, where King was concerned, she didn't even have to spell out the problem to herself there.

Quite simply, that crazy fever she had been suffering from as a hapless teenager had returned in full force, threatening to consume her with its intensity because she had no protection against it. His cruel words and actions then should have immunized her for life, and she thought they had until she had met him again the other night. How he made her feel was like an ever-changing strain of some deadly virus that couldn't be controlled, and the second time around it was even more potent and deadly than the first. It didn't help either, telling herself that she was a woman now and therefore should have known better. Known how to ride the torments of this lethal attraction until it passed. Because it wouldn't, she was shocked to realise. Because the only drug that would alleviate her symptoms was in the full-blown act of his possession of her. And then the relief, she thought, would only be short-lived, because once she had allowed herself to cross that line with him she knew she would never be able to have enough of King Clayborne. Like a drug, after its effects had worn off, the symptoms would return until she could indulge herself again, which would mean taking him into her until she could feel his power and his energy filling her up and seeping into every clamouring cell of her body, by which time she would be a hopeless addict.

No, she resolved, coming to a standstill at last on the beautiful pale Indian rug and making her decision.

First thing in the morning, she determined with a sudden painful contraction of her stomach muscles, she was going to let them both know exactly who she was and what she was doing there.

CHAPTER FIVE

'MONSIEUR CLAYBORNE? *Non*, he is not up yet,' the house-keeper informed Rayne when she enquired where he was. 'And Monsieur King…' Hélène Dupont always referred to him as that, Rayne noticed, as though to call him simply 'King' would somehow detract from the respect she felt he commanded '…I believe he is still giving an interview on the terrace.'

'An interview?' Rayne queried, her curiosity aroused.

'It's to do with the documentary he is sponsoring. The one about clean water for some African villages. I believe he is heavily committed to that. They rang early. It was unexpected,' Hélène told her before concluding, 'I think he will be about half an hour more.'

'Thanks,' Rayne responded, her smile strained, her insides knotted up, as they had been almost continuously since she'd made her decision to tell the truth, so much so that she'd scarcely slept last night.

Finding out about the charitable work that King was involved in didn't make her feel any better about deceiving him. In fact, it made her feel a whole lot worse.

She hadn't, until now, even considered him having a compassionate side. Not really compassionate. Not until he had comforted her on that cliff-top the other morning. But then hadn't he seen to it that her mother got her flowers when she was having difficulty ordering them? And rushed back from New York as soon as he'd been alerted to his father's state of health?

But then again, perhaps his main reason for coming back from New York was to suss her out, Rayne reflected disparagingly. After all, he'd already been forewarned that she was there. And as for the flowers? Well, he wanted to get her into bed, didn't he? And there could be other reasons for wanting to help people less fortunate than oneself. Like the publicity, for starters.

With his influence and money he could easily afford to help fund an irrigation programme for people in Africa. And it wouldn't do his company's image any harm at all to have favourable deeds associated with the Clayborne name.

And now she was being as cynical as he was, she thought, in willing herself to believe those things about him when, had she not known him better, and particularly after what Hélène had told her, she would have said he was a man of principle—a man who wouldn't stoop to stealing another man's intellectual property and helping to ruin his life.

But he had, she thought bitterly, standing there at the foot of the stairs and closing her eyes against the truth. That Kingsley Clayborne, the man who had broken her heart as a teenager and who now had her craving his attentions with every weak, betraying cell in her body, just wasn't the man she wanted him to be.

Half an hour later, Mitch still hadn't put in an appearance and King was still tied up with his visitor on the terrace.

Coming downstairs again into the deserted opulence of the sitting room, Rayne could still hear their muted voices drifting in from the sun-soaked terrace. The male interviewer's tones were rather even and uninteresting in contrast to the deeper, richer modulations of King's.

How could any woman not find herself drawn to him and in the most fundamental way? Rayne wondered, listening to him. When everything about him was unadulterated perfection? The way he looked, the way he conducted himself, the way he dressed. That sexy yet authoritative voice that had the power to make every woman he spoke to go weak at the knees.

Then there were the other traits of his personality, too. Determination and drive and that restless energy about him that made up the whole man, and amounted to a pretty formidable package which made him impossible to ignore.

In fact it gave her goosebumps all over her body, just as it was doing now. Goosebumps and a multitude of nervous flutters in her stomach from the thought of what she had to do and the consequences of what telling him the truth might be.

Hearing the scrape of chairs on the terrace, accompanied by phrases that warned her that the interview was drawing to a close, suddenly Rayne lost her nerve. Wasn't it Mitch she should be confronting first anyway?

She had almost reached the stairs when she caught the sound of the men's footsteps across the tiled floor and she quickened her own, keen to get away before they reached the hall.

'Oh, Rayne...' Too late, the honeyed resonance of King's voice drifted towards her, lifting the hairs at the nape of her neck, exposed by her loosely piled-up hair. 'Have you seen Hélène?'

'Not for some time,' she said shakily, turning round, her breath locking from the impact of his dark-suited executive image, from his poised elegance and commanding stature.

Why was it that other men seemed to diminish beside him? she wondered with painful awareness. She had only a fleeting impression of his younger, shorter companion because her gaze was held—against her will, it seemed—by the steel-blue snare of King's.

Beneath her simple white top and jeans, her body pulsed from the pull of his powerful magnetism and it wasn't until he broke the contact to say something to his tawny-haired visitor that Rayne, remembering her manners, turned to speak to the man.

As she did so, her greeting, like her smile, died on her lips and Rayne could feel her blood starting to run cold.

'What are *you* doing here?' the interviewer asked.

'Do you two know each other?' King enquired with a rather quizzical expression.

Rayne wanted to deny it, her mind chaotically processing what the chances were of the journalist who'd come to interview King being someone from her past. And not just someone. But Nelson Faraday!

'We worked together,' she admitted when she could wrench her tongue from the roof of her mouth, hoping against hope that the slick-talking journalist wouldn't give her away, not before she'd had the chance to do it herself.

'In what capacity?' King asked, still wearing that interested smile, but behind the urbane veneer Rayne could sense every sharp instinct honing in like a stalking tiger's.

'I was the office junior,' Rayne put in quickly. 'When I started, Nelson here was already destined for greater things.' So great that she'd packed him up after only a couple of evenings out with him because she hadn't liked his cut-throat methods of reporting. But this man knew more about her than was comfortable. In fact, it was downright mortifying, Rayne thought, in view of where she was and who she was with.

'You're too modest,' her ex-colleague told her, much to Rayne's overriding dread and dismay, because it was clear the man had picked up on her reluctance to talk. She could tell he was assessing what she might be doing in this billionaire's pad and, from the way his eyes took in both her and King, knew that his mind was already working overtime. 'She might have been the office junior when she started out on that provincial little rag, but everyone could see she had the nose of a bloodhound and that once she'd got going there'd be no one to touch Lorrayne Hardwicke for sniffing out a scoop.'

It was clear Nelson Faraday was still holding a grudge, Rayne realised, horrified, her eyes darting guardedly towards King.

There was tension in his jaw and in the sudden granite-like mask of his features. His cheekbones seemed to stand out prominently beneath the olive of his skin.

'Oh, dear...' The other man was putting up a good show of looking shamefaced, because he couldn't have failed to notice the atmosphere that had grown cold enough to freeze the heat of the Mediterranean day. 'Did I say something I shouldn't have?' he remarked with an award-winning performance of mock innocence.

'No, of course not,' Rayne put in quickly, wise to Nelson Faraday's tactics and to what he must be thinking. That she was either romantically involved with Clayborne's dynamic helmsman or she was there to dig up some dirt on the family. Which was too close to the truth, she thought, with her heart frantically pumping.

'You certainly didn't,' King remarked with a pasted-on smile, the cynicism with which he said it making Rayne shiver.

'Well, it's lovely seeing you again, Lorrayne.' The younger man was backing away, his eyes suddenly wary beneath the implacable steel of King's. 'I'll forward a copy of the article to you, sir.' Nelson was lapsing into total deference, as he always had with his most prized interviewees, and King Clayborne had to be among his most prized of all.

'You do that.' King's tone was clipped, lethally low.

His anger was roused and she was about to bear the brunt of it, Rayne realised, knowing she deserved no less. Knowing she should have told him—told them both—from the start.

Like a coward, though, as soon as the other man had left, she started towards the stairs, wanting to get away from King until he had calmed down.

'Oh, no, you don't!' Strong fingers suddenly clamped onto

her wrist, preventing her precipitous flight up the stairs. 'So you're Lorri Hardwicke. Well, well.'

'Let me go!' She could feel his white hot anger pulsing against her as those determined fingers tightened relentlessly around her soft flesh. 'I was going to tell you! Both of you!' she gasped as he pulled her towards him.

'You were? Well, that's very magnanimous of you!' he scorned. 'And when exactly were you going to do that? When you'd got your "scoop", or whatever it is you're after? What exactly is it you're after, Rayne?' His face was livid, his voice so dangerously soft that with one fearful yet furious yank she managed to pull free.

'What was rightfully my father's!' she shot up at him, massaging her wrist, numb from the pressure he'd applied.

'And what is that?' he breathed equally softly, every long lean inch of him powerfully intimidating, like a dangerous adversary she'd been unfortunate to cross. Well, he wasn't going to intimidate *her!*

'You know very well!' There were family loyalties at stake here. 'You stole that software from him! You and Mitch! You knew MiracleMed was his and you stole it!'

'And you, my dear young woman, have been very much misinformed if you think you can make a serious allegation like that.'

'I haven't been misinformed! I know the hours he put in— at home, as well as in the office. And don't speak to me like that. I don't need to be patronized by you!'

'Just the pleasure I can give that beautiful body when it suits you.'

'No!' Shame washed over her like scalding water.

'Don't deny it, Rayne. You're as enslaved by your desire for me as I am for you. Or was that all part of the act?' he tossed at her roughly.

'No!' What could she say? How on earth had they got on to this? 'That...that just happened,' she stammered, stepping back as he moved nearer, knowing that even now, if he touched her, she would have no defence or resistance against his particular brand of humiliation. And it would be humiliation. He'd make certain of that.

'I'll bet it did! And I'll bet you've been laughing all the way to the bank in thinking I was so taken in.'

'You were never taken in.'

'Maybe not. But Mitch was. So what is it you want?' he demanded. 'Money?'

'That's the only thing that matters to people like you, isn't it?' She was near to tears, but tears of anger and frustration which had been bottled up for so long. 'Well, it might surprise you to know that some of us put honour and respect before making ourselves rich at other people's expense.'

'Really?' A masculine eyebrow arched in obvious derision. 'There didn't seem to be much honour and respect in the way you engineered your scheming little way into this house. Those thieves didn't take your passport, did they, Rayne?'

His question, so direct and demanding, seemed to suck the air right out of her body. King Clayborne might be a lot of things, but a fool wasn't one of them.

'No,' she answered, inhaling again. 'It was in the glove compartment of the car with my driving licence.'

'And your credit cards? Where have they been while Mitch and I have been financing your every requirement? Your meals. Trips into town. The flowers for your poor ailing mother?'

The disparaging way he referred to Cynthia Hardwicke sent anger coursing through Rayne in red-hot shafts.

'My mother has been sick! Very sick!' she retorted fiercely. 'And don't you ever dare to refer to her illness like that again! And my credit cards *were* stolen! They took my bag. My traveller's cheques. All my money. Everything! It was only when Mitch jumped to the conclusion that I'd lost my passport as well and invited me back here that...well... that I let him think so. I felt he owed it to me. Or to Dad at least.' And it was her father who had said that windows of opportunity didn't just open on their own—that you had to create them. 'I needed to talk to him but I knew it wouldn't be easy, and it just seemed like the perfect chance I'd been waiting for.'

'I'll bet it did! So what have you been hoping to gain out of all this if, as you say, you're far too honourable to contemplate blackmailing him with the threat of selling some cracked-up story to the papers? Are you in league with this Faraday character? Is that it? Was that why he turned up here so coincidentally today?'

'That *was* only coincidence,' she retorted with bright wings of colour staining her cheeks. 'And I wasn't going to blackmail Mitch. I was hoping—if I could talk to him—let him know who I was and what my father went through—that it might prick his conscience in some way. That I might be able to appeal to his better nature.' Hotly then, she couldn't help adding, 'I didn't imagine for one moment I could ever appeal to yours!'

'So why didn't you tell him who you were? Right away? The day you got here?' he interrogated, ignoring her last derogatory remark about himself. 'Or was the prospect of sharing a house with such a newsworthy name too much for your journalistic instinct to pass up?'

'I didn't because he seemed so shaken up after those lads had taken his wheel,' she answered, ignoring him in turn, even though she was railing inside at his high-and-mighty attitude, 'I didn't want to do or say anything that might have upset him even more. And the day after that he still wasn't well.' And then you arrived, she remembered with her mouth firming in rebellion, although she didn't tell him that. Didn't let on that she feared and regarded him with far more respect than she feared and regarded his father, not least because of the frightening strength of her attraction to him. 'And then when Hélène said he had a heart problem and high blood pressure…' Her shoulder lifted in a kind of hopeless gesture. 'I didn't want to be responsible for making him ill.'

A thick eyebrow was lifting again in patent scepticism. 'Do I detect a conscience, Rayne? Surely not! And you'll have to excuse me,' he tagged on, with no hint of apology in his voice. 'It's Lorri, isn't it? But then it's difficult keeping up with the change of identity.'

'It isn't a change of identity. Rayne Carpenter's the name I write under,' she said, admitting it now.

'Why? So that your victims won't know who you are when they read the sensationalist dirt you've managed to dredge up about them?'

'I don't write that sort of news story.' Chance would have been a fine thing! She had never got beyond covering house-fires started from flaming chip pans and local demonstrations about library closures, whatever Nelson Faraday had led him to believe. 'I only write the truth.'

'Or your warped version of it.'

'Is it warped to expect some credit for my father's work? I'm not after any personal or financial gain, whatever you may think.'

'No. Just making strong allegations about a man who isn't well enough to defend himself. Well, I'll defend him, Lorri. And you'll find I'm not half so weak—or so smitten—as my father is. Grant Hardwicke did a lot of the work on MiracleMed. I believe I'm right in saying that. But he did it under a corporate umbrella.'

'Which was what you told him the night you came round and threatened him!' she reminded him. 'And just for wanting recognition for what was rightfully his! He created that software long before he ever joined forces with Mitch. He just didn't have the resources to launch it. He was honest and hardworking and never cheated or lied to anyone in his entire life. And you made him ill,' she uttered, aggrieved, and with such painful emotion in her voice it was difficult to breathe. 'You and Mitch! He might still have been alive today if you hadn't!'

Though she was saying it, some small part of her acknowledged that it wasn't strictly true. That there were other events that had contributed to the strain her father had been under. Like his bouts of drinking that had only made their family life harder. And the way he'd seemed to lose the will to do anything—even look for a job towards the end—which had only added to his increasing sense of worthlessness.

'I admire your loyalty to your father,' King surprised her by expressing. 'But I didn't see him as quite the paragon of virtue you obviously did. We're all human, dearest, and Grant Hardwicke could be as opportunistic and self-motivated as the next man.'

'That's a lie!'

'Is it?' King's mouth was a tight, inexorable line. Looking back, he still couldn't believe the man's crocodile tears when he'd told him about Mitch's accident. But then he hadn't been crying for Mitch—his closest friend and colleague. All he'd been concerned about was his own personal losses and all he might have stood to lose if his accusations of theft had ever been brought to the public's notice. 'Far be it from me to want to hurt you, but I can be every bit as ruthless as you're accusing me of being if—'

He broke off abruptly as a flushed-faced Hélène suddenly came rushing down the stairs towards them, her features looking pinched within their frame of greying bobbed hair. 'Oh, *monsieur*! You had better come quickly. It's Monsieur Clayborne!' Her hand went to her chest. 'He has the pain...'

King was springing away from them without any further prompting, taking the open staircase two steps at a time.

He was already at his father's bedside when Rayne raced up to Mitch's room with the housekeeper close behind her. One look at the elderly man who was sitting on the edge of the bed, still only half-dressed, revealed that he was in extreme pain.

'Call an ambulance!' King directed urgently towards Hélène.

While the housekeeper was summoning help on the bedroom telephone, Rayne hurried over to the bed.

Oh, please! she prayed. *Let him be all right! Don't let it be my fault that this has happened!*

'He needs to lie back,' she instructed, sensing that this was one occasion when King needed someone's help and advice, with all her basic first aid training rushing to the fore. And when he looked at her questioningly, 'It's all right. I know what I'm doing,' she assured him, suggesting how he could help, already plumping pillows and generally helping to make his father as comfortable as she could. Now wasn't the time to tell him how she had taken a first aid course after her father had died, when she'd read how anyone could make a difference in a medical emergency.

Glad that at least she hadn't contributed to this situation by actually telling Mitch who she really was, she watched King through eyes suddenly blurry with relief, gently easing his father back against the pillows, catching his deep, low murmurs of reassurance—despite his own concern—as he tried to put the older man's mind at rest.

Oh, to have him speak to her with that depth of emotion! She felt a surge of longing that was quite out of place in the current situation, or within the bounds of anything approaching logic. Why did she want anything more from him other than—as he'd pointed out to her downstairs—the pleasure her body craved from him? Surely she wasn't allowing herself to think of him in any capacity beyond that? Because if she were, she warned herself harshly, then she was being a total fool.

The ambulance didn't take long to arrive.

'Can I come with you?' Rayne appealed to King, hot on

his heels as he flew down the stairs while the medical team were bringing Mitch down in the lift.

'You?' he emphasised, his expression a contrary mix of surprise and blinding objection. She had been quick to help his father, King thought. And she looked concerned. Genuinely upset. But with a woman—particularly this woman—who could tell? 'That won't be necessary,' he told her succinctly, leaving her staring after his dark retreating figure and feeling as though she had been slapped in the face.

'What is it, King?' Mitchell Clayborne was staring at his son's broad back as King in turn stood staring out of the window of the private clinic. 'God knows I haven't been the best of fathers, but I would have thought the news that I'm not going to be consigned to the history books just yet would have made you a bit happier than you seem.'

Sighing heavily, King dragged himself away from an absent study of the clear evening sky, his mouth pulling down on one side at his father's dry remark. Mitch certainly sounded better, and his breathing was easier than it had been a few hours ago, but he had no intention of causing the man any undue distress.

'It's nothing that can't wait,' he answered.

'And it's nothing that I'm not man enough to take—even wired up like a puppeteer's blasted dummy! Tell me.'

It was clear to King that the man would be more likely to die of a heart attack from being kept in suspense rather than from being told the truth.

'It's about Rayne,' he breathed, the air seeming to shiver through his nostrils.

'What about her?' Mitch brought his head off the mountain of pillows, suddenly looking alarmed. 'She's all right, isn't she?'

King nodded. He couldn't believe how fond of her his father had become.

'What, then?' Mitch demanded with considerably less than his usual strength.

King hesitated, but only briefly. 'She's Lorri Hardwicke,' he stated, drawing another deep breath.

Mitch stared at him for a long worrying moment before closing his eyes.

'Shouldn't I have realised it!' he exclaimed somewhat breathlessly at length, with an unusual tremor in his gravelly voice.

'Do you know why she's here?'

'I think I can guess,' Mitch returned. 'But tell me anyway.'

'She's saying what Grant said all those years ago. That Claybornes took the credit for MiracleMed when it really belonged to him. In short, she's accusing us—but you in particular—of, at best, gross professional misconduct and, at worst, outright theft.'

Had he gone too far? King wondered anxiously, wanting to kick himself for telling him when he saw the pain that darkened Mitch's eyes and heard the way his breathing had suddenly became more laboured.

'She's right, King.'

'What?' Above the sound of footsteps hurrying along the corridor outside and the intermittent bleep of Mitch's monitoring machine, King's response was one of almost inaudible shock.

'I did steal that software.'

King's face was sculpted with harsh lines of bewilderment. 'What are you saying?' he whispered, his face turning pale, his mouth contorting in revulsion and disbelief.

'It's true,' Mitch admitted heavily. 'I know you thought I put a lot of my own time into it, but I didn't. I'm glad it's out. I'm glad you know, King. It's been hell keeping it to myself— and from you in particular—all of these years.'

For once King found himself unable to think straight. Had he really heard Mitch correctly? Was his own father admitting to being a thief? Was that what had been gnawing away at him for so long? Making him so bitter?

'You let me—let everyone—believe he produced the whole thing in the company's time. Or a large part of it, anyway. Under Clayborne's corporate umbrella!' King reminded him roughly.

'It was his word against mine—and he had no proof.'

'So you took it on yourself to call it yours? Another man's intellectual property!' King stared at his father, appalled. 'Didn't it occur to you that you might be robbing him of his livelihood? That he had dependants? A wife and a daughter?'

'So she's come after me,' Mitch murmured, sounding far away, as though he wasn't listening. 'After all these years! What a sparky little thing.'

'She's deceitful!' King rasped, feeling his earlier anger brewing, although he wasn't sure any more whether to be angry with her as well as his father, or just with himself. 'What I hadn't realised until now was that you were. My own father!'

He swung away towards the window again, massaging his neck, sightlessly watching the glittering sky mellowing with the lateness of the day. He didn't want to be speaking to his father like that. Not while he was so unwell.

He hadn't wanted to speak to Rayne as he had either, but the shock of discovering who she was with the knowledge that he had not only been ensnared by her beautiful face and body, but had also been made a fool of into the bargain had been much too much for his masculine self-esteem to take all in one go.

He couldn't forget though how fiercely she had defended Grant Hardwicke, standing up for him with all the loyalty and determination of a loving daughter. Nor could he forget the emotion in her face when she had asked him if she could come here today and he had point-blank refused to let her. After she had helped his father, too. After she could so easily have turned away and not got involved. Although she hadn't, he reflected, even though only minutes before she had been accusing Mitch of committing the worst possible corporate crime against her father. And in that, he thought, with his big body stiffening, she had been right...

'King?'

The weak appeal had him reluctantly turning to regard the semi-reclining form on the bed, the tension so gripping in his shoulders that he thought his spine would snap.

'Why?' he demanded of his father, his strong features ravaged by a complexity of emotions. 'Why did you do it, damn you? Why, Mitch?'

Amazingly, there was contrition and sadness too, King noted, in the watery blue eyes looking out of his father's loose-skinned, rather florid face. 'Do you—of all people— really need to ask?' He looked away, towards the ceiling and the metal curtain track that ran around his bed, sighing heavily. 'You *know* why.'

CHAPTER SIX

THE sky was changing from molten gold to burnished crimson.

In the grounds surrounding the house and on the forested hillside the crickets had struck up their shrill evening chorus, while in the distance, way below, Monte Carlo was waking up for the night.

From the terrace, her hand on the sun-warmed stone of the balustrade, Rayne watched the lights gradually come on in the hotels and apartments, and in the cafés and bars along the coast.

A thousand stars shining almost as brightly as the planet whose light seemed to be winking at her above the dark pointed spear of a cypress tree. One lonely star in a flaming universe, Rayne thought, which was how she felt right at that moment since Hélène had taken herself off to her rooms at least an hour ago, and Rayne hadn't heard anything from King since he'd left with his father and the paramedics that morning.

A sharp breath escaped her as she heard the low growl of a car turning in through the gates, which she couldn't see from the house as it was hidden by trees, and the next second saw the Lamborghini coming along the drive. The car drew up and her heart leapt when she saw King get out and hand his keys to a member of staff to garage it for the night.

She heard their muffled voices, King's low and congenial, the other man's infused with courtesy and yet genuine respect for his mega-rich, mega-influential employer. King was his employer, she had no doubt about that, since Hélène had told her that he oversaw most of his father's affairs these days.

She had tried ringing his cellphone several times to find out how Mitch was, but if it wasn't engaged it had been on voicemail. The one message she had left around lunchtime, asking King to call her, hadn't been answered, and Hélène hadn't been able to tell her anything beyond the fact that Mitch was still having tests.

Watching King's dark head disappear under the portico, she waited, breath held, for him to come into the house. A few moments later she swung round with her heart leaping absurdly as she caught the sound of his light footsteps moving towards her over the terrace.

'How's Mitch?' she asked without any preamble.

Bracing herself for some sarcastic response about her caring, his appearance, nevertheless, made her whole body go weak.

He was still dressed in the white shirt and dark suit trousers he had been wearing that morning, but his jacket was hooked over one shoulder. He was tie-less now and his shirt with the two top buttons unfastened was unusually crumpled. His hair looked as if he had been raking it back all day, but now there were dark strands falling loosely across his forehead as if he had finally given up trying to control it. His strong jaw was darkened by a day's growth of stubble and there were dark hairs curling over the open V of his shirt.

Never had she seen him look so dishevelled, Rayne realised. Nor so utterly and sensationally male.

'He had an angina attack. It wasn't a coronary.' The relief with which he informed her of that was almost tangible.

'So he's going to be all right?'

His eyes tugged over the golden slope of her shoulders beneath the shoelace straps of her dress, and Rayne felt as if the fine white chiffon would melt beneath the searing steel of his eyes.

'Do you truly care?' he murmured, so softly that she might have misheard him as he tossed his jacket unceremoniously down onto one of the heavily cushioned dining seats.

'Of course I care. I left a message,' she told him a little sharply, 'but you didn't answer.'

Because he hadn't known what to say to her after their antagonised scene this morning. Hadn't known then—when he was at the hospital—or now—when he was faced with the reality of telling her—exactly how to deal with the things his father had told him.

He merely dipped his head in acknowledgement of what she had said.

'They're keeping him in for observation, but hopefully he's going to be all right.'

He looked so weary—devastated, almost, Rayne would have said—that she had the strongest urge to go over and put her arms around him in the way he'd done with her the other day. Tell him that she understood the anguish in having a sick parent—of losing a parent, even—but she held back. This was King Clayborne, after all. Hard. Impervious. Impenetrable. And he had found her out in the web of deceit she'd been weaving ever since she'd been here. He'd have no sympathy for her. Or any member of her family.

Steeling herself against that imperviousness with her head held stiffly, she enquired, 'Have you come back to ask me to leave?'

'No.'

No? Surprise pleated her forehead. 'I thought you wouldn't be able to get rid of me fast enough.'

'That's what I thought,' he admitted with a heavy sigh.

Rayne's frown deepened. 'What's changed your mind? Or do you just want to keep me here to extract some sort of payment from me for lying to you?'

He came over to lean on the balustrade, looking out towards the sea beyond the twilit city. He chuckled softly, an almost self-derisory sound. 'What sort of man do you imagine I am, Lorrayne?'

She couldn't answer at first because all the replies that sprang to mind weren't very complimentary. And because he was so near that she could feel the power of his masculinity emanating from him, smell the faint hint of his animal scent beneath the lingering traces of his cologne.

'Tough. Determined. Implacable.' Her mouth pulled slightly as she finished reeling them off.

He made another self-deprecating sound down his nostrils as he angled his body towards her, his forearm resting on the still warm stone. 'Why do I get the impression that those adjectives were carefully chosen from the best of a bad bunch?'

Because they were, she thought, but remained silent this time.

'You also thought I was grossly unscrupulous in being party to some treacherous and probably very unlawful act against your father,' he stated, straightening up, 'but I want you to know categorically now that I wasn't.'

Strangely, she believed him, Rayne realised, shocked. But there was no room for anything other than truth in the deep intensity of his voice, nor, she accepted with a pulse-quickening heat stealing through her as she brought her head up, in the disturbing clarity of his eyes.

'And Mitch?' She looked quickly seaward to avoid his penetrating gaze, fixing hers on the light-spangled silhouette of a cruise ship moored way out in the distant harbour. 'Did you tell him who I was?'

Her voice was infused with resentment, King noted. Something she had held against Mitch—against *him*—for years. 'He knows who you are,' he disclosed.

'And what did he say?' She looked up at him again now, her lovely face pained and accusing. 'Did he admit that

MiracleMed was Dad's? And that he snatched it from under his nose?'

King took a deep breath. 'It wasn't quite like that, Lorri.'

'No?' Her head was tilted in rebellious challenge and her hair was as fiery as the Monte Carlo sunset. 'How was it?' she bitterly invited him to tell her.

King glanced away, way down across the scintillating Principality, watching a stream of red tail lights form a blur of colour along the highway following the curve of the coast.

This day had wreaked havoc on him, if any day could. First finding out that Rayne was Lorri Hardwicke. Then Mitch's suspected heart attack. And, to add to all that, those soul-sinking moments at the clinic when he'd believed his father was the worst kind of criminal. But Mitch's sin had been a moral one, rather than anything illegal. Even so, it still offended King's sense of propriety to realise that Grant Hardwicke had been treated so unfairly. And it wasn't going to be easy telling his daughter the truth when, either way, she wasn't going to want to hear the answer.

'Your father signed an agreement with Mitch just after they went into partnership together, to the effect that any work done for the company while they were directors of the company would be to the benefit of the company. I know. I've read the clause in that agreement. I had my secretary email it through to me today. Your father was the technical whiz-kid, but was lax when it came to business dealings or keeping vital records. If he hadn't been, he would have registered his right in that software prior to signing that agreement, but he didn't, which was a pity,' he said, sounding as though he meant it. 'And much to his cost, as it turned out.'

'And that's it?' she queried in protest. 'He signed his rights away and it's a pity! Why? Because it made Claybornes so much money!'

'Lorrayne, stop,' King advised gently, understanding her pain, her justified anger and bitterness. He wished he hadn't learned from Mitch today that he could have acknowledged the other man's concept of that software and that he had chosen not to. It had been an act of vengeance against a man who had been his friend and whom he had wound up hating. 'No one could have quite foreseen the impact that MiracleMed would make after it was launched.'

'But it did!' she complained. 'And Dad never received any credit for it!'

'And, believe me, no one regrets that more than I do,' King said somberly.

He didn't add that, for what it was worth, Mitch now regretted it too. That would be like openly admitting his father's wrongdoing, and if Mitch wanted to apologise to her then it was up to Mitch to do it himself.

He didn't know why his father had suddenly burdened him with this today, unless it was because he'd feared he was going to die and wanted to get it off his chest. But at least he could understand now why his father had become so bitter, and how shouldering such a weight of remorse could have contributed to making him ill.

'OK. So there's nothing I can do about it now,' she accepted grudgingly, 'because it was all signed, sealed and delivered legally! But that doesn't alter the fact that your father came by that software immorally and very conveniently, after that quarrel he obviously instigated, which made Dad walk out. And I know it wasn't Dad's fault, because Dad never quarrelled with anyone!'

'For heaven's sake, Lorri, stop being so naïve!'

'Naïve?' She gave a brittle little laugh. 'You think I don't know my own father?'

'Apparently not.'

She sent a sidelong glance up at him. 'What's that supposed to mean?' she bit out with her eyes narrowing.

'It means that, much as I believe my father exercised his rights under that agreement—whether ethically or otherwise—I also believe that it's time you, my misinformed lit-tle kitten, heard a few home truths about what really broke up their partnership.'

'I already know that,' Rayne tossed back assuredly. 'It was professional jealousy. He knew what Dad had created was going to be worth a fortune and he wanted to reap all the rewards for it himself!' She couldn't believe she was saying things like this about Mitch Clayborne. The man who had taken her in. Offered her food and shelter and a safe haven to get her affairs sorted out when she'd found herself virtu-ally stranded so far from home.

'Jealousy, maybe. But not so much professional as deeply personal, I imagine,' King was saying with a grim cast to his features. 'My father quarrelled with yours because of the af-fair Grant was having with Mitch's wife.'

'You're lying!' She couldn't believe King could dream up something so despicable.

'Am I? Then why do you think there were never any proper claims made by your father to try and secure the rights to his software?'

'Because you threatened him! I was there when you did it!' she reminded him passionately.

'And you think that was enough to stop him pursuing any claim against the company if he thought he could have, un-less he hadn't something to hide?'

She wanted to protest, but his words rang with something so akin to the truth that they left her speechless. There were times when she had wondered why her father hadn't fought harder to try and get the rights to MiracleMed into his name. Sometimes she had begged him to, but he hadn't, and she'd thought it was because he just hadn't had any fight left in him.

'I came round that night—rightly or wrongly—to tell him to stay away from my father. I had very little else on my mind except that my stepmother had been killed and that Mitch was more than likely to be in a wheelchair for life. He'd known about the affair for weeks, which had led to Grant leaving the company. But it was the shock of being told by Karen that she was leaving Mitch to run away with your father that caused him to lose control of the car that night and swerve into that tree. He was going to leave you, Lorrayne. You and your mother. The dear, devoted husband and father.' The censure which dripped through his words was evidence of just how little respect he had for Grant Hardwicke—or the institution of marriage. 'Did you really not know?'

Mortified, Rayne could only stare up at him. Finally she made a small negative gesture with her head.

How could it be true? Her parents had loved each other, she reflected achingly. Or had King been right in calling her naïve? Had Cynthia Hardwicke known? Been aware of her husband's infidelity? But no, she couldn't have been!

Painfully, she recalled her mother's constant assurance that it was Grant's memory that had given her the strength to fight through her recent illness. So what would it do to her now if she found out that all that love and devotion she'd thought he'd shown her had been just a sham? It would destroy her!

'I'm sorry I've had to be the one to destroy all your illusions about love and commitment, my dearest.'

'I'm not your dearest.' She wasn't ready yet to accept endearments from him after he had opened her eyes so cruelly.

'Maybe not,' he conceded which, contrarily, hurt her even more, 'but you're feeling bruised and cut up about it, naturally.'

How do you know how I feel? she wanted to fling at him, but bit the words back. It wasn't his fault that everything she'd believed in seemed to have crumbled to dust within the space of a few short minutes, even if it felt like it right at this moment.

She turned away from him, her hands resting limply on the top of the balustrade.

'He lied,' was all she could say, staring out at the darkening sea, hurting so much she didn't think she'd live to trust anyone ever again. 'To me. To Mum…'

'I'm sorry,' he murmured deeply. And, after a few seconds, 'Passion makes us do the most unprincipled things,' he said.

Didn't she know it!

'It's the second strongest animal force in the universe.'

'Only the second?' she uttered disdainfully.

'Perpetuation of the species.' His tone was flat—unsentimental. 'Preceded only by self-survival.'

He made it all seem so cold. So basic.

He laughed rather harshly when she told him so. 'Isn't it?' he suggested with unyielding scepticism.

'Is that all you think love is for?' she challenged, wondering how she had got on to this subject with him as she faced him again. 'Just to create babies?'

'Yes, but then we aren't actually talking about love, are we…Lorri?'

He caught her hand, his fingers strong and warm, but angrily she tugged out of their grasp.

'Don't call me that!' It was her father—her father, whom she had loved and trusted and looked up to, who had first started using that name. Everyone else had simply called her Lorrayne. 'It's Rayne to you!'

Which suited him fine, King thought, having been used to calling her that. It suited the woman she had become and who had changed so dramatically from the thin and stammering—at least with him, he remembered wryly—little scarecrow whom he'd known as Lorri, and who had graced the office for a time with her quiet presence.

'Then don't hate me, Rayne, for simply acquainting you with the facts.'

'I don't hate you.' Hate was just the flip side of a coin that suggested far too intense an emotion than she was prepared even to think about. 'Why should I hate you?'

'For knocking your gallant knight down off his horse?'

'I'm getting used to it,' she murmured with unshed tears in her eyes. Her emotions were too raw at that moment to stop herself from tagging on, 'After all, you did it to me once before.'

A frown knitted his brows as his gaze probed the moist hazel-green of hers.

'I was mad about you,' she admitted, not caring what she said any more.

'I know.'

His deep revelation shocked and surprised her. Had she been that obvious?

'You noticed me?' she breathed, having never beyond her wildest teenage dreams ever dared to hope.

'You were a child,' he remarked succinctly.

'I was eighteen!'

'As I said—a child,' he repeated with a soft chuckle, lifting her chin with his forefinger, his thumb lightly brushing her pouting lips. 'A little girl with big hungry eyes...' Because he knew now why those eyes had kept tugging at something inside him ever since that night he'd walked in and saw her standing here on the terrace. 'Huge hungry eyes,' he continued, 'that I remember thinking even then that one day some man would drown in. But which right then belonged to a love-sick teenager whose main reason for agreeing to help out in that office, I suspect, was to try and make me want to take her to bed.'

'I wasn't love-sick,' she denied with embarrassed colour flaring in her cheeks, overwrought from the feelings that had been building in her for hours because of his keeping her in suspense, because of his opinion of her father. Because she had been aching to see him—and talk to him—all day when she should have been hating him, convinced as she had been of just how ruthless he was. And when all she wanted him to do right now—and from the first moment she'd seen him walk in here tonight—really was to take her to bed. 'Anyway, if I had been, it wouldn't have worked with you, would it,' she murmured with her blood suddenly pounding in her ears because the touch of his hands sliding lightly across her shoulders and down over her bare arms seemed to be setting her insides on fire. 'Most of the time you ignored me.'

'I wasn't knocked out by spiky bleached hair and dark purple lips and eyes,' he stated with his mouth moving wryly. 'And what would you have preferred me to have done? Taken you over my knee for even thinking about it with a man way out of your age group?'

'You were only twenty-three!' she reminded him, breathless from her galloping emotions, wanting to run away from them—from him—and all the things he was saying that was sending a reckless excitement leaping through her. 'That's only five years.'

'And those five years made a world of difference,' he said sagely.

Which they would have, she accepted in hindsight.

Riveted by a desire that was stronger than her will, she looked up at him now to ask in a voice that was huskily provocative, 'So what are you saying? That I'm too young for you?'

She heard the sharp catch of his breath above the chorus of crickets and, from the lights that had just come on around the terrace, saw the sensuous pull of his lips before he answered thickly, 'Not any more.'

Common sense should have told her to stop this insanity before it got too far out of hand but, as his mouth came down over hers, it was already too late.

CHAPTER SEVEN

As King wrapped his arms around her, Rayne felt herself melting against him.

His jaw rasped against hers where he hadn't shaved since that morning, but she rejoiced in its roughness and in his hard warmth that was driving every last trauma—of the day, of the past week and of the longer past—from her mind.

The only thing that mattered was him—here and now, the desire that had her clinging to him, as the only sure, secure thing in her crumbling universe.

She had wanted this—so much! Wanted it now a thousand times more than she had ever wanted it before. It was as if all the feelings she had had for him as a teenager hadn't died but had been shut away inside her, brooding and intensifying so that now they overwhelmed her like a flood, gushing through her from her toes upwards and spreading along every nerve and sinew of her being.

He had called her a child then, but she was a woman now and she wanted to prove it to him, angling her body so that her needs were obvious—the craving for his hands against her naked flesh.

He read her like a book, following each silent sentence her body was conveying to him as long tanned fingers slipped the fine straps off her shoulders so that the chiffon bodice rippled like a waterfall down over the betraying fullness of her breasts.

King groaned deeply in his throat, his body hardening from her perfect femininity. He felt like ravaging her, driving them both wild in his need to blot out all the things that Mitch had revealed to him today. To lose himself inside the warm, slick wetness of her glorious body. But he forced himself to exercise all his powers of restraint, knowing that she wouldn't thank him for that.

This woman needed to be handled with kid gloves, her beautiful body served and pleasured with the skill and tenderness it deserved.

She had deceived him, it was true. But only because she'd believed him to be party to a gross misdemeanour against her father—a father who hadn't been wholly worthy of her trust and fierce loyalty. Nevertheless, the fact that she *had* deceived him made him glean a delicious thrill in inflicting some sensual punishment upon her in making her wait for all her body—and his own!—craved.

Dipping his head, he drew the hard peak of one pink begging nipple slowly into his mouth, taming the urge to pull her against him as his strong hands rested on the firm, gentle curves of her straining hips.

He was driving her crazy, Rayne thought headily, clutching at his shoulders, wanting to rip off his shirt, feel the hardness of his muscles and his hair-roughened chest against her breasts.

'Easy,' he advised softly, his breath fanning the wet swollen tip he had just released from its torturous pleasure. 'What is it you want? Show me what you want.'

Maybe she should have been embarrassed, she thought distractedly, but hunger had stripped her of all inhibitions, so that now she had no qualms about doing as he'd asked.

Thrusting her neglected breast towards him, she uttered a deep, guttural sob when his mouth closed over it, sending sensations plummeting down through the centre of her body.

'Is this it?' he broke off to murmur against the pale fleshy mound after a few moments. 'Is this what you want?'

No, I want you! All of you! Around me! On top of me! Inside me!

She heard her brain screaming out those phrases and couldn't believe that any man could reduce her to thinking them. But this wasn't any man, she assured herself hectically. This was King.

His hands on her hips were warm and firm, yet still holding her away from him when all she wanted was to *feel* him, feel the evidence of just how much he wanted her.

But he was controlling the pace, she realized, wanting more of what he was doing to her and yet crazy for this particular sensuous torture to end as he burned a slick, hot path between the valley of her breasts with a teasingly slow caress of his tongue.

'I hate you, King Clayborne,' she groaned.

She could say it now. Now, when the conflagration of need that was burning inside her raged so fiercely that there could be no turning back because what was there to lose? He knew how much she wanted him. Needed him.

'No, you don't,' he murmured thickly against her ribcage.

He knew that too, she accepted helplessly, because she couldn't fool him any more than she could fool herself. But to express what she was feeling in any other way would be no less than sheer folly, she realised, despairing at herself for wanting—needing—him so much.

With a deep groan from the depths of his throat he caught her to him then, and from that moment he was no longer in control.

Hungrily his mouth captured hers, their breath mingling, tongues blending in an urgent mimicry of the ultimate outcome of where all this was leading, as Rayne let her head fall back in wanton acquiescence to all that was about to happen.

They were equal now. Mouth to mouth. Pulsing body to

pulsing body. Locked in the most fundamental act between a man and a woman.

Below them, beneath the darkening Mediterranean sky, Monte Carlo pulsed with a life of its own but they were oblivious to it, the sound of their impassioned breathing like an extension of the exotic chorus outside.

His teasing had backfired on him, Rayne realised with her heart singing. He was desperate to make love with her, a scenario she had only ever dared to dream about seven years ago. But now it was happening and the reality was sending shock waves of pleasure through her body way beyond any she could ever have imagined.

With a small sob of need and urgent trembling fingers, she tugged at the buttons of his shirt.

His chest was bronzed and beautifully contoured, as she had imagined it would be, the feathering of hair that ran down and disappeared inside his shirt igniting a fire in her as she ran her hands across it.

'You're beautiful.' It seemed as natural to say it as it did to breathe, as very softly she pressed her kiss-swollen lips to his heaving chest. He smelled of pine and a masculine musk that acted like an aphrodisiac on her already heightened senses. His skin tasted slightly salty when she brought her tongue across the hard wall of muscle and bone.

'Not nearly as beautiful as you.'

Did he really think that? Or was it just sex talking? How could she compare with the super-model type of woman his name was usually linked with? At that moment, though, she didn't care—only that he was with *her*. Like this.

'Take this off,' he urged raggedly, already tugging her dress down over her hips. 'I want to see you. All of you.'

Before she could murmur an objection, having thought about his type of woman and feeling extremely self-conscious about not living up to all he expected her to be, the whisper of fabric was nothing more than a pool of light around her ankles and she was standing there in nothing but her flimsy white sandals and a white lacy string that left very little hidden from the dark intensity of his gaze.

'King,' she breathed, hiding her sudden embarrassment against the warm hard wall of his shoulder. Gently, though, those warm strong hands held her away from him.

'Let me look at you,' he exhaled in a way that was half an entreaty, half a command.

Allowing it, she stood stock-still and closed her eyes against the starkly visual images of what she knew he would be seeing. Red hair cascading like a dark waterfall over one shoulder, the urgent rising of pale breasts with their rosy tips still hard and turgid from his exquisite attentions.

She wondered if he'd think as she did. That her breasts were slightly too full for her tiny waist and the less curvy flare of her hips. But he was smiling when she opened her eyes, the smile of a man well gratified with the gift he was being given.

He reached out then, cupping the undersides of her breasts as tenderly as if each were a rare treasure, and Rayne gave a small moan, her lashes coming down over her eyes against the excruciating pleasure that ripped through her lower body as his thumbs lightly stroked the sensitised peaks.

'Look at me.'

She didn't want to! How could she stand here like this and let him see the naked longing in her eyes? Face him, knowing that her body was betraying the extent of her need of him? But his voice was as much her master as the sensations that were holding her in thrall and very slowly her lashes fluttered apart.

He looked flushed and tousled and as much a slave to his desire as she was, she realised, feeling the burn of his gaze like a brand on her body as it slid leisurely down over her rapidly rising breasts and ribcage, over the flat plane of her belly to the white triangle of lace at the apex of her creamy thighs.

'Such loveliness should be rejoiced in. Worshipped,' he

emphasised heavily, his massaging hands leaving her breasts to follow the same path down over her midriff, her hips and her trembling thighs before coming to rest on the taut mounds of her bare buttocks, the beauty he had just spoken of with the heat of his desire bringing him finally to his knees.

Rayne gazed down on his thick dark hair as his hot mouth sought the heart of her femininity, concealed behind the last barrier of her string.

His moist heat burned into her, mingling with her hot wetness through the wisp of lace, and Rayne plunged her fingers into his hair to clutch him to her and with a groaning need thrust her throbbing centre hard against him.

He groaned his satisfaction as she squirmed above him.

'I think we can dispense with this, don't you?' he murmured huskily.

His smile was excitingly sensual when he tilted his head to look up at her, although the strong masculine face was flushed with the desire that was making his eyelids heavy and lent his mouth the brooding look of a man in the grip of passion.

Rayne sucked in her breath as his fingers made short shrift of removing the little scrap of nonsense. His hands were dark and long and extremely masculine against the smooth, silky sheen of her legs.

Blindly she saw him toss her string down alongside her dress.

Both scraps of nonsense, she thought, if she'd imagined that either could protect her from her own weakness for him, or from his potent masculinity and his determined, exciting hands.

His clothes were unbelievably arousing on her nakedness as he pulled her to him and, where she had tugged his unbuttoned shirt out of his waistband, his chest hair rasped deliciously against her swollen breasts.

'Oh, King…' Involuntarily, she was wriggling against him,

wanting even closer contact. She had never felt more wanton or more feminine.

'Easy, darling,' he said softly, and though she knew that the endearment might have been used with any woman he had been making love to, she was too driven by her need for him to be anything but happy to pretend that just for tonight she really meant something to him. 'Don't you think I feel it too?'

In fact he had never felt so hot or so hard in his entire life, King realised, with such an intense burning throb in his groin it was almost akin to pain.

He hadn't intended this when he had come back from the clinic tonight, bearing the brunt of two men's total disregard for each other. Or having to tell Rayne—while personally appalled at Mitch's lack of ethics—that, legally, she had no claim against his father, and then to go on and shatter all her illusions about love and loyalty into the bargain. But it had been a hell of a day and he needed to lose himself in the pleasure of everything she was offering. And heaven help him if he was behaving like a sex-starved teenager! But this lovely woman couldn't begin to know just how much pleasure it was going to give him to make love to her.

Claiming her mouth once more, he ground his hips against hers to show her just what she was doing to him and laughed softly into her mouth—a satisfied sound—when she gasped from the evidence of his arousal and pressed herself against his hardness in answering need.

Dragging his mouth from the drugging warmth of hers, it was only to rasp against the perfumed silk of her hair, 'Come to bed with me.'

Her murmur of acquiescence was muffled by the depth of her wanting, but he understood.

Cupping her buttocks to lift her, he felt her warm eager legs wrap around him and, like that, somehow they made it up to his suite of rooms.

Monte Carlo was a blur of lights through the panorama

of the open windows, its busy Corniche a blazing snake that led sinuously who-knew-where? Just like where making love with this man would be taking her tonight, Rayne thought distractedly, although she was in far too deep now to care.

From over his shoulder, on The Rock on the south side of the harbour, she glimpsed the palace, floodlit as a beacon against the dark velvet of the night.

Clarity against confusion. The thought rang through her brain. Like common sense against a wild, abandoned pleasure such as she had never known.

As King laid her down on the bed, she let the pleasure take her over—the excitement of him removing his clothes, the hard shadowed potency of his thrusting manhood and the heart-leaping anticipation as he came down to join her.

She reached for him at once and knew the heady thrill of touching him intimately for the first time.

'Go easy,' he advised raggedly and she could tell from his laboured breathing how close he was to losing control. 'I don't want to waste this. I want to savour every minute of these hours with you.'

That it sounded like the prelude to something final, she didn't even want to think about. She couldn't think anyway because, in moving away from her to remove her sandals, he was suddenly employing his tongue to trace a slow sensuous trail along each thigh.

Except that now he had found the secret parting between them and, lying there, breath held in shuddering anticipation, she almost screamed with pleasure when his teasing tongue flicked across her ripe swollen bud.

She had had just two lovers in her life, but she had never permitted such intimacy, and now she knew why no other relationship had ever been enough for her. Because there was only one man she wanted! Only one man she had ever wanted. And she knew that after tonight she would be spoiled for any other man who ever came after King.

As he drove her mindless with his mouth, her hands clutched the soft fabric of the coverlet beneath her to try and stem the tide of pleasure that was building in her. A small guttural murmur escaped her. She didn't want to climax yet.

'What is it? What is it you want, Rayne?' he murmured with his lips softly brushing the soft flesh of her inner thigh. They left a slick trail of warmth where they'd touched, moist from the nectar of her body.

You! her mind clamoured, begging, silently appealing to him. *It's all I've ever wanted—for so long!*

Too unsure of him to actually say as much, she used the language of her body to show him by reaching down to entice him back across her.

'Ah, is that all,' he said softly and, even in the grip of passion, she realised, there was still room for sensual teasing in his voice.

As he reached across to open the drawer of the bedside cabinet, it hit her that he was continuing to call her Rayne. Rayne, not Lorri, because Lorri, the girl he had once ignored—silly, trusting, naïve Lorri—was gone, killed off by the crumbling of everything she had trusted and believed in. By the harsh reality of life as it really was.

King's muttered oath as he pushed closed the drawer he had been groping in suddenly woke Rayne to what was wrong.

'Don't you have any?' she asked breathlessly and a little coyly, despite how far their intimacy had come.

'I thought I did.' He let out a frustrated sigh and then, with a wry pull of his mouth, 'It's been a while,' he admitted to her.

Later, Rayne would glean some comfort from that statement. Right now, though, all she felt was frustration, agonizing and raw.

'I'm sorry, Rayne.' She was lying there with her hair spread like dark fire across his pillow, her beautiful body flushed from the fever-pitch he had brought her to, and which was mirrored by the febrile glitter in her slumberous eyes. 'I should have checked.' He swore again, quite viciously this time. 'Don't look at me like that,' he said, noticing the anguish on her lovely face. 'Or you'll make me lose my mind and all my principles will be shot to the winds, and I've no intention of putting you at risk like that.'

He meant from an unwanted pregnancy.

She could see the effort it was taking for him to honour those principles he'd spoken of. His face, as he drew away from her and sat up, was ravaged by his own frustration. Even in the dim light she could see the flush that darkened the skin across his cheekbones, and his darkened jaw appeared clenched against his thwarted sexual desire. But there was a bleakness to his superb profile that made him look vulnerable and weary.

Of course, she thought, reasoning through the depths of her wanting. He had been worrying about Mitch all day...

With her heart going out to him, she wondered how she could ever have doubted that he was anything other than trustworthy, and that that integrity he was showing her now would extend to every aspect of his life. And her intuition must have recognised that for her to have still found herself so attracted to him, even when she'd wanted to believe the worst about him.

She wanted to tell him she was sorry she'd misjudged him so completely, but she was still too aroused and racked with need for him to speak. She laid tentative fingers on his forearm. 'It's all right,' she assured softly, with wild impulses leaping through her from the sensation of his skin beneath her fingers. 'We don't need one.'

'You're protected?' The disbelief that chased away some of the shadows from his face was worth a month of birthdays, Rayne thought, smiling shyly, too aroused to tell him why. That weeks ago she'd been given the Pill to correct her erratic cycle, thrown out of kilter through worrying about her mum.

'We'll be perfectly safe—I promise,' she breathed, her

simmering desire beginning to bubble over again just from caressing the superbly contoured muscle of his upper arm. It felt firm and solid. As solid as the rest of his body as he came down to her again, causing her to gasp from the weight and power of him, and then from a breath-catching expectancy as he gently parted her legs.

But he didn't enter her right away. Instead, with his hot, hard flesh merely nudging at her moist softness, he treated her to a torturous game of re-arousal that had her sobbing at the ecstasy of his tormenting lips and hands until she spread her legs fan-like and raised her hips uninhibitedly to his in a frenzied and unequivocal invitation to him to take her.

And that was more than he could take, she realised, gasping and overcome by sensation when one long, hard thrust had him sinking deeply into her eager warmth.

Pushed over the limit, she started to climax at once, bucking and sobbing until she was nothing but an abandoned mass of writhing sensations, propelled to greater and greater heights by King's driving and increasingly deeper penetration.

Her zenith when it came was a starburst of colour and spell-binding pleasure in which she felt she was being catapulted to another planet. And then the moment came when King's own climax burst and he was flowing into her, joining her with him and to him, sending the earth spinning off its axis as they floated together—one mind and one body—in some glorious parallel universe.

When she awoke, she was alone in the big bed and the blinds were drawn up to reveal the cloudless Mediterranean blue sky.

She was in a very masculine room, with plain soft furnishings and heavy designer furniture, in contrast to the pale and more delicate fitments of her own room.

Her stomach flipped now as she remembered what had

transpired, the tender spots on the most intimate places of her body an exciting reminder of a long and rapturous night.

Now, though, remembering why she had come here and all that had transpired yesterday, she wondered just how wise she had been in letting it happen.

The Claybornes had as good as destroyed her family—or at least Mitch Clayborne had, even if Grant Hardwicke *had* brought it on himself in incurring Mitch's wrath by planning to run off with his wife. But Rayne's mother wasn't aware of that, and Rayne vowed she would do her best to keep her from ever finding out. However, where King was concerned, her mother still believed, as Rayne had, that he was just as guilty as Mitch of stealing her father's work. So whatever would her mother say if she knew how little it had taken for her daughter to wind up in bed with King? She'd be horrified and hurt beyond belief, Rayne thought, as she would if she knew about Grant's affair. And how could she explain to her mother that King had played no part in hurting her father, when she didn't think Cynthia Hardwicke would even survive knowing the whole truth?

All she could do, she reasoned, was not tell her mother anything—not even let her know that she had been here.

As for Mitch Clayborne...

Turning over in bed, she let out a low groan. She didn't think she could stand the embarrassment of ever facing him again.

She was just about to step out of bed but, hearing the door opening and realising she was entirely naked, she slipped back in, pulling the single sheet up over her breasts.

Despite her concerns, her heart leaped to see King striding in wearing a white dressing gown and leather slippers. He had combed his hair, but his unshaven jaw was even darker this morning and his tanned chest and legs contrasted deeply with the robe.

'You slept well,' he commented, and his smile was so warm

that all her worries were in danger of melting like the winter's last snows. 'Hélène's cooking breakfast, but I thought you might like a glass of orange juice to revive you,' he said.

Thanking him, Rayne took the crystal glass and drank from it gratefully. She couldn't believe how thirsty she was—or how hungry. Obviously making love with him had stirred her appetites, she realised, in more ways than one.

'King… About last night,' she began when she came up for air, hardly able to look at him after all they had shared.

'What are you going to tell me?' He looked at her knowingly. 'That it shouldn't have happened?'

'Something like that,' she murmured sheepishly, finishing her juice.

'Too late, my sweet. It did.' He sounded fatalistic as he removed the empty glass from her hand. 'Not once—but twice—' his mouth was pulling sensually '—if I remember correctly. So what excuse are you going to give me for virtually ripping off my shirt and then nearly driving me out of my mind with your wicked ways?'

The dark intensity of his eyes was making her throb in every intimate part of her that he had made his own, which meant that her 'wicked ways', as he'd called them, still weren't satisfied. Because she still craved him, and even more so as she remembered every tender caress of his skilled and wonderful hands and the burning heat of his mouth on the most secret places of her body.

In a voice tremulous with desire she said, 'I didn't rip off your shirt.' And because this whole scenario was too embarrassing for her she said, 'I think I should go.'

'Go?' He frowned. 'Go where? To the bathroom? Or home?' he enquired flippantly.

'Home, of course,' she responded seriously. 'It's much too embarrassing to stay here now that Mitch knows who I am.'

'Is that the only reason?' he purred with sensuality curling his fantastic mouth again and, before she could answer, too ashamed to know how to respond, he said, 'He's expressly requested that you stay. So do I. In fact, I insist upon it.'

'*Insist?*' Rayne echoed with her rebellious nature surfacing through her unquenchable desire.

'All right, then. I invite you to stay,' he amended.

'Why?'

'Because I think you must be feeling a little overwrought and probably much too tired after...last night,' he reminded her with his irises darkening, although he was still smiling, 'to be in any fit state to go anywhere.'

'I'm surprised, after all you called me yesterday—deceitful, lying, naïve—' she took a warped pleasure in reminding him equally '—that you should even care.'

'Of course I care.'

A glimmer of something deep inside her responded too eagerly to that heavily breathed statement. A throwback to her teenage years. That was all it was, she told herself chaotically.

'You're under my roof,' he went on, surprising her because she'd thought it was Mitch's house. 'I wouldn't want to be responsible for driving you out.'

'*Your* roof?' she enquired obliquely, while reluctantly processing the fact of his merely feeling responsible for her.

'Does that surprise you?'

'No.' Nothing about him surprised her.

'My roof. My house...' her breath caught sharply as the mattress suddenly depressed beneath his weight '...and my bed.'

His voice was arousing in itself, even without the things he was saying, and she thought of those couple of lovelorn weeks she had spent in his office, listening to his voice from behind that glass partition, wondering what it would be like to hear it roughened by desire.

'If Hélène's getting breakfast, we don't have time,' she said breathlessly because he was already turning back the sheet, making her whole body scream in anticipation.

He laughed softly. 'Oh, yes,' he said, pressing his lips against her forehead, and his voice was so soft she had to close her eyes because she couldn't deal with the depth of feeling it aroused in her, 'I think we do.'

CHAPTER EIGHT

RAYNE decided she had to go and visit Mitch at the clinic as soon as possible, since it had all come out now, who she was and why she was there.

She didn't feel like seeing a man who had used the terms of a signed agreement as a payback to ruin his ex-partner because, no matter how bad or naïve a businessman Grant Hardwicke had been, that was what Mitch had effectively done. But although she was still in shock over the things King had told her about her father, she still felt she owed it to Grant Hardwicke to hear the facts first-hand from Mitch himself.

At King's insistence, Rayne allowed him to drive her to the hospital, where a handful of reporters who had learned of Mitch's condition leaped on them like locusts as soon as they arrived at the main doors.

'Is it true, Mr Clayborne, that this health scare of your father's is more serious than the clinic is saying?'

'Is there any improvement in his condition?'

'Does this mean Clayborne shares in all areas are set to rise further with the expectation of your taking outright control?'

Questions came thick and fast, with microphones being thrust towards them, so that Rayne realised just how influential and newsworthy the Clayborne name was.

'You've heard the clinic spokesman's statement. My father's condition is stable,' King answered, pressing forward unperturbed, taking it in his stride. 'I've nothing more to add.'

'Mr Clayborne!' a female journalist shouted over the jos-tling heads. 'Can we deduce from your arriving here accom-panied this morning…' her gossip-hungry gaze fell pointedly on Rayne '…that your relationship with super-model Sophie Ringwood is well and truly over?'

Rayne gave a small gasp as a flashbulb suddenly went off in her face.

'No comment,' King said, his arm coming instinctively around her.

Rayne was glad of his shielding strength, turning her head into the immaculate pale jacket covering his shoulder as the camera flashed again before he hustled her inside the building.

'I'm sorry about that.' His face was grim as they came into the bright modern efficiency of the airy clinic. 'It comes with the territory, I'm afraid.'

'Naturally,' Rayne returned, breathless from all the com-motion, feeling the sudden loss of his arm around her shoul-ders. She didn't think she could ever get used to living life in the spotlight as he obviously had, she thought, trying not to dwell on what that reporter had said about his super-model girlfriend as he guided her towards a waiting lift.

'Remember he's ill,' King warned when she refused his offer to accompany her into Mitch's room as they were step-ping out of the lift, insisting on going in alone. 'And it won't do either of you any good to get into a stew.'

'As if I would!' she breathed. 'Unlike your father, I do have ethics,' she added under her breath as a passing nurse, looking interestedly at King, gave Rayne the remainder of her smile.

The stark reminder of just how attractive he was to the opposite sex, coupled with nerves over how she was going to broach the subject with Mitch, made her look flushed and uneasy as she steeled herself to enter the man's room.

It was light and beautifully furnished, with only the bleep of a machine and other necessary equipment around the bed where Mitch was lying, propped up by pillows, reminding her that this wasn't some luxury hotel.

'How are you?' she asked with genuine concern, despite everything. He looked less florid and much more relaxed than she'd seen him before.

'No need for preliminaries, child.' Still his impatient self, he was waving her concern aside. 'You can see how I am. Alive! And you, I believe,' he went on, his watery blue eyes unsettlingly direct, 'have something you want to say to me.'

'All right, then.' Now she wondered why she had been worrying about exactly what she was going to say, but she should have known how much he was like King. Love them or hate them, the Clayborne men always made things easy by cutting to the chase. Always taking command. Well, like it or not. She could do that too! 'Why did you do what you did to my father?' she demanded with her breasts lifting rapidly under the light fabric of her flattering yet simply tailored shift. 'I don't care how many agreements he signed. You could have acknowledged that MiracleMed was his concept and you didn't.'

Mitch's mouth twisted as though he was considering how best to answer. 'Did King tell you that?' he enquired. 'That I could have done the decent thing and decided not to?'

'No. He didn't have to,' she murmured torturously, guessing that Mitch must have told him that yesterday, which was why King had looked so…what was it?…devastated, almost, she decided, when he had returned from here last night. But he hadn't told her because, of course, he would have wanted to protect his father, even though deep down he must have been shocked and thoroughly appalled. She didn't know how she knew that. She just did.

'Oh, I know about your…wife.' It hurt excruciatingly to say it. To have to accept that her father had been having an affair. 'And yes, King did tell me that. But surely that wasn't enough reason to…' She couldn't go on. Pain and resentment, anger and betrayal—it was all there in the anguish marring her face.

'Have you ever been in love, Rayne?' The man's tone had softened as his silver head tilted to study her. 'No, don't answer that.' His breath seemed dragged from him. 'That wasn't any excuse. But Karen was the only woman I'd loved since King's mother deserted me—deserted both of us—for an Australian rancher. I couldn't bear it when I saw the whole thing happening again. I was demented with anger—and jealousy.' His voice sounded even more gravelly than usual from his emotion. 'I figured that Grant had stolen from me—and something that no amount of money could buy—although I've realised since that I was half-crazed and too dim to see that she'd only married me for my money. I thought I was justified in taking something that belonged to him, but it's haunted me all these years in having done that to a colleague and a friend and, for what it's worth, I am truly, truly sorry.'

Feeling rooted to the spot, Rayne didn't know what to think—to say. What could she say? she demanded of herself, hurting unbearably.

With tears burning her eyes, her emotions riding high, she did the only thing she could.

She fled.

Only to bump into something warm and solid as she rounded the corner at the end of the corridor.

'What the…?'

King's hands were steadying her, his eyes scrutinizing her face and, seeing the tension and the tears she was battling to control, he said merely, understandingly, 'Come on.'

They were out of the building before she had even realised it.

The reporters were still there, eager for news of a budding romance.

King, however, shouldered his way through them, ignoring their intrusive questions until, finally, and much to Rayne's relief, he brought her—unmolested, but feeling the worse for wear—back to the car.

'Would you care to tell me about it?' he invited when they were on the road again in the exclusive, quiet haven of the Lamborghini.

'No,' was all she said.

To her relief, he didn't press the point. Silently, she thanked him for that.

Maybe in time she would forgive Mitchell Clayborne, she thought, sinking against the luxuriously padded pale leather upholstery. And even forgive her father. But right then all she could do was sit there with the sun filtering through the tinted windscreen, staring sightlessly out at the palm-fringed road and the glittering waves of a teal blue sea, wishing she had never come to Monte Carlo, wishing she could simply escape.

And perhaps King was wise to exactly how she was feeling, she speculated, surprised when, without a word, he took her for a long drive along the dramatically sculpted coast.

Above them, pastel-coloured houses seemed in places to cling precariously to cliff ledges among the forested mountains, while parasol pines, their branches spread with welcoming shade, grew abundantly amidst fig and date palms, interspersed with vibrant splashes of colour from the Mediterranean flowers.

She was beginning to feel better by the time he pulled onto the harbourside of an ancient port lined with a mixture of fishing boats and dinghies and exclusive yachts. A row of craft shops, galleries and cafés had been converted out of the old buildings beside the quay.

'Watch your footing,' he cautioned when they were out of the car, taking her hand to guide her safely past tethered ropes and crates of provisions being loaded onto vessels that amazed her with their sheer size. But it was those cool fingers around hers that left her breathless, with a sharp thrill running through her as she thought of the passion they had shared both that morning and the previous night.

His yacht was moored at one end of the ancient harbour and, after he had settled Rayne on board, leaving her brewing coffee in the well-equipped galley, King popped back to the quayside shops for some provisions.

The coffee had just brewed when Rayne heard him step back on board.

She was reaching up for two mugs in one of the modern cupboards just as he came down into the galley. His arm going around her waist made her gasp, as did the arrangement of white perfumed blooms he was holding against her breast and which were filling the air with their heady fragrance.

'Roses!' She laughed in breathless surprise.

'A peace offering,' King told her, 'for being such an overbearing oaf—and for jumping to all the wrong conclusions.' And when she looked enquiringly over her shoulder with a velvety eyebrow raised, he said, 'Mitch's previous record with a woman young enough to be his daughter resulted in devastating consequences. You couldn't blame me for being on my guard.'

'On your guard?' She gave a censorious little laugh. 'You've been like a prowling tiger!'

'Because I knew you were hiding something,' he said. 'You confirmed that the first morning when you said Mitch had told you I was in New York, because Mitch hadn't known. But also, I suspect, because I wanted—' He broke off, exhaling heavily as he pulled her back against him. 'Correction. Want you myself.'

Want. Nothing else, Rayne forewarned herself as every nerve leapt in response to the lips that were suddenly caressing the sensitive skin exposed to him by the slashed neckline of her simple shift.

'I just didn't want to be turned out before I was able to speak to Mitch. That's why I didn't tell the truth,' she murmured with a sensuous little shudder because of what he was doing to her.

'If you'd come to me—explained how you felt—I'd have at least looked into it,' he told her softly against her cheek now. 'Instead, I was left to pre-judge.'

'Without knowing anything about me,' she scolded gently. 'And you still don't know anything about me. Or very little,' she tagged on, with colour appearing along the crest of her cheekbones as she reminded herself that after last night and this morning, physically, at least, he knew her very, very well.

'Don't I?' He was smiling as though hugging some secret he wasn't prepared to share with her. Or perhaps, she thought, he was just remembering their time in bed together too...

'All right, so I rip men's shirts off and then take advantage of them when I've got them at their most vulnerable,' she conceded jokingly, loving the heat of his hand through the fine fabric of her dress and the warm strength of him pressing into her back.

Seriously, though, she couldn't help thinking about how shattered he had looked when he had returned from the clinic last night, after what had been an obviously gruelling day. Shattered, not just from worrying about Mitch, but by the things Mitch must have told him. Realising he'd been wrong about her, too, probably hadn't helped lessen the load.

'If that was taking advantage of me, then I can't wait for the next time,' he drawled, and pretended to double up when she gave him a gentle nudge in the ribs with her elbow.

'You're right. Enough of this or we'll starve,' he said, laughing, as she took the flowers and stood them in the centre of the dining table that curved around its seating area next to the galley. 'And then I do have an hour or so's work to do,' he apologised. 'But first...'

She hadn't realised it until then, but in his other hand he had been clutching the strap of a square insulated cooler, which he lifted up now onto the counter beside the cooker.

'Oysters in Madeira with cheese sauce for starters,' he told her, opening the bag and looking very pleased with himself. 'Fresh tuna steak—to be seared, of course—with salad and crusty bread and fresh raspberries and passion fruit coulis to follow.'

'Goodness!' Rayne laughed, realising she'd been expecting something far less exotic. 'When you go to town—you go to *town*!'

But of course he would, she thought, watching those long deft hands unpacking the carefully selected items. A man like Kingsley Clayborne would never do things by half measures.

'Oysters *and* passion fruit? Aren't oysters supposed to be an aphrodisiac?' she remembered with a sidelong provocative glance up at him. 'As for passion fruit…what sort of afternoon are you planning?'

'If you keep looking at me like that, not a very productive one,' he responded with a feral smile.

'And don't tell me…' she laughed again, thinking how wonderful it was to feel so at ease with him '…Clayborne's shares will drop like a stone and the whole global workforce will be on the dole because the company's CEO stopped to enjoy himself for a while.'

'That's about the size of it,' he replied dryly, although there was a hint of seriousness in his voice that made her realise how hard he worked and how dedicated he was in what he did, which helped provide a living for so many thousands of people across the globe.

'So how did you come by all this stuff for such a gourmet meal?' Rayne asked. After all, he hadn't been gone *that* long.

'The owner of that restaurant over there…' this with a sideways toss of his head towards the quayside '…is a very good friend of mine. I rang him earlier and told him to expect me.'

'You…' *dark horse*, she finished silently, warmed by the knowledge that he'd been planning all this even before they had left the clinic. Probably even the roses too.

She couldn't remember much of what they talked about during the meal, which they ate out on the lower deck under the awning. Their conversation was light and casual and surprisingly easy. Then afterwards, with the dishwasher humming away in the galley and King working in the salon on his laptop, she lazed on the upper deck in her burgundy satin bra and panties because she didn't have her bikini with her.

Listening to the deep resonance of his voice, hanging on every word he uttered as he conducted his international business over the phone and arranged meetings, her gently tanning body pulsed from the memory of their lovemaking, and throbbed in reckless anticipation of what might be to come.

Her cellphone rang while she was lying there. She didn't recognise the caller as anyone she knew, answering it rather uncertainly.

'Hello, Lorrayne,' Nelson Faraday began. 'I got your number from an old associate of ours...' He named a mutual colleague with whom they had worked on the same paper and with whom Rayne still sometimes kept in touch. 'He told me your mother had been ill. I hope she's feeling better.' Preliminaries over with, he dived straight into the reason why he was ringing her. 'I understand you were seen looking more than chummy with Kingsley Clayborne. Want to tell me about it?'

A trickle of unease ran through Rayne like a paralysing poison. 'No.'

'Just good friends, eh? Or is there far more to your being here with him than meets the eye?'

'I don't know what you're talking about,' she said tremulously, knowing this man could spell trouble for her.

The journalist chuckled softly, without a trace of humour. 'Don't you? You have a short memory, Lorrayne.'

'If you think I've forgotten the methods you use to dig up your stories, then trust me—my memory's as long as an elephant's!'

Laughter came again, a little more sincerely now. 'That sounds more like the fiery creature I knew. Look, I think we should talk. How about meeting me for drinks at the Café de Paris?'

The man had to be joking! 'How about barking up some other tree, Faraday? I've got nothing to say to you. Goodbye!'

She found she was shaking as she cut him off and tossed down her phone on the sunbed.

'What's wrong?' King asked, choosing that exact moment to emerge from the lower deck.

His shirt was partially unbuttoned with the sleeves rolled up to the elbows, and with those light beige trousers moulding themselves to his hips and very muscular thighs he looked no less than utterly magnificent.

'Nothing,' Rayne fibbed, trying to restore her agitated features into some semblance of order.

'Nothing?' He glanced down at her cellphone, dark brows knitting together. Numbly, she wondered exactly what she might have said and how much he might have heard.

'Just someone ringing up enquiring about Mum,' she supplied, which was partly true at any rate. She even managed a smile.

'She's all right, isn't she?'

The concern lining his face with that strong hand on her shoulder had the effect of melting her worries like butter over a hot stove.

'Of course,' she murmured, tilting her head back, her smile genuine this time, her peach-tinted lips inviting—craving— the pressure of his.

'Do you think if I kiss you I'll be able to finish what I'm doing down there?' he suggested dryly, touching a finger to his lips and pressing that to her yearning mouth instead.

Sensations ignited in her like a bush-fire even from that simple gesture from him as he handed her one of his clean white shirts.

'You've had enough sun for one day,' he remarked solicitously, doing nothing to quell the fire raging inside her as his fingers brushed her sun-warmed shoulder. 'Put it on.'

She obeyed as he disappeared below. She'd been thinking of going inside anyway, but she'd been too ensnared by some kind of sensual torpor from imagining doing all sorts of delectable things with him to move.

Perhaps it was true. Perhaps oysters *were* an aphrodisiac, she thought, lounging back and putting Nelson Faraday from her mind. Or perhaps it was just the warmth of the sun on her body. Even so, just the sight of King had rekindled all the outrageously sensual things she had been thinking about him before her cellphone rang, so that it was twenty minutes or so before, aching for his company, she picked up her bag and phone and the suncream she'd found in the shower room and went below.

Now, as she stepped down into the air-conditioned comfort of the salon, she saw him lounging back on the luxuriously padded sofa, having just closed his laptop for the day. There was music coming from the hi-fi system, which was in fact what had brought her in. A plaintive, achingly beautiful melody that was as familiar to her as it was moving.

'The New World Symphony,' she identified, smiling broadly. 'I love this piece!'

'I know.'

'What?' She looked down at him quizzically. 'How can you?'

'Because I just happened to be there the morning your father came into the office and said you'd bought this CD with some birthday money you'd been given and that he was glad to get back to work as you'd been playing it non-stop all that weekend.'

'And you remembered that?' Rayne marvelled with an amazed little laugh. After all, it was seven years ago!

'Only because I recall thinking that it wasn't the type

of music I associated with the half-scarecrow, half-vampire image,' he drawled.

Rayne laughed again. 'Was I really that bad?'

'You were really that bad,' he admitted, his mouth moving wryly. Yet, strangely, there had been something about her willowy shape behind that glass partition during her short spell in that office that had acted like a magnet on his eyes.

'I was also a beanpole,' she remembered. Underdeveloped and rake-thin from always being on an unnecessary diet. 'No wonder you ignored me!' And she'd thought she looked so lovely, she remembered self-mockingly. If only she'd known! 'You weren't averse to my music, though, were you?' she reminded him coquettishly, with a toss of her head towards the music system. Then, with a soft pout to her mouth, 'Even if you would have preferred to spank me than to take me out.'

His lips twisted in mocking censure of what he had said the previous night.

'I couldn't be,' he responded, and smiled then, so warmly it made her heart miss a beat. 'It's a personal favourite of mine too.'

For some reason that pleased her more than anything else he could have said. It meant that he shared her taste, created a mutual rapport between them.

'I read that the composer was trying to convey a feeling of homesickness in this part,' she remembered aloud as the music swelled poignantly through the luxurious vessel. 'It's supposed to be about someone who'd gone to America looking for a better life, looking out at unfamiliar mountains and longing for home.'

'Quite possibly,' King agreed. 'I believe Dvořák wrote it while he was in New York—himself a stranger, many, many miles from home.'

'I didn't know that.' There was something so pleasurable in talking with him like this after all the animosity there had been between them. 'Don't you think the feeling comes over well?'

He nodded and said, 'Brilliantly.'

'So what does it make *you* think about?' she pressed, unable to imagine a man like him romanticising and going off into some dreamy fantasy world like she had whenever she had played it.

Pursing his lips, King dragged his gaze from the two scraps of burgundy lace beneath the gaping shirt—which looked a hell of a lot better on her than it did on him, he decided—before considering her question.

Quite simply that music always reminded him of his mother. It had been her favourite piece, too. Her albums were just some of the many personal things she had left behind when she had walked out that day, what seemed a lifetime ago, never to return.

He'd been five years old and nursing homesickness so acute he'd thought he'd die from the ache inside him. Because that was how it had felt when she had left. As if she'd ripped out his heart and taken it with her, or as if someone had robbed him of his home. He remembered standing at the window, day after day, with Mitch constantly playing and replaying that music, waiting for her to turn the corner of the street as if she had just been to the shops, waiting for her familiar smile, her wave—waiting for her to come home.

But Rayne had asked him what it made him think about and he had to give her an answer.

'Things I couldn't have,' he replied heavily, but honestly now.

The rawness in his voice had Rayne searching his face for any clue to his emotions as he leaned back against the cushions, staring out of the oblong window at the sun-streaked water. He looked so distant and so bleak that she wanted to stretch out a hand and touch his cheek, ease the loneliness she sensed lay hidden inside him, buried in a place too deep for her to reach.

'What sort of things?' she whispered, wise enough to realise that he wasn't talking about anything that money or influence or power could buy.

He smiled then, giving her his full attention, shrugging off what she knew was a moment of regretted weakness.

'Never you mind,' he dismissed lightly. 'So what about you?' he prompted from behind that impervious shell of his, although the teasing crept back into his voice as he continued, 'What did you dream about when you drove your family and friends—and probably the whole neighbourhood,' he said with a grimace, 'mad with Dvořák's New World Symphony?'

You.

She couldn't say it as she met those steel-blue eyes. Couldn't tell him that she used to imagine him sweeping her up in his arms one day when she had pretended to lose her way and wandered deliberately into his office. Imagined him carrying her off to a luxurious bed somewhere where he would slowly undress her, kissing and stroking each area of sensitive flesh he had uncovered. And all the time this music would be playing, its swelling crescendo the moment he made her his, with his deep voice whispering between kisses the one thing she craved to hear him say.

I love you.

From her wild imaginings, those three words suddenly took on a startlingly new meaning, coming as they did from the depth of her own feelings and shocking her with their intensity.

I love him, she thought, *which is why I never stopped hurting when I believed how much he had hurt Dad. I've always loved him! I love him now! And I always will!*

The feeling swelled and grew, the realisation of how little she knew about him, not to mention for how short a time, not mattering one iota. She'd been made for him and she had known it from the second she had first laid eyes on him all those years ago.

The knowledge held her rigid, every second that she stayed conveying to him how hopelessly ensnared she was, but she couldn't move or tear her gaze from the mesmerising depths of his.

She knew what a temptation she must look with the shirt he'd lent her hanging open and revealing her scanty underwear. And she knew he obviously thought so too when his mouth compressed with some inner satisfaction as he allowed himself a visual journey of her rapidly rising breasts to the dark triangle of satin at the juncture of her thighs, his eyes flickering with masculine appreciation beneath the dark sweep of his lashes.

'Come here,' he commanded softly.

The next second he had caught her hand and electrifying sensations ripped through her as he tipped her off balance, tugging her down across his lap.

'What are you doing?' she gasped, pretending to look shocked, wild impulses crackling through every nerve-ending from the heat that was pulsing through her veins.

'You accused me of not giving you any attention in the past,' he proclaimed, his mouth set with exciting purpose. 'I wouldn't want you thinking I was holding out on you now.'

Galvanized by his actions and by the excitement that was licking through her blood, Rayne clutched him to her with a throaty sob of pleasure as their mouths met and his hand found the eager heat of her body beneath the open shirt, massaging and moulding as it moved over her waist, along her ribcage, up and up until it found her straining breasts.

The satin cups were a hindrance to him—to them both—and, sliding a finger inside, he pulled each one down in turn to expose her breasts to his fervid gaze, accentuating their aching fullness.

She let out a shuddering gasp when he ran his hand across

them and watched the way her eyes darkened with desire as he caressed each warm mound in turn.

She had always wished her breasts were smaller, but she didn't any more. She was suddenly proud of her voluptuous curves, knowing they emphasised her femininity, proud of the pleasure she was giving King as well as receiving in turn as he lifted her eager body to taste each tingling crest with a circling tongue.

'Not bad for a beanpole,' he murmured teasingly.

Twisting around so that he was half lying on top of her, his lips were suddenly following his hands on a path of sweet torture along her body, driving her crazy for him, bending her to his will.

She murmured her pleasure, arching her body in involuntary response. But there was something she needed from him before she let this happen again. Something she needed to know...

'What about...'

She couldn't say it at first, her silence bringing his dark head up for a second from somewhere around her middle.

'What about what?' he prompted, his lips over her midriff refusing to be stilled.

'Sophie Ringwood.'

'What about her?'

'Are you still involved with her?' she uttered on a shuddering breath because he'd moved back along her body and his hands were making possessive claim to her breasts once more.

'No. It was over between us months ago,' he murmured, his warm breath on the inner edge of her ear driving her crazy, even though she needed to be serious for a few moments, to stay in control.

'The press didn't seem to think so.'

'The press just sensationalize to sell newspapers,' he breathed along the perfumed column of her throat. 'Surely you know that.'

'True,' she admitted in a voice almost strangled from the pleasure of what he was doing to her. 'But I also believe that there's never smoke without fire.'

Her persistence dragged him back from his sensational exploration of her body, compelling him to sit up and take notice of what she was saying. His features were flushed from his arousal and he was breathing heavily. 'Then you'll just have to trust me when I say that, much as the media like to make a song and dance about every woman I'm seen with, I've always thought it less than politic to involve myself with more than one woman at a time.'

He was trailing his fingers along her inner thigh, seeking access to that most secret part of her that was aching for his touch. But suddenly she clamped her legs together, trapping his hand between them as she asked the question which seemed ludicrous in the circumstances, but which she needed to ask.

'Are you saying *we're* involved?'

His irises were darkened with desire as he gazed sombrely down at her where she lay draped over his arm, but something flared in their depths beneath his heavily lidded eyes.

'Don't you think lying here naked in my arms constitutes an involvement?' he put to her incredulously. 'And that this...' a low, almost agonised moan escaped her as his probing fingers sought and found the wet warmth of her femininity '...marks us as lovers?' he suggested, sounding unashamedly possessive. 'Unless there's something you're not telling me. Like you have a boyfriend back home in England—and then I think I really *will* turn you over my knee.'

He wouldn't, of course. Intuition alone told her that. There was a reckless excitement, though, in knowing he had said it simply because he wanted her for himself.

He might have known quite a few women intimately, if the papers were to be believed. But he obviously abhorred cheating in a relationship—which was why he'd sounded so unforgiving last night towards Grant Hardwicke and his step-mother, she realised, loving him for his morals and how principled he was, hardly daring to hope that she might have some sort of future with him.

Would he fall in love with her? Eventually? Decide that he'd had enough of top models and actresses and hard-nosed, beautiful businesswomen and settle for someone who wasn't always vying for position with him and getting her name in the papers?

But she didn't want to think about that because that was getting too far ahead of herself. And, anyway, she couldn't think about anything else because his long practised fingers were working their magic and driving her crazy for him.

There was something incredibly erotic in what he was doing to her, she realised, feeling like a puppet being worked by her puppeteer. He was in control and all that was required of her was to do his bidding, which right now was to writhe against him and show him just how much pleasure he was giving her.

With her nails sinking into his arm, she clutched at him like someone drowning, sobbing and bucking as the sensually induced rhythm sent breath-quickening tingles licking along her thighs.

She had never felt so abandoned or so ungoverned as she did at that moment when, with one last thrust of her hips towards his deeply penetrating fingers, she climaxed and collapsed against him, sobbing and gasping, while he cupped her femininity and held her until the tensions throbbed out of her body.

CHAPTER NINE

KING awoke and reached automatically for the woman lying in the big bed beside him.

Rayne was still sleeping peacefully, with her slender body turned towards him, and for a few moments he lay simply watching her, his hand still, yet resting possessively on the gentle curve of her hip.

He had made love to her almost endlessly since that first time, two nights ago, when he had come back from the clinic, having realised he had been wrong about her—that she wasn't a gold-digger, out for her own ends—having already discovered who she was.

He marvelled now at how he hadn't recognised her earlier. Or perhaps he had—subconsciously—he thought in retrospect. Perhaps that was why she'd got under his skin from that very first evening he had come back here and seen her standing out there on the terrace. Perhaps a part of him had been yielding to a long-lost attraction that had ended before it had even begun, although he'd never have acknowledged it then. At twenty-three he had been too busy getting his life mapped out—dating women closer to his own age, who promised to fulfil a part of him that could never be fulfilled—to really notice Lorri Hardwicke. But after she had gone he'd missed her, he realised now. Missed the way she'd looked at him like an adoring young fawn whenever he spoke to her, missed her smile, her quiet presence. Though he would never have consciously acknowledged that either, seven years ago, he thought with a self-deprecating smile.

She stirred for a moment, snuggling closer to him, and he waited for her to open her eyes, but she didn't. Her mouth was curved slightly as though whatever she was dreaming about pleased her, and he couldn't help hoping that it was him.

She was warm and gentle and caring. He already knew that from the past. And whatever she had done to get herself into Mitch's—and consequently *his*—life, she had done only with her father's interests at heart. In fact, he found himself admiring the drive and spirit it must have taken to motivate her to act in such a way—to even think about taking on someone as intimidating and hard-bitten as Mitch.

'I've lost her, King,' he'd lamented when King, after driving Rayne back from the yacht last night, had made a flying visit to the clinic to check on his father's condition—which he'd been grateful to learn was improving—and Mitch had told him what had transpired between him and Rayne earlier in the day. 'Lost any respect she might have had for me— or what I thought she had for me,' he'd corrected with a grimace, 'when I didn't know who she was. Can you persuade her not to think too badly of me?' he'd appealed to King. 'I was a mad fool—in love—when I did what I did. But what's the point of telling that to you? I can't expect you—least of anyone—to imagine what that's like, can I?'

No, he couldn't, King thought now, because he'd never been in love. And his father knew it. Knew better than anyone how he had learned from childhood—and in the cruellest way possible—the folly that lay in putting his trust in a woman. And neither Mitch's second marriage nor any of his own cautious relationships had changed his views on that.

That didn't stop him wanting, however. And since Lorrayne Hardwicke had unintentionally stepped into his life last week he'd been almost permanently aroused.

Just like now, he thought wryly as he lay there, hot and

hard, studying the gentle curvature of her face, framed by that wild mass of red hair, finding himself unable to stop thinking of all they had done and what he still wanted to do to her.

Do with her, he amended shamefully, because he wanted her with him for more than just good sex. He wanted to take her places, and not just to show her off as the Sophie Ringwoods of this world always wanted him to do, but to keep her all for himself. Show her new things and experiences she might be interested in and that they could discuss together— for however long it might last—while he discovered everything he didn't already know about her. Which surely made her a pretty high contender on his list of special women, he realised, of which there had been only one or two in his adult life. And, as he still couldn't deny, the sex was pretty good. In fact it was more than that. It was sensational.

It didn't help cool his libido in any way to remember the way she had been with him yesterday. As if she had been on that yacht solely to give him pleasure…like when he had brought her to orgasm that first time and her wild response to him had made him feel like a billion dollars. And afterwards, when he had suggested that they go to bed, she had undressed him slowly and provocatively, caressing and adoring his body as if it were a temple, using her lips and hands and finally her soft mouth…

Feeling he was going to explode if he didn't do something to temper his urges, he slid out of bed and abandoned all thought of waking her for the invigorating effects of a cold shower.

Rayne awoke to see the sun blazing around the edges of the blind, a fierce Mediterranean sun that regained its strength so early each day that it could have been seven a.m. or noon.

The other side of the bed was empty, she discovered, rolling on to her side, only the rumpled sheet with the imprint of King's head on the adjoining pillow assuring her that she hadn't dreamed the smile-inducing pleasures of the previous night.

She felt like someone who had died from too much loving and gone to heaven, remembering how King had made himself master of her body, time after glorious time and time again.

But it wasn't just that that had her spirits soaring this morning. It was because of knowing how compatible they were, as well as discovering that vulnerable side to King—not only over the past few days, but particularly yesterday—and the secret pleasure of having realised just how much she loved him.

She knew he had been scarred quite badly. It must have been excruciating as a small boy to be deserted like that by his own mother, she sympathised, and then not to have had a close relationship with Mitch. It was no wonder he had turned out so hard-bitten and self-sufficient, evident from the way he hadn't yet loved anyone enough to settle down. Hadn't taken on the role of husband and father and got himself involved in the joys and sorrows of having children of his own. But instinctively she knew that deep down he was a very lonely man, and that she could change all that if he would only let her. And to do that she had to convince him of how deeply he could trust her—convince herself that one day she could make him fall in love with her...

Having showered and dressed in lemon shorts and a lemon and white T-shirt, Rayne found King in the study, browsing through some paperwork by the filing cabinet.

'Ah, there you are!' he said, the smile he gave her heating her blood from the hair she'd twisted loosely on top of her head to her softly golden feet in her Indian flip-flops. 'I thought I was going to have to come up and tickle those delightfully painted toes.'

'Why didn't you?' she crooned provocatively, sidling up to him and inhaling the tantalising scent of his cologne, which emanated from beneath the white T-shirt stretched across his wide muscular chest. He'd teamed it with pale lightweight trousers that hugged his powerful hips and legs and the whole image emphasised his fitness and hard virility.

'Because if I had I wouldn't have stopped with just your toes,' he admitted with a wry tug of his mouth. 'And where do you think we would be now?'

In paradise, Rayne thought with a secretive little smile but, running idle fingers down the exciting contours of his arm, she murmured, 'It *is* only seven o'clock.'

He checked his watch, which was gleaming gold against the black strap spanning his wrist. 'And have you any idea how long we were in bed?'

Not long enough, she thought, wondering how, after all their hours of lovemaking, she could want him with an almost insatiable hunger that was still demanding to be fed.

'I had a rough night. I needed my beauty sleep,' she declared with a mischievous twinkle in her eyes.

'No, you didn't.' He folded her gently into his arms, pressing his lips against the ridge of her nose. 'You're beautiful enough,' he breathed. 'As for rough…' He chuckled softly. 'I wasn't aware of hearing any complaints on that score last night.'

Because he was a consummate lover, Rayne marvelled, being as exquisitely tender as he was passionate.

'Then shut up and kiss me,' she ordered playfully, thinking she'd die of wanting if he didn't hurry up and do so. 'Otherwise I might—'

As his mouth swooped down over hers, cutting her off in full flow, suddenly he was the one taking command. She felt the surge of his body as he pulled her hard against him, thrilling her with the knowledge that she could have this effect on such an incredible man.

'I think,' he rasped, coming up for air, 'that I'm going to have to take you out for breakfast. Otherwise, we're just going to wind up back in bed. And, much as I'd welcome that diversion right now, there are a number of administrative things that require my attention before the day's out.'

'Is there anything I can help you with?' she volunteered, wanting as much as she wanted his lovemaking to be useful to him.

'You? Help?' He looked both surprised and amused.

'Why not?' she suggested. 'I type. I can do your letters for you. I'll even edit them if you want me to.'

Of course, King thought, smiling reflectively. She was a journalist, which required using all her powers of initiative. Even so, he was touched by her desire to help him, especially on a beautiful day like this. Most women he'd known—particularly Sophie Ringwood—used to complain that he was always working and that he wasn't giving them enough attention. This woman, however—despite how pig-headedly he had treated her to start with—was offering him her time and effort and her intellectual skills, not just the generosity of her beautiful body.

'If you could, it would cut the time in half,' he said. 'And then I'm yours for the rest of the day.'

A little frisson ran through Rayne, not just from the thought of helping him, but also from what he'd said about being hers.

'Promise,' she purred, touching her tongue alluringly to her top lip, and though she knew he'd meant having him sexually, her heart wanted to interpret it as much more than that.

There was a warming satisfaction in sharing the more serious aspects of his life with him, Rayne decided a little later, hugging the feeling to her as she filed a copy of the letter she had recently typed for him just as he finished making some highly important international call.

'Whoever put this away put it in the wrong file,' she observed, waving the errant copy letter she had just removed from its clip over her shoulder.

'Thanks for noticing. It was probably me,' King remarked,

coming across to the filing cabinet to take it from her, and she guessed that even if it hadn't been his own mistake, he wasn't the type of man who would openly blame his secretary in front of anyone else.

Impressed with her efficiency, taking the letter from her, King stooped to press his lips to the inviting nape of her beautifully exposed neck, feeling his urges rising almost instantly.

She was clearly bra-less beneath her top, and the warmth of her, with that faintly exotic perfume, was driving him just short of insane.

'Do you usually do this to all your secretaries?' she asked with a delicious little shiver when his arm, coming diagonally across her breasts, drew her back against him so that she could feel the potent warmth of his superbly masculine body.

'No,' he responded deeply. 'Nor have I ever made love to one on my desk before.'

'You're not!' she squealed excitedly, her breath shortening because he'd swung her up into his arms and was striding back with her across the room, before stooping to sweep papers aside with a careless arm and setting her down on the hard green leather surface. 'Someone might come in! One of the maids. Hélène...'

'To hell with Hélène and the maids,' he ground out through a jaw clenched rigid with sexual tension. 'To hell with work, with business and the whole darn world!' Because that was how she made him feel.

Heat radiated through Rayne's blood as he leaned across her, taking her mouth and reaching up to tug the pins out of her hair.

'That's better,' he approved breathlessly, his eyes burning with feverish satisfaction as the fiery swathe tumbled wildly about her shoulders. 'That's how I like you. Looking hot and dishevelled. Like you've just spent all night in my bed.'

But there was more to this, he thought. Much more than this. She had the power to make him lose control like no other woman had ever been able to do—the power to make him feel things that he had never allowed himself to feel. He didn't know where it could lead—or how. He only knew that over the past few days he had allowed her to get under his well-protected skin and that she didn't look like surfacing from it at any time soon.

Nor did he want her to…

'Promise me you'll always be here when I need you like this,' he rasped, his sentence broken by the fevered kisses along her cheek, her throat, against her hair.

Was he proposing? Rayne's mind swam from the staggering possibility.

But no, he wasn't, her common sense quickly kicked in to assure her. He just wanted her in his bed, although instinct told her that he wasn't a man who would make a suggestion like that lightly.

I promise, she breathed silently, so close to agreeing to become his mistress that she wasn't sure how she would have answered if the intercom beside them hadn't buzzed—and kept on buzzing until King threw up a switch when it became clear that the person on the other end wasn't going to be ignored.

'Yes. What is it?' he demanded in a voice roughened by passion.

'There's a bunch of reporters outside the gates,' the voice of the English security guard Rayne had seen around the place announced, sounding particularly harassed.

'Have you told them my father's condition is stable? That he isn't giving them the satisfaction of dropping off the planet just to give them a story?' King's words were strung with impatience.

There was a fairly long pause before the other man said, 'I think it's more about you and Miss Hardwicke, sir.'

A rising tension started to grip Rayne before King swore under his breath and sat up.

'For heaven's sake, Peters! You've dealt with this sort of thing often enough to know what to do.'

'Yes, sir. But this is different. I think you'd better come down.'

'What is it?' Rayne asked nervously, the thought of having her affair with King reported by the press abhorrent to her. But a deep-buried fear—a fear that had surfaced when she'd seen Nelson Faraday here the other day and then spoken to him yesterday—made her stomach start to feel queasy and her mouth go dry.

'Welcome to the rich man's world, Rayne,' King muttered with a grimace. 'You'll get used to it, but it still doesn't make it acceptable or any less annoying.'

She had to admit he looked annoyed—very annoyed—as he got to his feet.

'I should have gone.' She didn't intend to say it, except that she had this feeling that her whole world was about to explode.

'No, you shouldn't.' King's brows were drawn together as he bent down and kissed the top of her head. 'Stay here,' he advised calmly, straightening his clothes and running hasty fingers through his hair because someone had started rapping on the door.

'Hélène?'

She looked as flustered as the morning she had come and told them that Mitch wasn't well, Rayne thought as King opened the door.

Already on her feet, Rayne felt the dubious glances the housekeeper was casting her way.

'It is this article, Monsieur King. In the English paper.'

Rayne could see that it was folded at a particular page as King took the newspaper from her.

'Mon dieu!'

'All right, Hélène. I'll deal with it.'

The housekeeper seemed on the verge of tears as King closed the door behind her.

'What the...?'

'What is it?' Rayne whispered, hardly daring to breathe, watching the strong masculine features that had been flushed from their lovemaking turn pale as he continued to read.

'Would you care to explain *this?*' he seethed when he'd finished, thrusting the newspaper at her.

Rayne's blood seemed to freeze in her veins as she recognised the photograph of herself and King and read the bold headline above it.

IN BED WITH THE ENEMY?

Her fingers were trembling so much she could scarcely clutch the page as her darting eyes digested what had been written about them.

It seems that this century's Captain of Commerce and Technology, Kingsley Clayborne, might have switched his allegiance from the sex kittens of screen and catwalk for the deadlier claws of the tabloid press.
Small-time journalist Lorrayne Hardwicke, seen here arriving at the hospital with Clayborne's illustrious CEO yesterday, is reported to have allegedly accused the corporate giant of purloining the software, MiracleMed, while her father was an employee with the firm.

To her horror, it went on to mention Grant Hardwicke and his exact position with the company.

If there is any truth in these rumours—and our undisclosed source suggests that there is—then what is the lovely twenty-five-year-old doing with King, anyway? Or does it, as this picture suggests, mean that

*all those allegations have been put to bed, because it
certainly looks as though these two have finally kissed
and made up?*

Rayne could only stare at the photograph of the two of
them together, which depicted her walking with her face
turned towards King, while he had a protective arm around
her shoulders, trying to shield her from the glare of the camera.

'I...I can't,' she stammered, shaking her head in disbelief.

'Oh, come on, Rayne!' King's anger was white-hot, barely
controlled. 'You can do better than that!'

'I can't! I didn't know anything about this!'

'Well, someone did! Who else would have known about
those allegations only forty-eight hours after I'd found out
the truth myself if you hadn't told them?'

The chill that had been gripping her spread slowly out-
wards from her heart to her very extremities. She knew
without even reading the by-line. It was the work of Nelson
Faraday!

Ice trickled through her veins as all her worst fears were
manifested in the article she was holding. It was what she had
been dreading ever since the morning she'd come down and
seen who King's interviewer was.

'What's the matter, darling?' There was no warmth in the
way he said it. 'Were you planning to be gone before this...'
he was snatching the paper from her '...this gutter-mongering
came out?'

'No!'

'Then can you look me in the eyes and tell me honestly
that you had nothing to do with this? That you never contacted or discussed the facts about your father and this company with Faraday?'

She wanted to say no. To sweep away the hurt, anger and

disbelief with which he was looking at her. But how could she? she asked herself, agonised.

Dropping her head into her hands with her loose hair tumbling around them, she just stood there and groaned.

'I see,' King rasped, and it was all there in his voice. Condemnation. Disillusionment. Disgust.

'No, you don't,' Rayne sighed, dragging her fingers down her face as she brought her head up in an all but vain attempt to change his harshening opinion of her.

'Then enlighten me, sweetheart.'

His false endearments and his cutting tone pierced her to the heart after all they had shared, and especially after his tenderness of only a few minutes ago. 'Tell me what bizarre coincidence has suddenly led to this article coming out if you're as innocent as you're trying to lead me to believe.'

She shook her head. 'The only coincidence is that he's here,' she murmured, remembering how sick to the stomach she had felt when she had seen him coming in that day with King from the terrace.

'So you thought you'd capitalise on your fortuitousness and get your story to him while he was still here.'

'No!'

'When exactly did you do it, Rayne? The day you saw him here? Yesterday? Wasn't it him you were speaking to on the boat when I came up on deck?'

'Yes, but—'

'So while we were making love and you were driving me insane by making me feel like I was the only man you ever wanted to be with, you'd already been up there playing both sides of the coin and plying him with...this!' The way he stabbed the newspaper with an angry finger made her visibly flinch.

'No. That isn't true!' she protested, hurting, unable to imagine how he could reduce something as incredible as what they had had on his boat yesterday afternoon to something so low.

'Really? Then tell me what is? Or would you actually know the truth if it hit you, Lorrayne?'

He couldn't believe he was standing here speaking to her like this. But then he hadn't reckoned on being played for such a fool. Neither had he reckoned on how close he had come to trusting her, or how much he had wanted to trust her. The fact that he couldn't was like a knife twisting inside him, gouging out scars that even a lifetime's immunity hadn't healed.

'I did tell him about MiracleMed,' she admitted shakily. 'But not yesterday. And not recently. It was years ago, when we worked together. And I did it without even thinking. I didn't know he'd ever use it in any way to hurt anyone. To hurt me… I was as naïve as they came. Dad was going through a bad time and drinking heavily. I just needed someone to talk to and…well…he was there.'

'And he just happened to resurrect all that? Risk a lawsuit over something someone of little more importance than the office junior told him goodness knows how many years ago?' He looked and sounded incredulous and, put like that, she could see why he didn't believe her.

'He came here. He saw me with you.' And suspected there was something amiss about her being here when he realised she wasn't using her real name.

'So?'

'It obviously jogged his memory.'

'Obviously!' King wasn't giving any quarter.

'And he's always been one to bear a grudge.'

'And why would he do that? Did you rob him of a story? Is that it?'

'No.'

'Then you'd better give me a reason, Rayne, and you'd better make it good!'

'Because I wouldn't sleep with him!' she hurled back, wounded by his inexorable interrogation. 'Satisfied?'

For a moment he just stood there, looking as though she had just taken the wind right out of his sails.

'You slept with me. The so-called "enemy",' he reminded her with disdain in the hard, twisting line of his mouth.

'That's different.'

'Why? Because I'm a much better proposition?' he suggested cruelly.

Because I love you! her mind screamed, although she couldn't tell him that.

'Believe that if you want to,' she murmured instead, feeling his contempt like an arrow piercing her heart. 'I've told you the truth. Why won't you believe me?' she appealed to him, and knew the answer even before he replied.

'Give me one good reason why I should.'

He was standing there with his fists balled against his hips, the offending crumpled newspaper still clutched in his hand.

Because it's the truth, she wanted to say again, but knew that it would be futile. She had deceived him in the beginning. By lying about her passport. Her reason for being there. By not coming clean about who she was.

'If you trusted me, I wouldn't have to,' she said resignedly, knowing she'd done nothing to earn that trust, nor would she ever be likely to. It was written all over his hard, handsome face, in the bleak, steely depths of his eyes.

She couldn't stay there and look at him any longer. She brushed past him and ran up to her room, where she collapsed on the bed in a state of total despair.

If she left now she would have to run the gauntlet of reporters, but even that was preferable to staying here and suffering the torture of King's contempt.

He didn't love her, and she'd been a fool to imagine that there could ever have been any chance of him loving her, she thought, castigating herself for being so stupid.

She'd been a fling. A way of distracting himself from everything else that had happened over the past week. But what she had thought had begun to grow between them would never have stood the test of time if what little respect and belief he had had in her could be pounded into the ground at the first hurdle.

She heard the growl of the Lamborghini as she was dragging her suitcase up onto the bed, rushing to the window in time to see it tearing down past the curve in the drive towards the electrically operated gates.

It didn't stop to appease the paparazzi who would have had to leap aside to let it pass, and her only thought, as she visualised the gates closing behind the powerful car and heard the sound of its throbbing engine roaring away, was that she would probably never see Kingsley Clayborne again.

CHAPTER TEN

PREGNANT? How could she be? Rayne asked herself over and over, as she had been doing since it had been confirmed over a week ago now.

She had been taking the Pill. A low dosage one, it was true. But she'd believed it to be a foolproof contraceptive. Apart from which, when she'd made love with King over those wild few days in Monaco, she'd felt an added security in the knowledge that it was probably the safest time of her cycle.

But Nature, it seemed, was mocking her in its triumph over seeing her impregnated with King Clayborne's seed. Against all the odds. Against their best intentions. And against—she was certain where King was concerned, anyway—his strongest wishes. She was only relieved that he wasn't around to find out.

Queasily, she wheeled her supermarket trolley to the check-out and started unloading its contents.

It had been over ten weeks since she had left the Monaco mansion, fleeing in a cab—doing as King had done and ignoring the paparazzi—intent only on getting the first flight home. Ten weeks since she had left a note for him, propped up on his bedside cabinet, to the effect that she'd been telling him the truth and wishing him well.

He hadn't responded. Nor had she expected him to. She was just a girl he had had a good time with, for as short a time as it had been doomed to last.

The press had hounded her for a couple of weeks, but when she refused to comment on the alleged accusations, or on her relationship with King, they had backed off and it had all blown over. Probably, she guessed, because she wasn't newsworthy enough to warrant any more attention, since it was obvious she wasn't one of his *favoured* women.

And now she was carrying his child. A child whose two grandfathers had wound up hating each other, and whose father certainly didn't have any love for its mother.

Inserting her credit card into the machine when the assistant gave her the total amount of her bill, Rayne felt the bite of anguished tears behind her eyes as she attempted to key in her pin number.

'Take it out and try again,' the checkout girl told her in a sing-song voice when the machine refused to accept the number she had given it.

She did, only to have the same thing happen again—twice.

She heard the girl muttering something about getting it authorised when a deep voice from the queue behind her suggested, 'Allow me.'

Rayne swung round and found herself looking up into the steely gaze of two heart-wrenchingly familiar blue eyes.

'King!' Every self-destructive nerve pulsed into life and everything else around her seemed to melt away, leaving her breathless from his tall, dark, imposing masculinity. 'You don't have to,' she uttered croakily, trembling so much she was hardly able to speak. But he was already reaching around her and inserting his credit card in the slot that had rejected hers with comparatively steady fingers, making Rayne catch her breath from his suffocating nearness and the achingly familiar scent of his cologne.

The girl with the sing-song voice looked up at him dreamily as she handed him the till receipt, with nothing having dared question his credit-worthiness!

'Have a good day, sir,' she said deferentially, beaming up at him and completely ignoring Rayne.

'You can't do this,' she protested as he tucked the till receipt with his credit card into the inside pocket of the dark suit jacket he was wearing. A hand-stitched, impeccably tailored suit worn with a white silk shirt that made her feel positively drab in comparison. Her beige cropped trousers with an elasticated waist and her one-size-too-big black T-shirt she'd bought to accommodate her tender and already expanding breasts just didn't compete.

'It seems I just did,' he remarked dryly. Already, with one arm, he was scooping up her tote bag, which was so full that she'd have had to carry it in both of hers, and with his other hand at her elbow, without any preamble, he said, 'Come on.'

'Where?' she demanded, flabbergasted.

Who did he think he was that he thought he could just march in here and start taking over her life? But as they were passing the counter in front of the in-store bakery, the sweet smell of the cakes was so cloying that a wave of nausea suddenly surged up inside her and had her fleeing towards the merciful sign she spotted just inside the Exit door.

When she emerged a little later, looking pale and with every trace of lipstick she had been wearing wiped clean away, King was waiting just a few steps from the door she had disappeared through.

A thick eyebrow climbed his forehead as Rayne approached. 'I thought you'd taken off through a back window or something,' he drawled, looking faintly amused. But then his eyes scanned her pinched wan face and those devastatingly handsome features took on a serious cast. 'You look dreadful,' he commented, his examining gaze too probing, too disconcertingly shrewd. 'Are you all right?'

No, I'm not! I'm having your baby! she wanted to fling at him bitterly, but knew that he wouldn't welcome hearing that.

'I thought about it,' she parried in response to his remark

about disappearing out of a window. 'But I thought I might get myself arrested, having already tried to use a pin number that wouldn't work.' It dawned on her now that she'd had so much on her mind she'd obviously inserted the wrong card.

'That isn't funny,' he chided softly.

'No, it isn't. It was downright embarrassing,' she expressed, feigning a tight little laugh. 'But I needn't have worried because you were on hand to compensate for my inadequacies.' With a sideways tilt of her head, she was unable to stop herself from adding, 'Just like old times, hmm?'

'And, just like old times, you're determined to keep me at arm's length and treat me like I'm your bitterest enemy.'

Well, what did he expect? Rayne thought poignantly. Instead, though, with the barest movement of her shoulder, she said, 'How's Mitch?'

'He's fine,' he said impatiently, as though he had no inclination to discuss his father just at that moment.

Rayne merely nodded, relieved at least that his father had recovered from his heart scare and she looked away from his indomitable son towards a stand of mixed doughnuts marked 'Tuesday's Best Buys', biting her lower lip.

'Why did you run away from me, Rayne?'

With her eyes downcast to hide the pain in them, she said flippantly, 'I needed the Ladies.'

His chest lifted on an impatient sigh. 'I didn't mean now. You know exactly what I'm talking about.'

'What did you expect me to do?' she queried accusingly. 'You thought I was a two-faced liar, to put it bluntly, and I couldn't convince you otherwise. Oh, I can understand why I hadn't exactly earned your undying trust, but I didn't deserve the things you said to me, so I thought it was best to leave.'

'Without telling me?' The disbelief he must have felt when he'd come back that day and realised that she'd gone was still apparent in his voice. 'By leaving me a polite little note?' She thought at first that it was pain pulling his features into tight, tense lines until, torturously, she reminded herself of how little he cared for her.

'OK.' She shrugged, trying to sound nonchalant rather than as if she were dying inside from her unrequited love for him. 'So I should have been grown-up and mature and told you I was leaving, and if the way I did it offended you then I apologise. I'm sorry. But you didn't exactly make me feel like sticking around.'

Yet that didn't stop her from wanting him now as fiercely and as desperately as she had ever done. Now, when he stood before her with that breath-catching vitality that paid homage to everything that was fit and strong and so intensely masculine, and which was making her weak with longing for his arms around her. Now, when she looked her worst and didn't have a chance in hell of ever securing his love. Now, when she was carrying his child...

She felt as if she would choke on her emotions—which, with the cloyingly sweet smell of confectionery that was wafting towards them, brought another wave of nausea rising up in her.

'Oh, heaven...' she breathed, bringing her hand to her mouth to try and curb the sickness, not wanting to make a fool of herself here in public. In front of him. Not wanting him to know...

'What the...?'

She steeled herself against his hard scrutiny, fighting her reaction to him, which wasn't helping her queasiness at all as strong masculine fingers caught her hand and brought it down from her face so that he could study her tense, wary features.

She looked pale. Too pale, he thought. In fact he would have said washed out, King decided, noticing the dark smudges under her eyes that made her appear fragile and exceedingly tired. And yet, even like that, she was still able to produce that familiar kick in his loins, he realised as his gaze slid over her body.

She was wearing an unflatteringly loose T-shirt over less than flattering trousers and beneath her top her beautifully full breasts seemed to be straining against the inadequate cups of her bra. Yet she was still the most beautiful woman he knew, with that long, sensuous red hair that was inviting him to run his fingers through it and those guarded green eyes that were half-veiled from him by her thick lashes as though she were concealing…

And suddenly it hit him with a force that for a few moments seemed to leave him winded.

'Are you pregnant?' he whispered huskily when he could speak again, his eyes narrowing into steel-blue speculative slits.

Rayne swallowed, grateful that the nausea was subsiding. 'What makes you think that?' she hedged.

'I wasn't born yesterday.'

It was no good denying it, she realised. He could calculate just as well as she could.

She tossed her head up, throwing caution to the winds. 'And what if I am?'

'If you are, then we've got rather a lot to talk about, don't you think?' he proposed, his half-veiled eyes inscrutable, his mouth grim.

'What is there to say?' She gave a hopeless little shrug. 'It wasn't supposed to happen.' Pray heaven he wouldn't think she would ask him for anything, she worried, mortified.

'But it clearly has. And, as the father…I take it I'm not being presumptuous in deducing that I *am* the father. All right,' he capitulated, putting up a hand to ward off the silent attack in her eyes. 'That wasn't intended as an insult.'

'*No?*' she uttered with biting accusation.

'No,' he underscored. 'And, as I was about to say…as your child's father, I think you'll agree that that gives me some rights as to how we proceed.'

'We?' Rayne emphasised, so bowled over by how he was

suddenly taking control that she was scarcely aware of being guided outside until they were in the car park.

The warmth of the late summer afternoon hit them after the cooling air-conditioning inside.

'Why didn't you tell me, Rayne?' he enquired, ignoring her last comment and aiming his remote control switch at the familiar black beast of the Lamborghini parked just a few strides away.

The vehicle's immediate response had heads turning to look, first at the car and then at the man who was rich enough to be driving it. Several pairs of feminine eyes feasted on him before sliding to Rayne, whom they quickly dismissed as too insignificant to be the lover of such a stupendously attractive man.

'It wasn't your fault,' she responded, unable to tell him that she had ached to hear from him again. That since finding out she was pregnant she had wanted to contact him but had balked at such a rash action, fearing what his reaction might be. He might think she had allowed herself to get pregnant to try and trap him, or just to get money out of him. After all, it wasn't as if they had even had a proper relationship...

'I hadn't realised in these circumstances that it was customary to apportion blame.'

She had told him she was on the Pill and he hadn't doubted her for a moment, even though she had been less than forthcoming with the truth about herself in the beginning. Still, his own behaviour towards her had been less than exemplary, when he had suspected her of just being after his father's money. Nor could he quite forgive himself for being so determined to get her into bed, even when he had felt that badly about her, even if his opinion of her had changed when he'd found out who she was and by the time they had eventually made love. The fact remained, though, that those abandoned few days had resulted in a child being conceived between them, and finding out as he'd just done had floored him.

'Aren't you angry?' Rayne enquired, watching his cool, economical movements as he opened the boot and placed her groceries inside.

'What's the point of being angry?' he stated with the descending boot lid punctuating his remark.

So he was, she thought, noticing a muscle pulling in his tight, tense jaw. And realising what he had just done, she said, 'I did bring my own car, you know. I can't leave it here.'

'We'll come back for it,' he told her, moving round the side of the car to open the passenger door. 'Because if you think I'm letting you get away from me again—and this time pregnant with my child—you can think again.' He gestured for her to get in.

'I was pregnant the first time,' she reminded him dryly, settling herself onto the luxuriously upholstered seat.

'Except that you didn't know. Otherwise, yes, I would have been exceedingly angry with you,' he assured her through the open door, slicing her flippant attempt to ease the awkward situation between them to pieces with the precision of a scythe.

'I suppose you think I engineered this as well, don't you?' she contested hopelessly when he slid onto the driver's seat beside her, guessing he would never ever accept her for the person she really was.

He could have, but he didn't, King thought, knowing her far better than she realised. He also knew that a woman of her calibre who had had enough gumption to do what she had for her father would never dream of stooping to such a thing, regardless of the insults he had flung at her that last morning in Monaco, which made him cringe now as he remembered them.

'I didn't come here to fight with you,' he stated, with one touch of his fingers bringing the powerful engine throbbing into life.

'Why did you come?' Rayne asked, trying not to think

about what those long skilled hands could do to her as she stared almost belligerently at the windscreen.

Seeing her chin raised in proud challenge against him, King wanted to take her in his arms and kiss her. But if he did, he knew she would probably only view his action as purely sexually motivated, and what he felt for this beautiful and complex woman was a lot more complicated than that.

'I wanted to see you,' he admitted heavily, restraining the impulse. 'We didn't exactly part on very amicable terms.'

'And whose fault was that?' Rayne looked directly into his dark brooding features now and, against all her powers of resistance, felt her heart lurch in her chest. 'You were horrible to me.'

'I was angry,' he told her truthfully, drawing his seat belt across his shoulder. 'That article had me doubting you. As it probably intended me to do,' he added with a self-effacing grimace. 'I know I overreacted and that I should have listened to you, but I never thought you'd leave—just like that.'

'Perhaps some people just don't like being treated as though they're the lowest of the low,' she said bitterly, wrenching her gaze from his dangerously handsome face and fastening her own seat belt with trembling hands, because just sitting here in such a confined space with him was making her so painfully aware of what they had shared.

'And for that I'm very sorry,' he expressed, wishing he'd swallowed his wounded masculine pride long before this instead of driving himself crazy with wanting to see her. 'It was wrong of me. That's why I came. To tell you to your face— and, in the circumstances, it's a good thing I did.'

He meant because of her pregnancy, because she couldn't imagine him being a man who would shirk his responsibilities.

'I don't want anything from you, if that's what you're imagining,' she put in quickly before he could say anything else.

'We'll see about that,' was all he said, reversing out of the space.

His features were set with purpose as the car roared away from the car park.

All he could think about was how his father—his family—had screwed up her family's life. And how they owed them big-time.

'Where are we going?' she asked, her forehead pleating.

'Just somewhere where we can talk.'

About the pregnancy. About how he could help support and maintain her and their baby, she decided from the way he was taking control. Unless, of course, he was simply intending to offer her the funds to ease the situation in what might possibly be—to him, at any rate—a far more convenient way, because he hadn't expected this outcome when he had come looking for her today.

'How did you know where to find me, anyway?' she asked tremulously when they were driving through the traffic, because the thought of him even entertaining that last scenario was making it almost painful to breathe. 'Did you just happen to be in that supermarket at the same time I was? Or do you have some sort of extra-terrestrial powers that homed in on me as soon as I stepped through the doors?' It occurred to her suddenly that she hadn't seen him buying anything for himself back there at the checkout.

'Neither,' he clarified. 'I called at your home and your mother told me where you were. I gather she wasn't too happy finding out from one of her neighbours on her return from Majorca that her daughter had been photographed with me in one of the tabloids.'

'No, she wasn't,' Rayne admitted, still cringing from the memory of both that article and her mother's response to it.

In fact, Cynthia Hardwicke had been horrified when Rayne had explained that she'd gone to Monaco to try and get the truth out of the Claybornes. 'Oh, Lorrayne!' the woman had expressed with an almost defeated slump to her shoulders. 'Why did you have to go and get involved?'

'And what did she say when you told her you were having my baby?' King asked, indicating to take a side road off the main highway.

Rayne drew in a deep breath. 'I haven't yet.'

The lifting of a masculine eyebrow expressed surprise and disbelief in equal measure. 'Don't you think it's time you did?'

'I'm going to,' Rayne returned with a niggling unease in her stomach. 'I just haven't wanted to give her anything else to worry about.'

'Anything else?' He sliced a glance her way. 'I take it she's all right? Health-wise?' he enquired succinctly.

Her forehead puckering, Rayne glanced quickly away from those far too perceptive eyes, saying in a rather unconvincing way, 'She's fine.'

She couldn't bring herself to tell him the truth. That Cynthia Hardwicke had developed further worrying complications. It was much too personal and painful to share with him at that moment. And anyway, there was the baby to talk about.

'I'm going to bring the baby up on my own, but I will allow you visiting rights, if that's what you want,' she managed to say quickly before her confidence failed her, and to let him know exactly what she was going to do. Let him know where he stood, in case he had any differing ideas as to what she should do about the precious little bundle of life she was carrying inside her. Because it was precious to her, regardless of the unfavourable circumstances in which it had been conceived.

'What do you mean?' he asked. 'If that's what I want?'

'I was only just saying—'

'No.'

'What do you mean? Don't you want visiting rights?' She couldn't believe he wouldn't want to see any child he might have created—even with her—and her eyes defied him to say anything that might indicate that he expected she might want to hurt her baby in any way.

'I think we should get married,' he said.

It was so far from what she had been expecting that she just sat there staring at him as he brought the car to a standstill in a quiet road beside the ancient iron gates of a local park.

'Because of the baby?' she croaked, hardly daring to hope that there might be some other motive driving him to suggest such a drastic step.

'Can you think of a better reason?' he suggested.

Only love, she supplied achingly, but she didn't say it, staring sightlessly through the open gates with their peeling blue paintwork at an enormous oak tree just inside the park, which looked as though it had stood like that, looking down on people, with their joys and sorrows, for centuries.

'I've known what it's like to go through childhood with only one parent,' he was reminding her now. 'And it wasn't a bowl of cherries, I can tell you. I don't want any child of mine having to go through what I did,' he stated grimly.

'It wouldn't. It would have two loving parents, even if—'

'With its time with them apportioned out, just how and when they thought fit?'

'We don't even know each other,' she reminded him, overwhelmed that he could decide such a thing after being acquainted with her for such a short time. Her legs felt weak and her heart was hammering like a drum-roll through her body.

'Couples wind up in the divorce courts after knowing each other for decades,' he commented dryly. 'I would have thought—for our child's sake, at least—you would be prepared to give us a chance.'

'And supposing we wound up hating each other? Or just not wanting each other…in that way any more?' Colour suffused her cheeks just from mentioning the passion that had gripped them both so profoundly while they had been in Monaco together.

'I don't think there will ever come a time when I won't want you—when *we* won't want each other—in that way, Rayne. The magnetic pull, or chemistry, or whatever you want to call this thing between us is far too strong. But, as for hating each other…well…if it doesn't work out within a few years we can always call it a day. But I want my child to be born legitimate, with two united parents and with my name.'

So that was all he was really concerned with. Legitimising his heir and protecting his rights and the rights of his child. Never mind about her. About how much she loved him! She didn't think she could enter into a marriage with him like that, knowing that if it didn't work out, if he wasn't happy, he would simply be prepared to 'call it a day'! Surely it would be better to walk away from him now, with her pride and her dignity intact, rather than at some later date when she realised that he couldn't love her, and when she was even more enmeshed in her feelings for him than she was now?

'I can't,' she heard herself uttering.

'How can you say that?' He was looking at her incredulously. 'Discount it just like that? I'm not only offering you a stable and comfortable home life for our child, but the best possible outcome in view of past…hostilities,' he supplied, finding the word he'd been searching for, 'between our families. Don't you see? This child we've created between us will not only have two loving parents to care for its welfare, but he'll also inherit the rewards of everything both our fathers—but particularly yours—created and missed out on. Doesn't he or she deserve that?'

Yes, Rayne thought, realising the poetic justice that lay in her marrying King and her children being the heirs to the Clayborne fortune—in combining their genes, their blood. In uniting their families.

But how could she, when she would only be tying herself

down to a man who was only marrying her because he'd made her pregnant? When he had come looking for her today, to do what, exactly? Express his regret for the way he had treated her—doubted her—and to take up where they had left off? Which was right back where they both wanted to be—in his bed! Instead of which, he now found himself faced with a child's future to plan, as well as having what he'd presumably hoped would be a willing mistress as his reluctant wife.

'I can't,' she murmured again. 'It wouldn't be right. We don't love each other, for a start.'

'Fair enough,' he agreed, not realising how deeply those two words had the power to hurt her. 'But we will have respect for each other—and loyalty, if we work at it—and perhaps this "love" that you're so wrapped up in will take care of itself.'

If only she could believe that! Rayne thought poignantly, but told him, 'You're not going to bully me into it.'

'And I wouldn't want to,' he expressed. 'All I'm asking is that, first and foremost, you consider the welfare of our child. And if that's not enough to persuade you into doing what's best for your baby, perhaps you'll be more inclined to come out from behind this idealised fantasy you're obviously harbouring about romantic love and think about how it could benefit your mother.'

'What do you mean?' she queried cagily, her tone both challenging and hurt.

He wasn't sure until then whether what he had garnered earlier when he had visited Cynthia Hardwicke's home was right. But now, from the pain that darkened those beautiful, yet guarded, eyes, and that same pain he'd seen on her face when he'd asked after her mother a few minutes ago, he wasn't left in any doubt.

'Your mother needs further treatment. Treatment, I suspect, that can only be paid for, and which neither of you can afford. How are you going to do it, Rayne? On the salary of a struggling freelance journalist? I can help you, if you'll let me. I can see to it that she receives all the necessary treatment and care she needs to help her optimize her chances of a good recovery.'

'Did she tell you that?' She sat looking out of the window, absently watching a squirrel foraging for food around the base of the oak tree and biting her lower lip to stem the emotion he knew she was battling against.

'Not in so many words,' he enlightened her. 'She said one or two things quite unintentionally that made me wonder and, seeing the way you were as soon as I spoke about her, it didn't take much to work it out.'

So what he was saying was that if she didn't marry him, not only would she be denying her child the best possible start in life, but also jeopardizing her mother's chances of a full recovery as well?

'And if you're thinking what I think you are,' he said, surprisingly astute, 'as things stand between us now, I doubt that she would even consider accepting any financial help from me, so I wouldn't insult her by trying to persuade her to. But, as her son-in-law, I think she'd be more inclined to accept what I was offering—particularly if the persuading came from her newly wedded and supposedly blissfully happy only daughter, with the means to give her mother everything she needed. I'd have to insist, though, that we get married with no time to lose, since it's imperative that she's taken care of as quickly as possible.'

So, in short, if anything happened to her mother when she could have had the chance to prevent it, she'd have it on her conscience for the rest of her life.

'Put like that, I don't really have much choice, do I?' she murmured, resigning herself to her fate of becoming King Clayborne's wife. It was something she had once longed for and yet now, when faced with the reality of it happening, she was just left feeling numb and chilled by an aching regret. 'As you say, there's far more to consider in all this than simply what either of us really wants, isn't there?' she uttered with a false show of bravado.

'Yes, there is.' His own regret was clear from the way his breath shivered through him. He was simply doing the right thing. Nothing more. 'But not as I say, Rayne. As circumstances beyond our own desires, thoughts and feelings dictate.'

So he would be legitimising the Clayborne heir and seeing that all the treatment her mother needed from now on would be taken care of, which was a relief and a mercy, Rayne realised, beyond her wildest hopes. But King Clayborne was a high-flyer and used to associating with beautiful and celebrated women. Supposing he got bored with her and chose to end the marriage at some later date? What then?

Then he would have secured his rights to his child and ensured that he would always be a part of that child's life, but what about her? Could she bear the pain of losing him when it felt as if her very reason for having been born was simply to love him? She had to, because he was offering her mother the chance she needed, and she knew that any amount of personal unhappiness that might follow would be worth it to see her mother well again. There was no question of that.

She only knew that while she and King were man and wife she would give it everything she had to make their marriage work—to try and make him love her. After all, if she could, she thought, and they had a lovely baby to focus on as well, would there ever be any reason for him to go?

CHAPTER ELEVEN

THE register office wedding had been booked for two weeks ahead, and it was to be a small private affair with just a handful of guests attending.

King had already been having discussions with a top consultant about Cynthia Hardwicke's condition. Just as he had predicted, at first she had been strongly opposed to accepting any financial help.

But, after being told that she was going to be a grandmother—something she admitted to having guessed, despite Rayne's secrecy about it—and then being told that King—whom she had also guessed was the father of her future grandchild—actually intended to marry her daughter, it wasn't long before she finally gave in. Wooed, Rayne suspected, not only by the prospect of the coming baby, but also by King's inimitable charm.

In the meantime, regarding her only daughter's wedding, Cynthia Hardwicke was determined to offer all the maternal help and support she could.

'You don't mind, do you?' Rayne asked her a couple of days later, when they were browsing together around the bridal department of the exclusive London store.

'About you marrying a Clayborne?' Her mother's mouth tugged speculatively. 'I want whatever you want for yourself, Lorrayne. I just wish you'd told me you were having his baby. Told me you were pregnant without my having to guess.'

'I just didn't want to say anything to upset you,' Rayne told her ruefully. 'You aren't too disappointed in me, are you?'

'I could never be disappointed in you, darling. Just as long as you're happy,' her mother emphasised.

'I love him, if that's what you mean.'

'And does he love you?'

Rayne glanced away.

'I see.' Her mother's softly spoken statement held a wealth of understanding. 'Oh, darling…'

'But he will,' Rayne told her nonchalantly, feigning an interest in the billowing ivory satin yards of one of the extortionately priced wedding dresses she was fingering on the rail. 'I've got enough love for both of us,' she tagged on as determinedly as she could. 'And the welfare of his baby means everything to him. We can't fail to make it work,' she stressed, trying to convince her mother, even if she couldn't quite convince herself. And suddenly, from nowhere, the question sprang into her mind so that, before she knew it, she was asking, 'Mum…were you always happy with Dad?'

Cynthia Hardwicke's interest in the fabric her daughter was holding seemed to be as distracted, Rayne thought, as her own. 'We had our ups and downs.'

'But wasn't there ever a time when…when you thought it just wasn't going to work out?' She deliberately kept her attention on the dress but out of the corner of her eye saw the way Cynthia Hardwicke's forehead creased.

'Why all these questions?' Her mother sounded, Rayne thought, just like she did when she used to pat her on the head and tell her brightly that everything was going to be all right when she didn't really know if it would be. 'Are you really so unsure of King?'

'No.' Because how could she doubt the package that he'd laid out for her in black and white? She knew exactly how he felt—and where she stood. 'I just wanted to be certain that you're all right with what I'm doing because…' she couldn't look at her mother at all now as she said '…because you and Dad were so happy. And because you thought, like I did, that King had supported Mitch in stealing Dad's ideas from him and—'

'Which is why you went over to see Mitch Clayborne when I was away. Which is why, had I known, I'd have stopped you getting involved in what happened. For a start, Lorrayne, I've never held anything against King.'

'You haven't?' Now it was Rayne's turn to frown.

'Your father signed something which, on paper, gave us no legal right to pursue any claim for that software. Mitch and your father had agreed to launch it in their joint names but there were reasons why King's father didn't honour his promise. I don't know if I should be telling you this or any good way to say it, but Mitchell's wife and your father…'

As Cynthia hesitated, Rayne looked at her quickly now, clarity dawning in her wide, shocked eyes.

'You *knew* about that?' she said.

'Yes, darling, I did. And I gather that you now know about it too.'

'Oh, Mum!' Emotion welled into Rayne's eyes as she hugged her mother, regardless of who might be watching, not that there were more than one or two other customers browsing around the spectacularly designed gowns. 'Why didn't you tell me?'

'I didn't want to hurt you, darling. Or do anything to destroy the picture you had of your father. I know how much you loved him—and how much he loved you. And apart from that one foolish indiscretion, he was a good man.'

'You should have told me,' Rayne remonstrated softly, releasing her, wishing her mother hadn't had to bear the brunt of her heartache alone.

'Just as you should have told me when you first suspected you were pregnant,' Cynthia scolded gently, tenderly cupping Rayne's cheek. 'I suppose that makes us both a pair of stubborn, independent women—and both far stronger than each of us have given the other credit for being.'

'I'm sorry,' Rayne breathed, comforted by that maternal strength that made her realise just how precious her mother was to her. 'I thought you were totally blinded by love and would have cracked up if you'd ever found out what Dad had done. Oh, Mum! Why did you stay?'

'I stayed because he needed me—and to hold our home together,' Cynthia told her philosophically. 'Without that, our little family, which meant everything to me, would simply have fallen apart.'

And she'd thought her mother was the shrinking violet of her two parents! The one who had needed all the help and support and protection from any emotional stress when, in fact, it had been the other way around.

She only hoped that she would have the same kind of strength to support her husband and her child or children whenever they needed her as her mother had done throughout those difficult years, and she thanked her lucky stars that Cynthia Hardwicke would be given the chance to enjoy having grandchildren.

And that surely had to compensate for the fact that had she not gone to Monaco—which she wouldn't have done, Rayne decided painfully, had she known the truth—she wouldn't now be suffering agonies of doubt about marrying the man she loved, a man who was only marrying her because she was carrying his child.

It was proposed that after they were married they would live in King's country home, which was within commuting distance of London. The house took Rayne's breath away the day King first took her there.

An exclusively designed and totally modern building constructed mainly of glass, the faultless architecture of its various storeys seemed to grow out of the hillside, rising up with the trees that gave it its privacy and seclusion. The garden wrapped itself around the house, a garden filled with nooks and secret pathways, which would be a dream, Rayne decided, for children to explore, while a terrace at the back gave onto manicured lawns which tumbled down to the River Thames and a private mooring where King kept his boat.

'How the other half live,' she remarked dryly, with a grimace, because she couldn't imagine herself ever living in such a stupendous place, let alone as King Clayborne's wife.

'No. How *we're* going to live,' he corrected her, with his arm going around her as he guided her to the front door. 'You're going to be my other half, Rayne. We're going to be a unit. A family.'

'Based on accidental pregnancy and physical attraction?' she reminded him pointedly, with her head cocked at an angle.

'Based on two people pulling together to do what's best.'

And that was that, she realised with a little shiver of longing, wishing she could have taken more pleasure in the luxury of her surroundings. The type of pleasure any bride-to-be who loved with the knowledge of how much her future husband loved her would have taken in being told that this was going to be her future home, she thought. But even so, she still couldn't help being bowled over by the immediate impact of wealth combined with exquisite taste as he let her into the house.

This place had it all, from the touches of ebony and Italian marble to the exclusive antiques, body-sinking sofas and the Chinese silks that hung from the endless windows, which allowed one to feel part of the great outdoors while maximising the use of light. There was even a white baby grand piano standing in its own acres of floor space, enhanced by a couple of the many large and luxuriant plants that were growing about the place, obviously thriving because of all the light.

'I didn't know you played!' she exclaimed gleefully, moving over to the piano, considering then how little she did know about him.

'I don't.'

The lid was open, exposing the keys, and she'd started running her fingers lightly over them. But, realising what he'd just said, she looked up at him quickly, her gaze questioning as he came and stood beside her.

'Then why…'

But it had already dawned and her heart skipped a beat when she saw the almost amused twist to his lips.

She remembered telling him that day on the yacht that she'd learned to play the piano as a child, and that her parents had sold theirs when she'd lost interest. She hadn't told him that it had been sold to help pay off their debts, but she had said that she intended to take up the instrument again as soon as she could. One day. One day when she had saved up enough money to afford one that wasn't too expensive, but she hadn't told him that either. And now…

'I can't believe you've done this,' she breathed, standing there with tears in her eyes.

'Then believe this.'

Suddenly his arm was around her waist and he was pulling her against him.

Every nerve leaped in answering response.

As always, when they started to kiss, it was never enough and hungrily, drowning in the scent and touch and feel of each other, they started ripping one another's clothes off, Rayne's chequered tie-blouse and jeans, King's jacket and shirt and tie strewn over the floor leading from the opulent sitting room to the foot of the huge round bed two storeys up, where they made love as if it was the first time for each of them.

Afterwards, lying there in the crook of King's arm amongst navy-blue satin sheets and cushions and watching the sun dappling the trees which seemed as much a part of the magnificent bedroom as its coved ceiling and windows,

Rayne thought of all King was offering her besides marriage. Security for her child. Help for her mother. He had even put in a bid for a beautifully restored cottage nearby so that she wouldn't have to worry about being too far from her mother. And on top of everything else—the piano.

Even if he could never give her his love, Rayne mused, silently anxious, it was obvious he would be generous with everything else. And whatever else was lacking in their marriage, she wasn't in any doubt that he wanted her physically at least. She only hoped that she could be content to let that be enough.

King flew up to Edinburgh the next day for a couple of days, while Rayne carried on with plans for the forthcoming wedding.

She put a deposit on a gown—something simple with a lacy bodice and an A-line skirt that needed a bit of adjustment on the waist to take account of her pregnancy—and which she had arranged to collect at the beginning of the next week. Then she spent a couple of hours wandering around shelves of cuddly toys and wallowing in aisles of miniature jumpers and dresses and smart little dungarees, wishing that, while she was looking forward to this coming baby with so much love and expectation, the thought of her imminent wedding wasn't churning her up so much inside.

The following morning brought a letter from Mitch, back in his own home in the Loire, full of regret that she had left Monaco in the way she had before he had returned from the clinic and—in a rather roundabout way—for what had happened in the past between him and her father. The letter then went on to express his surprise at hearing that she would be tying the knot with, as he put it, *his only son*, although he sounded thrilled that King would be giving him an heir, and equally thrilled that it was going to be with her.

His letter continued on a rather self-congratulatory note.

I told you you'd be a good match for him and that he needed someone like you to stand up to him once in a while, didn't I? And now you have, and I can't think of anyone I'd rather have as the mother of my grandchild, or as my daughter-in-law, little Lorri.

That last bit was gratifying but, contrarily, it lowered her spirits a little too.

The way he had addressed her reminded her of being young and optimistic about love and romance and life in general, and of those days she'd spent in her father's office, hungry for any chance meeting with King. She'd ached for him then, but not as she ached for him now—with a woman's passion. It was a lonely, desolate aching for him now, even though she was carrying his child, because she knew that he wasn't marrying her for the right reasons. Such as love and mutual trust and respect. Such as the fact that he couldn't live without her. How could he be, when they had known each other for such a short space of time? No, he probably felt guilty and as though he owed her something for what his family had done to hers, and so he couldn't just abandon her with his child on top of that.

With that less than flattering thought, she took the train out to her future home, walking from the village because the day was so beautifully warm and mellow, although she felt all-in by the time she had let herself into the magnificent house.

King was still away on business in Edinburgh and, as Cynthia Hardwicke was feeling well enough to accompany her friend to see a West End show and had decided to spend the night in town, Rayne felt it was a good opportunity to do some measuring up in what she had chosen to be their baby's room, and then stay at the house until King returned the following afternoon.

He had given her carte blanche to do whatever she wanted in terms of redecorating or refurnishing the house, but when she'd taken a leisurely appraisal of his home she realised with surprise that his taste suited her perfectly.

It was dark by the time she finished her measuring up.

Pleased at finding that the little pieces of white furniture she'd picked out for the nursery would fit the spaces she had designated for them perfectly, she decided, as she was feeling extraordinarily tired tonight, to run herself a warm bath in the luxuriously appointed master bathroom at the top of the house, then take herself off to bed.

Its gargantuan proportions and its abundance of dark scattered satin cushions and pillows made the bed look sensuously inviting.

Too inviting, Rayne decided when the memory of making love there with King and the thought of how many times he would make love to her again between those billowing sheets had her aching for him with a need that darkened her eyes and put a pink tinge across her cheeks.

Having soaked in a long, luxurious bath, she stepped out and wound a huge white fluffy towel around herself.

She felt heavy and aching, and wished that King was there. And suddenly, glancing absently at the towel with which she had been drying herself, she froze, shock ripping through her with the trembling realisation of what was happening.

CHAPTER TWELVE

'You have to tell King,' Cynthia Hardwicke advised, already in a taxi on her way over. 'If you're losing the baby he has a right to know—and now!'

'I can't. Not yet,' Rayne told her, fighting back tears.

How could she tell her mother that she couldn't bear to drag him back from Edinburgh? That, on top of all her fear and misery about starting a miscarriage, she wouldn't be able to bear hearing him saying all the things he thought he should say to her when she guessed that, deep down, he would probably be nursing a huge sense of relief?

Because what man would be crazy enough to tie himself down to a woman he didn't love—and after so short an acquaintance? Particularly a man in King's position, unless he felt he had to—which he clearly did.

She hadn't even wanted to tell her mother, not only because she hated having to worry her. But also because, ridiculously, she'd felt that until she did tell someone, it might not be happening.

But it was, and so finally she had rung her friend Joanne in France because she had felt so frightened.

'You must tell your mother,' her friend had urged when she'd found out King was away. 'You can't stay there on your own.'

So she had, and shortly afterwards Cynthia Hardwicke

arrived, not long after the doctor who Rayne had called to ask for advice.

'If there's no pain and you're not haemorrhaging, then I won't rush you off to hospital,' the out-of-hours locum told Rayne briskly. 'At this early stage of a pregnancy there will be nothing anyone can do to prevent a miscarriage happening once it's already started,' the woman informed her a little more sympathetically. 'But if there are any problems—' she reeled off a few '—don't hesitate to call A & E.'

So that was that, Rayne thought numbly, hearing the woman's car pulling away, thinking about what she'd advised if things got any worse.

Later, with her mother having taken herself off to bed in one of the guest rooms at Rayne's insistence, she tried to get some sleep, but her thoughts wouldn't let her. Because what could be worse than losing the baby she already had so much feeling for? Unless it was to be told what she already knew deep down inside—that she was going to lose King as well?

Unable to rest, she got up and, slipping on the long ivory silk robe she had brought with her over her short matching nightdress, she stole quietly downstairs to the kitchen.

The fridge was well-stocked by the woman King employed to come in twice a week to clean and, pouring herself some juice, Rayne moved into the sitting room, where a full harvest moon was throwing a shaft of amazingly bright light over the white and ebony keys of the piano.

After losing her father—and then with her mother being ill—life had suddenly become so precious to her. And now...

She dropped down onto the piano stool, her fingers tense around her glass. She had desperately wanted this baby, she thought achingly. After getting over the initial shock of finding out that she was pregnant, she had welcomed the baby as part of them, but especially as part of King—a man she had been in love with since she was eighteen. But he wouldn't have wanted her as his wife if he hadn't unintentionally—and probably very regrettably, she decided with an acute ache in her chest—made her pregnant in the first place. She'd welcomed it as a symbol of her newly rekindled love for him— the love she knew she would always feel for him—even if that love was never reciprocated—and she had wondered over and over again during the past two and a half months when exactly it was she had conceived.

Was it that night he had come back to the house looking so devilishly dishevelled and yet devastated, too? The night when her intuition alone had told her that he was every bit the man she had always hoped he was? Or the next day on his yacht, when she had glimpsed the loneliness in him and when, rediscovering her love she had ached to fill the void she had sensed deep down inside him?

The day he had surprised her by playing her favourite music...

Setting her glass aside, with one finger she absently picked out the first few bars of the poignant theme until, tortured beyond belief, she threw the piano lid closed and collapsed, sobbing, over it, pouring out her grief with the pain of her loss and the agony of even more loss to come.

Why would he still want to marry her when he discovered that she was having a miscarriage? What was there to keep him with her when there was no other reason for him to stay?

She must have fallen asleep like that—a pale figure slumped over the piano with her head resting on her arms— because that was how King found her an hour or so later when he came quickly and silently across the room.

She hadn't been upstairs when he'd come in, making straight for the bedroom, having driven back from Edinburgh like a madman, though the bedclothes were rumpled and the lamp on the cabinet on her side of the bed was on, as though she'd only just got up.

'Rayne?' He wanted to reach out and touch the pale slope of her shoulder but was afraid that if he did he would startle her, and he wanted to avoid that. 'Rayne,' he repeated in a tone that was soft and deep.

She made a soft sound like a whimper as she lifted her head, and anxiously he wondered if she was in pain.

'You're home,' she murmured weakly, with a surge of relief and then sadness washing over her as everything came back to her. She couldn't believe he was standing there right beside the piano. She'd thought he was coming back tomorrow.

'Cynthia rang me.' The moonlight had shifted since she'd first come in here, slashing across the wooden floor behind him so that his face was in shadow. 'Why didn't you?'

So her mother had telephoned him after all! He sounded so pained that she looked up at him questioningly as she angled herself around towards him on the stool, absently remembering that she'd given Cynthia his cellphone number in case her mother couldn't reach her at any time.

'I couldn't,' she sighed, unable to tell him the reason why. 'I didn't want you dashing home.' As he evidently had. 'I thought it would be best to wait until the morning to tell you.'

'That you were losing our baby?'

There was incredulity in his voice. But the way he bracketed the two of them together brought emotion welling up in her again, and it took every ounce of willpower she possessed to restrain it.

'Shouldn't you be in bed?' As he laid a gentle hand on her shoulder he heard her catch her breath as though she didn't welcome the contact and was recoiling from it, although she gave no physical indication of doing so. 'You're cold,' he observed, horrified, touching his hand to her cheek. He couldn't believe how cold. 'Here.'

Rayne heard rather than saw him shrugging out of his jacket.

She sucked in a breath as the warmth of it came around her back and shoulders. His body warmth, she thought achingly, drowning in the familiar scent of him that clung to it, sitting there like a limp doll while he pulled it around her as though she were a small child.

He dropped to his haunches in front of her.

'Are you sure?' he whispered, holding on to her, his eyes almost level with hers.

He meant about the baby and she nodded. 'The doctor seemed to think so and I...I don't feel pregnant any more.'

She heard him draw in a breath and saw, in the dim light, his lashes come down as he nodded his head. Accepting it, she thought. Before she could. Without any problem.

Even so, as his arms came around her, offering her the comfort she guessed he thought she would need, she couldn't stop herself from straining towards him, clinging to him, breathing in the scent of him first-hand this time, and wondering how many more times he would hold her like this before he finally released her from their commitment.

'You know what this means, don't you?' she said, making herself deal with it—say it—before he could. 'It means we don't have to get married any more.'

Whatever it was King had been expecting, it wasn't that, and coming as it did so soon after being told that the child he had anticipated wasn't going to be, felt like a double slap in the face. Like the one she'd given him when they were in Monaco, only harder and more incisively targeted. He wondered how much duress she must have felt under to have agreed to marry him in the first place.

'We'll talk about that later,' he said thickly, getting to his feet, 'but first of all I think we should get you back to bed.'

She didn't protest as he lifted her up as effortlessly as if she were the child she had envisioned herself as a few moments ago. She wanted these last moments with him. To memorize how it felt to have her arms around his neck, his warmth, his latent strength, to be this close to him when there would be so many cold and lonely days to follow that would find her forever wondering what might have been, and what being King's wife and the mother of his children would have been like.

Perhaps it couldn't cling on because it knew you didn't love me, she thought, torturing herself, and drew no consolation from the knowledge that pregnancies of women who were happily settled with their partners could often end in miscarriage. Especially with a first pregnancy, the doctor had said when she had been trying to reassure her, but she hadn't been listening, concerned only with what was happening to *her* baby, the little life she had been nurturing inside her.

King bore her up the four flights of stairs without bothering to switch on the lights. The moon shining in the long and wide windows on each landing put a silvery wash over the stairs, throwing their shadows onto the side wall that ran up from the lowest storey.

They looked like tragic lovers, he thought with unrestrained cynicism, aware of the straining bulk that was his own body and the slender arms wrapped around him, of the way the feminine head was angled so that it looked to be almost touching his.

He was mourning this child, he realised in that moment, and found himself acknowledging that he *had* wanted it— and more than he could ever have imagined possible. He had wanted the responsibility of another human being to care for. Part of himself. Someone he could always be there for in the way that neither of his own parents had ever been there for him. It had felt like a chance to redress the balance. A chance to put things right. And it had seemed like a good enough reason for accepting its existence when he'd given Rayne little option about marrying him and had hustled her through the arrangements for the wedding day after day.

But was it? he asked himself as he carried her into the softly lit, splendid opulence of the master bedroom. Because how much thought had he given to what she might want? And what was right for her? And now he answered himself truthfully. Very little.

But now, as he set her on her feet and she turned to let his jacket slip off her shoulders onto the bed, he saw from the lamplight, and for the first time, how shockingly desolate she looked. Her face, cleansed of make-up, looked pale and gaunt, and he could see that her eyes were red-rimmed and puffy with crying.

And suddenly it dawned on him how much she must have wanted this baby. Wanted it—even though she hadn't wanted him.

'Oh, my poor love...' His arm was still round her middle and now he caught her to him, not caring how weak it might make him seem or how he sounded as he buried his lips in her hair and, in a voice that seemed wrenched from him, he uttered, 'I'm sorry. I'm really so very, very sorry.'

For what? Rayne wondered wretchedly, aching to clasp him to her but only allowing her hands to rest lightly on the straining contours of his muscled back. For making her love him in the first place? For making her pregnant and having to watch her lose the most precious gift he could ever have given her? Or for not being able to love her and for leaving her just as soon as he considered it felt right for him to do so?

'Don't,' she demurred, and wished it had come out sounding less like a plea when he didn't let her go, but urged her gently down to sit on the bed beside him.

Just as gently, then, he put an arm under her knees and lifted her legs onto the mattress so that she could relax against the mountain of cushions that were still stacked up on his side of the bed.

'It meant everything to you, this baby. Didn't it?' he said with a surge of hope that was quickly quashed when she looked down and away from him with her lips pressed almost mutinously tight.

'What did you imagine?' she invited him to tell her, and

with such a wobble in her voice that he realised it was threatening emotion that was making her look like that.

She didn't look at him, but kept staring at some point between the door and the mirrored wall of endless wardrobes, waiting for him to tell her that she was young and strong. That one day she'd have more babies, and with someone she really wanted to be with, but he didn't. He just kept looking at her with that fathomless emotion etching his face, understanding at least that that wasn't what she needed to hear right now.

Unless, of course, he'd guessed that she'd only ever wanted his, and that this baby was so special to her because of all they had already shared and because of how hopelessly she loved him. In which case, was that emotion she would have so dearly liked to believe was shared anguish in him really only generated by sympathy for her?

'You're going to have to cancel the wedding,' she advised him, choked, because if pity was all he felt for her then she couldn't bear it.

He didn't look at her as his breath shuddered through his lungs. 'We'll talk about it tomorrow,' he said, starting to get up.

Rayne shot out a hand to stop him and, feeling the bunching muscles of his arm, quickly retracted it, reminded too poignantly of how exquisite he was and of just how much pleasure they had known together.

'No, now,' she stressed, steeling herself against the emotional pain.

'All right, then.' His shoulders seemed to slump from the heavy breath he exhaled, a resigned posture that matched the note of resignation in his voice. 'Fire away.'

'We're going to have to lose some deposits. And I know this hasn't exactly gone the way you planned...' She dragged in a breath, finding it took every ounce of her mental strength to put on a brave face. 'I can bear some of the expense myself, but I can't yet pay you back for what you've already arranged for Mum. But if you let her treatment go ahead, I'll slave…I'll slave day and night to save up and—'

'Enough!' His fist came down on his knee, punctuating his barely rasped command and, through her misery, Rayne was amazed to realise that he was trembling. His voice was trembling too and his eyes were darkened by an emotion she could almost touch. 'What sort of hard, insensitive individual do you think I am?'

He had asked her something like that before. Ten weeks ago. When they were in Monaco. But she couldn't think about that right now, only why the groan that seemed to come from deep in his chest sounded like that of an animal in pain.

'Have you ever considered for one moment that I might be just as cut up over losing this baby as you are? Why can a woman only feel pain? Loss? Regret? And had it even occurred to you that I might not want to cancel the wedding?'

'What?' Through the mire of her unhappiness, his question awakened a spark of something in her not unlike hope.

'Yes,' he affirmed on a laboured breath. 'Crazy though that might seem to you, I still want to go ahead and do everything we were planning.'

'Why?' Rayne enquired, stupefied. Then, as it suddenly dawned on her, 'Because you feel sorry for me?' she remembered, hurting. 'Because you think you owe it to me?'

His body had been half-turned away from her, but now he shifted his position so that he was facing her full on and she could see the pained incredulity in his eyes.

'Hadn't it occurred to you either that I might…just might…' it was a soft reprimand '…be in love with you?' he rasped.

Now it was her turn to look incredulous, and yet there was warmth starting to trickle through the cold emptiness she had been feeling inside.

'But…how can you be?' she challenged breathlessly. Her head felt cloudy and yet her heart was racing. 'I mean…we haven't…'

'Haven't known each other long enough?' he supplied. The ghost of a smile was trying to play around one side of his mouth now. 'You already admitted to being mad about me before. And if your response to me whenever I touch you is anything to go by, I'd say you still are,' he took the chance on saying. After all, he thought, what was there to lose? 'All right,' he went on, bolder now that he could see incredulity being dissipated by the warmth that lit her eyes. 'You might think I'm crazy. And perhaps I am,' he said with a self-mocking pull of his lips. 'But I've never been in love before so I can't judge what this feeling is. But if love is never wanting to let you go, that it would devastate me if I were to lose you, and wanting you—and only you—to be the mother of my children, then I'm in love.'

'Oh, King...'

She sat forward and grasped his arm, laying her head against the strong, hard support of his shoulder. There were tears in her eyes as his arms came round her now, but they were shining with love and warmth and the knowledge that while she was losing something so precious, she could bear it if he was beside her, loving her. Sharing, not just the good times, but times like now, when she needed him. So much...

'There's no one who's ever made me feel like you do,' he murmured huskily into the perfumed silk of her hair, holding her as though he would never let her go.

'You mean drive you to distraction,' she suggested, sniffing back emotion, feeling suddenly that there was so much to hold on to, even if right now there was such a dark cloud hanging over her—over them both.

'Like I want to take care of you,' he scolded softly, proving it to her as he set her tenderly back against the pillows just in case it might be harming her to give into this need to hold her and keep her sitting there, locked in his arms. 'Like I want to grow with you. Learn with you and from you—because we both have so much to learn from and about each other, dearest. Comfort you—as you so badly need that from me now...' His voice was thickened by emotion and when he placed his hand lightly over her abdomen she could so easily have wept. But she didn't, for his sake as well as her own, battling against her hormones and a whole flood of feeling for this wonderful man as he murmured, 'Would you let me do that for you, Rayne?'

'Oh, King,' she expressed again. 'If you only knew how much I want that. Have wanted it. And not like the lovesick teenager you called me and that I know I was, but as I am— as we are—now. I feel I've known you all my life. Even when you thought I was too young for you and you weren't even aware of me.'

'Oh, I was aware of you,' he confessed, smiling down at her from where he lounged, his head resting on his bent arm, his long length stretched out on the bed beside her now. 'Or at least of your presence. And very much so,' he admitted, trailing an index finger down the soft curve of her cheek. 'From the first time I saw you, until the last. While you were there in the office for that short time I couldn't stop looking at you— or at least the outline of you—through that frosted glass, and I had to keep pulling myself up short and reminding myself that I shouldn't. You were a crazy kid and I was just starting out. And, to test my resistance even further, when you weren't there your father never stopped talking about you,' he remembered wryly.

Her eyes darkened a little as he mentioned her father. 'Talking about me?' she asked, curious. 'In what way?'

'Like how, after slipping a disc and losing the use of its legs, you sacrificed a trip to the States with your friends to look after the family dog. Which meant carrying him everywhere,' he outlined, sounding impressed, 'until he could walk again.'

'Well, he recovered,' she stated assertively, remembering now that rare moment in the office when King had singled her out to enquire about the spaniel; remembered how she'd hugged that moment to her for weeks.

'But only thanks to you,' he reminded her. 'The same girl who wanted to support every children's and animal charity that posted a flyer through her door, while training to run a half marathon for Oxfam. The girl who looked like a cross between the scarecrow in the Wizard of Oz and the Bride of Dracula. The girl who was crazy about Dvořák's music...'

A flush touched her cheeks from the pleasure of knowing how King had retained so much about her. It surprised her, too, to learn about all her father had said.

'No matter where he was planning to go, or how much he might have thought he wanted my stepmother, he never stopped loving you, Rayne,' King told her, cannily sensing everything that she was feeling. 'And I don't think *I* have— subconsciously,' he admitted candidly—amazingly—to her, 'because it was one hell of a testimonial to deal with for a young man who was trying to stay immune. I was planning to ask you out—given a year or two. When you'd grown up a bit and I didn't have so much on my mind. But within weeks your father and Mitch had that blow up. And then, after that night when I called round to your house to see Grant and you flew at me like I was some sort of demon, I knew I'd blown whatever chances I'd had of getting to know you better.'

What he was saying amazed her and, looking up at him now, she wondered how any man could be so handsome, as well as having such inner strength and tenderness, as she allowed her fingers to revel in the texture of his dark, un-shaven jaw.

'I know I came over all possessive and overbearing about... the baby,' he went on with some hesitancy, 'but ultimately I knew it was the only chance I had of keeping you with me— in my life,' he disclosed hoarsely, making her tremble with the depth of her feeling for him as his thumb moved lov-

ingly over the soft outline of her mouth. 'Can you ever forgive me?' he asked.

'Only if you'll promise to always stay as determined to
keep me with you,' she murmured, feeling as if her heart
were overflowing. 'I couldn't bear it if I lost you.' And realising that she hadn't actually told him in as many words, she
whispered from the depths of her soul, 'I love you, King.'

'I promise,' he whispered back, bending to kiss her, oh,
so softly on her mouth. 'And now, my love, I think it's time
you got some rest.'

The wedding was going ahead as planned for the end of the
following week but, sitting there in the waiting area of the
pregnancy unit while Rayne had gone for her ultrasound scan,
King wished fervently that she wasn't having to go through
all this beforehand. Seeing doctors. The check-ups. Having
to be prodded and poked about. All quite routine and happily anticipated when it was to assess how your little one was
developing, but not under these circumstances. Agitatedly,
he tossed down the magazine he had been thumbing through
without having read a word. Not like this.

He had wanted to be with her but she had insisted that he
wait outside and, very reluctantly, he had complied with her
wishes. He guessed she didn't want him to see how upset it
made her to be told categorically that her pregnancy was over.

She'd need a lot of care and consideration over the weeks
ahead, he realised, hiding his own regret and disappointment
behind his usual practised calm as he promised himself he
would do everything it took to make this difficult time easier for her.

She was crying when she came out of the room beyond.

She'd promised him she would be brave, but he could see
at once that the ordeal had proved too much for her, even if
she was doing her best to hide it from the other happily ex-
pectant couple who had been sitting opposite him.

'I should have been there with you,' he said, berating himself as he reached her side and put a consoling arm around her shoulders. 'I shouldn't have listened to you. I should have come in.'

He took her hand in his—the one with the emerald and diamond engagement ring he had brought back from Edinburgh and placed on her finger this morning—a token of his love, a sign that he was marrying her for who she was: the woman he was crazy about—and understood how, right then, she was too over-wrought to speak.

It wasn't until they were outside in the mellow sunshine that she finally gave rein to her emotion, sobbing against his shoulder while he held her close and felt each convulsive sob like a pain in his heart.

At last she managed to get a grip on herself and, as she looked up at him now, he could see that she was trying to shrug off her outpouring of emotion, to even smile at him through the mist of her tears.

'Our baby...' She was trembling; choking on the words. 'They found a heartbeat. It was visible on the ultrasound! They said it was good and strong and it's got the right number of beats per minute! I'm still pregnant, King! That doctor was wrong.'

If she could have described the effect those words had on his face then she would have said it was like coming out into brilliant sunshine after being in a long, dark tunnel. But then she still couldn't quite believe herself that they had both been handed back such a beautiful miracle. 'They said it *could* have been a threatened miscarriage but, if it wasn't, then what happened isn't entirely uncommon. It could have been caused by possible hormone fluctuation, which is why I stopped feeling pregnant. And they said that that's not uncommon either, particularly at this stage of our pregnancy.'

King could scarcely believe what she was saying. He was

still going to be a father! He felt like jumping up with a terrific *Whoop!* and reaching for the sky.

It also touched him immensely how she had said 'our' pregnancy. It meant that she was going to share every part and every minute of his child's development with him over the coming months. Meant that this wonderful woman, who had started out as just a flitting figure he wanted to deny being attracted to, was having his baby, and was never going to shut him out of her life—or be separated from him—again. Meant that whatever problems lay ahead, they could deal with them. Together. Her mother's health. Mitch. And any other trials and tribulations that came their way.

'I love you,' he told her, placing a hand on the yet gentle swell of her middle. 'Both of you,' he murmured, and the depth of his unmistakable love produced an answering emotion in Rayne.

When she responded, standing on tiptoe to kiss him, her face was glowing, King noticed, her eyes moist and sparkling, but sparkling now, he acknowledged, with tears of joy.

'Do you realise the papers are going to have a field day when they realise that, not only are we married, but that we've already started a family?' she breathed, slightly in awe of all the attention that the news would attract initially.

'Let them!' King invited, smiling broadly, locking her to his side as they moved leisurely back to the car, and from the pride and happiness she could see and feel emanating from him at the prospect of being a husband and father, Rayne knew that he was going to enjoy shouting it out to the world.

* * * * *

THE GIRL HE'D OVERLOOKED

BY
CATHY WILLIAMS

Cathy Williams is originally from Trinidad, but has lived in England for a number of years. She currently has a house in Warwickshire, which she shares with her husband Richard, her three daughters, Charlotte, Olivia and Emma, and their pet cat, Salem. She adores writing romantic fiction, and would love one of her girls to become a writer—although at the moment she is happy enough if they do their homework and agree not to bicker with one another!

PROLOGUE

JENNIFER looked at her reflection in the mirror. She had died and gone to heaven! Fantastic restaurant, fantastic food, even the ladies' room was fantastic. Beige marble everywhere and delicate little hand towels, a basket of them, to be picked, used and discarded. Could things get any better? Her cheeks were pink, her eyes were glowing.

She leaned forward and for the first time her physical shortcomings did not rush towards her in a wave of disappointment. She was no longer the too tall, too big-boned girl with the hair that was slightly too unruly and a mouth that was too wide. She was a sexy woman on the brink of the rest of her life and, best of all, James was out there, waiting for her. James, *her date.*

Jennifer Edwards had known James Rocchi all her life. From the small window of her bedroom in the cottage that she had shared with her father, she could daily look out to the distant splendour of his family home—The Big House, as she and her father had always called the Rocchi mansion, with its sweeping drive and imposing acres of stunning Victorian architecture.

As a kid, she had worshipped him and had trotted behind him and his friends as they had enjoyed themselves in the acres and acres of grounds surrounding the house. As a teenager, she had developed a healthy crush on him, blushing and awkward whenever he returned from boarding school, although, several years older than her, he couldn't have been more oblivious. But she was no longer a teenager. She was now twenty-one years old, with a degree in French firmly behind her and a secondment to the Parisian office of the law firm in which she had spent every summer vacation working only days away.

She was a woman and life couldn't have felt any better than it did right now, right here.

With a little sigh of pleasure, she applied a top up of her lip gloss, patted her hair, which she had spent ages trying to straighten and mostly succeeded, and headed back out to the restaurant.

He was gazing out of the window and she took a few seconds to drink him in.

James Rocchi was a stunning example of the sort of aggressively good-looking alpha male that could turn heads from streets away. Like his father, who had been an Italian diplomat, James was black-haired and bronze-skinned, only inheriting his English mother's navy-blue eyes. Everything about him oozed lethal sex appeal, from the arrogant tilt of his head to the muscled perfection of his body. Jennifer had seen the way other women, usually small blonde things he had brought back with him from university, had followed him with their eyes as if they couldn't get enough of him.

She was still finding it hard to believe that she was actually here with him and she took a deep breath and reminded herself that *he had asked her on a date*. It gave her just the surge of confidence she needed to walk towards him and she blushed furiously as he turned to look at her with a slow smile on his face.

'So…I've arranged a little surprise for you…'

Jennifer could barely contain her breathless excitement. 'You haven't! What is it?'

'You'll have to wait and see,' he told her with a grin. He leaned back, angling his body so that he could stretch his legs out. 'I still can't believe that you've finished university and are heading off to foreign shores...'

'I know, but the offer of a job in Paris was just too good to pass up. You know what it's like here.'

'I know,' he agreed, understanding what she meant without her having to explain. Wasn't this one of the great things about her? he thought. They had known each other for so long that there was hardly any need to explain references or, frankly, sometimes, to finish sentences. Of course, Paris for a year was going to be brilliant for her. Aside from her stint at university, which, in Canterbury, had hardly been a million miles away, he couldn't think of a time that she had ever left here and, however beautiful and peaceful this slice of Kent was, she should be champing at the bit to spread her wings and fly farther afield. But he didn't mind admitting to himself that he was going to miss her easy companionship.

Jennifer helped herself to another glass of wine and giggled. 'Three shops, a bank, two offices, a post office and no jobs! Well, I guess I could have thought about travelling into Canterbury...seeing what I could land there but...'

'But that would have been a waste of your French degree. I guess John will miss having you around.'

Jennifer wanted to ask if *he* would miss having her around. He worked in London, had taken over the running of his father's company when, in the wake of his father's death six years previously, the vultures had been circling, waiting to snap it up at a knock-down price. At the time he had barely been out of university but he had skipped the gap year he had planned and returned to take the reins of the company and haul it into the twenty-first century. London was his base but he travelled out to the country regularly. Would he miss having her around on those weekends? Bank holidays?

'I won't be gone for the rest of my life.' Jennifer smiled, thinking of her father. 'I think he'll manage. He has his little landscaping business and, of course, overseeing your grounds. I've been working to get him computer literate so that we can Skype each other.' She cupped her face in her hands and looked at him. He was only just twenty-seven but he looked older. Was that because he had been thrown into a life of responsibility at the highest possible level from a very young age? He had had little to do with his father's company before his father had died. Silvio Rocchi had barely had anything to do with it himself. While he had carried out his diplomatic duties, he had delegated the running of the company to his right-hand men which, as it turned out, had not been the best idea in the world. When he died, James had been the young up-start whose job it had been to sack the dead wood. Had that forged a vein of steel inside him that had turned the boy quickly into the man?

She could have spent a few minutes chewing over the conundrum but he was saying something, talking about her father.

'And it's just a thought but he might even enjoy having the place to himself, who knows?'

'Well, he'll get *used to it*.' But enjoy? No, she couldn't really see that happening. Her earliest memories were of her and her dad as a unit. They had weathered the storm of her mother's death together and had been everything to each other ever since.

'I think,' James murmured, glancing over her shoulder

and leaning towards her to cover her hand with his, 'your little surprise is on its way…'

Jennifer spun around to see two of the waiters walking towards her and felt a stab of sudden disappointment. They were holding a cake with a sparkler and huge bowl of ice cream liberally covered with chocolate sauce and coloured sweets. It was the sort of thing a child would have been thrilled by, not a grown woman. She glanced over her shoulder to James, and saw that he was lounging back, hands clasped behind his head, smiling with an expression of satisfaction so she smiled too and held the smile as she blew out the sparkler to an audience of clapping diners.

'Really, James, you shouldn't have.' She stared down at more dessert than anyone could hope to consume in a single sitting, even someone of her proportions. The awkward girl she had left behind threatened to return as she gazed down at his special gesture.

'You deserve it, Jen.' He rested his elbows on the table and carefully removed the sparkler from the cake. 'You did brilliantly at university and you've done brilliantly to accept the Paris job.'

'There's nothing *brilliant* about accepting a job.'

'But Paris…when my mother told me that you'd been offered it, I wasn't sure whether you had it in you to take it.'

'What do you mean?' It seemed rude to leave the melting ice cream and the slab of cake untouched, so she had a mouthful and looked away from him.

'You know what I mean. You haven't strayed far from the family home…university just around the corner so that you could pop in and check on John several times a week, even though you were living out…'

'Yes, well—'

'Not that that's a bad thing. It's not. The world would be a better place if there were more people like you in it. We

certainly would be reading far fewer stories in the newspapers of care homes where ageing relatives get shoved
and forgotten about.'

'You make me sound like a saint,' Jennifer said, stab-
bing some cake and dipping it into the bowl of ice cream.

'You always do that.'

'What?'

'Somehow manage to turn cake and ice cream into
slush. And you always manage to do...*that*...'

'What?' She could feel her irritation levels rising.

'Get ice cream round your mouth.' He reached over
to brush some ice cream off and the fleeting touch of his
finger by her mouth almost made her gasp. He licked the
ice cream from his finger and raised his eyebrows with
appreciation.

'Very nice. Bring that bowl closer and let's share.'

Jennifer relaxed. This was more like it. Three glasses
of wine had relaxed her but she hadn't been able to banish
all her inhibitions. His treating her like a kid was probably
going to bring them all back but clinking spoons as they
dipped into the same bowl, exchanging mouthfuls of ice
cream and laughing...

Once again she felt intoxicated with anticipation.

She made sure to lean forward so that he could see her
cleavage, which was daringly on display. Normally, she
wore much plainer clothes, big jumpers in winter and loose
dresses in summer. But, for this date, she had splashed out
on a calf-length skirt and although the silky top was still
fairly baggy, its neckline was more risqué.

It was strange but, although she had no qualms about
wearing tight jeans and tight tops at university, the standard uniform for students, the thought of wearing anything
tight in front of James had always brought on a mild panic
attack. The feel of those lazy blue eyes resting on her had

always resulted in an acute bout of self-consciousness. His girlfriends were always so petite and so slim. In her head, she had always been able to hear his comparisons whenever he looked at her. Loose clothes had been one way of deflecting those comparisons.

'So,' he murmured, 'will you be leaving any broken hearts behind?'

It was the first time he had ever asked her such a directly personal question and she shivered pleasurably as she shook her head, not wanting, *under any circumstances*, to let him get the impression that she wasn't available.

'Absolutely no one.'

'You surprise me. What's wrong with those lads at university? They should have been forming a queue to ask you out.'

Jennifer blushed. 'I went on a couple of dates, but the boys all seemed so young, getting drunk at clubs and spending entire days in front of their computer games. None of them seemed to take life seriously.'

'At eighteen and nineteen, life is something not to be taken seriously.'

'*You* did when you were barely older than that.'

'As you may recall, I had no choice.' Jennifer was the only woman who could get away with bringing his private life into the conversation. She was, in actual fact, the only woman who knew anything at all about his private life and, even with her, there was still a great deal of which she was unaware.

'I know that and I know it must have been tough, but I honestly can't think of anyone who would have risen to the occasion the way you did. I mean, you had no real experience and yet you went in there and turned it all around.'

'I'll make sure that you're the first on the guest list when I get knighted.'

Jennifer laughed and pushed the plate of melting ice cream away from her, choosing instead to have a bit more wine and ignoring James's raised eyebrows.

'I'm being serious,' she insisted. 'I can't think of a single guy I knew at university who would have been capable of doing what you did.'

'You're young. Life shouldn't be about looking for a guy who can take the world on his shoulders. In fact, it should be about the guy who hasn't grown up yet. Believe me there's plenty of time to buckle down and realise that life's no picnic…'

'I'm not young!' Jennifer said lightly. 'I'm twenty-one. Not that much younger than you, in actual fact.'

James laughed and signalled to the waiter for the bill. 'You haven't done justice to those desserts.' He changed the topic when she would have had him pursue this tantalising personal conversation. 'I've always admired your sweet tooth. So refreshing after some of the girls I've dated in the past, who think that swallowing a mouthful of dessert constitutes an offence punishable by death.'

'That's why they're so skinny and I'm not,' she said, fishing hopefully for a compliment, but his attention was on the approaching waiter and on the bill being placed in front of him.

Now that the evening was drawing to a close, she could feel her nerves begin to get the better of her, although the copious amounts of wine had helped. When she stood up, she swayed ever so slightly and James reached for her with a concerned expression.

'Tell me you haven't had too much to drink,' he murmured. 'Hang onto me. I'll make sure you don't topple over.'

'Of course I'm not going to topple over! I'm a big girl. I need more than a few glasses of wine to topple over!' She loved the feel of his arm around her waist as they strolled out of the restaurant. It was August and still balmy outside. The fading light cast everything into shadow but the street lights had not yet come on and the atmosphere was wonderfully mellow and intimate. She surreptitiously nestled a little closer to him and tentatively put her arm around his waist. Her heart skipped a beat.

She was five ten and in heels, easily six foot, but at six foot three he still made her feel gloriously small and feminine.

She could have stayed like this in silence but he began asking her about Paris, quizzing her about the details of her job, asking her what her apartment would be like and reassuring her that, if it wasn't up to scratch, she was to remember that his company had several apartments in Paris and that he would be more than happy to arrange for her to stay in one of them.

Jennifer didn't want that. She didn't want him doing the big brother thing and imagining that she wanted him to take care of her from a distance so she skirted around his offer and reminded him that she wasn't in need of looking after.

'Where has this sudden streak of independence come from?' he asked teasingly, and his warm breath rustled her hair. He was smiling. She heard it in his voice.

They had reached his car, and she felt the loss of his arm around her as he held open the passenger door for her to step inside.

'I remember,' he said, still smiling and turning to look at her as he started the engine, 'when you were fifteen and you told me that you couldn't possibly get through your maths exam unless I sat and helped you.'

Never thinking that he had better things to do, just

pleased to be able to bask in his attention for a couple of hours as he had patiently helped her.

'I must have been a complete pain,' she said truthfully.

'Or a pleasant distraction.'

'What do you mean?'

'I was buried under work trying to fish my father's company out of its woeful state of affairs. Helping you and listening to all your school gossip often gave me a much-needed break from the headache of running a company.'

'But what about your girlfriends?'

'I know,' James said ruefully. 'You would have thought that they would have provided a distraction, but at that juncture in my life I didn't need their demands.'

'Well, that was such a long time ago. I can't even remember any of that school gossip.'

'And if I recall, you went on to get an A in your maths…'

Jennifer didn't say anything. The restaurant was only a matter of thirty minutes away from the house. In the blink of an eye, they would be back at the cottage and she would be able to show him that she really and truly was no longer the kid who had asked for help with her homework or filled him in on the silly happenings in her life whenever he happened to be down for the weekend. Maybe he wouldn't be entirely surprised…? After all, he *had* asked her out on a date!

She replayed that lovely feeling of having his arm around her and resisted the temptation to reach out and cover his hand with hers.

They drew up to the cottage in comfortable silence. Set in the grounds of the manor house, it was originally designed to house the head butler, but it had been annexed years before the Rocchis had moved in by a wily investor who had seen it as an efficient way of making some additional money. It was a happy coincidence that her father had bought the tiny two-bedroom place at around the same time as the Rocchis had moved into the manor house. Her own mother had died when she, Jennifer, had been just a toddler and Daisy Rocchi, unable to have any more children after James, had become a surrogate mother, bypassing all rules and conventions that predicated against two families of such differing incomes becoming close.

'Dad's not in.' Jennifer turned to look at James and cleared her throat. 'Why don't you…um…come in for something to drink? You barely had any of that wine tonight.'

'If I had thought ahead, I would have booked a taxi for us instead of driving myself.'

'Well, I know there's some wine in the fridge and I think dad's got a bottle of whisky in the cupboard. His once-a-month vice, he tells me.' She wasn't sure what she would do if he turned down her offer but he didn't and she breathed a sigh of relief as he said no to the alcohol but opted for a cup of coffee instead.

Inside the cottage, she switched on the lamp in the sitting room instead of the harsher overheard light and urged him in while she prepared them coffee with shaking hands. She was trying very hard to recapture the excitement and confidence she had felt earlier on in the restaurant as she had gazed at her reflection in the mirror and told herself that this *date* had arrived at just the perfect time, when she was still riding the crest of a wave, with her finals behind her and an exciting new job ahead of her.

She was so lost in her thoughts that she almost sent both mugs of coffee crashing to the ground as she turned to find James lounging in the doorway to the kitchen. Very carefully, she rested the mugs on the pine kitchen table and took two steps to close the distance between them.

Now or never, Jennifer thought with feverish determination. She had nurtured this crush for way too long. All through her time at university, she had tried to make herself like the boys who had asked her out, but her thoughts had always returned to James. His heart-stopping sex appeal and their shared history were a potent, heady combination and she had never quite managed to break free of its spell.

'I…I liked what you did earlier…' The palms of her hands were sweaty with nerves.

'You mean the cake and ice cream?' He laughed and looked down at her. 'Like I said, I know what a sucker you are for sweet things.'

'Actually I was talking about after that.'

'Sorry. I'm not following you.'

'When you put your arms around me on the way to the car. I liked that.' She slid her hand over his chest and nearly fainted at the hard body underneath her fingers. 'James…' She looked up at him and before she could chicken out she closed her eyes and tiptoed up to reach him. The first taste of his cool mouth sent a charge of adrenaline racing through her body and with a soft moan she kissed him harder, reached up to wind her arms around his neck as her body curved against his.

Her breasts were aching, her heart was beating like a drum. Every nerve in her body was alive with sensations she had never felt with anyone in her life before. Every kiss she had ever shared with other boys was drowned out by the scorching heat of this kiss. She felt his response as he kissed her back and that response was enough for her to take his hand and guide it underneath the loose shirt, up to the lacy bra that she had worn especially.

She was so lost in the moment that it was a few seconds before she realised that he was gently but firmly detaching himself from her and it was a few more seconds before it sank in that this was not a gesture preparatory to taking her upstairs. This much-longed-for evening was not going to end in her bedroom, making love while candles flickered in the background. She had agonised over her choice of linen, ditching her usual flowery bedcovers for something plain instead. He wasn't going to see any of it.

'Jennifer...'

Unable to bear the gentleness in his voice, she spun around with her arms tightly clasped around her body.

'I'm sorry. Please go.'

'We need to talk about what...what happened just then.'

'No. We don't.' She refused to look up as he circled round to face her. She kept her eyes pinned to his shoes while her body went hot and cold with mortification. She was no longer a sexy woman on a date with the guy for whom she had spent years nursing an inexhaustible infatuation. She bitterly wallowed in the reality that she was an awkward and not particularly attractive woman in a stupid, newly purchased outfit who had just made a complete fool of herself.

'Look at me, Jen. Please.'

'I got the wrong end of the stick, James, and I apologise. I thought...I don't know what I thought...'

'You're embarrassed and I understand that but—'

'Don't say any more!'

'I have to. We're friends. If we leave this to fester, things will never be the same between us again. I enjoy your company. I wouldn't want to lose what we have. For God's sake, Jennifer, at least *look at me*!'

She looked up at him and for the first time the sight of him didn't thrill her.

'Don't beat yourself up, Jen. I kissed you back and for that I apologise. I shouldn't have.'

But he had and she knew why. What man wouldn't suc-

*cumb to a woman who flung herself at him? It was telling
that he had come to his senses in a matter of seconds. Even
with everything on offer, she hadn't been able to tempt him.*

'You're young. You're about to embark on the biggest
adventure of your life—'

'Oh, spare me the pity talk,' Jennifer muttered.

'I'm not *pitying you*.' He stuck his hands in the pockets
of his trousers and shook his head in frustration.

'Yes, you are! I've been a complete idiot and I've put
us both in an awkward position and none of it is your
fault! Okay, so when you asked me out to dinner tonight, I
thought it was more than just two friends having a meal. I
fooled myself into believing that you might have begun to
see me as a woman instead of the girl next door! Instead
of the clumsy, ungainly, unappealing, borderline unat-
tractive girl next door.'

'Don't put yourself down. I don't like it.'

'I'm not putting myself down.' She managed to meet his
eyes without flinching although it cost her every ounce of
will power. 'I'm being honest. I've had a crush on you—'

'And there's nothing wrong with that…'

'You knew.'

'It was endearing.'

'Well, a pleasant distraction from when your pocket-
sized blonde bombshells were being too demanding, at
any rate.'

'You had a schoolgirl crush and there's nothing sinful
about that,' James told her with such sincerity that she
itched to slap him. 'But you're young. I know you said that
you're only a few years younger than me, but in terms of
experience we're light years apart. Trust me when I tell
you that in a year's time you'll have forgotten all about
this. You'll have met some nice lad…'

'Yes,' Jennifer parroted dutifully, wanting this entire

conversation to be over so that she could go upstairs and bury herself under the freshly laundered covers.

He sighed and shook his head. This was a Jennifer he didn't recognise. Gone was the smiling, malleable girl. Had he known that she had a crush on him? Yes, of course he had, although he had never openly addressed the issue. Now, for the first time, he could sense her locking him out. He understood but it was a strange sensation and he didn't like it.

'Your feelings for me are misplaced,' he told her roughly. 'I wasn't lying when I told you that you want to enjoy your youth with boys who are uncomplicated and fun-loving.'

'You make it sound as though I was looking for... looking for something more than just...'

'A romp in the sack?'

Mortified, Jennifer shrugged.

'You deserve a lot more than I could give you.'

By which, she thought, *you mean that there's nothing you're interested in giving me aside from a peck on the cheek every now and again and lots of good advice about how to live my life.*

He was being patronising and the worst of it was that he wasn't even aware of it.

'Don't worry about me, James,' she said with a forced smile, relieving him of the obligation to keep thinking about her feelings because he was a decent human being. 'I'll be fine. These things happen.' Two steps back, putting distance between them. 'I probably won't see you before I leave.'

'No.'

'Of course I'll keep in touch and I'm sure we'll bump into one another now and again.' One more step back.

'You'll be all right, will you?'

Jennifer chose to interpret this at face value and she looked at him with a polite, unfocused expression. 'Of course I will. As I told you, the job I'll be doing over there isn't going to be substantially different than what I've done over the summer vacations. Naturally, I'll be following through on a lot more and there'll be a great deal of translating but I'm sure I'll be able to handle it.'

'Right. Good.'

'So.'

James hesitated and raked his fingers through his hair. 'Thanks for dinner, James…and I'll see you…'

She remained frozen to the spot as he brushed past her, pausing fleetingly, as though hesitant to leave.

What did he think she was going to do? Jennifer wondered. Fling herself out of her bedroom window because he had rejected her? Was she so pathetic in his eyes that he doubted her ability to get over the slight?

The soft click of the front door closing signalled his departure and it was only once she was certain that he had left the cottage that Jennifer slumped.

She closed her eyes and thought of the excited girl who had bought a new outfit especially for her big date. She remembered her anticipation at having him all to herself over dinner. She had dreamt of seduction and of finally having this crazy crush of hers fulfilled. It suddenly felt like a million years ago and, although a year wasn't long, it was long enough to say goodbye to that person.

CHAPTER ONE

EXCEPT one year became two, which became three, which became four. And in all those four years, Jennifer had not once set eyes on James. Each Christmas, she had contrived to bring her father over to Paris for the holidays, which he had loved. What had begun as a one-year placement, during which she could consolidate her French, had seen her rise through the company, and as she had risen so too had her pay cheque. She found that she could afford to holiday with her father abroad, and on those occasions when she *had* returned to England she had been careful with her visits, always making sure that they were brief and that James was nowhere in the vicinity.

He had walked out of the cottage four years previously and she had fled to Paris, her wounds still raw. She couldn't imagine ever facing him again, and not facing him had developed into a habit. He had emailed her, and she had been happy enough to email back, but on the occasions when he had been in Paris she had excused herself from meeting him on grounds of being too busy, prior engagements, not well, *anything* because the memory of him gently letting her down remained, that open wound quietly hurting somewhere in the background of her shiny new life.

Except now…

She had nodded off on the train and woke with a start as it pulled into the station.

When she looked through the window it was to see that the flurries of snow that she had left behind in London were a steady fall here in Kent. The weather was always so much harsher out here. She had forgotten.

At six-thirty in the evening the train was packed with commuters and fetching her bags was chaotic, with people jostling her on all sides, but eventually she was out of the train and braving the freezing temperatures and snow on the platform.

She wasn't planning on staying long. Just long enough to sort out the problems in the cottage, problems she had learnt about via an email from James who had been checking his house in his mother's absence and had happened to walk down to the cottage to take a look only to find water seeping out from under the front door. Her father was away on his annual post-Christmas three-week holiday to visit his brother in Scotland. The email had read:

You can pass this on to your father, but I gather you're in the country so you might want to check it out yourself instead of ruining your father's fishing trip. This, of course, presupposes that you can interrupt your busy schedule.

The tone of the email was the final nail in the coffin of their enduring friendship. She had run away and, never looked back, and over time, the chasm between them had become so vast that it was now unbreachable terrain. His emails, which had been warm and concerned at the beginning of her stint in Paris, had gradually become cooler and more formal, in direct proportion to her avoidance tactics. It occurred to her that she actually hadn't heard from him at all for at least six months.

In Paris, she could tell herself that she didn't mind, that this was just the way things had turned out in the end, that their friendship had always been destined to run its course because it had been an unrealistic union of the inaccessible boy in the manor house and the childishly doting girl next door.

But now here, back in Kent, his email was a vaguely sexy reminder of how things used to be.

She wheeled her suitcase out to where a bank of taxis was only just managing to keep the snow on their cars from settling by virtue of having their engines running. Everywhere, the snow was forming a layer of white.

The water had been cleared, James had informed her, but there was a lot of collateral damage, which she would have to assess for the insurance company. He had managed to get the heating started. So at least when she arrived at the cottage, she wouldn't freeze to death. She hoped he might have left her some fresh provisions before he cleared off, on his way to Singapore for a series of meetings, he had politely informed her in his email, but she wasn't banking on it.

That was how far their friendship had devolved. When Jennifer thought about it for too long, she could feel a lump of sadness in her throat and she had to remind herself of that terrible night when she had made such a fool of herself. Someone better and stronger might have been able to survive that and laughingly put it behind them so that a friendship could be maintained, but she couldn't.

For her, it had been a devastating learning curve and she *had* learnt from it.

She gazed out of the window of the taxi but could barely see anything because of the snow. Deep in the heart of the Kent countryside, the trip, in conditions like this, would take over an hour. She settled in for the long haul and let her thoughts drift without restraint.

It had been a while since she had returned to the cottage for any length of time. She and her father had spent summer in Majorca, two weeks of sun and sea, and every six weeks she brought him over for a weekend. She loved the fact that she could afford to do that now. She knew that there was a part of her that was reluctant to return to the place that held so many memories of James, but that was fine because her father was more than happy to travel out to see her and she always, always made sure that she met Daisy, James's mother, for lunch in London when she was over on business. She had politely asked about James and given evasive non-answers whenever Daisy showed any curiosity as to why they no longer seemed to meet. Eventually his name had been quietly dropped from conversations.

To think of him moving around in the cottage made something in her shiver. Sometimes, a memory of the scent of him, clean and masculine and woody, would surface from nowhere, leaving her shaken. She hoped that scent wouldn't be lingering in the cottage when she got there. She was tired and it was too cold to run around opening windows to let out an elusive smell.

By the time they reached the cottage, driving was becoming impossible.

'And they predict at least a week of this,' the driver said bitterly. 'Business is bad enough as it is without Mother Nature getting involved.'

'Oh, this won't last,' Jennifer said airily. 'I've got to be back in London by day after tomorrow.'

'Lots of clothes for an overnight stay.' The driver struggled up to the door with the case, unable to wheel it in the snow.

'I'll be leaving one or two things behind. Clearing out old stuff.'

She paid him, thinking of the task that lay ahead. Aside from sorting out the cottage, she would be bagging up all those frumpy clothes that had once been the mainstay of her wardrobe. None of them would fit any more. In the space of four years, she had been seduced by Parisian chic. She had lost weight, or maybe, thanks to her daily run, the weight had just been reassigned. At any rate, the body she had once avoided looking at in the mirror now attracted wolf whistles and stares from strangers and she was not ashamed to wear clothes that accentuated it. Nothing revealing, that would never be her style, but fashionable and figure hugging. Her untamed hair had been tamed over the years, thanks to the expert scissors of her hairdresser. It was still long, longer even than it used to be, but it was cleverly layered so that the frizz had been replaced with curls.

The cottage was in complete darkness although the door was surprisingly unlocked. She lugged the suitcase through and slammed the door shut behind her, luxuriating for a few seconds in the blissful warmth, eyes closed, lights still off because she just wanted to enjoy the cottage before she could see all the damage that had been caused by the flood.

And then she opened her eyes and there he was. Lounging against the door that led into the kitchen.

The cottage hadn't been in complete darkness, as she had first thought. No, one of the kitchen lights had been switched on, but the kitchen was at the back of the house and the door leading to it had been shut when she had entered.

She literally froze on the spot.

God, he hadn't changed. He was still as beautiful as

he always had been, still the man who towered over other men. His hair was shorter than it had been four years ago and she could tell from the shadow on his jawline that he hadn't shaved. In the space of a few seconds, during which time Jennifer felt her breath catch in her throat, she took in everything. The lean, long body in a pair of jeans and an old striped rugby jumper, the sleeves of which were shoved up to the elbows, those amazing deep blue eyes, now focused on her in a way that made her head swim.

Disastrously, she felt herself catapulted back to the young, naive girl she had once been.

'James. What on earth are you doing here?' She knew that her hand was trembling when she hit the light switch. 'You told me that you would be leaving the country!'

'I should be in the air right now but the weather got in the way of those plans. It's been a long time, Jennifer...'

The silence stretched and stretched and stretched and she had to fight to maintain her self-control. Four years of independence, of cutting herself free from those infantile ties that had bound her to this man, and she could feel them melting and slipping away. She could have wept. Instead, she let the little ball of remembered bitterness and anger form into a knot inside her stomach and she began to get rid of her coat, which was heavy and damp from the snow.

'Yes. Yes, it has. How are you?' She forced a stiff smile but her heart was thumping like a sledgehammer.

'I thought I'd stay in the cottage until you got here, make sure you arrived safely. I wasn't sure whether you were going to drive or take the train.'

'I...I took the train.' Her car was parked outside her friend's house in London where she stayed every time she came back to the city. 'But there was no need for you to hang around here. You know I can take care of myself.'

'You've certainly been doing a very good job of that

while you've been in Paris. My mother frequently regales me with news of yet more promotions.'

She still hadn't taken a single step towards him because her feet appeared to be nailed to that one spot in the hallway.

He was the first to break the spell, turning away and heading into the kitchen, leaving her to follow him.

He hadn't said a word about how much she had changed. How could he have failed to notice? But then, why was it so surprising when he had never really noticed her? The ease she had once felt in his company was nowhere to be found and it was a struggle thinking of polite conversation to make.

'It's been a very successful posting for me,' Jennifer said politely. 'I never thought that I'd end up staying over there for four years but as I accepted more and more responsibility, the work became more and more challenging and I found myself accepting their offers to stay on.'

'You look like a visitor, standing there. Sit down. You might as well forget about getting anything done tonight. We can work on detailing what will need to be done to the cottage tomorrow.'

'*We?* Like I said, there's absolutely no need for you to help me with this. I plan on having it all finished by tomorrow afternoon and I'll be leaving first thing the following morning.' This was not how two old friends, meeting after years of separation, would act. Jennifer knew that. She could hear the sharp edge to her voice and, while she was dismayed by it, she was also keenly aware that it was necessary as a protective tool, because just looking at him rooting around in the fridge with his back to her threatened to take her down memory lane and that was a journey she wasn't willing to make.

'Good luck arguing with the weather on that score.'

'What are you doing in the fridge?'

'Cheese, eggs. There's some bread over there, bought yesterday. When the snow started, I realised I might find myself stuck here and if I was stuck here, then you would be as well, so I managed to make it down to the shops and got a few things together.'

'Well, that was very kind of you, James. Thank you.'

'Well, isn't this fun?' He fetched a bottle of wine from the fridge, something he had bought along with the food, she was sure, and poured them both a glass. 'Four years and we're struggling to pass the time of day. Tell me what you've been up to in France.'

'I thought I just had. My job is very invigorating. The apartment is wonderful.'

'So everything lived up to expectation.' He sat back in the kitchen chair and took a deep mouthful of wine, looking at her over the rim of the glass. God, she'd changed. Did she realise just how much? He couldn't believe that the last time he'd seen her had been four years ago, but then she had made sure to be unavailable whenever he'd happened to be in Paris, and somehow, whenever she'd happened to be in the UK, he'd happened to be out of it.

She had cut all ties with him and he knew that it had all happened on that one fateful night. Of course, he didn't regret the outcome of that evening. He had had no choice but to turn her down. She had been young and vulnerable and too sexy for her own good. She had come to him looking for something and he had known, instinctively, that whatever that something was he would have been incapable of providing it. She had been trusting and naive, not like the hard-edged beauties he was accustomed to who would have been happy to take whatever was on offer for limited duration.

But he had never suspected that she would have walked out of his life permanently.

And changed. And had not looked back.

'Yes.' Jennifer played with the stem of her wine glass but there was no way that she was going to drink any of it. 'Everything lived up to expectation and beyond. Life has never been so good or so rewarding. And what about you, James? What have you been up to? I've seen your mother over the years but I really haven't heard much about you.'

'Shrinking world but fortunately new markets in the Far East. If you like, I can go into the details but doubt you would find it that fascinating. Aside from the challenging job, what is Paris like for you? Completely different from this neck of the woods, I imagine.'

'Yes. Yes, it is.'

'Are you going to expand on that or shall we drink our respective glasses of wine in silence while we try and formulate new topics of conversation?'

'I'm sorry, James. It's been a long trip with the train and the taxi and I'm exhausted. I think it's probably best if you went up to your house and we can always play the catch-up game another time.'

'You haven't forgotten, have you?'

'Forgotten what?'

'Forgotten the last time we met.'

'I have no idea what you're talking about.'

'Yes. Yes, I think you do, Jen.'

'I don't think there's anything to be gained by dragging up the past, James.' She stood up abruptly and positioned herself by the kitchen door with her arms folded. Not only were they strangers, but now they were combatants, squaring up to each other in the boxing ring. Jennifer didn't dare allow regret to enter the equation because just looking at him like this was making her realise that on some deep, instinctive level she still responded to him. She didn't know whether that was the pull of familiarity or the pull of an attraction that refused to remain buried and she was not willing to find out.

'Why don't you go and change and I'll fix you something to eat, and if you tell me that you're too exhausted to eat, then I'm going to suspect that you're finding excuses to avoid my company. Which wouldn't be the case, would it, Jen?'

'Of course not.' But she could feel a delicate flush creep into her cheeks.

'Nothing fancy. You know my culinary talents are limited.'

The grin he delivered was an aching reminder of the good times they had shared and the companionable ease they had lost.

'And don't,' he continued, holding up one hand as though to halt an interruption, 'tell me that there's no need. I know there's no need. Like I said, I'm fully aware of how independent you've become over the past four years.'

Jennifer shrugged, but her thoughts were all over the place as she rummaged in the suitcase for a change of clothes. A hurried shower and she was back downstairs within half an hour, this time in a pair of loose grey yoga pants and a tight, long-sleeved grey top, her hair pulled back into a ponytail.

It had always been a standing joke that James never cooked. He would tease her father, who adored cooking, that the kitchen was a woman's domain, that cooking wasn't a man's job. He would then lay down the gauntlet—an arm-wrestling match to prove that cooking depleted a man of strength. Jennifer used to love these little interludes; she used to love the way he would wink at her, pulling her into his game.

However, he was just finishing a remarkably proficient omelette when she walked into the kitchen. A salad was in a bowl. Hot bread was on a wooden board.

'I guess I'm not the only one who's changed,' Jennifer said from the doorway, and he glanced across to her, his eyes lazily appraising.

'Would you believe me if I told you that I took a cookery course?'

Jennifer shrugged. 'Did you?' She sat at the table and looked around her. 'There's less damage than I thought there would be. I had a look around before I went to have a shower. Thankfully, upstairs is intact and I can just see that there are some water stains on the sofa in the sitting room and I guess the rugs will have to be replaced.'

'Have we finished playing our catch-up game already?' He handed her a plate, encouraged her to help herself to bread and salad, before taking up position opposite her at the kitchen table.

Jennifer thought that this was the reason she had avoided him for four years. There was just *too much* of him. He overwhelmed her and she was no longer on the market for being overwhelmed.

'There's nothing more to catch up on, James. I can't think of anything else I could tell you about my job in Paris. If you like I could give you a description of what my apartment looks like, but I shouldn't think you'd find that very interesting.'

'You've changed.'

'What is that supposed to mean?'

'I barely recognise you as the girl who left here four years ago. Somewhere in my memory banks, I have an image of someone who actually used to laugh and enjoy conversing with me.'

Jennifer felt the slow burn of anger because *he* hadn't

changed. He was still the same arrogantly self-assured James, supremely confident of their roles in life. She laughed and blushed and he basked in her open admiration.

'How can you expect me to laugh when you haven't said anything funny as yet, James?'

'That's *exactly* what I'm talking about!' He threw his hands up in a gesture of frustration and pushed himself back from the table. 'You've either had a personality change or else your job in Paris is so stressful that it's wiped out your sense of fun. Which is it, Jen? You can be honest with me. You've always been open and honest with me, so tell me: have you bitten off more than you can chew with that job?'

'I know that's what you'd like me to say, James. That I'm hopelessly lost and can't handle the work in Paris.'

'That's a ridiculous statement.'

'Is it? If I told you that I was having a hard time and just couldn't cope, then you could be the caring, concerned guy. You could put your arm round my shoulder and whip out a handkerchief for me to sob into! But my job is absolutely brilliant and if I wasn't any good at it, then I would never have been promoted. I would never have risen up the ranks.'

'Is that what you think? That I'm the sort of narrow-minded, mean-spirited guy who would be happy if you failed?'

Jennifer sighed and pushed her plate away.

'I know you're not mean-spirited, James, and I don't want to argue with you.' She stood up, began clearing the dishes, tried to think of something harmless to say that would defuse the high-voltage atmosphere that had sprung up.

'Leave those things!' James growled.

'I don't want to. Tomorrow's going to be a long day and

the less I have to do in the kitchen, tidying up stuff that could be done now, the better. And by the way, thank you very much for cooking for me. It was very nice.'

James muttered something under his breath but began helping her, drying dishes as she began washing. Jennifer felt his presence as acutely as a live charge. If she stepped too close, she would be electrocuted. Being in his presence had stripped her of her immunity to him and it frightened her, but she wasn't going to give in to that queasy feeling in the pit of her stomach. She launched into a neutral conversation about their parents. She told him how much her father enjoyed Paris.

'Because, as you know, he stopped going abroad after Mum died. He once told me that it had been their dream to travel the world and when she died, the dream died with her.'

'Yes, the last time I came here for the weekend, he was waiting for the taxi and reading a guide book on the Louvre. He said it was top on the agenda. He's been ticking off the sights.'

'Really?' Jennifer laughed and for an instant James went still. He realised that the memory of that laugh lingered at the back of his brain like the refrain from a song that never quite went away. Suddenly he wanted to know a lot more than just whether she enjoyed her job or what her apartment was like. She had always, he was ashamed to admit to himself, been a known quantity, but now he felt curiosity rip through him, leaving him bemused.

'You've opened up a door for John,' he drawled, drying the last dish and then leaning against the counter with the tea towel slung over his shoulder. 'I think he's realised what he's been missing all these years. He was in a rut and your moving to Paris forced him out of it. I have a feeling that he's going to get bored with weekends to Paris pretty soon.'

'We don't just stay in Paris,' Jennifer protested. 'We've been doing quite a bit of Europe.' But she was thrilled with what James had told her. It was a brief window during which, with her defences down, they were back to that place they had left behind, that place of easy familiarity, two people with years and years of shared history.

She glanced surreptitiously at him and edged away before that easy familiarity could get a little too easy, before her hard-won independence began draining away and she found herself back to the girl in the past who used to hang onto his every word.

'In fact, I've already planned the next couple of weekends. When the weather improves, we're going to go to Prague. It's a beautiful city. I think he'd love it.'

'You've been before, have you?'

'Once.'

'And this from the girl who grew up in one place and never went abroad, aside from that school trip when you were fifteen. Skiing, wasn't it?'

Yes, it certainly was. Jennifer remembered it distinctly. James's father had just died and he had been busy trying to grapple with the demands of the company he had inherited. He hadn't been around much and when, after the skiing trip, she had seen him for the first time after several weeks, she had regaled him with a thousand stories of all the little things the class had done. The cliques that had subdivided the groups. The quiet girl, usually in the background, who had come out of her shell because she was one of only a handful who had been any good at skiing.

'Yes, that's right.'

'And who did you go to Prague with?' James enquired casually. 'I've actually been twice. Romantic city.' He

turned to fill the kettle and found that he was keenly await-
ing her response.

Jennifer frowned. She was relieved that he had his back
to her. Her first instinct was to tell him that her private
life was none of his business. She quickly decided that it
was one thing being scrupulously polite, but if she began
to actively push him away he would start asking himself
why and they would be back to the subject she was most
desperate to avoid: her mistimed, unfortunate pass at him.
He would really be in his element then, she concluded bitterly, holding her hand and trying to assure her that she
shouldn't let the memory of it interfere with her life, that
their friendship was so much more important than a silly
non-escapade. She would be mortified.

'Yes. It's a very romantic city. I love everything about
it. I love the architecture and that terrific feeling of a place
almost suspended in time. Don't you agree?'

'So who did you go with? Or is it a deep, dark secret?'
He chuckled and turned round to face her, moving to hand
her a mug of coffee and then sitting down and pulling one
of the chairs in front of him so that he could fully relax,
using the spare chair as a footrest.

'Oh, just a guy I met over there.'

'A guy!'

'Patric. Patric Alexander. Just someone I met at a party
a while back...'

'Well.' He didn't know why he was so shocked at this.
She had always been sexy, although it was fair to say that
she had never realised it. She was still sexy and the only
difference was that Paris had made her realise just how
much.

'French guy, is he?' James heard the inanity of his question and his lips thinned although he was still smiling.

'Half French. His mother's English.' She gulped down

her coffee and stood up with a brisk smile. 'Now, I really think it's time for you to head back to your house, James. I have unpacking to do and I want to be up fairly early to make a list of what needs doing. Hopefully not that much. I noticed that the rug in the sitting room's already been rolled. Thank you for that.'

'Thank God there's no carpet downstairs. The joys of flagstones when there's a flood! Why didn't this Patric guy come to help you?'

'Because he's in Paris.' She moved to the door and frowned when he remained comfortably seated at the table.

'The name doesn't ring a bell. I'm sure your father would have mentioned him to me in passing—'

'Why would he?' Jennifer snapped.

'Because I'm his friend…? How long have you been going out with this Patric guy?'

'I really don't want to be having this conversation with you.'

'Because you feel uncomfortable?'

'Because I'm tired and I want to go to sleep!'

'Fair enough.' James took his time getting to his feet. 'I wouldn't want to be accused of prying and I certainly wouldn't want to make you feel uncomfortable in any way…' He walked towards her and, the closer he got, the tenser she could feel herself becoming.

'I'm perfectly comfortable.'

'I just wonder,' he mused, pausing to invade her personal space by standing only inches in front of her, a towering six-feet-three inches of pure alpha male clearly hell-bent on satisfying his curiosity, 'whether you avoided me over the years because you were reluctant to let me meet this man of yours…'

'I was not *avoiding you* over the years,' Jennifer muttered uncomfortably. 'I thought we corresponded very frequently by email...'

'And yet every time I happened to be in Paris, you were otherwise occupied, and every time you happened to be in this country, I was out of it...'

'The timings were always wrong.' Jennifer shrugged, although she could feel hot colour rising to her face and she stared down at the ground with a little frown. 'Patric and I are no longer involved,' she finally admitted, when the silence became unbearable. 'We're still very good friends. In fact, I would say that he's my closest confidant...'

This time she did look at him and James knew instantly, from the genuine warmth of her smile, that she was being completely truthful.

The girl who had always turned to him, the girl who had matured into a woman he hadn't seen for nearly four years, now had someone else to turn to.

'And what about you?' she asked, because if he could ask intrusive questions then why shouldn't she? 'Is there anyone significant in your life at the moment, James?'

James was still trying to get over a weird feeling of disorientation. He tilted his head to one side, considering her question.

'No. No one at the moment. Until recently, I was involved with an actress...'

'Blonde?' Jennifer couldn't resist asking and he frowned at her and nodded.

'Petite? Fond of very high heels and very tight dresses?'

'Did my mother mention her to you? I got the impression she wasn't bowled over by Amy...'

'No, your mother didn't mention anyone to me. In fact,' she added with a hint of smugness, 'your mother and I haven't really discussed you at all. I'm just guessing because those are the sort of girls you've always been inter-

ested in. Blonde, big hair, small, very high heels and very
tight dresses.' Jennifer couldn't help herself, even though
dipping into this subject would be to open a door to all
the insecurities she had felt as a young woman, pining
for him and comparing herself incessantly to the girls he
would occasionally bring back to the house. Amy clones.
She took a deep breath and fought her way through that
brief reminder of a time she would rather have forgotten.

James flushed darkly.

'Nothing changes,' she said scornfully.

'Really? I wouldn't say that's true at all.'

'You still go out with the blonde airheads. Daisy still
despairs. You still only have relationships that last five
seconds.'

'But you don't still have a crush on me...'

That softly spoken remark, a lazy, tantalising question
wrapped up in a statement, was like a bucket of freezing
water thrown over her and she stepped back as though she
had been slapped.

What had she been thinking? Had she been so shocked
to find him in the cottage that she had forgotten how efficiently he could get under her skin? She had managed to
keep her distance so how was it that they had somehow
drifted into a conversation that was so personal?

'That was all a long time ago, James, and, like I said,
there's nothing to be gained from rehashing the past.'

'Well...' He finally began strolling to where his coat
was hanging over the banister. She wondered how she
had managed to miss that when she had walked in but, of
course, she hadn't been expecting him. 'I'll be heading
off but I'll be back tomorrow and please don't tell me that
there's no need. I'll roll the other carpets. Get them into
one of the outbuildings and keep them dry so that they can

be assessed for damage when this snow decides to stop and someone from the insurance company can come out.'

'I'm sure that can wait,' Jennifer said helplessly. 'I won't be here long. I plan on leaving…well…if not tomorrow evening, then first thing the following morning…'

James didn't say anything. He took his time wrapping his scarf round his neck, then he pulled open the front door so that she was treated to the spectacular sight of snow swirling madly outside, so thick that she could barely make out the fields stretching away into the distance.

'Good luck with that.' He turned to her. 'I think you'll find that we might both end up being stuck here…'

With each other. Jennifer tried not to be completely overwhelmed at the prospect of that. He wasn't going to stay cooped up in his house when he thought that she needed help in the cottage. He would be *around* and she had no idea how long for. Certainly, the snow looked as though it was here for the long haul and the house and cottage were not positioned for easy access to handy, cleared roads. They were in the middle of nowhere and it would not be the first time that heavy snow would leave them stranded.

But maybe it was for the best. She couldn't hide away from him for ever. Sooner rather than later she would be returning to the UK to live. Her father wasn't getting any younger and she had enough on her CV to guarantee a job, or at least a good prospect of one. When that happened, she would be seeing him once again on weekends.

She decided that this was fate.

'You could be right,' she said with more bravado than she felt. 'In which case, thank heavens you're here! I mean, I adore Patric, but I have to be honest and tell you that an artist probably wouldn't be a huge amount of practical help at a time like this…'

CHAPTER TWO

AN ARTIST? Jennifer had gone out with *an artist*? James could scarcely credit it. She had never shown any particular interest in art, per se, so how was it that she had been enticed into an affair with an artist? And who else had there been on the scene? He was disconcerted to find that she had somehow managed to escape the box into which he had slotted her and yet why should he be? People changed.

Except, there had been something smug about her tone of voice when she had implied that *he* had changed very little over the years. Still going out with the same blonde bimbos.

He was up at the crack of dawn the following morning and one glance out of the window told him that neither of them would be going anywhere, any time soon. If anything, the snow appeared to be falling with even greater intensity. Drifts of it were already banking up against the sides of the outbuildings and his car was barely visible. It was so silent out here that if he opened a window he would have been able to hear the snow falling.

Fortunately, the electricity had not been brought down and the Internet was still working.

He caught up with outstanding emails, including informing his secretary that she would have to cancel all meetings for at least the next couple of days, then, on the spur of the moment, he looked up Patric Alexander on an Internet search engine, hardly expecting to find anything because artists were a dime a dozen and few of them would ever make it to the hall of fame.

But there he was. James carried his laptop into the sprawling kitchen, which was big enough to fit an eight-seater table at one end and was warmed by the constant burn of a four-door bottle-green Aga. Mug of coffee in one hand, he sipped and scrolled through pages of nauseating adulation of the new up-and-coming talent in the art world. Patric was already garnering a loyal following and a clientele base that ensured future success. The picture was small, but James zoomed into it and found a handsome, fair-haired man surrounded by a bevy of beautiful women, standing in front of a backdrop of one of his paintings.

He slammed shut the lid of the computer, drained his coffee and was in a foul mood when, minutes later, he stood in front of the cottage and banged on the knocker.

It was barely eight-thirty and so dark still that he had practically needed a torch to find his way over. Even with several layers of clothing, a waterproof and the wellies he had had since his late teens, he could feel the snow trying to prise its way to his bare skin. His mood had slipped a couple of notches lower by the time Jennifer eventually made it to the door and peered out at him.

'What are you doing here so early?'

'It's too cold for us to make conversation in a doorway. Open up and let me in.'

'When you said you were going to come over, you never told me that you would be arriving on my doorstep *with the larks*.'

'There's a lot to do. What's the point in sleeping in?' He looked at her as he removed his coat and scarf and gloves and sufficient layers to accommodate the warmth of the cottage. She was in a pair of faded jeans and, yes, she really *had* changed. Lost weight. She looked tall and athletic. She had pulled back her hair and it hung down her back in a centre braid. 'I hope I didn't wake you? I've been up since five-thirty.'

'Oh, bully for you, James.' The day suddenly had the potential to be unbearably long. He followed her to the kitchen, sat down and seemed pleasantly surprised when she began cracking eggs into a bowl. He hadn't had any breakfast. Great if she could make some for him as well. Did she need a hand?

'I thought you said that you had made sure to buy some food?'

'Oh, the fridge at home is stocked to capacity but I didn't think to make anything for myself.'

'Even though you were up *at five-thirty*? It never crossed your mind that you could pour yourself a bowl of cereal? Grab a slice of toast?'

'When I start working, nothing distracts me. And small point of interest…I don't eat cereal. Can't stand the stuff. Just bits of cardboard pretending to be edible and good for you.'

Jennifer had spent a restless night. This was the last thing she needed and she turned to him coolly.

'This isn't going to work, James.'

'What?'

'*This!* You strolling over here and making yourself at home!'

'It's impossible to stroll in this weather.'

'You *know* what I mean! If you think that you need to help, to get the rugs to the outbuildings, then that's fine, but you can't just waltz in here for the day. I have things to do!'

'What?'

'I have to clear some cupboards and I have lots of work to catch up on if it turns out that I can't leave tomorrow as planned!' She felt his eyes on her as she turned round to pour some eggs into a frying pan.

'It makes sense for us to share the same space, Jen. What's the point having the heating going full blast in my house when I'm the only person in it?'

'The point is *you won't be under my feet!*'

'I'm going to be doing some heavy lifting on your behalf today, Jennifer. It's hardly what I would call *being under your feet.*'

'I'm sorry,' she muttered with a mutinous set to her mouth. 'I'm very grateful for the practical help you intend to give me but—'

'Okay. You win, Jennifer. I don't know why you want to draw battle lines, but if that's what you're intent on doing, then I'll leave you to get on with it.'

He stood up and Jennifer spun round to look at him. Was this what she really wanted? To make an enemy out of the person who had always been her friend? Because she found it difficult being in the same room as him?

'I don't want to draw battle lines,' she said on a heavy sigh. 'I just don't want you to…to think that nothing's changed between us.' She flicked off the stove and moved to sit at the table. The past was still unfinished business. That clumsy pass had never been discussed and she had carried it with her for four years. The memory of it was still so bitter that it had shaped all her relationships over the past four years, not that there had been many. Two. The first, to a young French lawyer she had met through work, had barely survived three months and, although he had laboured to win her over, she had been hesitant and eventually incapable of giving him the commitment he had wanted.

Patric had been her soul mate from the start and they had had three years of being friends before they decided to take that step further. It was a relationship that should have worked and yet, try as they had, she had not been able to capture the sizzle, the breathless excitement, the aching anticipation she had felt for James.

She knew that all of that was just a figment of her imagination. She knew that she had to somehow find it in her to prise herself out of a time warp that had her trapped in her youth, but eventually she and Patric had admitted defeat and had returned, fortunately, to being the close friends they had once been.

He had laughingly told her that there was no such thing as a friend with benefits. She had told herself that she needed to find a way of blocking James out of her head. She wasn't an impressionable young girl any more.

James looked at her in silence.

'I know I…I made that awful pass at you all those years ago. We never talked about it…'

'How could we? You left the country and never looked back.'

'I left the country and then life just became so hectic…' Jennifer insisted. 'I suppose to start with,' she said, conceding an inch but determined to make sure that an inch was the limit of her concessions, 'I *did* think that it might be awkward if we met up. I *may* have avoided you at first but then, honestly, life just became so busy…I barely had time to think! I guess I could have come back to England more frequently than I did, but Dad's never travelled and it was fun being able to bring him over, take him places. It was the first time I've ever been able to actually afford to take him on holiday…' The egg she had been scrambling had gone cold. She relit the stove and busied herself resuscitating it, keeping her back to him so that she could guard her expression from those clever, perceptive deep blue eyes, which had always been able to delve into the depths of her. She couldn't avoid this conversation, she argued to herself, but she wasn't going to let him know how much he still affected her.

She was smilingly bland when she placed a plate of toast and eggs in front of him.

'I think what I'm trying to say, James, is that I've grown up. I'm not that innocent young girl who used to hang onto your every word.'

'And I'm not expecting you to be!' But that, he realised, was exactly what he had been expecting. After four years of absence, he had still imagined her to be the girl next door who listened with eagerness to everything he had to say. The smiling stranger he had been faced with had come as a shock, and even more surprising was the fact that his usual cool when dealing with any unexpected situation had apparently deserted him.

'Which brings me to this: I don't want for there to be any bad feeling between us, but I also don't want you thinking that because we happen to be temporarily stranded here, that you have a right to come and go as you please. You've seen to the little flooding problem in the cottage and I'm very grateful for that but it doesn't mean that you now have a passport to my home.'

'Point taken.'

'And now I expect you're angry with me.' She hadn't wanted to say that but it just slipped out and she could have kicked herself because, as the new woman she claimed to be, would she still care what he thought of her? Why couldn't she be indifferent? She hadn't seen him for *four years*! It seemed so unfair that after all this time her heart still skipped a beat when he was around and it was even more unfair that she inwardly quailed at the thought of antagonising him.

'I'm glad you said what was on your mind. Honesty being the best policy and all that.' He dug into his breakfast with relish. 'Did your father tell you that he's thinking of doing a cookery course? This, incidentally, is my way of trying to normalise the situation between us. Because you've changed doesn't mean that we've lost the ability to communicate.'

Jennifer hesitated, apprehensive of familiarity, but then decided that, whether she liked it or not, there were too many strands of their lives that were interwoven for her to pretend otherwise.

'He told me,' she said, relaxing, with a smile. 'In fact, the last time he came over, just before Christmas, he brought all his prospectuses so that I could give him some advice. Not that I would be any good at all when it comes to that sort of thing.'

'You mean being in Paris, surrounded by all that French cuisine, wasn't enough to stimulate an interest in cooking?'

'The opposite,' Jennifer admitted ruefully. 'When there's so much brilliant food everywhere you go, what's the point trying to compete at home?'

'You must have picked something up.' James saluted her with a mouthful of egg on his fork. 'This scrambled egg tastes pretty perfect.'

'That's the extent of it, I'm afraid. I can throw a few things together to make something passable for an evening meal but no one I've ever entertained has really expected me to produce anything cordon bleu. In fact, on a couple of occasions, friends in Paris actually showed up with some store-bought delicacies. They always said that they wanted to make life easier for me but, personally, I suspected that they weren't too sure what they might be getting.' She laughed and their eyes met for a few seconds before she hurriedly looked away.

There was no way that she was going to return to her comfort zone but this felt good, chatting to him, relaxing, dropping her guard for a while.

'And what about you?' she asked. 'Do you still avoid that whole domestic thing?'

'Define *avoid that whole domestic thing.*'

'You once told me that you always made sure that the women you dated never went near a kitchen just in case they started thinking that they could domesticate you.'

'I don't remember saying that.'

'You did. I was nineteen at the time.'

'Remind me never to have conversations of a personal nature with any woman who has perfect recall.' He had forgotten just how much he had told her over the years, superficial stuff and yet stuff he probably would never have told any other woman. 'Your father has been trying to lure me into cooking. Every time I've popped over, he's shown me one of his new recipe books. A few months ago I came for a few days to oversee some work my mother was having done in the house, and your father asked us both to dinner here. We were treated to an array of exotic meals and I was personally given a lecture on the importance of a man having interests outside work. Have you any idea how difficult it is for a man to defend himself from a dual-pronged attack? Your father preached to me about learning to enjoy my leisure time and my mother made significant noises about the correlation between hard work and high blood pressure.'

Jennifer laughed again, that rich, full-bodied laugh that reminded James of how much he had missed her uncomplicated company over the years. Except now…nothing was as uncomplicated as it once was. They could skim the surface with small talk and reach a place in which they both felt comfortable, but he realised that he wanted to dig deeper. He didn't want to just harp back to the good old days. He didn't want to just keep it light.

'I thought I'd see if that Patric guy of yours had a presence on the Internet.' He changed the subject, standing up and waving her to sit back down when she would have helped him clear the table.

Jennifer went still. Why, she wanted to ask, would he do that?

'Oh?'

'He's well reviewed.'

'Why would you want to check up on him?' she asked abruptly. 'Did you think that I was lying? Made him up?'

'Of course I didn't!' He shook his head in frustration as they teetered back to square one after their fragile truce.

'Then what? Why the curiosity?'

He looked at her closed, uninviting expression and scowled. She might have loosened up for a few minutes, but the bottom line was she wanted their relationship to remain on the safe, one-dimensional plane it had always occupied.

He thought back to that crossroads moment, when, four years ago, she had offered herself to him. Hell, he could still taste her mouth on his before he had gently pushed her away. In fact, thinking about it, he wondered whether he had ever really put it behind him.

'Call it human nature,' he gritted. 'Is it a taboo subject? Am I getting too close to showing a perfectly normal interest in the person you are *now*?'

Jennifer couldn't argue with that. *She* was the one at fault. It was only natural that he would want to exchange more than just polite pleasantries about their past or idle chit-chat about their parents. It wasn't his fault that she felt threatened whenever she thought about him getting too close and the reason she felt threatened was because she still had feelings for him. She didn't know what exactly those feelings were, but they were defining the way she responded. It was crazy.

It was going to be very tiring if they continually veered between harmless small talk and bitter arguments. Worse, he would wonder why.

'Patric isn't a taboo subject. I just think that I already told you everything there is to know about him, and what I didn't you probably gleaned from the Internet. He's a big name in Europe. Or at least, he soon will be. His last exhibition was a huge success. Everything sold and he has a number of galleries vying to show his work.'

James had read all of that in the glowing article on the computer. They had not stinted in their praise.

'You were never into art.'

'I…I…never really thought that it would be something practical to do so I dropped it at school and really, around here…well, museums and art galleries aren't a dime a dozen. I think I started realising how much I loved art when I went to university…so it was easy to fall in love with it in Paris where it's all around you…'

'And the French guy was all part and parcel of the falling-in-love process?'

Jennifer shrugged. 'We were close friends first. Maybe I got caught up in his passion and enthusiasm over the years. I don't know.'

'And it didn't work out in the end.'

'No. It didn't. Now, why don't you start getting the rugs together and I'll give you a hand? There's a great wad of tarpaulin in the coal shed at the back of the cottage. If I get that, then we can cover the rugs and hopefully they won't get too wet when we lug them over.'

What little personal conversation she had submitted to was over. James was receiving that message loud and clear. He had never been one to encourage touching confidences from women. Events in his past had conspired to put a cynical spin on every relationship he had, although that was something he kept to himself. It was weird that he was now increasingly curious to find out more about Jennifer. It was almost as though he had suddenly discovered that his faithful pet could spout poetry and speak four languages.

He wondered whether his sudden interest was a result of being marooned with her by the snow, compounded by the fact that he hadn't seen her in years. Had he met her at his mother's house, would they have skirted over the same ground, played their usual roles and then parted company to meet again in three weeks' time and repeat the process?

Hauling rugs into an outbuilding seemed an inadequate substitute to having his curiosity sated, but he dropped the subject and, for the next couple of hours, they worked alongside each other in amicable companionship, exchanging opinions on what would and wouldn't need to be done to the cottage. It was an old place and prone to all the symptoms of old age. Things needed replacing on a frequent basis and an updating process was long overdue.

'Right,' Jennifer said, once they were back in the cottage. 'You're going to have to go now, James.'

The past couple of hours were a warning to her that she had to be careful around him. She had always found his charm, his wit, his intelligence, irresistible and time, it appeared, had not diminished his appeal in that area. He could still make her laugh, and wading through the fast-falling snow was a great deal safer than sitting in a cosy kitchen where they had eye-to-eye contact.

What alarmed her were those casual touches, the brush of his gloved fingers against her arm, the feel of his thigh next to hers as they had manoeuvred the rug into the outbuilding, laughing and looking at the collection of junk they had had to shift to make room.

Her body had felt alive; her skin had tingled. She had been that twenty-one-year-old girl again, yearning to be touched. At least, it had felt like that. What if this whole unforeseen situation, trapped in the snow, made her do something regrettable? It was barely a thought that she allowed to cross her mind, but she knew that it was there, like an ugly monster shifting lazily underneath the defences she had laboured to pile on top of it. What if, on the spur of the moment, she let her hand linger just a little bit too long on his arm? What if she held his look for too long?

He was no longer the cardboard cut-out hero of her youth. She had moved on from blind infatuation and now, here, she was beginning to see the complex man who told her how tough it was moving from being a carefree student to a man who needed to run a company. He shared thoughts about his mother, getting older and living in a house that was too big for her, and she could see the worry etched on his face.

She didn't like it or perhaps, scarily, she liked it too much. He was easy and relaxed with her because he still considered her a friend. She was wary with him and she had to be because, beyond any friendship, there were still feelings buried there and they frightened her.

So spending the afternoon in the cottage together, because *it made sense*, just wasn't going to do.

'I have some clothes I need to box up and also some work to do because, you're right, it doesn't look likely that

I'm going to make it back to London tomorrow. In fact, I'll be lucky if I get out of here by the weekend. So…'

Neither of them had had a chance to change and her hair was damp from the falling snow. Dark tendrils curled around her face. Her cheeks were pink from the cold and the woollen hat she had put on was pulled down low, almost down to her eyes, huge and brown and staring purposefully at him. Unlike the babes he dated, she had a dramatic, intelligent face, a face he found he liked looking at.

'I can't think of the last time I was chucked out of a woman's house,' he said, raising his eyebrows. 'Come to think of it, I can't think of the last time I did anything manual with a woman.'

'I doubt any of your girlfriends would be any good in conditions like these. Deep snow and kitten heels don't go well together. And I'm not a woman, I'm a friend.'

'Thanks for reminding me,' James murmured. 'I was in danger of forgetting…'

Jennifer drew in a shaky breath. What did that mean? No. She refused to waste time speculating on the things he said and reading meanings into throwaway remarks. She knew from experience that that was a road that led nowhere and, anyway, she *didn't care about him*. She had spent *four years* putting him behind her!

'Perhaps later this evening we can share a quick meal. Or I could come up to the house. It *does* seem silly for us to eat on our own when we could join rations.'

'And I could cook for you.' His voice was warm and amused. 'Adding yet something else to the steadily growing list of things I don't do with women but I do for you.'

Was he flirting with her? 'You can if you want to,' she countered sharply, 'but if not you're more than welcome to come here and have something with me or we could just reconvene in the morning and take it from there. You have my mobile number, don't you?'

'I think it's one of the things you omitted to give me when you left...' Once upon a time his charm would have swept her off her feet. Now, it slid off her, leaving her unaffected. In fact, leaving her irritated.

'Then let's exchange mobile numbers now just in case there's a change of plan. If I find that I'm behind with all the stuff I want to do, then I'll contact you.'

'And are you going to get in touch with John and let him know what's happened?'

'No.' Tell her father? That she was holed up in the cottage in the middle of a snowstorm with James? His imagination would be on overdrive if she did that! He had been all too aware of her childish crush! She had been so young and disingenuous...incapable of hiding her emotions, wearing her heart on her sleeve like any impressionable teenager. He had never known about that disastrous final dinner she had had with James. At least, he had never known the details but he was as sharp as a tack. He had known that it hadn't lived up to expectations because the following day she had been quiet, avoiding his questions. And then she had left for Paris and never seen James again. 'No. You were right to get in touch with me and leave Dad out of this. He doesn't get to see Anthony often and he looks forward to his three-week holiday up there. Anyway, the transport links are terrible at the moment. He would have a hard time returning and there's nothing he can do here that I can't manage.'

'How does it feel?' James asked softly and she stared at him with a perplexed frown.

'What are you talking about?'

'To be in charge.'

'I'm not in charge of anything,' Jennifer mumbled,

dipping her head. She wondered whether it was a compliment to be seen as a woman *in charge*. Maybe from someone else it would have been, but from James…? 'Well, maybe I *am* in charge,' she amended, refusing to be drawn into thinking that there was something wrong with not being a helpless feeble woman incapable of doing anything useful in case a nail got chipped. 'Dad's not getting any younger. He's going to be sixty-eight on his next birthday and he's been complaining about tiring more easily. He jokes about it, but I can tell from when we've been walking around Paris that he's not as spritely as he used to be.'

'And where does that leave you, I wonder?'

'I'm not saying that Dad has suddenly become old and feeble!'

'I'm curious as to how long you intend to work in Paris…'

'That's a big subject for us to suddenly start discussing,' Jennifer said, fighting the irresistible temptation to confide. Patric might be a wonderful friend and a sympathetic confidant, but he wasn't James. James who had known her for most of her life and who knew her father better than anyone else.

'Is it?' He shrugged and shot her a crooked smile. 'Am I stepping too close to something personal?'

'Of course not,' Jennifer said uncomfortably, hating the way he found it so easy to return to their familiarity while she continued to fight against it tooth and nail because in her head it represented a retrograde step. 'I…yes, I've been thinking about that, wondering whether it might not be time to return to England…'

'But you're worried that you've settled into a lifestyle that agrees with you and you might just get back here and have difficulty slotting back in. This isn't Paris.'

'I've made a lot of friends,' Jennifer said defensively.

'I know the work and I'm very well paid... I don't even know whether I'd be able to find a similar job over here! I keep abreast of the news. There are no jobs!'

'Plus you hate change and the biggest thing you've ever done is go to Paris and reinvent yourself...'

'Stop trying to shove me back in time. I'm not that person any more.' But yes, she had never liked change even though she had never had a problem adapting to different circumstances. Secondary school had been a challenge, but she had done it and it had been fine. University, likewise. However, she had had no choice in either of those. Paris, as he had said, had been her big step. Returning to England would be another.

'No, you're not,' James said quietly, while she continued to glare at him. 'I would have no problem giving you a job, Jennifer. There are a lot of opportunities in my company for someone fluent in French with the level of experience you've had. In fact, I have access to a number of company apartments. It would be an easy matter for me to sort one of them out for you...'

'No, thank you!' Jennifer could think of nothing worse than breaking out of her comfort zone only to be reduced to handouts from James Rocchi. In Paris, she had been her own person. She shuddered to think how it would be if she were to be working in his company and renting one of his apartments. Would he be dropping in every two minutes with one of his blonde Barbies on his arm to check up on her and make sure that she was okay? Nosing into her private life and expressing surprise if she happened to be dating someone? Maybe looking up this, as yet, fictitious someone on the Internet so that he could check for himself that she wasn't dating someone unsuitable? Or maybe just checking out of curiosity, the way he had with Patric?

'I mean,' she amended hurriedly, 'that's a generous

offer but I haven't made any decisions as to whether or not I'll be returning just yet, anyway. And when I *do* decide to return…well, I would want to find my own way. I'm sure my boss in Paris will supply me with excellent references…'

James tried not to scowl as she smiled brightly at him, a big, glassy smile that set his teeth on edge. He was so used to her malleability! Now, in receipt of this polite dismissal, he felt strangely impotent and piqued.

'I'm sure he would.'

'And I've managed to save quite a bit while I've been over there. I stayed in a company flat and they kindly let me carry on there at a very subsidised rate after my one-year secondment was at an end. In fact, I would probably be able to put down a deposit on a small place of my own after a while. Not in London, of course. I would have to travel in. But definitely in Kent somewhere. I could work in London, because that's where the jobs are, and commute like most people have to do. So…thanks for the offer of one of your company flats, but there's no need to feel duty-bound to be charitable.'

'And on that note, I think I'll leave.'

She let him. She saw him to the door, where they made polite noises about the continuing bad weather. He suggested that he come over to the cottage to eat because it would be easier for him to tackle the short distance in blizzard conditions; he was sure he had a pair of skis lurking in a cupboard somewhere from his heady teenage years. She smiled blandly.

Inside it felt so wrong to be closing the door on him with this undercurrent of ill feeling between them.

Her head was telling her to let go of the past and find new ground with him, as he obviously wanted to do with her. New, inoffensive ground. Her heart, however, was beating to a different tune.

She spent the remainder of the day clearing out cupboards and bagging old clothes. She couldn't believe the rubbish she pulled out of her wardrobe. The cottage was small and yet the cupboard in her bedroom was like the wardrobe in Narnia—never ending. She had binned the outfit she had worn all those years ago on their disastrous dinner date in a fit of humiliation and hurt, but the shoes were still there, stuffed at the back, and she pulled them out and relived that night all over again.

Then she worked on her computer. She didn't know how long the connection would last. Paris seemed like a million light years away and when she managed to talk to Patric, she found it hard to imagine that she had once thought that he might be the one for her.

She tried not to look at the clock and told herself that she honestly didn't care whether James came over to the cottage for dinner or not. Yes, sure, some adult company would be nice. Eating pasta for one while the snow bucketed down outside was a pretty lonely prospect. She told herself that she likewise didn't care if he had taken offence at her rejection of his offer of a job and a place to rent. She could have handled it differently, but the message would have amounted to the same thing whatever. On both counts, she knew that she was kidding herself. She was keyed up to see him later. Like an addict drawn to the source of her addiction, she craved the way he made her feel.

By six, she was glancing at the clock on the mantelpiece, and when her mobile vibrated next to her on the sofa, she had to fight back the disappointment at the thought that he would be at the other end of the line informing her that he had decided to give their arrangement a miss.

CHAPTER THREE

'IF YOU'RE calling to tell me that you won't be coming over tonight for dinner, then don't worry about it. Not a problem. I still have so much work to do, anyway! You wouldn't believe it! Plus I'm going to take the opportunity to catch up with some of my frie…'

'Jennifer, shut up.'

'How dare you?'

'You need to do exactly what I say. Get dressed in some warm clothes, come out of your cottage and head for the copse behind it. You know the one I mean.'

'James, what's going on? You're scaring me.'

'I've had a bit of an accident.'

'You…*what*?' Jennifer stood up, felt giddy and immediately sat back down. Every nerve in her body had gone into sudden, panicked overdrive. 'What do you mean?'

'There were some high winds here a couple of days ago. Just before you came. Some fallen branches in the copse behind the cottage and a tree that's about to go and is dangerously close to one of the overhead cables.'

'You tripped over a branch on your way here?'

'Don't be ridiculous! How feeble do you think I am? After I left you earlier, I got back to the house, did some work and then thought that I might as well see if I could bring the tree down, get it clear of the overhead power lines.'

In a flashback springing from nowhere, she had a vivid memory of him as a young boy not yet sixteen, strapped halfway up one of the towering trees that bordered the house, chainsaw in one hand, reaching for a branch that had broken, while underneath his parents yelled for him to get down *immediately*. He had grown up in sprawling acres of deepest countryside and had always loved getting involved in the hard work of running the estate. He had had a reckless disregard for personal safety, had loved challenging himself. She had adored that about him.

'I can't believe you could have been so stupid!' she yelled down the phone. 'You're not sixteen any more, James! Give me five minutes and *don't move*.'

She spotted him between the swirling snow, just a dark shape lying prone, and the worst-case scenarios she had tussled with as she had flung on her jumper and scarf and coat and everything else smashed into her with the force of a ten-ton block of granite. What if he had suffered concussion? He would be able to sound coherent, make sense, only to die without warning. That had happened to someone, somewhere. She had read it in the news years ago. What if he had broken something? His spine? Fractured his leg or his arm? There was no way that a doctor would be able to get out here. Even a helicopter would have trouble in these weather conditions.

'Don't move!' She had brought two tablecloths with her. 'You can use these to cover yourself with and I'm going to get that table thing Dad uses for wallpapering. It can be rigged up like a stretcher.'

'Don't be so melodramatic, Jen. I just need you to help me up. The snow's so soft that it's impossible. I seem to have pulled a muscle in my back.'

'What if it's more serious than that, James?' she cried, kneeling and peering at him at close range. She shone

her torch directly at his face and he winced away from
the light.

'Would you mind directing the beam somewhere else?'

She ignored him. 'What I'm saying is that you shouldn't
move if you think you might have done something to your
spine. It's one of the first things you learn on a first-aid
course.'

'You've done a first-aid course?'

'No, but I'm making an educated guess. Your colour
looks good. That's a brilliant sign. How many fingers am
I holding up?'

'What?'

'My fingers. How many of them am I holding up? I need
to make sure that you aren't suffering from concussion…'

'Three fingers and move the bloody torch, Jennifer.
Let me sling my arm around your neck and we're going
to have to hobble to the cottage. I don't think I can make
it all the way back to the house.'

'I'm not sure…'

'Okay, here's the deal. While you debate the shoulds
and shouldn'ts, I'm going to pass out with hypothermia.
I've pulled a muscle! I don't need the blankets and a make-
shift stretcher, although I'm very grateful for the suggestion. I just need a helping hand.'

'Your voice sounds strong. Another good sign.'

'Jennifer!'

'Okay, but *I'm still not sure…*'

'I can live with that.'

He slung his arm around her neck and she felt the heavy,
muscled weight of him as he levered himself up, with her
help. The snow was thick and their feet sank into its depth,
making it very difficult to balance and walk. It was little
wonder that he hadn't been able to prise himself up. Even

with her help, she could tell that he was in pain, unable to stand erect, his hand pressed to the base of his back.

They struggled back to the cottage. She had draped the tablecloths around him, even though he had done his best to resist and the torch cast a wavering light directly ahead, illuminating the snow and turning the spectral scenery into a winter wonderland.

'I could try and get hold of an ambulance service...' she suggested, out of breath because even though he was obviously doing his best to spare her his full weight, he was still six feet three inches of packed muscle.

'I never knew you were such a worrier.'

'What do you expect?' she demanded hotly. 'You were supposed to stroll over for dinner...'

'Didn't I tell you that it's impossible to stroll in snow this deep?'

'Stop trying to be funny! You were supposed to come to the cottage for dinner and the next time I hear from you, you're calling to tell me that you decided to chop down a tree and you're lying on the ground with a possible broken back!'

'I'm sorry if I worried you...'

'Yes,' Jennifer muttered, still angry with him for having sent her into a panic, still deathly worried that he was putting on a brave face because that was just the sort of man he was, 'well, you *should* be.'

'Have you cooked something delicious?'

'You shouldn't talk. You should conserve your energy.'

'Is that something else you picked up on the first-aid course you never went to?'

She felt her lips twitch and suppressed a desire to laugh. She got the feeling that he was doing his utmost to distract her from her worry, even though he would have been in a lot of discomfort and surely worried about himself. That simple generosity of spirit brought a lump of emotion to her throat and she stopped talking, for fear of bursting into tears.

Ahead of them the well-lit cottage beckoned like a port in a storm.

'Here at last.' She nudged open the door and deposited him on the sofa in the sitting room, where he collapsed with a groan.

He didn't have a broken spine. Nor was anything fractured. That much she had figured out on the walk back. He had pulled a muscle. Painful but not terminal.

She stood back, arms folded, and looked at him with jaundiced eyes.

'Now, admit it, James. It was very silly of you to think you could sort out that tree, wasn't it?'

'I managed to do what needed doing,' he countered. 'I fought the tree and the tree lost. The pulled muscle in my back is just collateral damage.'

Jennifer snorted in response. 'You'll have to get out of those clothes. They're soaking wet. I'm going to bring down some of Dad's. They won't be a terrific fit, but you'll have to work with it. Tomorrow I'll fetch some from your house.' She was resigned to the fact that they would now be stranded together, under the same roof.

James, eyes closed, grunted.

'But first, I'll go get you some painkillers. Dad keeps them in bulk supply for a rainy day. Or an emergency like this.'

'I don't do painkillers.'

'Too bad.'

Her father was shorter than James and thinner. She had no idea how his clothes would stretch to accommodate James's more muscular frame, but she chose the biggest of the tee shirts, a jumper and a pair of jogging bottoms

with an elasticated waist, which were a five-year-old leg-
acy from her father's days when he had decided to join
the local gym, which he had tried once only to declare
that gyms were for idiots who should be out and about.

'Clothes,' she announced, back in the sitting room,
where the open fire kept the room beautifully warm. 'And
first, painkillers.' She handed him two tablets with a glass
of water and watched as he reluctantly swallowed them.

'You make a very good matron.' He handed her the
glass of water and sighed as he began to defrost.

He grinned but she didn't find it very amusing. He had
been a complete fool. He had, as was his nature, been so
supremely confident of his strength that it would never
have occurred to him that sorting out a tree in driving
snow might have been an impossible mission. He had worried her sick. And beyond both those things, she was stu-
pidly annoyed to be compared to a *matron*. She privately
and illogically rebelled against being the friend upon
whom he could rely in a situation like this, the girl who
wouldn't baulk in a crisis and was used to the harsh east-
erly conditions, the tall, well-built girl who could tackle
any physical situation with the best of them. She wanted to
be seen as delicate and fragile and in need of manly protection, and then she was annoyed with herself for being
pathetic. Old feelings that she thought she had left behind
seemed to be waiting round every corner, eager to ambush
the person she had become.

'I'll leave you to get into some fresh clothes,' she said
shortly. 'And I'll go and prepare us something to eat.'

She turned to walk away and he reached out to catch
her hand and tug her to face him.

'In case you think I'm not grateful for your help, I am,'
he said softly.

Jennifer didn't say anything because he was absentmindedly rubbing his thumb on the underside of her wrist, and for the first time since she had been flung into his company she had no resources with which to fight the stirrings of desire she had been trying so hard to subdue. She could barely breathe.

'I don't know what I would have done if you hadn't been here.'

'That's all right,' Jennifer croaked, then cleared her throat, while she wondered whether to snatch her hand out of his gently, delicately, caressing grasp.

'I know you weren't expecting to find me here when you arrived but I'm glad I was. I've missed you.'

She wanted to shout at him that he shouldn't use words like that, which made her fevered irrational brain start thinking all sorts of inappropriate things.

'Have you missed *me* or was I replaced by your hectic life and new-found independence?'

'I...I don't know what you expect me to say to that, James...' But she wondered whether this was his way of reasserting the balance between them, putting it back to that place where he could be certain that he knew where she stood, a place where the power balance was restored.

'Of course—' she pulled her hand away from him and took a step back '—I thought about you now and again and hoped that you were doing well. I meant to email you lots more than I actually did and I'm sorry about that...'

He looked at her in unreadable silence, which she was the first to break.

'I'll leave you to change.'

'I think it would probably be a good idea if I were to dry off a bit. It won't take long, but it'll be easier to get these clothes off if they aren't damp.'

'Makes sense.' Her nerves were still all over the place

and those fabulous midnight-blue eyes roving over her flushed face felt as intimate as his thumb had on her wrist.

'You've just come from outside. Sit for a while and get dry before you think of cooking.'

'Well…maybe just for a few minutes…' She sat on the chair closest to the fire and nervously looked at him. She had thought he hadn't changed at all in the past four years but he had. There was a tough maturity about him that hadn't yet crystallised when she had last seen him. His rise in the world of business had been meteoric. She knew that because, just once, she had given in to temptation and devoured everything she could about him on the Internet. She had discovered that he no longer limited himself to the company he had inherited, he had used that as a springboard for taking over failing companies and had gained a reputation for turning them around in record time. And yet, he had continued to resist the lure of marriage. Why? Was he so consumed by work that women were just satellites hovering on the periphery? Or did he just still enjoy playing the field which, as an eligible, staggeringly rich, good-looking bachelor, would have been a really huge field?

She felt the urge to burst through her self-imposed barrier and ask him and stifled it. She remembered the last time she had misread a situation.

'You've grown up,' he said so softly that she had to strain forward to hear him. 'You've lost that open, transparent way you used to have.'

'People *do* grow up,' she said abruptly.

'Were you hurt by that guy? That's the question I've been asking myself.'

For a few seconds, Jennifer didn't follow where he was going and then she realised that he was talking about Patric.

'He's my best friend!'

'Not sure that says anything.' James slanted her a look that made her go red. 'Were you in love with him? Did he break your heart? Because you seem a lot more cynical than you did four years ago. Sure, people change and grow up, but you're much more guarded now than you were then.'

Jennifer was lost for words. His take on her was revealing. He might have known, years ago, that she had a crush on him, but he obviously had never suspected the depth of her feelings. *She* had not really suspected the depth of her own feelings! It was only as she began dating that she realised how affected she had been by James's rejection, how deep her feelings for him ran. And returning here… all those feelings were making themselves felt once again.

The last thing she needed was him trying to get into her head!

'I love Patric,' she told him tightly. 'And I don't want to be psychoanalysed by you. I know you're probably bored, lying there unable to do anything, but I can bring you your computer and you can work.' The devil worked on idle hands and right now James was very idle.

'My computer's back at my house,' he said irritably, 'and I won't have you braving the snow to get it. I've done enough work for the day, anyway. I can afford to take a little time off.'

'Your mother would be pleased to hear that. She thinks you work too hard.'

'I thought you never talked about me with my mother.'

Jennifer shook her head when he grinned at her and stood up. 'I'm going to go and fix us something to eat. Get changed when you feel your clothes are dry enough.'

'What's on the menu?'

'Whatever appears on the plate in front of you.' She left

to the sound of his rich chuckle and she sternly stifled the temptation to laugh as well.

Her head was full of him as she went about the business of turning a bottle of crushed tomatoes, some cream and some mushrooms into something halfway decent to have with some of the tagliatelle her father kept in abundant supply in the larder. James annoyed her and alarmed her the way no one else had ever been able to, but he also made her laugh when she didn't want to and held her spellbound when she knew she shouldn't be. So what did that say about the state of her defences? She had thought that by seeing him again, she would have finally discovered that his impact had been diminished. She had foolishly imagined that she would put her demons to rest. The very opposite had happened, and, although she hated the thought of that, she was practically humming under her breath as she prepared their meal.

When she thought about him lying on the sofa in the sitting room, a wonderful, excited and *thoroughly forbidden* heat began spreading through her and she couldn't stop herself from liking it.

She took him his food on a tray and he waved her help aside as he struggled into a sitting position.

'The painkillers are kicking in.' He took a mouthful of food and then wondered where the wine was. Oh, and while she was about it, perhaps she could bring him some water as well.

Halfway through the meal, about which he was elaborately complimentary, he announced that he was now completely dry. He magnanimously informed her that there would be no need to wash his clothes, even though she hadn't offered.

'I have more than enough at home to get me through an enforced stay,' he decided, and Jennifer frowned at him.

'How long are you planning on staying?' she asked, not bothering to hide the sarcasm, and then she looked at him narrowly when he shrugged and smiled.

'How long is a piece of string?'

'That's no kind of answer, James.'

'Well, weather wise, even if the snow stops in the next five minutes, which is highly unlikely, we won't be leaving here for another couple of days. We both know that this is the last port of call for the snow ploughs. It's too deep for either of us to drive through and, in my condition, I can't do much about clearing it. That said, I don't think it's going to abate for at least another twenty-four hours, anyway. Longer if the weather forecast is to be believed.'

'Well, you're certainly the voice of doom,' Jennifer said, removing his tray from him, putting it on top of hers and sitting back down because she was, frankly, exhausted, despite having had a very lazy day, all things considered.

'I prefer to call it the voice of reality. Which brings me to point two. I can't go back to my house. I'm going to need help getting back on my feet. I'm putting on a brave front, but I can barely move.' She hadn't exactly been the most welcoming of friends when she had discovered him in the cottage, but, hell, however hard she fought it, there was still something there between them. Friendship, attraction…he didn't know. He just knew that the frisson between them did something for him. As did looking at her. As did hearing her laugh and seeing her smile and catching her slipping him sidelong looks when she didn't think his attention was on her. He relished this enforced stay and, while his back was certainly not in a particularly good way, he silently thanked it for giving him the opportunity to get to the bottom of her.

Jennifer was torn as to whether to believe him or not. On the one hand, he had always claimed to have the constitution of an ox. He was known to boast that he never fell prey to viruses and that his only contact with a doctor had been on the day of his birth. He surely wouldn't lie when it came to admitting pain.

On the other hand, he didn't look in the slightest regretful about his circumstances. In fact, for someone in the grip of back pain, he seemed remarkably breezy.

Breezy or not, she couldn't send him hobbling back to his house although the thought of him in the cottage with her made her stomach tighten into knots of apprehension. Four years of hiding had been rewarded with such a concentrated dose of him that she was struggling to maintain the fiction that the effect he had on her was history. It wasn't. Anything but.

'So…as it stands, I'm going to have to fetch clothes for you for an enforced stay of indefinite duration, plus your laptop…plus I'm going to have to feed and water you…'

'There's no need to sound so thrilled at the prospect…'

'This just isn't what I banked on when I began this journey to the cottage.'

'No,' James said drily, 'because you didn't even expect to find me here.'

'But I'm glad I did,' she told him with grudging truthfulness. 'Four years is a long time. I was in danger of forgetting what you looked like.'

'And have I lived up to expectation?'

'You look older than you are,' Jennifer said snidely, because his ego was already big enough as it was.

'That's very kind of you.' But he grinned. That boyish, sexy grin that had always been able to set her pulses racing. 'Now you're going to have to do me yet another favour, I'm afraid.'

'You want coffee. Or tea. Or something else to drink. And you'd like something sweet to finish off the meal.

Maybe a home-made dessert of some kind. Am I along the right lines?'

'Could I trust you to make me a home-made dessert?' he asked lazily. 'Don't forget that my knowledge of your love of cooking goes back a long way…' He held her eyes and Jennifer, skewered by the intensity of his gaze, half opened her mouth to say something and discovered that she had forgotten what she had been about to say. Colour slowly crawled into her face and, to break the suffocating tension, she stood up to get the two plates and carry them into the kitchen.

'So tea or coffee, then,' she said briskly. 'Which is it to be? Dad has a million varieties of tea you could choose from. The larder seems to have had a massive overhaul ever since he decided to take up cooking. Apparently one brand of tea is no longer good enough.'

'I need you to help me undress.'

'I beg your pardon?'

'I can't manoeuvre to get the trousers off, even though the painkillers are beginning to kick in.'

Jennifer froze. For a few seconds all her vital functions seemed to shut down. When they re-engaged, she knew that, in the name of this friendship that they were tentatively rebuilding, she should think nothing of providing the help he needed. He had no qualms asking for it. He wasn't going into meltdown at the thought of her touching him. She had loftily told him that he should see her as a friend rather than a woman, so what was he going to think if, *as a friend*, she told him that she couldn't possibly…?

'Have you tried?'

'I don't need to try. Every time I make the smallest movement, my back protests.'

Jennifer took a deep breath and walked towards him. What choice did she have?

James slung his arm over her shoulders, felt the softness of her skin underneath the jumper she was wearing,
breathed in her clean fresh scent, the smell of the cold outdoors still lingering on her skin.

'Well, thank goodness I'm not one of these five-foot-
nothing girls you go out with,' she managed to joke, although her vocal cords felt unnaturally dry and strained.
'You would still be lying in the snow outside or else dragging yourself back to the house the best you could.'

'Why do you make fun of yourself?'

'I don't.' She helped him into a sitting position. His skin
was clammy. Underneath the breezy façade, he was obviously in a great deal of discomfort, yet he had not taken it
out on her. While she had been reluctantly catering to his
demands and not bothering to hide the fact that she wasn't
overjoyed at having him under her roof, he had been suffering in silence. Shame and guilt washed over her.

'You do. You've always done it.' He had unbuttoned his
shirt and he grimaced as she eased him out of it, down
to the white tee shirt underneath. 'I remember when you
were sixteen laughing at yourself, telling me about the
outfits your friends were wearing to go out, making fun
of your height and—'

'I can't concentrate when you're talking!' She was red-
faced and flustered because those were memories she
didn't want thrown at her.

'You're a sexy woman,' he said roughly.

'I'll help you to your feet so that we can get the trousers
off.' He thought *she was a sexy woman*. Why did he have
to say that? Why did he have to open a door in her head
through which all sorts of unwanted thoughts could find
their way in? He hadn't thought she was *a sexy woman*
four years ago, she reminded herself fiercely. Oh, no! Four
years ago he had shoved her away!

She didn't have to look at him as she began easing the trousers off. On their downward path, she was aware of black tight-fitting underwear, the length and strength of his legs, his muscled calves. She was in danger of passing out, and even more so when she heard his voice in her head telling her that she was a sexy woman.

Patric had never made her feel this way when he had told her that she was sexy. Hearing Patric tell her that she was sexy had made her want to giggle uncontrollably.

'This is crazy,' she said in a muffled voice, her face bright red as she sprang back to her feet and snatched the jogging bottoms she had earlier brought down.

'Why is it crazy?'

'Because you…you need a professional to help you. A qualified nurse! What if I do something wrong and you… you damage yourself?' She was mesmerised by the sight of his legs, the dark hair on them, the rock hardness of his calves. She didn't dare allow her eyes to travel farther up. Instead, she focused furiously on the jogging bottoms and his feet as he stepped into them, supporting himself by his hand on her shoulder.

'I thought you already gave me all the vital checks?'

'Not funny, James! There. Done!'

'Tee shirt. Might as well get rid of that as well.' He slowly sank back down on the sofa.

Jennifer wondered whether this would ever end. He thought she was *sexy*. What did he feel as her fingers made contact with his skin? Did it do anything for him, considering he thought that she was *a sexy woman*? She fought back the tide of inappropriate questions ricocheting in her head and pulled his tee shirt off, where it joined the rest of his now barely damp clothes on the ground, and helped him with the tee shirt she had grabbed from her father's chest of drawers.

None of the clothes fitted him properly. The jogging bottoms were too short and the tee shirt was too tight. He should have looked ridiculous but he didn't. He just carried on looking sinfully, unfairly, disturbingly sexy.

'Okay. I'm going to stick these in the wash and have a shower and then I'll make you some coffee. I'm sure Dad has some sleeping tablets somewhere in his bedroom from when he did his back in a few years ago. Shall I get them for you?'

'Painkillers are about as far as I'm prepared to go when it comes to taking tablets.'

Jennifer shrugged and backed towards the door, clutching the clothes in one hand like a talisman.

Anyone would imagine, he thought with sudden irritation, that she had been asked to walk on a bed of hot coals. She made lots of noises about friendship but her body language was telling a different story. This wasn't the girl upon whom he had always thought he could rely. This wasn't the girl fascinated by his stories and willing to go the extra mile for him. This was a woman inconvenienced by his presence, a woman determined to keep him at a distance. He had hurt her once and she had moved on, leaving him behind in her wake. The knowledge was frustrating. He wondered how well he had ever known her. She had skimmed over her relationship with the Frenchman and had mentioned no other guys, although he was sure that there would have been some. The woman was a knockout. But whereas once she would have happily confided in him, leaving no detail out, this was no longer the case. He could remember a time when she had laughed and told him little stories about the people she went to school with and, later, to university. No more.

Fair's fair, he thought. Did she know *him*? He was uneasily aware that a relationship flowed two ways. It was something he was poorly equipped for. His relationships with women were disposable and had always involved more effort on their part than on his.

James was not given to this level of pointless introspection and he pushed it aside.

'Well, it's up to you,' she was saying now with a dismissive shrug. 'I think, as well, that you should sleep down here. The sofa is big enough and comfortable enough and it'll save you the trip up the stairs. There's a downstairs toilet, as you know…I know the bath is upstairs but I'm sure you'll be able to manage things better…tomorrow…after you've had a good night's sleep…' She hoped so because she drew the line at helping him into a bath or under the shower. Just thinking about it made her feel a little wobbly.

Having delivered that speech in a surprisingly calm, controlled, neutral voice, she fled up the stairs, had a very quick shower, which was blissful, and then returned to the sitting room with an armful of bed linen. She had expected to find him still lying on the sofa but he wasn't. He had moved to one of the chairs and switched the television on. Wall-to-wall coverage of the weather.

Quickly and efficiently, she began making up the sofa with two sheets, the duvet which she had pilfered from her father's bed, likewise the pillows.

'You probably shouldn't be taxing your back too much,' she said, hovering by the sofa because she didn't intend to stay down and watch television with him. There was danger in this pretend domesticity and she had no intention of falling prey to it.

'The more I tax it, the faster I'll be back on my feet,' James said curtly, realising, from her dithering, that she had no intention of being in his company any more than was strictly necessary. Her body language was telling him that, whatever common ground they had managed to carve out for themselves, she still hadn't signed up to be stuck with him in the cottage for an indefinite period of time. That was beyond the call of duty.

'Aren't you going to relax and watch some television with me?' he asked, perversely drawn to hearing her confirm what was going through his head, and his mouth twisted cynically as she shook her head and stammered out some excuse about still having to clear the kitchen, being really tired after the day's events, needing to finish some emails she had started earlier in the afternoon...

'In that case,' he said coolly, 'I wouldn't dream of keeping you. If you make sure that the painkillers are at hand, then I'll see you in the morning.' He stood up, waved aside her offer of assistance and made his way back to the sofa, where he lay down carefully as she left the sitting room, closing the door quietly behind her.

CHAPTER FOUR

It DIDN'T take long for Jennifer to work out that James made a very demanding patient.

She awoke the following morning at seven-thirty and tiptoed downstairs to discover that the light in the sitting room was on, as was the television, which was booming out the news. James was on the sofa and she stood for a moment in the doorway to the sitting room with her dressing gown wrapped tightly around her, drinking him in. She had hoped to simply grab a cup of coffee and retreat back to her bedroom for a another hour's worth of sleep, but he noticed her and glanced across broodingly at her silhouette.

'There's no end to this snow,' were his opening words. The curtains had been pulled open as if to reinforce his darkest suspicion that they were, indeed, still stranded in a sea of white. 'The last time it snowed like this, life didn't return to normal for two weeks. I have work to do.'

'That goes for the both of us,' Jennifer muttered, ungluing herself from the doorway and stepping into the sitting room to toss a few logs into the now-dead fire.

She had exhausted herself wondering how she was going to deal with James under her roof. She had feverishly analysed the heady, unhealthy mix of emotions his presence generated, had shakenly viewed her loss of calm as a dangerous and possibly slippery slope to a place she couldn't even begin to imagine, a place where she once again became captive to feelings she had spent years stuffing away out of sight. Now she realised that, while she had been consumed with her own emotional turmoil, he likewise was counting down to when they could part company.

She sourly wondered if *making the best of things* was becoming a strain. Add to that the fact that he was now out of action and she could understand why he was contemplating the still-falling snow with an expression of loathing.

'I've had to let Paris know that I can't say when I'll be back. I'm missing Patric's next exhibition, which I had been looking forward to. You're not the only one desperate to get out of here!'

James wondered whether she could make things any clearer. If she had had skis, he would not have been surprised to find her strapping them to her feet so that she could use them.

And who cared whether she happened to be missing her ex-boyfriend's exhibition? He thought back to the fair-haired man with the earring and the fedora and scowled. They had gone out and broken up. Who, in God's name, remained good friends with their ex-partner? It was unhealthy. His mood, which had been grim the night before when she had made it clear that the last thing she wanted was his company, became grimmer in receipt of this unwanted piece of information.

'I've been up since five,' James told her, levering himself into a sitting position.

'Wasn't the sofa comfortable?'

'It's big but so am I. I wouldn't say it's been the most amazing night's sleep. My back was in agony.'

'I left some painkillers...'

By way of response, James held up the plastic tub and tipped it upside down. 'Not enough and I didn't have the energy to hobble into the kitchen to see if I could find more. Your father has an eccentric way of storing things.'

Jennifer, ashamed because she had spared little thought for his back in between her own inner confusion, instantly told him to wait right there, that she would get him some painkillers immediately, something stronger than paracetamol.

'Where am I supposed to go?' James asked sarcastically. 'I am literally at your mercy.'

Jennifer almost grinned. He was always so masterful, so much in control, the guy who was never fazed by anything and yet here he was now as sullen and as sulky as a child deprived of his Christmas treat because the body on which he depended had let him down.

'I like the sound of that,' she told him and he quirked an eyebrow and then reluctantly smiled.

'Really? So what do you intend to do with me?'

Jennifer didn't know whether there was any kind of double meaning to that soft drawl, but she felt the hairs on the back of her neck stand on end.

'Well…' be brisk and keep it all on an impersonal level, two friends thrown together against their will, two friends who had absolutely no history '…first of all I shall go and get you some painkillers. A full tub of them, although I don't have to tell you that under no circumstances are you to go over the allotted dosage—'

'There's a career in nursing crying out for you—'

'And then—' she ignored his interruption '—I shall light that fire because this room is pretty cold—'

'Fire went out some time around two in the morning.'

'You were up at two in the morning?'

'Between the sudden drop in temperature and the agony in my back, sleep was difficult.'

Jennifer, distracted from her list of things to do, wasn't sure whether to believe him or not. The advantage to their familiarity with one another was that there was no need to continually try and be entertaining or even talkative. The disadvantage was that he would see no need whatsoever to be on his best behaviour.

'And then I shall go up to your house and fetch whatever it is you want me to fetch.'

She didn't give him time to ask any questions. Instead, she went to the kitchen, located a box of strong painkillers and took them in with a glass of water.

'You'll have to help me into a sitting position.'

'Honestly, James, stop milking it.' But she helped him up and she knew, although she could barely admit it to herself, that she liked the feel of his body. She could tell herself that she had to be careful until the cows came home, but it was heady and treacherously thrilling to touch him, even if the touching, like this, was completely innocent.

Flustered, she turned her attention to the dead fire, and she began going through the routine of relighting it. It was something she had done a million times. More logs would have to be brought in from the shed outside. She hoped that they would have been cut. Her father was reliable when it came to making sure that they were well stocked over the winter months. Snow, at some point, was inevitable and it never paid to take something as simple as electricity for granted. Too many times it had failed, leaving them without heating.

James edged himself up a bit more and watched, fascinated, as she dealt expertly with the fire. He had turned down the volume on the television when she had entered the sitting room and the flickering light from the TV picked out the shine in her long, wavy hair, which fell across her face as she knelt in front of the fireplace.

She wasn't one of those useless, helpless women who thought that their role in life was to be dependent. Her slender hands efficiently did what had to be done. Her robe had fallen open and he could see her tee shirt underneath and the shorts that she slept in. Sensible sleeping wear and never, he thought, had he ever seen anything so damned sexy.

James was taken aback by the sudden ferocity of his arousal and he realised that it had been there from the start, practically from the moment he had laid eyes on her again. He whipped the duvet over him because she wouldn't have been able to miss the definition of his erection underneath the jogging bottoms that she had brought down for him the evening before and that he was still wearing.

His breath caught in his throat when, eventually, she stood up, all five foot leggy ten, and brushed her hands together to shake off some of the woody dust and ash. She had forgotten that she was supposed to clutch the dressing gown around her and now he had an eyeful of long, shapely legs and the brevity of a tee shirt that delineated full, firm breasts. He thought back to four years previously when she had offered herself to him, thought back to how close he had come to taking what had been on offer, only pulling back because he had known, instinctively, that a vulnerable girl with little experience didn't need a man like him. Desire for her now slammed into him and he half closed his eyes.

'No wonder you have to pull that duvet over you.' Jennifer walked towards him and James looked at her. She was resting her hands on her waist and wore a reproving expression. 'It's cold in here even with the heating on. You should have yelled for me to come down and light the fire. I would have understood that you couldn't do it yourself.'

James shifted and dragged his eyes away from those abundant orbs barely contained underneath the skimpy tee shirt. In resting her hands on her waist, she had pushed aside the dressing gown and was it his imagination or could he see, in the grey, indistinct light, the outline of her nipples?

'I was hardly about to do that when you made it clear that taking care of me for five minutes was a chore,' he said gruffly, dragging his eyes away from the alluring sight.

Jennifer flushed guiltily in the face of this blunt accusation. He couldn't even look her in the face and she could understand why. She had been a miserable friend, taking out her insecurities on him when he had done nothing but try and fix the gaping hole four years of absence had left in their friendship. In return, she had sniped, chastised and been grudging in her charity. God, he was probably close to truly disliking her.

When she thought about that, about him really not wanting to spend time in her company, she was filled with a sour, sickening anguish.

Although she had been at pains to avoid him for four long years, she had never, actually, thought about the simple truth, which was that she had engineered the destruction of a long-standing friendship. She had thought that the choice was a simple one. All or nothing. And in Paris she had managed to kid herself that nothing was achievable. It wasn't. Her heart picked up speed and she longed for him to look at her again instead of averting his eyes from her the way he would have averted them from a stranger who couldn't be bothered to help out in a crisis.

'I'm sorry if that was the impression I gave you, James. I didn't mean to. It's not a chore. Of course, it isn't.'

'You've made it perfectly clear that this is the last place on the face of the earth you want to be, especially when there's the exciting pull of Paris, parties and important exhibitions to view.'

'I never said anything about parties,' Jennifer mumbled. Disconcertingly, the exhibition that she had been looking forward to when she had left Paris now held little appeal. Technicolor reality was happening right here and everything else had been reduced to an out-of-focus, inconsequential background blur.

'And Patric will be fine hosting his exhibition without me. In fact, sometimes those things can be a little bit tiring.'

James, who couldn't think of the blond man without feeling distinctly uptight, pricked up his ears. He looked as she perched on the side of the sofa and picked absently at the tassel on one of the cushions, which she had rescued from the ground where it had landed at some point during the night.

'Really?' he asked in an encouraging voice and she shot him a guilty look from under her lashes.

James kept his eyes firmly fixed on her face because anywhere else would have been disastrous for the array of responses his body was having in her presence. Those were definitely her nipples outlined against the soft cotton tee shirt. He could see the tips of them. It was just one reason to make sure he looked directly at her face, although even that made him feel a little giddy.

'I love art and I just love going to exhibitions and, of course, I would do anything in the world to help Patric out, but sometimes it gets a little boring at those dos. Lots of glamorous people trying to outdo one another. The women are always dripping with jewellery and most of the men barely look at the paintings because they are into invest-

ment art. You see, Patric's parents are rather well connected so the guest list is usually...well...full of the Great
and the Good...'

'Sounds tedious,' James murmured. 'Can't stand that
kind of thing myself...'

'It *can* be a little dull,' Jennifer confided. 'But the
financial climate is tough out there and art is a luxury
buy at the end of the day. Patric has no option but to put
up with stuff like that.'

'Maybe he enjoys it...' James was keen to insinuate that
the wonderful best-buddy-confidante thing might have
been something of an illusion. People who go abroad could
be very susceptible to the kindness of strangers. 'He certainly looked on top of the world in those pictures I saw
of him. Big grin, lots of hot babes around him...'

'He always has a lot of hot babes around him.' Jennifer
laughed. 'He's that kind of person. Women are attracted
to him. He doesn't try to hide his feminine side.'

'You're telling me that the man's gay?'

'I'm telling you no such thing!' But she found herself
laughing, right back in that place where they had always
been so good together. 'He's just in tune with women, likes
talking about the things they like talking about, and he's
also a massive flirt.'

James wanted to ask her if that was why they had broken up. Had she, perhaps, caught him in bed with one of
those hot babes to whom he had been pouring out his heart,
showing his sensitive side, while simultaneously chatting
about clothes and shoes and feelings?

But regrettably she was standing up and telling him
that she would go and get changed and get the day started.

'I'll bring you some breakfast,' she said, 'just as soon
as I've had a shower. Er...' Should she ask him whether
he wanted a shower? A bath, maybe, if he was up to that?

She decided not to because just the thought of helping him get undressed made her feel light-headed and horribly, horribly turned on.

'Er…I won't be long…' She thought about helping him get naked, wondered what he would look like and felt faint at the thought of it. 'You can make a list of what you want me to bring back from the house for you and I'll need your key. I know Dad has one but I have a feeling he keeps it on his key ring, which he took with him to Scotland.'

For the first time since she had arrived at the cottage and run slap bang into James, Jennifer was feeling on top of the world as she quickly showered and changed into a pair of faded jeans, a vest, a tee shirt, a jumper and some very thick knee-high socks. She knew why. Keeping him at a continual distance was hard work. Of course, she wasn't about to start being overly chummy, giggling and forgetting that he was the guy who had broken her young heart, but it was just a hell of a lot easier to let him in just a little.

At any rate she had no choice, did she? He was laid up, unable to move. She *had* to physically help him! If she could open up and be friends with him once more, it would just prove that she had got over him! More or less! Those niggly, confused, tumultuous, excited feelings she was having would therefore be nothing to worry about!

The list was ready when she returned. On it he had written, 'laptop, charger, clothes'.

'But before you disappear,' he said, making it sound as though she were Scott of the Antarctic, 'I'm feeling a little peckish…'

She was still feeling strangely upbeat when, forty-five minutes later, she headed off to his house. The estate was so vast that no other dwelling could be glimpsed from any window in the house. In summer, the trees shielded the view of the house but those trees now were bare and

heavy with snow and it was a battle against the wind and
the snow to make it to the front door. She had been to the
house before but never to his bedroom, which she managed to locate by a process of elimination. The top of the
house was comprised of a suite of rooms, and was virtually closed off, used only for guests. Of the other bedrooms, only one, apart from Daisy's, resembled a room
that was occupied.

Deep burgundy floor-length drapes were pulled open so
that she could see, outside, the steady swirl of the never-
ending snow. Most of the pale carpet was covered by a
sprawling Persian rug and a massive four-poster bed dominated much of the room. It was neatly made up but, when
she leaned against the doorframe and closed her eyes, she
could picture James lying on it, wickedly, sensationally
sexy, with dark satin sheets lightly covering his bronzed
muscular body. Then she pictured him on that sofa, with
the duvet over him as she perched on the edge and chatted to him, so close that their bodies had been practically
touching. She blinked guiltily and the image was gone.

Locating a handful of clothes took no time at all but
it felt uncomfortable gathering them up, jumpers, trousers, tee shirts and underwear. Designer items neatly laundered and tossed into the drawer indiscriminately. She had
grabbed two plastic bags before leaving the cottage and
she stuffed all the items inside and then hunted down his
laptop computer and charger, both of which were in the
kitchen where he had left them before his heroic mission
to fell the tree.

She had left him lying on the sofa and he was still there
when she finally returned, although he had decided that
he couldn't remain prone for ever.

'I can manage to move a bit when the painkillers kick
in,' he announced, liking the way the wet made the waves

in her long hair turn into curls. Her dark hair was dramatic against the paleness of her skin and he didn't think he had ever noticed before how long her lashes were or how satiny smooth her complexion.

'But I don't think it's going to do any good if I try and work sitting up on the sofa,' he pushed himself up, flexed his muscles and grimaced when his back made itself felt. 'I should be upright. You'd probably know that if you'd done that first-aid course you never got around to doing.'

'So what are you suggesting?' Jennifer asked drily.

'Well…I can use that chair over there but you might have to bring me some sort of desk. We can position it by the bay window.'

'What sort of desk did you have in mind, sir?'

'Would it be asking too much for you to get the one I use at the house? It's roughly eight by four.' He grinned and felt a kick when she grinned back at him and shook her head with an elaborate sigh.

'I suppose I could bring down my dressing table. It's small and light and it'll have to do.' She glanced down at the clothes she had brought over in the plastic bag. 'Can you manage to change yourself?'

'Only after I've had a shower, but I figure I can just about make it up the stairs myself. If you could lend me a towel…'

She did and while he showered—she could hear the water and could picture him standing under it—she cleared the little dressing table and manoeuvred it down the stairs where she set up a miniature work station for him. An office away from his office with a view of the snowy landscape.

The cottage was small and, having avoided him the night before, leaving him to watch television on his own, she resigned herself to the fact that she wasn't similarly going to be able to avoid him during daylight hours. She could work in the kitchen and she would, but even stretching her legs would entail walking into the sitting room.

Far from feeling discomforted by the prospect of that, as she had the evening before, she felt as if something had changed between them. Despite her best efforts, she had stopped fighting herself and relaxed.

He had forgone the hassle of shaving and he emerged half an hour later with wet hair and just enough of a stubble so that he looked even darker and sexier. Reluctantly she was forced to admit that neither Patric nor Gerard, the erstwhile lawyer with whom she had tried to forge a relationship, were a patch on James when it came to sheer animal sex appeal.

He took himself off to the sitting room with a pot of coffee and Jennifer tried to concentrate on catching up with her emails in the kitchen. It was almost impossible. Eventually, she began reading some of her father's recipe books, amused when she noticed a number of pages creased, dishes he had either tried or else had put on a list to try at some stage.

In the midst of trying to decide whether she should just abandon all hope of concentrating on work and start cooking something a little more ambitious for their dinner, she was interrupted by the sound of a book hitting the ground with force and she yelped and jumped to her feet.

James was standing by the window with his hand pressed against the base of his back and scowling. He turned as she entered and greeted her with, 'Why do people resist doing something when they must know that it's for their own good!'

Jennifer looked down at the heavy book that had hit the floor. It was her father's gardening tome.

'Apologies. I had to throw something.'

'Do you throw something every time you get frustrated?' she asked, moving to collect the book and replace it on the little coffee table.

'My favoured way of releasing stress is to go to the gym and punch-bag it out of my system. Unfortunately that's impossible at the moment.' He felt a lot less stressed now that she was in the room. 'What are you doing in the kitchen? Are you working?'

'I'm reading a recipe book and wondering whether I should chance cooking something a little more ambitious a bit later. Shall I get you something to eat? Drink?'

'No, but you can sit and talk to me.' He gave up the chair in favour of the sofa and lay down with a sigh of intense relief.

'Your secretary must have a nightmarish time working for you,' Jennifer commented, moving to the comfy chair by the fire and tucking her legs under her.

She marvelled at how easy it was to slide back into this easy companionship and how much she was appreciating it, having feared it to be lost and gone for good. She tried not to think that it was no good for her and then decided that she was just, finally, dealing with things in an adult fashion. Not hiding, not fighting, just accepting and moving on. What could be dangerous or unhealthy about that? Besides, she enjoyed looking at him, even though she hated admitting that weakness to herself. She liked seeing him rake his fingers through his hair as he was doing now. It was a gesture that had followed him all through his teenage years.

'My secretary loves working for me,' he denied. 'She can't wait to start work in the mornings.'

Jennifer imagined someone young, pretty and adoring, following him with her eyes and working overtime just to remain in his company, and suddenly was sick with jealousy. 'She's in her sixties, a grandmother, with a retired husband who gets under her feet. Working for me is like having a permanent holiday.'

The relief that flooded her set up a series of alarm bells in her head and she resolutely ignored them. So that crush she had had might not have been quite as dead and buried as she had hoped, but she could deal with that!

He was grinning at her and she smiled back and said something about his ego, but teasingly, blushing when he continued to look at her with those fabulous deep blue eyes.

'So tell me why you threw the book,' she said, still feeling a little hot and bothered by his lingering stare. She knew that it wasn't good to feed an addiction, however much you thought you were in control, but she found she just couldn't stand up and walk back to the kitchen and carry on reading recipe books.

'A couple of months ago, we finalised a deal with a publishing company. On the whole a lucrative buyout with a lot of potential to go somewhere, but one of the subsidiary companies is having a problem toeing the line.'

Jennifer leaned forward, intrigued. She remembered reading about that buyout on the Internet. 'What do you mean *toeing the line*?'

'They need to amalgamate. They have a niche market but it makes no money. The employees could be absorbed into the mainstream publishing company and get on board with ebooks but they're making all sorts of uncooperative noises and refusing to sign on the dotted line without a fight. Of course, they could be made to toe the line but I'd rather not take on board disgruntled employees.'

Jennifer had worked with a couple of small publishing houses in Paris, one of which specialised in maps, the other in rare limited edition books. She had been fascinated to find how differently they were run from their mainstream brothers and how different the employees were. They were individually involved in their companies in a way ordinary employees tended not to be. Both had successfully broken away from the umbrella of the mother company and both were doing all right but hardly brilliantly. Without any security blanket, it was tough going.

She peppered him with questions about the legal standing of the company he was involved with, quite forgetting her boredom in the kitchen when she had been unable to concentrate on work.

Digging into her experiences with similar companies, she expanded on all the problems they had faced when they had successfully completed management buyouts.

'You want to work with them,' she said earnestly. 'You can exploit a different market. It doesn't all have to be about ebooks and online reads. I personally think it's worth having that niche market operating without interference because it really lends integrity to the bigger picture.'

James, who had had no real idea of what Jennifer did in Paris, had only known that whatever she did, she did extremely well, was impressed by the depth of her knowledge and the incisiveness of her ideas. She also knew all the legal ins and outs should this small arm of his publishing firm decide to break away. He found himself listening to her with interest and when, pink cheeked, she finally rounded up her rousing argument for not trying to force them to fit into a prescribed mould, he nodded slowly and frowned.

'Very good,' he said slowly, and she flushed with pleasure. 'So you think I should stop trying to close this minor arm of the business and let the employees do their own thing?'

'Not *do their own thing*,' Jennifer said, 'but with someone good in charge, you might be pleasantly surprised to find that there's room in this computerised world of ours to accommodate things that don't want to or can't be computerised. There are still people out there with a love of old things and we should encourage that.'

'And what would you say if I told you that I have just the person for that job in mind?'

'Have you? I guess I always thought that the people who work for you were bright young things who wouldn't want to get tied up with something they might see as old-fashioned.'

'Oh, some of the bright young things could be easily persuaded into tying themselves into something old-fashioned if the pay was right. Money is always the most effective arm twister.'

'Ye-es...' She dragged out that single syllable as she thought about what he said. 'But you also need someone who's really interested in what they're doing and not doing it just because the pay cheque at the end of the month is fat.'

'The person I have in mind is bright, passionate and would do a damn good job.'

'That's brilliant. Well...enough of me spouting my opinions. Do you feel a little less frustrated now or am I going to hear that gardening book hit the ground again? Not that I mind, but maybe you could give me a little advance warning so that I don't jump out of my skin when I happen to be holding a knife about to chop something up for our dinner!' She began standing up and he waved her back down.

'I like you spouting your opinions,' he said, which made her flush with pleasure again. 'The girl I knew just used to hang onto mine.'

And the guy I knew and with whom I was so infatuated never encouraged me to have my own...

The shift in their relationship now stared her in the face. Two adults finding ground that was equal, so different from what they once had, so different and *so much more rewarding.*

From nowhere floated those little words he had said when she had still been fighting him, still trying to prove to him how little he meant to her...

You're a sexy woman. Her heart skipped a beat and her skin began to tingle. He might respect her opinions, she thought, but that didn't mean that he had suddenly stopped seeing her as the girl next door. This time, when she tried to dredge up the hurt she felt she had suffered at his hands all those years ago, it eluded her. It was in the process of being replaced by something else. For the very first time, she thought back to that night and tried to see herself through his eyes. Young, naive, infatuated, gullible. What a poor proposition. She shook her head, clearing it of the muddle of thoughts now released to show themselves.

'I know. How boring for you.'

'Boring...never...'

'Who,' she said hurriedly, because that thoughtful look in his eyes was doing all sorts of weird things to her, 'do you have in mind for this job, then? And do you think he'll like being taken away from what he's doing to head up something that might not be a profitable concern?'

'It's a she...'

All at once Jennifer's overactive imagination, the very one she had tried to subdue, was back in play, throwing up images of a little blonde thing, cute and brainy, simpering and doing whatever was asked of her. One of his loyal employees, like his secretary only much younger and not married.

'The only fly in the ointment,' James said, watching her very carefully and marvelling at the fact that she still didn't seem to have a clue where this conversation was leading, 'is that she doesn't actually work for my company.'

'She doesn't?'

'Nope. In fact, she doesn't even work in the country.' He let those words pool in silence between them and smiled as it began to dawn on her that he was asking her to work for him.

'*I* can't work for you, James!'

'Why not? You said yourself that you were thinking of returning to England, that your father is getting older and will need you around more than he has done... Have you changed your mind about that?'

'No, but—'

'And this isn't a job offered to you out of charity. You talked yourself into it, as a matter of fact. Everything you said is spot on. It'll be the biggest challenge of your life and I guarantee you'll love every second of it.'

'Surely you have people within your company who are more qualified for the position.'

'None as passionate as you and certainly none with the required experience in dealing with a tiny, stubborn company that refuses to shift with the times.'

'I don't know what to say...'

'Then think about it.' He closed his eyes and listened to her soft breathing. 'Now what were you saying about that exciting meal you were going to prepare for me...?'

CHAPTER FIVE

'I NEVER said that it was going to be *exciting*...'

'And you'll give some consideration to my offer while you cook...'

'Are you sure you're being serious about this, James? You've never worked with me. I don't want you to get back to London and realise that you did the wrong thing because you weren't in your normal surroundings. I can't afford to jack my job in to discover that you've made a mistake.'

'I never make mistakes.'

'And you're never laid up, yet here you are. Laid up.'

'Do you ever do anything without putting up an argument?' But his slow smile addled her. 'I mean it. You'd be perfect for the job. You can join that little team and you can all argue together about the ills of capitalism and big conglomerates wiping out small concerns.'

'Is that what they've been saying to you?' She grinned, liking the sound of that team already.

'Something like that. I've never met a more stubborn bunch of people. They've been allowed to be fully self-accounting, thanks to their very woolly-headed, charming, eighty-two-year-old boss and, now that they face the threat of being held to account, they refuse to surrender. I think one of them may have said something along the lines of they'll go down fighting. None of them have realised that they've already been taken over and they don't have much choice but to get with the programme.'

'But you're not hard-hearted enough to force them.'

'Like I said, a disgruntled employee is worse than no employee at all.'

Her heart flipped over. James Rocchi might be powerful and ruthless, but he was also fair-minded and sympathetic. He was all those things she had always seen under the surface.

'And what about their eighty-two-year-old boss? Did they feel betrayed that he'd sold them out?'

'It wasn't a hostile takeover,' James said. 'Far from it. Edward Cable was a friend of my father's even though he was considerably older. He came to me for a rescue bid. One of the big publishing houses wanted them. They were a failing company but he was reluctant to sell out to someone who would pick them apart and throw aside the bits they didn't want without thought to the employees. I have next to no experience with publishing companies and no desire to add one to my stable but...'

'But you felt you had to do the decent thing.'

'Perhaps it was my sensitive, feminine side coming out...'

Jennifer wished he would stop doing that, making her laugh, making her see him as the three-dimensional man she had never glimpsed as a young girl.

'Edward was extremely grateful to me and I could afford to buy him out. In actual fact, like I said, the company has a lot of promise. There's enough there for them to carry that little wayward arm of their company which is what I suspect he's been doing all these years.'

'Then why the need to sell?'

'Because they were making less and less money and he's never had a family. No children to inherit. A family business in a fast-moving world that doesn't have much time for family businesses unless they're incredibly well run with top-of-the-range IT departments that can take them into the twenty-first century.'

'I'll think about it.' She stood up, flexed her legs and headed out to the kitchen with a lot on her mind.

Should she take a job that would require her to work for James? If that had been suggested when she had been in Paris, hunkered down with him out of sight, she would have run a mile from the idea, but out here, forced to face him once again, she was discovering that he was not the *bad guy* of her imagination. And the job sounded as though it could be fun. In fact, it sounded like a job that would be right up her street. Should she turn it down because it involved James? Should she let pride get in the way of a good deal?

She prepared a meal on autopilot. They were now running out of fresh vegetables and, with the snow still falling and no idea when she would next be seeing a shop, she made do with tinned vegetables. Her father's larder was well stocked. It was the sort of larder that would keep a small family in food for weeks in the event of a nuclear fall-out.

She was busily opening a can when she heard James's deep velvety voice at the door and she started and spun round to see him lounging indolently against the doorframe. Immediately her body went into overdrive. How was it that he was capable of dominating the space around him so that it was impossible to remain detached?

'I've come to lend a hand.' He pushed himself away from the door and sauntered into the kitchen to peer over her shoulder. 'What feast are you preparing?'

'Nothing.'

He picked up the recipe book that she was following in a half-hearted way and scrutinised it, reciting the ingredients and then checking them off on what he could spy on the counter.

Up close and personal, his presence next to her was making it impossible to think straight and she snatched the recipe book from his hands.

'You're not supposed to be in here!' she informed him. 'You're supposed to be out there. Working. I put a lot of effort in dragging my dressing table downstairs for you because you couldn't possibly make do with the sofa and the coffee table.'

'Now you make me sound fussy.'

Her eyes slid over to where he was picking up one of the onions, which he began to peel.

'You *are* fussy,' Jennifer grumbled. 'Most people would have made do.'

'These things are fiddly.'

'Have you never peeled an onion before?'

'Look at me and tell me what you think.'

Jennifer glanced at him. His eyes were watering and he wiped one with the back of his hand.

'You're the only woman who can make me cry like this,' he murmured. She felt warm colour flood her cheeks while she mentally slapped herself on the wrist because he was just teasing her. He'd always enjoyed teasing her. He had once told her that he liked to see her blush. Now that she had stopped sniping at him, he was once again comfortable teasing her. Still, she looked away abruptly and told him not to be silly, to leave the wretched onion alone, that too many cooks spoiled the broth…

'Ah, but many hands make light work,' he quipped, carrying on with the task, 'and it's only fair that we both share the cooking duties. Besides, it gives me an opportunity to try and persuade you to work for me. I want to lock you up and throw away the key before you have time to consider other options.'

'It's tempting,' Jennifer admitted. 'But I don't want to have anyone think that I got a job because of my connections to you. It wouldn't feel right and it would compromise my working conditions. There's such a thing as office politics, although you probably don't know that because you're the head of the pile.'

'I'd be your boss on paper but in reality you'd report through a different chain of command. The company isn't even lodged in my head office. They're housed in an old Victorian building in West London, far from the madding crowd, and I shall let them continue to lease the premises. Makes more sense than dragging them into central London. So you'd be far away from me.'

He'd moved on to the peppers and was making short work of cutting them into strips. He was quick but untidy. He was a typical male with a cavalier approach to food preparation. Bits of discarded pepper were flicked into the sink or else accidentally brushed onto the ground. He might be helping but she would spend an hour afterwards cleaning up behind him. Instead of finding the prospect of that frustrating, she had to conceal a smile of indulgence. God, what was happening to her? Were her brains in the process of being scrambled like the eggs she had cooked for him the day before?

'I don't know how much notice I would have to give my boss in Paris.' She was determined to ignore the increasingly potent effect he was having on her. 'It's usually one month but they've been very good to me and I wouldn't want to leave them in the lurch.'

'Naturally.' He looked around for something else to chop and decided to avoid the mushrooms, which looked grubby. Giving up on his good deed, he washed his hands and moved on to the less onerous task of pouring them both something to drink. A glass of wine. Rules of normality were suspended out here, so why not? He leaned against the counter and watched as she started putting things together. She didn't try and impress him with her culinary skills. Twice she apologised in advance for something she was sure would taste pretty appalling. She ignored the scales and the measuring cup. She was a breath of fresh air.

He didn't like women who went out of their way to try and impress him. He had fallen victim once, many years ago, to a woman's wiles and he had vowed never to repeat the mistake. He never had. Nothing was as off-putting as the woman who wanted to display her culinary talent. Behind that, he could always read the unspoken text. *Let me show you what a good catch I am and then maybe we could start talking about the next stage.*

For James, there was never a next stage. At least not in the foreseeable future. He supposed that one day he would start thinking about settling down, but he would recognise that day when and if it came, and so far it was nowhere on his horizon.

'And then there's the question of leaving your friends behind.' He sipped his wine and resisted the temptation to brush that wayward tendril of hair from her cheek.

'I think we'll all make the effort to keep in touch,' Jennifer said drily. She looked at her concoction and hoped for better things when it had done its time in the oven. For the moment, there was nothing else to add and she began tidying the counters, nudging him out of the way and allowing him to press the glass of wine into her hand.

James wanted to ask her how much she would miss the French fedora man but he couldn't work out how to introduce him into the conversation. Nor could he quite understand why he was bothered by the thought of her ex-boyfriend, anyway. She suddenly turned to him and he flushed to have been caught staring at her.

'So I'm assuming you're on board...'

'Yes.' She made her mind up. She wasn't going to let a once-in-a-lifetime prospect slip away from her for the wrong reasons. She wasn't going to let the past dictate the present or the future. 'I'm on board. Of course, I'll have to hear the complete package.'

'I think you'll find that it will be a generous one. Shame we have no champagne. We could have cracked a bottle open to celebrate.'

Jennifer wasn't sure of the wisdom of that. Alcohol, James and her increasingly confusing emotions didn't make good bedfellows. With the cooking out of the way, she edged to one of the kitchen chairs, sat down and watched him there by the kitchen sink, sipping his wine and contemplating her over the rim of his glass.

'And I expect you'll turn this down, but there will always be a company flat for you to stay in, should you choose.'

'You're right. I've turned it down. Ellie...my friend in London...I've maintained the rent on a room in her house. I always knew that I'd be back in London and it's there, waiting for me.' She wondered what his place was like. Did he live in a house? An apartment? She wanted the background pieces to slot together so that the picture in her head could be more complete. What did that mean?

'Do you know—' she laughed lightly '—that I don't actually know where you live in London?'

'Kensington.' And you could have known, James thought, if you had kept in touch. He pictured her in his sprawling apartment, wrestling with a cookery book and trying to turn a recipe into something appetising. He pictured her with a glass of wine in her hand, laughing that rich, full-throated laughter. The image was so sudden, so unexpected, that he shook his head to clear it and frowned.

'How lovely.' That slight frown reminded her that perhaps she was being nosy.

'Well, it's big although I'm not sure you would find it lovely.' *What would she look like sitting across from him at his dinner table? With her elbows resting on the glass surface? Laughing?*

'Why?'

'It's very modern and I know you've never liked modern things.'

'I could have changed.'

'Have you?'

'Not that much,' she admitted, swirling the drink in her glass and then taking a sip. 'That's one reason why I've continued to rent the room in Ellie's house. I love where it's located and I love the fact that it's small and cosy and Victorian. There's a garden and in summer it's absolutely beautiful.'

James thought that she would have loathed the company flat, which was modelled along the lines of his own apartment, although half the size. Pale walls, pale wooden flooring, pale furniture, abstract paintings on the walls, high-tech kitchen with all mod cons known to mankind.

'I think you should email your office and give them advance warning of your plan to return to the UK. The sooner we can get this sorted, the better.' Now that she had agreed to the job, he couldn't wait to get her to sign on the dotted line.

'And you're sure you don't want to interview anyone else for the position?'

'Never been more sure of anything in my life.'

'And how is your back feeling, James? I'm sorry I haven't asked sooner. I've just been thinking about this whole job thing...'

'A near lethal diet of painkillers is doing its job.' He walked towards her. He couldn't get images out of his mind, images of her in his apartment, images of her looking at him the way he knew he wanted to look at her, images of her turning to him, raising her lips to his, closing her eyes...

He remembered the feel of her from all those years ago when he had gently turned her away and was rocked by the realisation that he had never cleared his head of the memory. He wondered whether it was because she was so much taller and so much more voluptuously endowed than the women he had dated before and since. She had offered herself to him as a naive girl and he hadn't hesitated in turning her away because to do otherwise would have been to have taken advantage of her gullibility. Now, the offer was no longer on the cards but he wanted her. He wanted her as the woman she had become. Independent, outspoken, challenging. In every respect, so different from the airheads of his past.

When he thought about the Frenchman, he had to subdue the sudden surge of jealousy. He wasn't a jealous man and yet, there it was, the green-eyed monster buried underneath his cool.

'But the pain is still there. Might have to see the doctor when I get back to London. Might...' he leaned against the kitchen table, directly in front of her so that she had to look up to meet his eyes '...have to go to a physiotherapist. Who knows? When something happens to your back, the consequences can last for years...'

'Really?'

'Really,' he confirmed seriously. 'Which is why I'm thinking that it might be a good idea if you could maybe massage my back for me.'

'Massage your back?'

'It's a big ask but I don't want to wake up at two in the morning again in agony. I also don't want to find that when this snow's disappeared, I'm still laid up and can't get back out to work.'

'And you think a massage is going to help you?'

'I don't think it can do any harm. I wouldn't have asked you two days ago. I realise you had some kind of problem with me…'

'I didn't have a problem with you,' Jennifer said awkwardly. 'I was just surprised to find you here.'

'But we seem, thankfully, to have put whatever differences you may have had with me to rest, which is why I feel comfortable about asking you to do this…unless, of course, you'd rather not help me out here…would fully understand…'

'Well, just while the chicken's in the oven. I guess.' *Massage?* If he knew how disobedient her thoughts about him had been, that would be the last suggestion to leave his mouth. He had rejected her once. He would run a mile if he thought that there might be any temptation on her part to repeat her folly.

Not that she would. But she still felt uncertain about touching him, even in a way that wasn't sexual. What excuse would she give to shoot his request down in flames? As he had said, their differences had been overcome, they were back on safe ground, friends but without the complications of her having a crush on him… He felt nothing for her. He would wonder why she couldn't help him out, especially if, as he had intimated, the pulled muscles in his back could have lasting repercussions.

'Five minutes,' he agreed. 'It might make all the difference…'

Back in the sitting room, which was wonderfully warm with the open fire burning, James stripped off his top. In truth, his back still protested vehemently at any extreme movement, although he acknowledged that he had exaggerated just a little. He lay face down on the sofa and waited as she pulled a couple of cushions over so that she could kneel on the ground next to him.

His skin was cool as she began kneading his firm, bronzed back. He had the perfect physique. Broad shoulders, tapering to a narrow waist and long, muscular legs. There was a mantra playing in her head, one she was forcing herself to repeat: *He's just a friend, how nice to be pals once again, pals always help each other out...*

She could feel his body relax under the pressure of her fingers. She, on the other hand, couldn't be further from relaxed. Her pulses were in free fall and her heart was racing so fast that she could scarcely breathe properly. It was just as well his back was to her. If not, she was certain that he would be able to see the telltale traces of a woman...

Turned on. She stopped massaging and informed him that she would have to check the chicken.

'Surely it won't be ready yet.' He turned over before she had time to stand up and suddenly she was no longer safely staring at his back but instead looking straight at him, lying there, sexily semi clad. 'Raw chicken...not recommended by any major chef...'

'Yes...well...' There was no way that she would allow her eyes to drift down to his bare chest and even meeting his eyes with some semblance of self-control was a trial.

'That felt good.'

Jennifer licked her lips nervously. There was a subtle change in the atmosphere. He was holding her glance for too long and she couldn't tear her eyes away from his. The mantra had fragmented into worthless pieces and she was only aware of the changes in her body as he continued to stare at her.

'Sit.' He shifted his big body a little and patted a space next to him on the sofa. Idiotically, Jennifer obeyed. She wasn't quite sure why.

Her fingers were resting lightly on her lap and she nearly passed out when he reached to entwine his fingers with hers, although he didn't take his eyes away from her face.

Jennifer found that she was nailed to the sofa as he began doing that thing with his thumb, rubbing it gently on her hand so that her breathing became jerky and uneven and her mouth went dry.

When the silence became too much to bear, she finally found her voice and said, shakily, 'What are you doing?' She didn't want to look at their enmeshed fingers because to do that would have been to acknowledge that she knew exactly what he was doing. Caressing her. Was it some kind of weird *thank-you-great-massage* caress? Was he aware of what it was doing to her? Was this a *friendly thing*?

'I'm touching you,' James murmured in a voice that implied that he was as surprised by the gesture as she was. 'Do you want me to stop?'

Jennifer was having trouble getting past the first part of his statement. This was what she had seemingly spent a lifetime fantasising about. The four years she had spent telling herself that daydreams played no part in reality, that he had never been attracted to her, that she had to *wake up and smell the coffee*, floated away like early morning mist on a summer day.

'Yes! No…this isn't…isn't appropriate…'

'Why isn't it?'

'You know why...' There was a very good reason but she couldn't quite remember what exactly it was and, while she was trying to figure it out, he drew her slowly down towards him.

A buzz of nervous excitement ripped through her. She was the kid opening her eyes on Christmas Day, wondering if the much-longed-for present would live up to expectation... She knew that no good would come of any physical contact with him, that she wanted, had always wanted so much more than he could ever offer, and yet his pull was magnetic and irresistible and her curiosity and raw longing far too powerful.

She closed her eyes on a soft sigh and their mouths touched, a sweetly exploring caress, then he reached both his hands into her hair, brushed his thumbs along her neck and didn't give her the opportunity to surface as the gentle exploration turned into something wonderfully, erotically hungry.

Jennifer lowered herself onto him and her breasts squashed against his chest. In between drowning in his kisses, she surfaced to tell him in a shaky voice that they really shouldn't be doing this...that he wasn't himself... that the chicken in the oven was going to burn...

He, for his part, laughed softly and informed her that this was exactly what they should be doing.

His hand had moved from the nape of her neck to slide underneath her top. He stroked her back, his hand moving upwards until he was brushing her bra strap. He carried on kissing her while he unclasped it.

'I'm not one of your Polly Pockets...' Along with a shudder of intense excitement, she felt the hangover of self-consciousness that had always afflicted her in his presence. He liked them little. She wasn't.

'Stop talking,' James commanded huskily. 'Let me see you.'

Jennifer arched up into an awkward sitting position and he shoved her top up. Bountiful breasts tumbled out, breasts that were much more than a handful, breasts a man could lose himself in. He groaned.

'I've died and gone to heaven,' he breathed unevenly. Her nipples peeped over the unclasped bra. With her head flung back and her long, curly hair tumbling down her back, she was the epitome of sexiness, a wanton goddess the likes of which he had never seen before.

Once she had offered herself to him. Only now could he receive that offering. He touched the tips of her nipples with his fingers, circling them and trying not to explode with desire as the tips firmed and stiffened in response. She was panting and moaning softly, little noises that inflamed him. He didn't know how long he would be able to indulge in foreplay because he was losing his self-control fast. When she edged upwards on the sofa so that her breasts now dangled provocatively close to his mouth, he circled her waist with his hands, determined to take things as slowly as he could.

It felt like an impossible task, requiring heroic efforts beyond his control, as he gently levered her down so that he could suckle on a proffered nipple. He drew the pulsing bud into his mouth and luxuriated in tasting her. He was a big man with big hands and her lush breasts suited them perfectly. How could he ever have been satisfied with those thin women with jutting hip bones and small breasts?

The sofa was big but they still had to wriggle to find comfortable positions. While they did, he continued sucking her nipples and massaging her breasts. He could have carried on for ever.

'This sofa isn't ideal,' he broke free to tell her.

'I can lay the duvet in front of the fire…'

'Do it without your clothes on. I want to see every naked inch of your perfect body.'

Jennifer stood up and slowly stripped off her clothes. She wasn't inexperienced but removing every item of clothing while her man looked on with rampantly appreciative eyes was new to her. She felt deliciously, thrillingly wanton. He had been vocal in his praise for her body, had lavished attention on breasts that were big by anyone's standards, had hoarsely told her that she was beautiful. Any lingering self-consciousness she might have had had disappeared under the onslaught of his compliments. In fact, she felt heady and sexy and bursting with self-confidence.

As she began pushing aside the coffee table that sat in the centre of the room, making space for the king-sized, thick, soft duvet, he told her to take her time. When it was time for her to fetch the duvet from the sofa, he stood up and began undressing, more slowly than he might have had his back not still been aching.

The breath caught in her throat as the images she had stored in her head were replaced by the reality. When he was completely naked, he held her eyes and then motioned for her to look at him as he touched himself. He was a big man and everything about him was impressively big, including the erection his hand circled.

In her wildest, fiercest day dreams, she had never imagined that it could feel so good to be standing here, naked, on the brink of making love to this man. She walked over to him and removed his hand so that she could replace it with her own. To feel him throb against the palm of her hand…

Was she doing the right thing? Never had anything felt

so right. She stretched up to kiss him and this time they kissed long and tenderly.

'You'll have to do the work,' he murmured, breaking free and leading her towards the duvet. 'Don't forget that I'm a man with a bad back...'

'I wouldn't want to do further damage,' Jennifer returned, guiding his hand to her breast. 'I remember what you said about bad backs never going away...'

'I'd be happy to swap the health of my back for an hour in bed with you.'

How easy it would be to allow words she'd never thought she would ever hear to get to her. How easy to lose herself in the excitement of the moment. A little core of practical common sense cautioned her against jumping into this wonderful situation feet first, without any thought for rocks that might lie beneath.

This was what she wanted. She had waited a long time and she knew now that she had spent the past four years waiting. How long would she have waited? She didn't know. But that didn't mean that this was the beginning of every dream she had ever had coming true. That wasn't how life worked.

They lay down on the duvet, which was mercifully soft.

She curved her body against his, drawing her leg over his thigh, and riffled his dark hair with her fingers.

When she looked at his impossibly handsome face, she saw the past entwined with the present, the boy as he had been and the man he had become. The feelings she had had for him, which had started with the sweet innocence of infatuation, had grown and matured and had never gone away. Being thrown together in the cottage had made her realise that. What she felt for him was no longer infatuation. Neither had it been four years ago. Infatuation didn't have much of a life span; it would have faded over time, replaced by other experiences.

She loved him and she knew, without quite understanding why, that any mention of love would have him running for cover. She took this on board and knew that she still wanted to be right here with him, even if her feelings left her exposed and vulnerable.

'You are beautiful,' he interrupted her chain of thoughts and she smiled sadly.

'I don't want to kill the moment, but that's not what you said four years ago.'

'Four years ago you were a child.'

'I was twenty-one!'

'A very young twenty-one,' James murmured, stroking her hair away from her face. 'Too young for someone as jaded as me. You've grown up in the past four years, Jennifer.'

Grown up but still as vulnerable as that twenty-one-year-old girl had been. She nodded and kissed him and pushed uncomfortable thoughts to the back of her mind. Her nipple tingled and throbbed as it rubbed against his chest. She straddled him and eased her body up so that when she lowered it he could take her nipple into his mouth and suckle on it until her body was alive with sensation. She groaned as he slipped his hand between her legs and began caressing her, rubbing fingers along the sensitised, slippery groove until she could hardly bear the exquisite, agonising need to be completely fulfilled.

'Not fair,' she murmured into his mouth, but she moved her hips sensuously against his exploring hand and he laughed with rich appreciation.

'I want to taste you,' he groaned, easing her into an upright position so that she was kneeling over him and he could fully take in the beauty of her spectacular body.

Her heavy breasts were amazing, her nipples dark and perfectly formed and the patch of dark hair nestled between her thighs was as sweet and aromatic as honey. He clasped her from behind and nudged her closer to his mouth.

Jennifer rested her hands flat against his shoulders and shuddered at the first touch of his tongue tasting her. He took his time, licking and exploring and then falling back when she thought she couldn't take any more. She was cresting a wave except, just when the wave threatened to break, it simply ebbed and began building again. It was the most incredible experience. She had wondered what it would be like to be with him. Nothing like this. This was way, way better than anything she had conjured up in her head.

'I can't take any more of this,' she gasped, when he had, once again, brought her almost to the point of no return.

She slid off him to lie on her side where she could try and let her breathing return to normal, but how could it when he was nudging his thigh between hers and sending her right back to the brink?

'I can't take much more myself,' James admitted shakily. 'I never lose control but I'm in danger of doing so very soon.'

'Shall I see how much stamina you have…?'

She wriggled around so that while he explored her with his mouth, she could likewise explore him with hers. He was rock hard and tasting him made her want to swoon, as did his continuing exploration of the delicate groove between her legs.

Their mutual need was frantic by the time her mouth joined his in a wet, musky, greedy kiss.

'I need you. Now.'

And I love you so much, was the reply that flew through her head. 'I need you too,' she returned huskily.

'Are you protected?'

'I'm not at the moment but I can be…'

CHAPTER SIX

JENNIFER'S bag was lying on the ground next to the chair. She unzipped it and rustled in the side pocket where a memento of that non-event four years ago lay. The condom, optimistically bought and never used for a love-making session that had never happened, had been through a lot. It had jostled next to coins and make-up and packets of chewing gum. It had been transferred from bag to bag, a secret talisman and a permanent reminder of her youthful foolishness. It had even drowned and been resuscitated when, on a boat trip with her father in Majorca, she had accidentally dropped her bag in the sea.

Fetching it out of its compartment felt like fate.

'Not yet.' He caught her hand as she was about to tear open the little packet. 'My back feels up to a little bit more foreplay...'

In truth, he felt fighting fit and this time she was the one lying on the duvet as he explored every glorious inch of her succulent body. She tossed beneath him and he pinned her down, subjecting her to the onslaught of his mouth and tongue and hands. Their bodies were slick with perspiration when, unable to take any more, she cried out for him to enter her.

The condom that had been through the wars was finally serving its purpose and as he thrust into her she bucked and cried out in ecstasy. The feel of him inside her was beyond all expectations. He was big and powerful and he filled her in a way she would never have dreamed possible. It was as if their bodies were made for each other. They moved in perfect rhythm and her orgasm, when she finally came, was wave upon wave of such pleasure that her whole body quivered and shook from the strength of it.

The used condom joined the logs burning in the open fire and she curved her body against his with a gurgle of contentment.

'Amazing,' James murmured softly. 'It's done my back a world of good. I think we'll have to carry on with this method of physiotherapy if I'm to improve and suffer no lasting damage.'

Jennifer had never felt so blissfully happy and completely whole. For the first time in her life, her body was complete.

Then she wondered how long the physiotherapy was destined to continue. She glanced outside through the window and the snow reminded her that this was a snatched moment in time.

'Pretty incredible.' She brushed his cheek with her hand. He had shaved earlier but she could feel the stubble already trying to make a reappearance. She nuzzled his chin and settled on top of him so that she could feel every inch of his body underneath her.

'Everything you dreamed of?' There was laughter in his voice but the navy-blue eyes were solemn.

'I'm not going to feed your ego by telling you how great it was, James.' She unglued herself from him to allow his hands to wedge over her breasts where he could tease her nipples.

'Cruel woman.' He laughed out loud this time and continued to roll the pads of his thumbs over her nipples, which were already standing to attention even though it had only been minutes since they had been lavished with devotion. 'I'm tempted to punish you by not allowing you to get any sleep tonight. In fact, if I had my way I wouldn't let you leave my side...'

And he almost succeeded in doing just that. At least for the next forty-eight hours, during which the snow began to slacken in its fury and the unremitting leaden grey skies gradually showed glimpses of pale, milky blue.

Jennifer yielded to the bubble in which there were just the two of them, playing house like babes in the wood and making love wherever and whenever, which was everywhere and often. Her one condom had done its job but James had more at the house because he would never, she assumed, take risks of any kind with any woman.

He told her repeatedly that he couldn't get enough of her and, with every smile and every touch, she fell deeper and deeper into love. It consumed her and it was only when, lying on her bed, wrapped up with him, she looked outside and noticed that the snow had finally and completely stopped.

'It's not snowing any longer,' she said and James followed her gaze to see that she was right. He hadn't even noticed. In fact, over the past three days there was a great deal that he hadn't noticed. Starting with the state of the weather and ending with his work, which he had rudimentarily covered. Most of the time, his computer lay on the dressing table, which neither of them had bothered to relocate to the bedroom, untouched.

'If I know anything about the weather here, we'll wake up tomorrow morning to find bright sunshine and the snow melted.'

She couldn't prevent a certain wistfulness from creeping into her voice because with the end of the snow came the beginning of the questions that she had conveniently put to one side. What happened next? Where did they go from here? Was this a relationship or was it only a consequence of the fact that they had been cooped up for days on end?

She wasn't about to start asking questions, though.

James was adept at picking up the intonations in women's voices. He waited for her to continue and frowned when there was nothing forthcoming.

'I don't want you to return to Paris,' he surprised himself by saying, and Jennifer looked at him in astonishment.

'Well, we can't stay here for ever pretending the rest of the world doesn't exist,' she pointed out. She turned back to face the window, resting in the crook of his arm. The moon was big and fat and round and it filled the bedroom with a silvery glow.

James was accustomed to women making demands on his time. It irritated him that she made no attempt to demand anything. Having spent the past few days living purely for the moment, he was now driven to get inside her head and discover what she was thinking. He had just nailed his colours to the mast and told her that he wanted her to quit her job immediately for him, and was her only response to be that they couldn't stay put and block out the rest of the world? As if that were the only logical option to ditching her Paris placement?

'I'm not implying that we should do that,' he said edgily. 'But we're going to have to start thinking about leaving here…and we're going to have to decide what happens with us now.'

'Maybe we should go our separate ways,' Jennifer told him. He might want her to give up her job immediately but that was just him reaching out and taking what he wanted without a scrap of thought for what *she* wanted. She had been a keen observer of his girlfriends down the years. None of them had ever lasted longer than a holiday. He had taken what he wanted from them and discarded them when he thought that it was time to move on.

'You mean that?' He raised himself up and spun her round to look at him because he wanted her undivided attention.

'Look, you're not into long-term relationships—'

'And that's what you want?'

Of course it was! But she knew what would happen next if she were to say that. His pursuit, such as it was, would come to a grinding halt. She might play hard to get, but, really and truly, did she want this to end so abruptly? Eventually, it would, but why shouldn't she enjoy herself for as long as she could and let tomorrow take care of itself? She hated the weakness behind that choice but even more she hated the hypocrisy of pretending that it would be worthwhile to walk away now and become a martyr to her principles.

'Let me finish,' she inserted, picking and choosing her words very carefully. 'We…this…I guess, for me, this is unfinished business…'

'Unfinished business?' He flung aside the duvet and strode towards the window to glare outside at the picture-postcard winter scene before swinging around to scowl at her. 'I'm *unfinished business*?'

'Okay, maybe I didn't phrase that quite as well as I should have…'

She sat up and drew her legs up. 'Come back to bed. I…I…' Some truth forced its way out. 'I don't want to go back to Paris either,' she confessed, at which he slowly returned to lie down next to her.

'Then pack it in. Tell them something. Anything. I want you here with me.'

'Yes…it's fun…it would be nice to carry on seeing one another, I guess…' *But for how long?* That was a question that was definitely off the cards. 'I mean, no strings attached, of course…'

He could feel a return of that groundswell of dissatisfaction, the same dissatisfaction that had slammed into him when she had labelled him as *unfinished business*, and he couldn't understand why because what she was saying tuned in perfectly with his own personal philosophy. No strings attached had been his motto for a very long time. And wasn't she, in her own way, his unfinished business as well? Something had been started four years ago and it had now reached fruition.

'I never took you for a *no-strings-attached* kind of girl.'

Jennifer stilled. He knew her so well, but did she want him to ever suspect how much he meant to her? Did she really want to open herself up to being hurt all over again? She couldn't face his pity for a second time.

'It just shows how much you have to learn about me,' she murmured lightly.

'So you'll email your Paris office…bid them a fond adieu…?'

'I'll go and discuss the matter with my boss over there,' she said firmly.

'I don't know how long I can wait before you return. If we're talking in terms of months, then forget it. I'll go over there myself and drag you back to London.'

He propped himself up on one elbow, rested his hand on her stomach and traced the outline of her belly button. Jennifer, caught in the now familiar tide of longing, fought to stay in control.

'Do you always get your own way when it comes to women?' she asked breathlessly, staring straight up at the ceiling and not pushing him away when he dipped his fingers lower to sift the soft, downy hair between her thighs. Before he could start doing even more dramatic things to her body, things that always seemed to wreak havoc with her thought processes, she wriggled onto her side so that their bodies mirrored one another, both of them propped up on their elbows, staring directly into each other's eyes. She didn't want to get hopelessly lost in making love. She wanted to talk, really talk.

'I can't tell a lie...'

'What do they hope for?' she asked in genuine bewilderment. She knew what *she* hoped for, but she was a lost cause and had been from as far back as she could remember. Other women, women he had gone out with for a matter of a few weeks, surely they couldn't all be silly enough to think they could tie him down? Or was he only attracted to women like himself, women who wanted affairs and were happy to part company when the lust bit was exhausted?

'What do you mean?'

'Do they honestly think that you're going to offer them a lasting relationship?'

'How can they?' James said impatiently. 'The women I date always know from the beginning that I'm not interested in walking down the aisle. Why are we having this discussion, anyway? When we both agree that you're going to leave Paris immediately and come back here...'

Jennifer ignored his interruption. 'And they don't mind?'

'I suppose,' James admitted grudgingly, 'there are instances when one of them might have wanted to take things to another level, but, as far as I am concerned, if a woman chooses to go out with me, then she chooses what she's signing up for.' *No-strings-attached fun...* He swept aside the unsettling memory of how her easy acceptance of that had thrown him.

'And you've never been tempted?'

'You talk too much,' he growled.

'You'll have to get used to it.'

'You never used to ask so many questions.'

'I never used to ask *any* questions…but then again, we were never in the place we are now, were we?'

'I've never been tempted.' He lay back and shielded his face with his arm, then he pulled her against him and slung his arm around her shoulder so that the tips of his fingers were brushing her nipple, although his mind appeared to be far away.

'You probably don't remember when my father died,' he surprised her by saying. 'You would have been…what… fifteen? It was a pretty terrible time all round. Daisy was in pieces.'

'I remember. You abandoned your gap year and went to work. It was tough. I know.'

'They had just lost their figurehead. The employees were edgy and so was the bank. I'd worked there before, summer jobs…well, you know that.' He felt her nod against him and he inhaled deeply. He had always thought it a myth that confessions were good for the soul, so why was he telling her this? 'I knew a bit about the accounts but I was green around the ears. Like it or not, though, I was a majority shareholder and responsibility fell on my shoulders.'

'And you were still grieving for your dad… How hard that must have been, James…' Her heart went out to him because, however mature he might have been for his age, he had still only been a kid, really, one forced to grow up very, very quickly.

'It was…very hard. I was in a bad place. I got involved with a woman.'

'You *got involved with a woman*?'

'You say that as though I started growing two heads and five arms,' James said drily. This was new ground for him. This window in his life had always been kept a secret. No one, including his mother, knew about that indiscretion ten or so years ago. He had never been tempted to confide in any of the women he had dated, even though they had all pressed him for details of his personal life as though getting beneath the armour would guarantee a foot through the door.

Jennifer had a moment of feeling special until he continued in the same flat, neutral voice, 'And the reason I'm telling you now, aside from the fact that we go back a long way, is that I want you to understand why I've made the choices that I've made with women.'

Jennifer was still trying to work out which woman he was talking about. She remembered that time quite clearly, although it was many years ago. He had lost the easy banter and the light-hearted teasing and was beginning the transition to the man he would later become. Controlled, single-minded, adept at channelling his incredible intelligence towards a single goal and getting there whatever it took. For the first time he had been around and yet she had hardly seen him.

'I thought you were completely wrapped up with the company,' she said, looking at him. 'When would you have had time to go out socialising? Dad and I nicknamed you The Invisible Man because we knew you were around but we just never saw you.'

'Well, I didn't go out socializing. The socialising came to find *me*.'

'What are you talking about?'

'Anita Hayward was the accounts manager. She looked like something that had just stepped off the cover of a magazine. Long legs, long hair, long lingering looks whenever she came into my father's office where I had set up camp. She struck just the right note between sympathy and a matter-of-fact acceptance that, tragic though the circumstances were, life had to go on. It was a break from seeing the pity in everyone's eyes and hearing the sympathy oozing in their voices. It seemed to be what I needed at that moment in time. She made it her mission to fill me in on everything that was going on in the office. I was sharp enough to know the mechanics of how things worked but I knew nothing about the people and I needed to get them onside. Twenty-minute briefings at the end of the day turned into dinners out.'

'Your mum said that you were working at the company, making sure that loose ends were tied up…but you weren't working…'

'Nope. I was being worked over.'

'What do you mean?'

James had intended to throw her the bare bones. It was more than he had ever thrown anyone else. Now, as he lay flat on his back and stared up at the ceiling, he was reliving a time he had relegated to history.

'I should have been at home. At least, I should have been at home more than I was. Instead, I was being seduced by Anita Hayward of the long red hair and the slanting green eyes.'

'And you still feel guilty…' Jennifer deduced slowly.

'Very good, Sherlock.'

'But no one operates on all cylinders when they're experiencing great stress. We react in different ways. What… what happened…in the end?'

'In the end,' he said drily, 'I discovered that she was

after a promotion. It was as simple as that. I had been used by an ambitious woman who wanted to make sure that she got the top job when the cabinet was reshuffled. And by the way, she had a boyfriend. I caught them in one of the directors' offices when I happened to return to the building after hours because I'd forgotten something. Either the boyfriend was in on the game or else he was just another sap she was using for her own ends. The fact is that, at a crucial time in my life, I took my eye off the ball.'

He turned to her, cupped her breast in his hand and Jennifer covered his hand with hers.

'You use sex as a substitute for talking,' she told him and he smiled crookedly at her.

'And you talk too much.'

'So…because of one unfortunate experience, you decided…what…?'

'I like the way you describe that wrong turn as an unfortunate experience… Well, because of that unfortunate experience, I made a rational decision to steer clear of anything called uncontrolled emotional involvement.'

For Jennifer, the long line of airhead blondes now made a lot of sense. He had fallen in love, or *thought* he had fallen in love, with a woman who was sensitive, intelligent, beautiful and mature, and, for his trouble, he had ended up being manipulated at a time when he had been at his most vulnerable. He had emerged from the experience with the building blocks for a fortress and behind the walls of that fortress he had sealed away any part of him that could be touched. The women he had dated since had been disposable and she would be as well.

Realistically, she might last a bit longer because of their history, because they had slightly more going for them than just sex, but she, like the rest of them, would be disposable.

'What happened to her?' Jennifer asked, and when he replied she could hear the ice in his voice.

'She got the sack. Not immediately, of course, and not directly. There are all sorts of regulations pertaining to employee dismissal. No, she was treated to a series of sideways moves. The vertical line she had manoeuvred towards suddenly flattened out and became horizontal. Removing myself from the equation, she failed to realise that there was no way I could have someone working for me who was capable of deceit. Strangely enough, even after I caught them having sex on the desk, she continued to believe that she could patch things over and pick up where we had left off. When she realised that her career in my company was over, she decided to lay all her cards on the table. Not only had she slept with me to further her career but she was no young girl of twenty-four with a ladder to climb and a sackful of qualifications. She was thirty-three and I later found out that most of her qualifications had been fabricated.'

'I'm sorry,' Jennifer said quietly and he shrugged against her.

'Why? We all need a learning curve in our lives.'

Jennifer, resting against him, thought that she had already had hers except she seemed to have learnt nothing from it. He had once rejected her and she had thought she had learnt to keep away and yet here she was, in his arms and busy repeating the same process, except this time the hole she had dug for herself was a lot deeper.

'And you've told me this because…you want to warn me off getting too involved with you,' she surmised thoughtfully. 'You don't have to worry on that score.'

'Because I'm your unfinished business?'

'I'm sorry that you found that offensive. I'd always wondered…'

'You don't have to explain, Jen. I've wondered too.'

'You have?'

'I'm only human. Of course I have. I had very graphic dreams about you for a long time after that incident.'

'What was I doing in those dreams?'

'When you're back in London and we have the benefit of a bed with a wrought-iron bedstead and some cloth, I'll demonstrate…'

As she had predicted from past experience, the snow stopped abruptly overnight and the temperatures rose sufficiently for the settled snow to start thawing.

They went to sleep that night and by the following evening, the outlines and contours of the fields around the house and cottage were slipping back into focus. His back was still not in top condition but between them they could clear the drive and he disappeared up to the house to get his car, which he drove down to the cottage. There was snow on the roof and the bonnet but it was melting almost as she looked at it.

In the space of a few days, she felt as though her well-ordered life had been turned on its head. She had grown, developed, matured and become an ambitious, successful and single-minded career woman in Paris, but emotionally she now thought that she had been sleepwalking. She hadn't moved on from James, she had just held herself in abeyance until they met again.

He wanted her to quit her job but he had been careful to give her no promises of a future. They would be lovers. He had treated her the same way he had treated all the women he had ever gone out with. Up front announcing his lack of commitment, making sure she didn't get it into her head that long term was part of his vocabulary.

By the time they left the estate, the insurance company had been contacted and she had also spoken to her father and emailed him a list of things that would need doing when he returned.

As James drove them away she looked back at the disappearing cottage as though it had been a dream. When she turned to look ahead, she wondered how she was going to fare in the real world and, as though sensing her doubts, James rested his hand over hers and flicked her a sideways glance.

'I've been thinking. Perhaps I should come with you to Paris. It's been a while since I had a holiday...'

Jennifer had had time to think about everything. From her perspective, she had run into her past and discovered that she had never managed to escape it after all. Locked away in the cottage, she had found how fast a youthful crush could turn into hopeless adult love. She had had no weapons at her disposal powerful enough to protect her against the man who had stolen her heart a thousand years ago.

She wasn't, however, stupid. James liked her. He certainly adored her body. That was where the story ended. He had warned her off looking for anything more than sex and she had successfully convinced him that they were both on the same wavelength.

She didn't have enough good sense to walk away from him but she had enough good sense to know that when the time came for them to go their separate ways, she wanted to be able to do so with her head held high.

'Come with me to Paris?' she said now. 'James...Paris isn't going to be *a holiday*.'

James stifled a surge of irritation. 'I realise you're going to be working but it wouldn't be beyond the realms of possibility for me to arrange to be in Paris for a week or so.'

Bliss, Jennifer thought. That would be absolute bliss. Getting back to her little apartment, knowing that she

would be seeing him later. Cooking together and showing him all the little cafés and restaurants where the own-
ers knew her, taking him to that special *boulangerie* that
sold the best bread in the city and the markets where they
could stock up on fresh fruit and vegetables and tease each
other about who could concoct the most edible meal. She
could introduce him to her friends and afterwards they
could lie in bed and make love and he could tell her what
he thought of them in that witty, sharp, amusing way of
his... *Bliss*.

The pleasant daydream fell away in pieces. She knew,
without a shadow of a doubt, that if she was to take that
first step down the road of doing whatever he wanted it
would the first step down a very slippery slope.

'You've been out of your office for several days. How
on earth would you be able to wangle a week-long trip
to Paris?'

A slashing smile of satisfaction curved his lips.
'Because I'm the boss. I call the shots. It's an undeniable
perk of the job. Besides, I've always maintained the importance of having good people to whom responsibility can
be delegated. I have a queue of people lining up to prove
to me how capable they are of covering in my absence.'

'Well, I'm sorry but I don't think it would be a very
good idea.'

'Why not?' He slipped his hand between her legs and
pushed his knuckles against her and the pressure was so
arousing that she began to dampen in her underwear. The
past few days had taught her that he was an intensely physical man. He relied on his ability to arouse to make his
point and to win his arguments and it would have been so
easy to let him have his way.

He returned his hand to the steering wheel. He couldn't
keep his hands off her and he knew that she felt the same

way about him. There were times when he looked at her and he knew, from the faint blush on her cheeks, that if he reached out and felt her she would be hot and wet for him. So what, he wondered with baffled exasperation, was the problem in capitalising on the time they spent together?

'I feel badly enough about leaving everyone there in the lurch.'

'You're not leaving them *in the lurch*,' James pointed out irritably. 'They understood perfectly the circumstances surrounding your resignation. Your father's getting older... the emergency at the cottage further proof that you will be needed here more and more over time... The fact that there's the offer of a job that might not be on the cards for ever and you owe it to yourself and your father that you take it while it's there... You've offered to see in your successor and train them up. Why would you think that they're being left in the lurch?'

'Because I do.'

'That's insane feminine logic.'

Jennifer clicked her tongue and sighed because he could be so *black and white*.

'From my perspective,' he continued, proving to her how well she knew his thought processes, 'you've acted in the most sensible, practical way possible.'

'Well, I don't want you around distracting me.'

'But you know how much fun a bit of distraction can be...' James murmured, savouring that small admission of weakness from her. They were few and far between. Much to his annoyance.

'I'll be there for two weeks. Maybe three. Not long. Enough time to clear my desk, pack up the things in my apartment I've gathered over the years, go out with friends...'

Which, to his further annoyance, was something else

on his mind. The goodbyes to the old friends…everyone knew about *making love one last time for old times' sake*… He swept aside that ridiculous concern. Hell, she wasn't like that! But he was scowling at the mere hint of any such thing, the mere suggestion in his head that she might be tempted to go to bed with the good friend and ex-lover artist of the fedora and the earring.

Jennifer saw that scowl and smiled because, even though she knew where he stood on matters of the heart, his unrestrained possessiveness still gave her a little quiver of satisfaction. She hugged it to herself and savoured it for a few seconds.

'So let me get this straight,' he gritted. 'You don't want me in Paris and you also don't want either of us to tell our parents about what's going on…' It wasn't cool to behave like a petulant teenager and he forced a tight smile, which he was pretty sure wasn't fooling anyone.

'Well, I explained why I thought it wasn't such a good idea to tell Dad and Daisy,' Jennifer said vaguely. Her father knew her better than anyone else. He would never buy the fiction that she was the sort of girl who would indulge in something passing and insignificant with the guy who had stolen her vulnerable teenage heart. He would immediately know that she was in too deep. There would be questions and speculation and she wouldn't be able to wriggle out of telling him the truth.

'And I explained why I didn't get it.'

'I'm practical.' She began listing the reasons once again while her treacherous mind broke its leash and started imagining how wonderful it would be if she could shout her love out to the whole world. 'We both are…we know that this is just about having fun, so why drag other people into it?' She and James, lovers and in love, building a future together…she and Daisy planning a wedding,

nothing too big…just the local church…friends and neighbours… 'It would just make it awkward when the inevitable happened.'

'Nice to know you're planning the demise of what we
have before we've even begun.'

'These are *your* rules, James. You don't do involvement.' He couldn't argue with that. She was the perfect
woman for him. She challenged him intellectually, which
he found he enjoyed, and they were brilliant in bed together. In fact, they couldn't have been more compatible.
She also respected his boundaries. There had been no
coy insinuations about the importance of commitment,
no leading questions that involved long-term planning,
no shadow of disappointment when he had told her about
his ill-timed disastrous affair with Anita and the consequences of it. Nor had she tried to lecture him on the
importance of letting go of the past. In that respect, she
ticked all the boxes.

He wondered why he wasn't feeling more pleasantly
satisfied.

'Besides—' she thought it a good idea to move on from
the commitment angle, just in case he got scared that she
was hinting that *she did do commitment* and *preferably
with him* '—we've both agreed that we're not each other's
type…' Or something like that. The night before, when
the conversation had mysteriously returned to Patric, even
though he was no longer in her life *in that way*. James
seemed obsessed with Patric and she couldn't understand
why unless it was to confirm his singular position in her
life, with no spectres at the feast. He wanted her in place
and at his beck and call, without distractions from anyone, even an ex-lover, although, in return, she knew that
he would never give those assurances back to her. The
playing field would never be level as far as James went.

'So I'm not trying to sabotage what we have,' she concluded. 'We both know that this is just physical attraction. It'll pass in time and we'll both move on so why involve other people when there's no need?'

'Why indeed?' James grated.

'Let's just have fun. And no complications...'

CHAPTER SEVEN

JAMES glanced at his watch for the third time in ten minutes. She was running late, which was unusual for her, but he didn't mind. For the first time in nearly three and a half months, she had actually suggested meeting up, as opposed to waiting for him to take the lead. She had called him on his mobile and he had immediately booked dinner at an exclusive restaurant where, and this was just one of the upsides of wealth and power, his request for a secluded table at the back was instantly accommodated.

Of course, despite the fact that he had always loathed a woman who tried to insinuate him into a social life he didn't want and engineer arrangements without plenty of prior notice, it annoyed him that Jennifer was so completely the opposite.

She engineered nothing. She was impossible to impress. She declined his gifts. She was irritatingly elusive. Twice she had laughingly turned down his invitations to the theatre because *she was busy* and then failed to come up with an explanation why. Busy doing what? Once she had bailed on him claiming tiredness. Admittedly, he had telephoned her at short notice, in fact at eleven o'clock at night, but after a series of exhaustive meetings the only person he had wanted to see had been her. In fact, he had brought the meetings to a summary conclusion because visions of her lying naked in bed had been too much. He had failed to laugh along when she had told him, yawning, that he couldn't possibly come over because a girl needed her beauty sleep.

She wasn't playing hard to get. Far from it. When they were together, she was everything a man could wish for. She made him laugh, turned him on to the point where he was capable of forgetting everything, argued like a vixen if she didn't agree with something he said and had no qualms in teasing him on the grounds that everyone needed to be taken down a peg or two now and again. She didn't play games. She was up front in everything she did and everything she said. He had had no option but to swallow down his intense irritation when she failed to put him first.

And she never talked about a future. Everything was done on a spur-of-the-moment basis and he had gradually, inexorably and frustratingly come to the conclusion that, however sexy and accommodating she could be, he was a stopgap. When he thought about that for too long, he could feel a slow anger begin to build so he didn't think about it. Instead, he told himself that that was a good thing because stopgaps didn't lead to attachments and attachments, as he had made perfectly clear to her at the beginning of their relationship, were not on the horizon. Clearly they weren't on hers either.

A waiter came to refill his drink, a full-bodied red wine, asked him if there was anything, *anything at all*, they could bring for him while he waited for his companion. The chef, they assured him, would be more than happy to concoct some special delicacies, nothing heavy, perhaps something creative with the excellent fois gras they had only today taken delivery of...

James waved the man aside and turned on his iPad.

He sipped his red wine while lazily scrolling through

the pictures in front of him. Pictures of a house, neatly positioned in one of the leafy London suburbs, within handy commuting distance of the offices. Not a flashy apartment, which Jennifer accused his place of being… no porter sitting at the front behind a marble desk, which she found impersonal…no opulent artificial plants in the foyer, which she exclaimed weren't nearly as good as the real thing and must take for ever to dust, what a waste of someone's time.

A house in the suburbs that was already part of his vast property portfolio, which had last been rented out over a year ago and which had dropped off the radar since then. It couldn't compete with the ultra-modern places more centrally located, which appealed to expensive overseas executives. It had been brought to his attention by one of his people three weeks previously as just one of a batch to be considered for sale. He had pulled it out, seen it personally himself and made his decision on the spot to hang onto it. With some decent refurbishment, it would be perfect, and he had relished the thought of how delighted she would be at being able to move out of her poky shared house to a charming little cottage with a small but well-developed garden, a butcher, a baker and a candlestick maker within walking distance and a busy but distinct village atmosphere. Since then he had sent an expensive team of decorators in and it had been transformed, updated, modernised but retained its period style, which was the only stipulation he had made to the head of the design team. Perfect.

To think that six months earlier he might have sold it! Who said that life wasn't full of happy coincidences?

He sat back and contemplated, with satisfaction, the excitement on her face that he predicted he would see when he told her the good news. Whatever rent she was paying, he would make sure to charge less. In fact, he would happily charge nothing but he doubted she would accept that, given her stubbornness and her pride. It would be a done deal and he would no longer have to make allowances for her friend every time he visited her, tiptoeing just in case Ellie was asleep, making sure not to drink wine that wasn't Jennifer's or open beer that belonged to Ellie's boyfriend. Job done.

He glanced up, saw her hesitating by the door of the restaurant, casting her eyes around for him, and he turned off the computer, leaving it on the table next to him.

God, she was sex on legs. He had told her to don her finery, that the restaurant was one of the top ones in London, and she had. Winter was finally beginning to lose its icy winter edge as spring made itself felt and she was wearing a slim-fitting, figure-hugging dress in deep reds and browns with a pashmina artfully arranged loosely over her shoulders. Her curves seemed to grow more luscious by the day and his body was predictably reacting to the sway of her walk as she spotted him, to the sight of her cleavage, which even the modest neckline of the dress couldn't quite hide because her breasts were so lush and abundant.

For the first time, Jennifer watched James's lazy assessing smile and, instead of feeling thrilled, she felt the knot of tension in her stomach tighten.

How close she had come to cancelling out on this date! What an effort it had been to climb into clothes that had been so horribly inappropriate for her mood!

She had to force a returning smile on her face and by the time she made it to the table, her jaw was aching and her nervous system was in overdrive.

She slipped into the chair facing him, barely aware of the waiter pulling it out for her, and placed her hand over her wine glass, asking instead for a glass of fresh juice.

'You look stunning.' Deep blue eyes roved appreciatively over her. 'I'm going to enjoy taking that dress off you in a couple of hours…'

'I'm…sorry I'm a little late,' Jennifer said weakly, fiddling with the end of the pashmina.

'Traffic!' He threw his hands up in a gesture of frustration at the horrors of getting around London. He was picking up something, an uneasy atmosphere, something he couldn't quite put his finger on.

'Actually, the traffic was fine. I just…left my house later than I expected…'

'Woman's prerogative.'

'I'm never late, James. I hate it.'

'Well, you're here now. At least you haven't bailed on me because your house mate was feeling down and needed a shoulder to cry on.'

Jennifer flushed. Little did he know that her occasional cancellations had been carefully orchestrated. A sense of self-preservation had made her instil a small amount of distance and she was very glad of that now.

She fiddled with her hair, made a few polite noises about the restaurant, told him that there was no need to bring her to such an expensive place, that she was more than happy with cheap and cheerful.

'I've never been out with a woman who hasn't appreciated being taken to somewhere grand.'

'I'm not impressed by what money can buy, James. How many times have I told you that?' She heard the sharp edge in her voice and she watched as he frowned and narrowed his deep blue eyes on her.

'Are we going to have an argument?' He sat back and folded his arms. 'I should warn you that I have no intention of participating.'

Now that he mentioned it, an argument was just what Jennifer wanted, something to release the sick tension that had been building over the past few hours. An argument would be a solid staging post for what had to follow.

'I'm not having an argument with you. I'm saying that I'm not impressed by...*all this*. I mean, it's just one of the things that reveal how different you and I are. Fundamentally.'

'Come again?' James sat forward and this time the navy eyes were sharp. 'I thought you would like to be treated to a meal out somewhere fancy. I hadn't realised that you see it as a direct attack on your moral code and I certainly hadn't thought that I would be accused of...what is it exactly? That you're accusing me of...?'

'I'm not accusing you of anything. I'm just saying that this isn't the sort of place I would choose to eat. Waiters bowing and scraping, food that doesn't look like food—'

'Fine. We'll leave.' He made to stand up and Jennifer tugged him back down.

'Don't be silly.'

'What's going on?'

'Nothing. Nothing's going on. Well...'

'Well...what?'

'I've been thinking...' She drew in a gulp of air and had to fight a sudden attack of giddiness. Did he have to look at her like that? As though he could see straight into her head? Her heart was beating fast, a painful drum roll that added to the vertigo.

'Never a good idea.' His unease was growing by the second. 'My advice to you? Don't think. Just enjoy.'

'You don't know what I've been thinking.'

'I don't need to know. I can see from your face that whatever it is, I won't want to hear.'

'I just want you to know that I stick to what I've said all along, James. You and I aren't suited. We have fun together but, in the long run, we're like oil and water. We just don't have personalities that blend together. I mean, not in the long term.' She stared down at the swirling patterns of her dress.

'I have no idea what you're talking about and if you're going to say something, then I suggest you actually look me in the face when you say it.'

'This...' She looked at him. 'All of this...has been fun, really great and I appreciated every second of it, but I think...I think it might be time we call it a day.'

'I'm not hearing this.' He kept his voice very low and very even. If he gave in to what he was feeling, he thought he might end up doing untold damage to the exquisite, mind-blowingly expensive decor in the restaurant. 'You're breaking up with me. Is that what you're saying?'

'In a manner of speaking.'

'What the hell does *that* mean? I don't know what's going on here, but this is not the place for this conversation. We're going back to my apartment.'

'No!' Jennifer could think of nothing worse. The familiarity...the kitchen where they had prepared meals together reminding her of how much she was going to lose...the coffee table where they had sat only a couple of days ago playing Scrabble...which she had brought from the house with her and which she had forced him to play as a relaxation technique, although that had gone through the window when he had decided that there were other, more enjoyable ways of relaxing...the bedroom with the king-sized bed, which she would no longer occupy...

It would all be too much.

James held up both hands in surrender but his eyes were cool and questioning when they rested on her face.

'Look.' She splayed her fingers on the table and stared intently at them. 'There's something I need to tell you but, first of all, we need to get this whole relationship straight.

We need to admit that it was never going to stay the course. We need to break up.'

James raked his fingers through his hair and found that his hands were shaking. 'Between last night and tonight, you've suddenly decided that we need to *break up*...and you expect me to *go along with you*? I'm not admitting anything of the sort.'

'This isn't how I meant this conversation to be, James. This isn't where I thought I'd find myself, but something's...something's cropped up...'

'What?' With something to focus on, his mind went into free fall. It was a weird sensation, a feeling of utterly and completely losing all self-control. 'You've found someone else. Is that it?' His voice was incredulous. Break up? How long had she been contemplating *that*? Had there been some other man lurking in the background? One of those fictitious sensitive, emotionally savvy guys she had once told him made ideal partner material? He could think of no other reason for her to be sitting opposite him now telling him that *it had been fun but...*

'Don't be crazy. I haven't found anyone else. When would I have had time to go out looking?'

'Are you telling me that you think I've monopolised your life? Is that it? Because I'm perfectly happy to take things at a slower pace.' He could scarcely credit the levels to which he was willing to accommodate her.

Jennifer was sure that he would be. He hadn't emotionally invested. He could always tame his rampant libido until such time as it was no longer rampant.

'No, it's not that.'

'Let me get this straight. For no particular reason, you've suddenly decided that we can't go on. There's no one else on the scene, we've both been having fun and yet it's no longer enough. Am I missing something here? Because it feels as if I am.'

'There's no easy way of telling you this, James, so I'm just going to come right out and say it. I'm pregnant.'

She couldn't look him in the face when she said it so she stared down at her lap instead while the silence thickened around them like treacle.

'You can't be. You're using contraception. I've seen that little packet of pills in the bathroom. Are you telling me that you've been pretending to take them?' At some point, the wires in his brain appeared to have disconnected. In possession of one huge, life-changing fact, he found that he could only fall back on the pointless details around it. 'I can't talk to you here, Jennifer.'

'I'm not going to your apartment.'

'Why the hell not?'

'Because I want to deal with this situation in neutral territory.'

'Your choice of words is astounding.'

'How *else* do you want me to phrase it, James? Shall I start by telling you that I'm sorry? Well, I *am*. And before you even *think* of accusing me of getting pregnant on purpose, then I'm warning you not to go there because that's the *very last thing on earth* I would do.'

'Message received loud and clear!'

'I *have* been on the pill. I can only think that that first time…'

'We used a condom. We were protected. We were *always* protected. This is madness. I can't believe I'm hearing any of this.'

'Because you signed up for a life you could control!'

'It's not going to get either of us anywhere if we start arguing with one another!'

'You're right,' Jennifer whispered. 'And I didn't come

here to argue with you. I'm happy to take the blame. The first time we made love, I used a condom that I'd had for absolutely ages...' *Four years to be precise. How ironic that the condom she had bought to enjoy sex with him all those years ago had become the condom that allowed her to fall pregnant.* 'It may have perished. They can.' Salt water seeping through the foil would do that, she thought, and if not salt water when her bag had dropped into the sea, then an infinitesimal puncture with the sharp edge of a key, or nail clipper or tweezers or any of the hundred and one items she had flung in her bag next to it over the years.

She had gone on the pill the second they had returned to London because he had laughed and told her that he would be a pauper at the rate they went through condoms, little knowing that by then it had been too late.

'I did go on the pill when we got back here so I never noticed that I hardly had any kind of period at all and nothing a couple of weeks ago, so I decided to go and see the doctor just to make sure that I was on the right dosage. Anyway—'

'You're pregnant.' It was finally sinking in. 'You're going to have a baby.'

'I'm sorry.' His face was ashen. 'You're in shock. You must be. I understand that and I'm sorry that I've spoilt the meal but it's been on my mind all day and I just wanted to get it out of the way. And now that I have, I think the sensible thing to do would be for me to leave and for you to take a little time out to adjust to the idea, so...'

He was going to be a father!

'But why didn't I notice?' he asked, dazed.

'We never notice things we aren't expecting. Not really. And I'm not one of those rake-thin types who show every ounce of weight they put on. Apparently someone with a fuller figure can hide a pregnancy for a lot longer.' Part of her wished that he would be open with his displeasure. Instead, he looked like someone who had been punched in the stomach and, instead of reacting, decided to lie on the ground and curl up instead. It wasn't him! That in itself was proof of how thrown he was and of course he would be! She had had a head start in the shock stakes. She had had several hours in which to absorb the news. The accusations would come when it really and truly sank in, the reality, the consequences, the potential to throw his neatly ordered life out of sync for ever. The waiter came and was waved away.

'You're going to have my baby and you greet me with the opening words that you want out of the relationship?'

'We don't *have* a relationship.' Jennifer tensed as she sensed the shift in the atmosphere. He had looked glazed but now his eyes were sharpening and focusing on her. 'We have…had…a passing physical interest in each other. And don't look at me like that. You know that I'm just being honest.' Was he aware of the fleeting pause she allowed, a window in which he could contradict her, tell her that things had changed, that he might not have entered their relationship with a future in mind but had found commitment along the way? The brief silence went unfilled. 'Neither of us counted on this,' she said abruptly.

'You're going to have my baby and the only way you can think of dealing with the problem is by breaking up…'

Jennifer stiffened at his use of the word *problem*.

'It seems the best solution,' she said coolly. 'You didn't ask for this to arise and I'm not going to punish you, or me for that matter, by putting you in a position of having to stand by me whether you like it or not.'

'I don't believe I'm hearing this. We're lovers but have you forgotten that we also happen to be friends?'

She had forgotten neither but how could she explain

that a baby needed more than a couple united by passion? Or even, for that matter, friendship?

'So tell me,' James said with increasing cool, 'how do you see this panning out? Perhaps you'd like me to walk away from you and leave you to get on with it?'

'If that's what you want to do, then I'll accept it.'

'If you really think that that would be an option I would consider, then you don't know me very well, do you?'

Which was why, of course, she had pre-empted any re-action by breaking up with him. She had known that he wouldn't walk away from the situation. She could never have fallen head over heels in love with a man capable of doing that, and that in itself was the problem. James would want involvement. He would want to do the right thing but his heart wouldn't be in it. Any affection he felt for her would eventually wither away under the strain of having to deal with a child he hadn't asked for and being stuck with a woman he had never envisaged as long term.

'We'll have to get married.' Something powerful stirred inside him, something he could scarcely identify.

'And that's exactly why I opened this conversation by telling you that it's over between us,' Jennifer said quietly. 'I know you want to do the right thing, but it wouldn't be fair on either of us to be shackled to each other for the sake of a child.'

They both broke off while the waiter came to take their orders. James didn't bother to consult the menu. He ordered fish and she followed suit, not caring what she ate. Her appetite had deserted her.

'And marriage!' She leaned forward to continue where she had left off. 'I bet you've never given a passing thought to the idea of getting married, have you?'

'That's not the point.'

'It's exactly the point,' Jennifer cried. 'Marriage is

something serious. A commitment between two people who see their lives united for ever.'

'At least that's the romantic interpretation of it.'

'What other interpretation could there possibly be?'

'Something more pragmatic. Think about it. One in every three marriages ends in the divorce courts and all of those bitter, sad, divorced couples probably sat across each other at a dinner table holding hands and waxing lyrical about growing old together.'

'But for two out of those three, the holding hands and waxing lyrical works. They end up together.'

'You're an eternal optimist. Experience has taught me to be a little more cautious. But none of that matters and we could argue about it for the remainder of the evening. The fact is, we're in a situation where there's no choice.'

Jennifer's heart sank. If she didn't love him, maybe it would have been easier to settle for the solution that made sense, but if she married him, she would be torn apart.

'I'm sorry, James,' she said shakily, 'but the answer has to be no. I can't marry you because you think it makes sense. When I get married, I want it to be for all the right reasons. I don't want to settle for a reluctant husband who would rather be with someone else but finds himself stuck with me. How healthy would that be for our child, anyway?'

How could life be suddenly turned on its head in the space of a few short hours? Very easily was the conclusion he was reaching as he looked at her stubborn, closed expression.

Rage at her blinding intransigence rushed through him in a tidal wave. 'And tell me this. How healthy would it be for our child to grow up without both parents there? Because that's something you need to consider! This isn't about you and your romantic notions of fairy-tale endings!'

Jennifer flinched and looked away. 'You're not going to make me change my mind,' she said, gathering all the strength at her disposal.

'No? Then let me provide you with an alternative scenario. Our child grows up in a split family and in due course finds out that both of us could have been there but you wouldn't have it because you were determined to look for Mr Right, who may or may not come along. And if he does coming along…well, I'm telling you right now that he won't be involved in bringing up my child because I'll fight for custody.'

Battle lines had been drawn but Jennifer could scarcely think so far ahead.

'And your father. What do you intend to tell *him*?' This before she had had time to digest his previous statement.

'I haven't thought—'

'Because don't even think about insinuating to your father that I haven't offered to do the decent thing. I intend to make it perfectly clear to my mother and to John that I've proposed to you and that you have in your wisdom decided that the best course of action is to go it alone. We can see what they make of that.'

'I don't want to fall out over this—'

'Then maybe you should have thought about broaching this bombshell in a slightly different way!'

'It wouldn't have made any difference. The result would have been the same and I'm sorry about that. Look, I can't eat any more. I've lost my appetite. I think I should go back home now.' She half stood, swayed and sat back down. In an instant, James was at her side, all thoughts of pursuing his argument forgotten.

Jennifer was barely aware of him settling the bill, leaving a more than generous tip for the waiter, who had sensed an atmosphere and had patiently left them alone. She had her head in her hands.

'Honestly, I'm fine, James,' she protested weakly as soon as they were out of the restaurant.

'How long have these giddy spells been going on?'

'I get them now and again. It's nothing to worry about...' But it was comforting to have his arms around her, supporting her as he hailed a black cab and settled her inside as though she were a piece of porcelain.

'What did the doctor say?'

'I didn't mention them. I was too shocked at finding out I was pregnant!'

'You should go back. Have a complete check-up. What's with these people? Don't they know how to do their jobs?'

'Don't worry. It's nothing!'

For the first time since finding out about the pregnancy, she wondered whether she was making the right decision in turning down his proposal. Whether he loved her or not, he was a source of strength and when would she need that strength more than right now? When she was facing motherhood? He wanted to do the right thing. Was it selfish of her to hold tight to her principles? Or in the big scheme of things, was *he* right? Could his suggestion of a loveless marriage be the right one?

The questions churned around in her head for the duration of the trip back to her house although by the time they got there, the giddiness had disappeared, replaced by utter exhaustion.

'We can talk about this tomorrow,' she told him by the front door and James looked at her in glowering frustration, his hands jammed into his pockets.

'We weren't talking back there. You were dictating terms and I was supposed to listen and obey.'

'It's hard for me too, James, but marriage is a big deal

for me and I want to marry a guy who wants me in his life for all the right reasons.'

'Weren't you happy when we were together?' he asked gruffly and, taken aback by the directness of the question, Jennifer nodded.

'So now that there's a baby, why would that change?'

'Because,' Jennifer said helplessly, 'it's not just about having lots of sex until it fizzles out and we say goodbye to one another and move on.'

'But the having lots of sex is a start.'

'You're so physical, James.' She could feel her body quivering at the hundreds of memories she had of them making love. She would never forget a single one of them. 'The cab driver's going to start getting impatient.'

'Why? It's good money sitting there with the meter running. We still need to talk this one through. In fact, let me get rid of him. I could come in with you. The lights are all off, which means your house mate probably isn't here. We could discuss this in private...'

What he meant was that they would make love. It was the language he spoke most fluently and she knew she couldn't trust herself if they climbed into bed together.

'We both need to think about this.' She placed her hand on his chest to stop him from following her into the house. 'Tomorrow we'll think about the practicalities. And by the way, I would never tell Dad that you weren't taking the responsible attitude, James,' she returned to the insinuation she had never protested.

He nodded, at a loss for anything else to say. What did she mean about right reasons? Wasn't a child a good enough reason for them to be married? It wasn't as though they didn't get along, weren't fantastically suited in bed. He was genuinely bewildered at his failure to convince her.

He wondered whether he should have taken a step back,

led up gently to the notion of getting married. She had stated from the very beginning that she wasn't looking for commitment and yet he had jumped in, feet first, arrogantly assuming that she would fall in line with what he wanted. But how could she fail to see that getting married was the most practical solution to the situation? And what about *them*? Was what they had about to dissolve because a baby on the way had crystallised the fact that she didn't see him as a long-term partner? He felt hollow and angry and impotent.

At any rate, there was nothing to be gained by continuing to push her into the decision he wanted her to take. It was clear that she wasn't about to let him into the house and she looked utterly shattered. For her own good, he knew that he should go and let her get some rest, but he still hesitated because he couldn't think of her walking away from him. It wasn't going to happen. He would make sure of that.

His mind returned to that picture-perfect house, bristling with new furniture, updated to within an inch of its life, perched in its very own garden, a stone's throw from all those quaint village services she had always raved about. He had intended to present it to her with casual indifference, a little something he had pulled out of his portfolio. He would have offered it to her at a laughably low rental and suggested that it would hit the open market if she decided not to take it because of her pride. Faced with that, he had known that she would not have been able to resist.

Well, the house was still there but now it would be his trump card.

The sick feeling of helplessness that had earlier gripped him began to dissipate. He was a man who thought quickly and made decisions at the speed of light. He was a man who found solutions. He had extended the obvious solution and had been knocked back, but now he had another solution up his sleeve and thank God for that. For a few minutes back there, he had not been able to think clearly.

'You're right,' he said heavily. 'Although I don't like leaving you like this. You look as though you're about to collapse.'

'It's been a long day.' For one craven, cowardly moment Jennifer was tempted to open the door for him, let him in so that she could curl up in his arms and fall asleep. She just wanted to hold him close because he made her feel safe.

'Tomorrow, then,' he murmured, badly wanting to touch her but instead pushing himself away from the doorframe. 'If you still want to meet on neutral territory, then we will. If you're agreeable to coming to my apartment, I will get my caterer to prepare something. We can talk about what happens next...take it from there...'

CHAPTER EIGHT

TAKE it from there...yes. Discuss the practicalities...of course. But are you excited...even just a little...?

That was the question Jennifer would really have liked to have asked him. Once she had recovered from the shock of being told that she was pregnant, she had been thrilled at the thought of having a baby, of having *James's* baby. In the space of twenty-four hours, she had managed to wonder what the baby would look like, what sex it would be, whether he or she would attend a single-sex school or a mixed one, what career path he or she would follow, what his or her girlfriends or boyfriends would do for a living and at what age he or she would be married.

She was *excited*.

She didn't think that excitement would feature on James's chart of possible reactions to the news. She thought that the best she could hope for would maybe be *acceptance* and its close relation, *resignation*.

How could he not see that any marriage based on a situation where those two damning words were involved would never be anything more than a marriage of convenience? Destined to eventually fail because the last thing a marriage should ever be was *convenient*?

Nevertheless, that didn't stop Jennifer wondering what it would be like to be married to him. She marvelled, sitting in the back of the chauffeur-driven car he had sent for her, how close she could be to everything she had ever dared hope for while still being so far. She wondered whether his anger and disappointment at what had happened would have gathered steam overnight. Had he lain awake thinking that, thanks to her idiocy, his plans for his life were now lying in ruins at his feet? Without a roomful of unwitting chaperones to keep the full extent of his reactions at bay, would he feel free in the privacy of his own apartment to really let rip when she showed up?

At any rate, they were going to have to reach some sort of agreement with regards to the way forward because she couldn't keep her father in the dark for ever. She was due to visit the following weekend and she intended to break the news then that he would be a grandfather.

With the days getting longer, it was still bright by the time she got to his apartment at a little after six and there was no time to brace herself for the sight of him because he was waiting for her in the marbled foyer as she entered. Fresh from work and still in his suit, although without a jacket and with the sleeves of his white shirt rolled to his elbows and his tie loosely pulled down to allow the top two buttons of his shirt to be undone.

'Oh.' Jennifer came to a dead stop as she was buzzed in. 'Have you just arrived from work? You should have called and asked me to get here a bit later. I wouldn't have minded.' All over again, she felt that powerful sensual tug towards him, as though her body had a will of its own the second she was in his presence.

James frowned. He had grown accustomed to her exuberance. Her awkward formality was a jarring reminder of the situation in which they had now found themselves. He shoved his hands in his pockets and took a few seconds to look at her. She was wearing a stretchy knee-length dress in shades of green and was it his imagination or could he now see evidence of her pregnancy? More rounded curves, breasts that would be substantially bigger than a handful... On cue, he felt himself harden and, given the inappropriateness of the moment, he dealt with that by walking towards her and keeping his eyes firmly focused on her face.

'Don't worry about it. Plans have changed. We won't be heading up to the apartment.'

'Where are we going?'

'Should you be wearing such tight dresses?' He cupped her elbow with his hand and hustled her back towards the front door. 'Now that you're pregnant?' Hell, she looked even sexier than ever. What man wouldn't run into a lamp post trying to catch a backward glance at her luscious body. 'Your breasts are spilling out of the top of that dress!'

'Yes, I've put on some weight.' Jennifer felt herself flush at the thought that he might be turned off at the sight of her increasing size. He was, after all, a man who was primarily concerned with the whole 'body beautiful' rubbish. If he wanted her to hide herself in smocks now, then what on earth was he going to do when she reached the size of a barrage balloon?

'I don't need to get into maternity frocks just yet,' she snapped, watching as the chauffeur hurried to open the passenger door for her. 'Some women *never* buy maternity clothes! Have you seen how unappealing they can be?'

'You won't be one of those women.' He grimaced in distaste at the memory of a certain recent magazine cover that had been lying around his apartment, courtesy of Jennifer. It had featured a semi naked actress, heavily pregnant, in a few shreds of clothing that had done nothing to conceal her enormous belly.

'You can't tell me what I can or can't wear!'

'I just have. Tomorrow we'll go shopping. Get you some looser stuff.'

'Is that one of the *practicalities* you were planning on talking to me about?' She spun to face him as soon as the passenger door had slammed behind him. 'Because if it was, then you can consider it discussed and struck off the list!'

James gritted his teeth in frustration. Not the perfect start to the evening.

In the ensuing silence, Jennifer debated whether she should apologise for overreacting and decided firmly against it.

'Where are we going?' she asked eventually.

'There's something I'd like to show you.'

'Really? But I thought we were going to discuss…how we're going to deal with the situation…'

'Consider what I show you as part of the ongoing conversation on the subject. Were you all right when you got back to your place last night?'

'What do you mean?'

'You felt faint at the restaurant.'

'Oh, yes. Well, that was just my nerves.' She rested her head against the window and looked at him from under her lashes. 'I know you think that I'm being unreasonable, James…'

'This is a debate that can only end up going round in circles, Jennifer. Let's put it on the back burner for the moment and concentrate on a more productive way forward, shall we?' They had cleared the centre of London in record time and were now heading south west. 'Question—when do you intend to break the news to John? I'd like to be there.'

'I don't see why—'

'Is every suggestion I make going to end in a point-less argument?'

'I'm sorry. I don't mean to be difficult.'

'Good. At least we agree on one thing. It's a start!'

'There's no need to be sarcastic, James. I'm trying my best.' She looked away quickly. Honesty forced her to admit to herself that that was hardly the strict truth. So far he had risen admirably to the occasion and she had re-lentlessly shot him down in flames. Was it his fault that he couldn't supply her with the words that she wanted to hear? He had not once apportioned any blame on her shoulders, even though he must surely be blaming her in his head. He had offered to do the decent thing and was probably baffled by her refusal to even consider the possibility of marriage. He had no intention of leaving her in the lurch even though he doubtless wanted to run as far as his feet could take him to the farthest corner of the earth because fatherhood, for the man who couldn't commit, would have been the final albatross around his neck. His *one hundred per cent innocent* neck.

He wanted to do what was best for the baby growing inside her, *their baby*, and all she could think was that he didn't love her, that she would become a burden, that he would end up hating her. He was thinking of the baby. She, on the other hand, was thinking about herself.

Consumed by a sudden attack of guilt, Jennifer lapsed into nervous silence and watched as they cleared through the busiest part of London, heading out until increasing patches of greenery replaced the unremitting grey of pave-ments and roads.

She still had no idea where they were heading and was surprised when, eventually, the car weaved through a se-ries of small streets, emerging in front of a house that looked as though it had leapt out of a story book.

'Where are we?' She looked at him with bewilderment and James offered her a ghost of a smile.

Thirty-six hours ago, he thought, this would have been a terrific surprise for her. Now, it was part of his back-up plan.

'We're in one of the leafier parts of London.'

'I didn't think they existed. At least, not like this...' She couldn't take her eyes off the picture-perfect house in front of her. The small front garden was a riot of flowers on the verge of bursting into summer colour. A path led to the front door of the house, which was small but exqui-site. A child's painting of a house, perfectly proportioned with massive bay windows on the ground floor, flanking a black door, a chimney minus the smoke, beautiful aged stone awash with wisteria. To one side was a garage and to the other one mature tree, behind which peeped a lawn swerving away towards the back of the house.

'Who lives here?' she asked suspiciously. 'If you had told me that we would be visiting friends of yours, then I might have worn something different.' She was annoyed to discover that she was already thinking about chang-ing her wardrobe, stocking it with baggier, more shape-less garments even though she had protested otherwise.

'It's one of the properties in my private portfolio.' He was already unlocking the front door, pushing it open and standing aside to let her brush past him.

'You never mentioned this!'

'I never saw the need.'

'It's wonderful, James.' Flagstones in the hallway, cream walls recently painted from the looks of it, a deep burnished wooden banister leading up to the first floor. Jennifer tentatively took a few steps forward and then, be-coming braver, began exploring the house. It was much bigger on the inside than it looked from the outside.

Downstairs, a range of rooms radiated from the central hallway. There was a small but comfortable sitting room, a dining room, a box room with built in shelves and cupboards that had clearly been used as an office, a separate television room and, of course, the kitchen, which had been extended so that it was easily big enough to fit a generous-sized table as well as furniture. It was a kitchen and conservatory without the division of walls. French doors led out to a perfectly landscaped garden. Whoever had owned the house previously had been a keen gardener with an eye for detail. Various fruit trees lined the perimeter of the garden and between them nestled a bench from which you could look back towards the house and appreciate the abundance of plants and flowers.

'Gosh.' Eyes gleaming, Jennifer turned back to James. 'I can't believe you would ever choose to live where you do when this place could have been an option.'

'It's very country cottage. Why don't you come and see the upstairs? I think you'll like the four-poster bed in the master bedroom. Everything has been done to the highest possible standard while maintaining the period of the place. Did you get a chance to see the Aga in the kitchen? I can't think that there would be many properties in London boasting one of those.' He wondered what on earth someone would do with one of those. He had no idea. It looked like a baffling piece of kitchen equipment, but she had wistfully mentioned them in the past and he had taken mental note. In fact, he had furnished the house with her in mind. He had been surprised at how many details of her likes and dislikes he had gathered and stored over time.

'You sound like an estate agent.' But for the first time since she had broken the news, James could see laughter in her eyes. Where he had failed, the house appeared to be succeeding, and before she could remember that she was fighting him he ushered her up the stairs so that she could gasp and admire the bedrooms, the bathrooms, the walk-in dressing room in the master bedroom.

'So,' he said, once they had returned to the kitchen and taken up position at the wooden kitchen table, wooden because she had previously expressed a dislike for all things chrome and glass, 'what do you think of the place?'

'You know what I think, James. I imagine it's been written all over my face.'

'Good. Because this is one of the practicalities I want to talk to you about. A shared house isn't going to be suitable for a baby. This, on the other hand...' He made a sweeping gesture to encompass the cottage while keeping his deep blue eyes firmly fixed on her face.

He could see the indecision on her face and had to fight down the desire to tell her that she had no choice in the matter. Laying down laws and trying to browbeat her into submission hadn't worked. 'I firmly believe,' he carried on smoothly, just as she was about to say something, 'that children benefit from a more relaxed lifestyle than living in the centre of London can provide for them. Don't you remember how much fun it was for you growing up in the countryside? Granted this is nothing like the countryside but there's a garden, quite a big one by London standards, and all the shops you might need are within walking distance.'

'But don't you have plans for this place? I mean, was it rented out before? I hope you didn't turf out any tenants, James.'

'Your faith in me knows no bounds,' he said drily, knowing that part one of the battle had been won. 'I didn't turf anyone out. You like the place and I think it would be ideal. It's within commuting distance from London. In fact, surprisingly convenient for the underground...which brings me to the small matter of your job.' Which, he could see from the expression on her face, was something she had given no thought to.

'My job…I hadn't really thought…'

'It's going to be awkward.'

'Are you telling me that I'm out of a job?' Jennifer demanded, bristling.

'Far be it from me to tell you anything of the sort. But think about it. You're pregnant. You won't be able to keep it under wraps and sooner or later it's going to emerge that I'm the father. Might not be the most comfortable situation in the world for you…'

'So I leave and do what?'

'Practicality number two. Money. Naturally, if you want to stay on at the company then there's no way I would stand in your way. I have no problem dealing with whispers behind my back and if you think you can deal with that as well, then I'll support you one hundred per cent in staying on.' He allowed a few seconds of silence to follow that statement. It took a strong person to survive the toxicity of office politics. 'At any rate, whether you continue working or not, I intend to open a bank account for you and, just in case you want to argue with me over this, I'm telling you right now that no child of mine will want for anything because you're too proud to accept money from me.'

'I have no objection to you paying for our child, James,' Jennifer muttered awkwardly as she feverishly played in her mind the scenario of her co-workers gossiping behind her back. She could be a genius at her job and would still not be able to fight the rumours that she had got where she was because she had been sleeping with her boss. Pregnant by him would stoke the fires from a slow simmer to a blazing inferno.

'*You* come as part of the deal, Jen,' James said gently. 'I intend to ensure that your bank balance allows you freedom to choose what you want to do. Carry on working for the company, go ahead. Find another job closer to this place, then feel free. Give up work altogether, then I'm one hundred per cent happy with that solution. It's up to you. Of course...' he appeared to mull over his next few words '...I'm jumping the gun here, assuming that you don't have a problem moving out here...'

'It might be better all round to be out of central London,' Jennifer concurred, trying hard not to show her relief at leaving the house. Ellie was free, single and disengaged. She played loud music and entertained her boyfriends with exuberance. It was her house. In between all the other stresses, Jennifer had wondered how a baby would feature in that set-up. She sneaked a glance at the super modern kitchen, the granite work surfaces, which blended so harmoniously with the old-fashioned dresser and the mellow kitchen table with mismatched, charming chairs. She could get a kitten.

'And the job?'

'I'll have to think about that.'

'But not for too long, I hope. Your replacement would have to be found,' he murmured. 'Could take ages...but moving on from there to the thorny subject of our parents...'

'I told you...I'm going to break it to Dad on the weekend.'

'I'd also like my mother to be present...'

'Yes. Of course.' She hadn't actually dwelled on that particular horror waiting round the corner, but, of course, Daisy would have to be present.

'How do you think they're going to take the news?'

'Why are you talking about this,' she said with a hint of desperation. 'I'm just living one day at a time.'

'Which doesn't mean that tomorrow isn't going to come.'

'I know *that*.'

'Do you?'

'Of course I do! I'm not a complete idiot. I know there are going to be lots of complications to sort out along the way but at least we've managed to do something about the first one. I mean, I *had* actually wondered whether sharing Ellie's house was going to be suitable for a baby. And it's a busy road. I've always felt sorry for those women pushing buggies on crowded streets, trying to get them on and off the buses…'

'The cottage is vacant. I'll make sure that you're moved by the end of next week. You won't have to lift a finger.'

Hearing him say that was like heaven to her ears. She didn't want to feel burdensome to a man who didn't love her, but, still, she could feel his strength seep into her and the temptation to close her eyes and lean on him was so great that she felt giddy.

James stood up, walked to the fridge and told her that he had taken the liberty of getting his caterers to prepare a light supper for them.

'Sit,' he ordered, when she automatically began rising to her feet. 'I've got this.'

'I feel like I'm on a roller-coaster ride with someone else manning the controls,' Jennifer mumbled, but half-heartedly, and he glanced across at her with a crooked smile.

'Go with it.'

'But I don't want you to feel that you've got to play the responsible role,' she protested, clinging to her principles by the tips of her fingers. 'You haven't listened to what

I've said. You don't have to *take care of me*. It's enough
that you're allowing me to move to this cottage.'

'And you haven't listened to *me*. I intend to be fully
involved. I have no intention of letting you play the independent woman, keeping me at a distance while you wait
for Mr Right to come along.' Just thinking about that set
his teeth on edge. Food ready, James took it to the table in
its original containers, which he had stuck in the micro-
wave, and placed two plates and cutlery alongside them.

'We have to get past this…atmosphere…' he gritted,
sitting back and waiting as she dished out some of the one-
pot dinner for herself. He had had a little time to think
about the change in her attitude towards him and he had
worked out the reason behind it. Where their relationship
had always been one of easy-going friendship, which had
developed into something even more so after they had
become lovers, the fact of her unexpected pregnancy had
thrown up all the downsides to what they had. She could
no longer relax with him because she now felt trapped,
hemmed in by a situation she couldn't reverse and, in
one way or another, stuck with someone she had always
planned on moving away from eventually. She wasn't in it
through free choice. She was in it through lack of option.

Which didn't mean that he was going to allow himself
to be shunted aside so that she could start her search for
her knight in shining armour the second their baby was
born. No way.

Which, in turn, brought him to the delicate part of the
proceedings.

He thoughtfully worked his way through the meal in
front of him, half listening as she tried to assure him that
there was *no atmosphere*, that she was *just tense, that's
all*, that she was very pleased that they were both being

so adult about everything. In mid-sentence, he cut her short by raising his hand, and Jennifer stuttered to silence.

'Why don't we go and relax in the sitting room?'

'It feels odd…when someone's probably just left this place…'

'Let me dispel that myth,' he drawled, getting to his feet. 'The house was last rented out over ten months ago. It's just been recently refurbished.'

'Has it? Why? Were you going to put it on for rental again?'

James flushed darkly. 'It doesn't matter.'

'So…all this furniture is new?' Jennifer stood up, marvelling that there was not a single thing in the house that she wouldn't have chosen herself.

'Yes, I had my people equip it,' he allowed, omitting the fact that he had personally instructed them in what to buy.

'They couldn't have chosen better.' Jennifer gazed admiringly at the deep, plush sofa in the sitting room, the broad comfortable chairs on either side of it. Every detail took her breath away, from the rich burgundy drapes to the intricate Persian rug covering the polished wooden floor.

She flopped onto the sofa and curled her legs under her. Disturbingly, because she was determined to keep her distance, James sat next to her, then turned, his arms along the back of the sofa and behind her.

'So…'

'So…?' She could feel her heartbeat pick up and a fine film of perspiration break out over her body.

'So I want you to tell me why the atmosphere has changed so fast between us…'

'Well, isn't it obvious?' Jennifer stammered. She blinked rapidly to try and stabilise her nerves, which were suddenly in wild free fall. Two days ago, she would have been in his arms right now, two days ago they would have been making love. Yes, things had changed, but he would still be bemused by her retreat. Without the complication of being emotionally involved, lust, for him, would still be intact.

'Nope.' He inclined his head and continued staring at her.

Jennifer wished that she had some sharp retort to counter that, but she didn't. She was suddenly hot and bothered and flustered and very much aware of his proximity.

'Then it should be...'

'Why is that?' He sighed and raked his fingers through his hair in a gesture that was so familiar that Jennifer felt her heart tug painfully. 'Has pregnancy done something to your hormones? Turned you off sex? Or have you suddenly found that you're no longer attracted to me because you're carrying my baby?'

'No!' The hot denial was out before she had time to think about it and swallow the shaming truth back down. 'I mean...'

'You mean you *are* still attracted to me,' James murmured with satisfaction.

'That's not the point!'

'The point being?'

'The point being that there's more at stake than just the two of us being attracted to each other and *having fun*, no *strings attached*.'

'You say *having fun* as though it's a crime against humanity.'

'Stop confusing me,' Jennifer cried, standing up agitatedly and pacing the sitting room, aware of his deep blue eyes thoughtfully following her. She paused to stand in front of him. She was fired up with a tangle of confusing emotions. She could barely think properly. She wasn't expecting him to reach out and place his hand gently on her stomach. She froze.

'I want to feel it,' James said unevenly. Children had never appeared on his radar but now that he knew that she was carrying his child, he was driven to have tangible evidence of it, wanted to feel the more rounded stomach.

'When will you feel it moving?'

'James, please…'

'I took part in the creation…surely you wouldn't deny me the chance to feel it?' He slipped his hands under her dress and gently tugged it up to expose her stomach. He felt her release her breath on a shudder but she didn't move away. How oblivious had he been? She was by no means big but she was certainly bigger than when they had first become lovers, her stomach smooth and firm but no longer flat. She was wearing little cotton briefs and they were low enough for him to see the shadow of soft, downy hair peeping above the elastic band.

He closed his eyes, faint with an overwhelming surge of intense, driven craving. It was like nothing he had ever felt in his life before. He had had friends who had wittered interminably about the joys of parenthood, who had reliably informed him that having a baby was like nothing on earth. He had always listened politely and promptly shoved the rhapsodies into the waste disposal unit in his head. Now, he wondered…was this what it was all about? This weird feeling that left him shaken and uncharacteristically out of control?

He would savour the moment and not question its origin. He felt her fingers settle into his hair as he shoved the dress farther up so that her bra was just visible.

With a soft tug he pulled her towards him onto the sofa and she fell with a little thud into the squashy cushions.

Jennifer knew that this was not how the evening was

supposed to proceed. She was *vulnerable* and should be *protecting herself*. That certainly did not include letting him pull her dress over her head, which he was now doing, not to mention unhook her bra so that he could ease it off her shoulders to expose breasts that were sensitive and tingling with wanting him to touch them.

Which, of course, he did, but not until he had told her how her body had changed.

He grazed his teeth against her nipples, sending a compulsive shiver rippling through her body. 'How couldn't I have seen the changes to your body?'

'You weren't looking,' Jennifer breathed unevenly. 'Nor was I and, like I've said, we just don't really notice what we're not expecting.' In fact, she had known that she had put on weight, but she had assumed that it was because she had been eating more, enjoying the domestic life with a man who refused to be tamed.

James barely heard her. He was too busy licking and tasting her, circling the stiff buds with his tongue before lavishing his attention on them in turn. She arched up, eyes closed, with her hands clasped behind her back.

His mouth was clamped on one nipple and as he sucked it she twisted and moaned, automatically parting her legs, inviting his hand to cup the throbbing mound between her thighs.

He could feel her dampness seeping through the cotton underwear but he was in no hurry to take off the flimsy garment. Instead, he pressed down and kept up the insistent pressure as he continued to lose himself in her glorious breasts. He liked the way she writhed every time he dipped his fingers deeper into her wetness. How could she hold herself at a distance from him? How could she deny that what they had together was good? Beyond good? He slipped his hand underneath the briefs and she groaned as his searching fingers began stroking her, over and over and over again, rubbing her clitoris until she wanted to pass out with pleasure.

They made love slowly, as though they had all the time in the world, and afterwards she almost dozed off in his arms.

'We shouldn't have done that,' was what she said instead, hating herself for having succumbed and terrified that it would just be the start of a pattern. He would get too close and she would give in because she was weak. She scrambled to push herself away from him but he yanked her back.

'Try and say that with conviction and I might start believing you.'

'I mean it, James. It's not on.'

'That's not what your body spent the past hour telling me.'

'And I don't *want* to let *my body* deal with this situation!' She pushed against him and scrambled around for her clothes, ashamed of herself.

James propped himself up and looked at her as she wriggled into the dress.

'I know you don't,' he agreed gravely, and Jennifer shot him a suspicious look from under her lashes.

'You do?' She looked at him uncertainly.

James sat up, strolled to where his boxers had been tossed, put them on and then turned to look at her.

'You're still attracted to me but you don't want that to get in the way of making what you think is the right decision.'

'Well…yes.' She sat back down, although this time on one of the chairs instead of on the sofa. Her body was as stiff as board and her hands rested primly on her knees as she continued to warily look at him. Fading light made his half-clothed body look as sculpted and as perfect as a classical Greek statue. She thought it would help if he could stick a shirt on.

'And I apologise unreservedly if I took advantage of your weakness and seduced you.'

'Well, you're not entirely to blame...' Jennifer was driven to admit, looking away with a guilty flush.

'Of course you're not going to want to get back into the situation we had, given the circumstances.'

'No-o-o...' Jennifer dragged out that one syllable for as long as she could while she tried to figure out where his speech was going.

'In a matter like this, you simply don't see the value of thinking with your head.'

'It's not *that*—'

'And I won't waste time trying to make you see that this is *just* the time when you *should* be thinking with your head. You don't want to marry me and I accept that.'

'Really? You do?' Why did that hurt so much?

'Why do you sound so surprised?'

'Because you seemed so convinced that getting married was the only option we had. As if we were still living in Victorian times and you had to make an honest woman of me, however unhappy we might both have ended up being!'

James held his cool and continued to look steadily at her. 'Let's just say that I'm willing to make compromises in that area.'

'What sort of compromises?'

'You move in here and I move in with you. No marriage, but I think we should see how it works out, give this a chance for the sake of the baby. If it doesn't work out, then we do the modern thing and walk away from each other.' He flushed darkly and looked away. 'We were happy…before this all blew up,' he said in a rough undertone. 'What's to say that we couldn't be happy again?'

CHAPTER NINE

JAMES didn't realise just how happy life with Jennifer was until he got her panicked call in the middle of a meeting.

When he had suggested that they live together, he had had no idea what he had been letting himself in for. He was a man accustomed to freedom of movement and independence, fundamentally unanswerable to anyone. Of course, he acknowledged that that state of affairs had undergone some change in the weeks after they had become lovers. He had also acknowledged that had she agreed to his original terms they would probably have been married by now, but somehow the fact of marriage had seemed less daunting than the fact of living together.

With a sense of duty no longer in the equation, living together had struck him as more of a commitment, even though he couldn't fathom why.

He had engineered a smooth transition for her from apartment to house. Despite her reassurances that she was as healthy as a horse, waving aside the occasional giddy spell as nothing to worry about, insisting that she continue working until a suitable replacement was found for her position, he made sure that she had as little to do as humanly possible during the actual move. Packing a few personal items into a suitcase was just about all he allowed her to get away with.

Clearing his own apartment had been a far weirder experience. The enormity of what he was doing only struck him when, after two days and a lot of overtime from engineers kitting out an office space in the house, he finally closed the front door on the outside world and joined her in the kitchen for their first meal as…a couple living together.

It had felt like a massive step but he had made sure to conceal any trepidation from her. He knew that she remained wary and hesitant and pregnancy appeared to have made her unpredictable. It happened. He knew. He had surreptitiously bought a pregnancy book and had read it cover to cover. He now felt equipped to start his own advice column.

'James…do you think you could get here?'

'What's wrong?' Few people had his private cell number. He had felt his phone vibrate in his pocket and her name had popped up. Immediately he had silently indicated to the assembled financiers that they should continue with the meeting and he had left the conference room. When she had started working at the little publishing company that he had inherited as part of the much bigger takeover package, Jennifer had never contacted him. She had quit two weeks previously and not once had she called him at work, even though he had repeatedly told her that she was more than welcome to interrupt his working day.

If the tone of her voice hadn't alerted him that something was wrong, the mere fact that she had called would have.

An emotion shifted into gear that he almost couldn't recognise. It was fear.

'I'm bleeding…I'm sure there's nothing to worry about—'

'I'm on my way.'

Jennifer lay back on the sofa with her legs raised and

tried to stay calm. Looking around her, she took in all the small touches she had introduced to the house that had very quickly felt like a home. The vases filled with flowers picked from the garden, the framed photos on the mantelpiece, the ornaments she had picked up from Portobello Market a couple of weekends previously. She wasn't entirely certain that James even noticed them and she hadn't wanted to point them out.

She had been gutted when all talk of marriage had been dropped so quickly. Had he been relieved that that final act of commitment had been avoided? Living together was so different and, of course, she had no one but herself to blame for not grabbing his marriage proposal when it had been on the cards.

Not that she regretted it. She still believed that without love a marriage was nothing more than a sham and yet...

Hadn't he been just the perfect partner ever since they had moved in together? She constantly told him that there was no need for him to treat her as though she could break at any given moment, and yet hadn't she loved every minute of it? Hadn't she begun to hope that the love he didn't feel for her might begin to grow from affection?

And now...

Jennifer didn't want to think that she might lose this baby. She wished that she had paid more attention to those dizzy spells she had been having off and on. If she lost the baby, then what would happen to her and James? It was a question she didn't want to think about because the answer was too agonising to deal with.

She closed her eyes and kept as still as possible but her mind continued to freewheel inside her head, irrespective of her desperation to keep it under control. She had already invested so much love into this unborn baby. How would she cope if anything happened?

She sagged with blessed relief as she heard the sound of James's key being inserted into the door, and he was in the act of removing his jacket as he pushed open the sitting room door and strode towards her, his face grey with worry.

'I shouldn't have bothered you—'. She smiled weakly as he snapped out his mobile and began dialling.

'And hurry!'

'Who have you called?'

'The doctor.'

'I panicked. I'm sorry, James. I'm sure all I need is a bit of rest.'

James knelt down next to her and slipped her hand into his. 'You're not a doctor, Jen. You don't know what you need. Gregory is the top guy in London and a personal friend of the family. I asked him whether I should get an ambulance to take you to hospital but he said that he'll give you the once-over first. You scared the hell out of me.'

'I didn't mean to.'

He asked her about her symptoms, detailed questions to which she produced a series of clinical answers, and she smiled when he confessed to the pregnancy book languishing in his briefcase.

'A little knowledge is a dangerous thing, James.'

'Why didn't you tell me sooner that the giddy spells hadn't stopped?'

'I didn't want to worry you. I didn't think that there was anything to worry about...' And besides, she could have added truthfully, she hadn't wanted to rock the boat. She hadn't wanted to face up to anything that might cast a shadow over the picture-perfect life they had been living for the past few weeks. Except uncomfortable questions couldn't be put to bed by ignoring them and they were out of the box now, demanding attention.

'I know you're going to tell me that this isn't the right time to have this conversation, James, but—'

'It's the right time.'

Jennifer's eyes fluttered and she felt her heartbeat quicken.

'You don't know what I'm going to say...'

'I do.' He smiled crookedly at her. 'Do you think I don't know you a bit by now? Whenever you want to broach a delicate topic of conversation, you lick your lips for courage and begin to play with your hair.'

'I didn't think you noticed stuff like that.'

'You'd be surprised what I notice.' *About you.* 'You won't lose this baby.'

'You can't say that and what if I do?' There. It was out. She closed her eyes and calmed herself by taking deep breaths. Deliberately, she stuck her hands by her sides and fidgeted with the baggy tee shirt she was wearing.

'Then the time is right for us to talk about what happens. Before Gregory gets here. Stress isn't good for you and I don't want to stress you out but I need to say something.'

Jennifer looked at him with resignation. She wanted to put her hand over his mouth and hold the words back but he was right. He needed to tell her that their arrangement would not survive a miscarriage. The stress of hearing it would be a great deal less than the stress of lying here pretending that everything was just fine. And if she didn't lose the baby, then it would be good to know the next step forward. She realised that through the happiness and joy of the past few weeks, there had remained a poisonous thread of doubt that things would continue the way they were for ever more. That just wasn't how life worked. Now, he would put a face to those doubtful shadows and, yes, there would be disappointment all round, because their respective parents had accepted the situation and given their full support, but life was full of disappointment, wasn't it?

'I know that sharing this house with me probably wasn't what you had in mind when you realised that you were pregnant. You were only just coming into your own and suddenly…fate decides that it's time for you to have another learning curve…'

'What do you mean *coming into my own*?'

'I mean—' he sighed heavily and raked his fingers through his hair '—you'd led a sheltered life and then you go to Paris and return a changed person. You're sexy as hell and you're on a journey of discovery.'

'I hadn't realised that I was that adventurous.'

'You fell into a relationship with me to fulfil some youthful infatuation but I know you still want to get out there and discover what the world has in store for you.'

'I do?'

'Of course you do. You said as much when you told me that I was unfinished business. Unfinished business comes to an end eventually.' He looked away, his broodingly handsome face flushed. 'I guess I maybe ambushed you when I suggested we live together… You'd already turned down my marriage proposal. I'll admit that there was a certain amount of blackmail involved when I suggested that we live together. How could you turn down marriage *and* turn down the other reasonable alternative on the table without appearing utterly selfish?' He threw her a challenging look.

'It was a good idea,' Jennifer murmured, heart beating fast.

'And it *has* been…hasn't it? Good?'

Jennifer nodded, because it required too much effort to try and work out how much of herself she should give away. Should she tell him that it couldn't have been better?

He had been affectionate, supportive, reassuring and, as she had always known, wonderfully funny and entertaining. He had returned from work early so that she could put her feet up while he had cooked. He had put up with Ellie coming round every few days and had only given her the occasional dry look when her best friend had launched into colourful stories about her love life. He had indulged her sudden taste for soaps on television and brought her cups of tea whenever she wanted. She had been spoiled rotten and that was the problem. It had felt like a *real* relationship. But there was no ring on her finger and she was now terrified that if there was no baby to provide the glue that kept them together, it would all come crashing down around her ears. Had she been too greedy in holding out for perfection?

'I'm going to tell you something, Jennifer, and it may shock you but it needs to be said before Gregory gets here.' James looked at her and felt the ground shift under him. He had always been able to predict the outcome of the things he did and the decisions he made. But then, his biggest decisions had always involved deals and business. He had come to realise that, where emotions were involved, there was no such thing as a predictable outcome, which made it a hell of a lot scarier.

Jennifer braced herself for the shock. She reminded herself that it was better to get it all out of the way.

'If you lose this baby—and I don't think for a minute that you will. In fact, you're probably right, there was probably no need to get Gregory over at all, but better safe than sorry—'

'Just say what you have to say,' she told him gently. 'Between the two of us, I'm the only one allowed to babble when I'm nervous.'

James opened his mouth to tell her that he wasn't

nervous, that nerves were a sign of weakness. Except he *was* nervous.

'Whatever the outcome, I want to marry you, Jennifer. Okay, I'll settle for living together. I don't want to rush you into anything and living together at least gives me a shot at persuading you that we can make this work. But I want to persuade you of that whether or not there's a child involved.'

She looked at him in silence for so long that he began to wonder whether he had got it all wrong. The signs had all been there. Hadn't they? He had a talent for interpreting nuances. Had that talent let him down now?

'We've been happy. You said so yourself.' A defensive tone had crept into his voice.

'Very happy,' she finally whispered, which he thought was a start. She could feel tears begin to gather in the corners of her eyes. Pregnancy had sent her emotions all over the place. Now she wondered whether they had interfered with her hearing as well.

'Are you saying that you want us to be married… whatever…?'

'Whatever.'

'But I don't understand why.'

'Because I can't imagine that there could ever come a day when I wouldn't want to wake up with you next to me, or return from work knowing that you'd be waiting for me. I love you, Jennifer, and, even if you don't return the feeling, I wanted to lay my cards on the table—'

'When you say you *love* me…'

'I love you. With lots of strings attached. So many strings that you'd tie yourself up in knots trying to work your way out of them.'

'I love you too.' She tried to hold back the tremulous grin but failed. 'And what strings are you talking about?'

'I'll tell you later.' The consultant had arrived, a very tall, very gaunt middle-aged man with a severe expression that only relaxed into a smile once his examination was completed and he accepted the cup of tea offered to him.

Some slight concern but nothing to worry about. Blood pressure was a little on the high side but nothing that some rest and relaxation wouldn't sort out. The bleeding would stop and, although he could understand her worry, rest assured that it had not been a dramatic bleed. He had examined and listened and everything was in order. And she was in good hands. He had known James since he was born because he had delivered him.

Jennifer smiled and listened, relieved that her panic had been misguided. Her mind was all over the place. Relief that everything was all right. Wonder mixed with disbelief that James had told her that he *loved her*. Had he just said that because he had thought it might calm her? Had he known that that was what she had wanted to hear? She caught his eye and tried to still the nagging doubts from trying to get a foothold.

Everything in that warm glance he had given her made her heart soar but acceptance of the fact that he didn't love her was so deeply embedded that she was cautious of letting herself get wrapped up in silly dreams.

He could read her mind. The second the consultant had left, he settled her comfortably back on the sofa, tucking the cushions around her and tutting when she told him that she wasn't an invalid.

'I'm not sure I can believe you in any matters to do with health when you decided to keep those giddy spells to yourself,' he chided, and Jennifer half sat up and drew him towards her.

'And I'm not sure I can believe what you said before...'

'I could tell that that was playing on your mind.' He

sighed and pulled one of the chairs towards the sofa and sat on it, taking her hand in his. 'And I don't blame you. I know I made it clear from the start that I wasn't into long-term relationships and I had the history to prove it. My life was my work and I couldn't foresee a time when any woman would take precedence over that. I never realised how big a part you played until you left. I had become accustomed to having you there.'

'I know,' Jennifer said ruefully. 'I always felt like the girl in the background you could relax with but never really looked at. I just saw a procession of gorgeous little blondes and it didn't do anything for my confidence levels. And then I got my degree, got that job in Paris…and best of all, you asked me out to dinner. I thought it was a date. A proper date. I thought you'd finally woken up to the fact that I wasn't a kid any more. I was a woman. I was so excited.'

'And then I knocked you back.'

'I should have known that nothing had changed when you ordered cake and ice cream as a surprise, with a sparkler on top.'

'I'd do the same thing now,' James told her with a slow smile that made her toes curl. 'You love cake and ice cream and I love that about you. I didn't knock you back because of how you looked.'

'It felt that way to me,' Jennifer confessed.

'You were on the brink of going places. When you kissed me, I felt like a jaded old cynic taking advantage of someone young and vital and innocent. You had stars in your eyes. I honestly thought that you deserved better, but it was hard. I'd never touched you before. I was so turned on… We should have had all this out in the open a long time ago.'

'I couldn't. You were right about me. I was very innocent and very young. I wasn't mature enough to handle a discussion about it. I just knew that it felt like the ultimate rejection and I ran away.' She sighed and looked at him tenderly. 'I thought I'd built a new life for myself in Paris and, in a way, I had.'

'You're not kidding. I had the shock of my life when I saw you again at the cottage. You weren't the same girl who'd made a sweet pass at me four years before. I couldn't take my eyes off you.'

'Because I had changed my outward appearance...'

'That's what I thought,' James confessed ruefully. 'I wasn't into the business of exploring my motivations. One and one seemed to add up to two and I took it from there. I never stopped to ask myself how it was that you were the most satisfying lover I'd ever had.'

'Was I? Really?' Jennifer shamelessly prodded him encouragingly and he favoured her with one of those brilliant smiles that could literally make her tummy do somersaults.

'You're fishing.'

'I know. But can you blame me? I spent years daydreaming about you and then just when I thought I'd mastered it, we meet again and I discover that I've always been daydreaming about you. When we finally became lovers... it was the most wonderfully perfect thing in the world.' She thought back to the moment the bubble had burst. 'I never thought for a second that I would get pregnant and the really weird thing was that it was the fault of my condom, the condom I'd bought four years ago...'

'To use with me?' James looked at her in astonishment. 'You're kidding.'

'No, I'm not. I hung onto it for so long that it went past its sell-by date. Actually, I think drowning in salt water and being bashed about in my bag can't have helped prolong its useful life.'

'Well, I'll be damned.'

'When I found out, I had to face up to the truth, which was that you found the sex amazing and you liked me because we'd known each other for such a long time, but you didn't *love* me.'

'The whole business of love was something I hadn't got my head around. I just knew that you turned up holding a bombshell in one hand and a Dear John letter in the other and I couldn't seem to find a way of getting through to you. When I proposed to you, I didn't pause to think that you might actually turn me down.'

'If I'd known…'

'Shall I confess something?'

'What?'

'This house was never renovated to be rented or sold on.'

'What do you mean?'

'It came to my attention because it had been out of action for a while. It must have slipped through the net somewhere along the line but, the second I saw it, I knew I wanted it for you and that was long before I found out that you were pregnant. God, I was a fool. I should have known from the very second I started thinking about you and houses in the same breath that I had fallen in love with you. In fact, I was going to tell you about it when you broke the news.'

Pure delight lit up Jennifer's face and she flung her arms around his neck and pulled him towards her.

'I thought when you dropped all talk about getting married that you were relieved to have been let off the hook… Most men would have been if they found themselves landed with an unwanted pregnancy…'

'Relieved to have been let off the hook?' James laughed and stroked her hair. 'All I could think was that you wanted out, you wanted to be free to find this perfect guy of yours and all I could think was that I needed to put a stop to that, needed to show you that *I* was that perfect guy... I knew that the thought of marriage had sent you into a tailspin. You didn't want to marry me and I wasn't going to try and force your hand and risk you pulling back completely.'

'But I *did* want to marry you. You don't know how much. I just didn't want to be married for the wrong reasons. I hated the thought that you would put a ring on my finger because you couldn't see any other way round the situation. I didn't want to be your lifelong obligation.'

'So now I'm asking you to be the lifelong love of my life. Will you marry me...?'

The wedding was a quiet affair, with family and friends, and, after the scare with the pregnancy, baby Emily was born without any fuss at all. She was plump and pink, with a mop of dark hair, and for both Jennifer and James it was love at first sight.

For a commitment-shy guy determined never to be tamed, James was home promptly every evening. It was very important to delegate, he told her—delegation ensured that employees were kept on their toes and it motivated them in their careers, and if he had taken to working from home now and again, then it was simply because modern technology made it so simple, virtually mandatory in fact.

She would have to get used to having him under her feet because, he further informed her, he was tiring of the concrete jungle. It was no place to bring up all the children he planned on them having. It was a cut-throat world and, besides, there was just so much money a man could use in a lifetime and, that being the case, why waste time

pursuing more when there were so many other, more rewarding things to do with one's time?

And there was no doubt what those other things were.

Jennifer teased him about the man he had become
and she knew that she would spend a lifetime ensur-
ing that the happiness he gave her was returned to him
a thousandfold…

* * * * *

STEPPING OUT OF THE SHADOWS

BY
ROBYN DONALD

Robyn Donald can't remember not being able to read, and will be eternally grateful to the local farmers who carefully avoided her on a dusty country road as she read her way to and from school, transported to places and times far away from her small village in Northland, New Zealand. Growing up fed her habit. As well as training as a teacher, marrying and raising two children, she discovered the delights of romances and read them voraciously, especially enjoying the ones written by New Zealand writers. So much so that one day she decided to write one herself. Writing soon grew to be as much of a delight as reading—although infinitely more challenging—and when eventually her first book was accepted by Mills & Boon she felt she'd arrived home.

She still lives in a small town in Northland, with her family close by, using the landscape as a setting for much of her work. Her life is enriched by the friends she's made among writers and readers and complicated by a determined Corgi called Buster, who is convinced that blackbirds are evil entities. Her greatest hobby is still reading, with travelling a very close second.

CHAPTER ONE

HEART thudding more noisily than the small plane's faltering engine, Rafe Peveril dragged his gaze away from the rain-lashed windows, no longer able to see the darkening grasslands of Mariposa beneath them. A few seconds ago, just after the engine had first spluttered, he'd noticed a hut down there.

If they made it out of this alive, that hut might be their only hope of surviving the night.

Another violent gust of wind shook the plane. The engine coughed a couple of times, then failed. In the eerie silence the pilot muttered a jumble of prayers and curses in his native Spanish as he fought to keep the plane steady.

If they were lucky—*damned* lucky—they might land more or less intact...

When the engines sputtered back into life the woman beside Rafe looked up, white face dominated by great green eyes, black-lashed and tip-tilted and filled with fear.

Thank God she wasn't screaming. He reached for her hand, gave it a quick hard squeeze, then released it to push her head down.

"Brace position," he shouted, his voice far too loud in the sudden silence as the engines stopped again. The woman huddled low and Rafe set his teeth and steeled himself for the crash.

A shuddering jolt, a whirlwind of noise...

And Rafe woke.

Jerking upright, he let out a sharp breath, grey eyes sweeping a familiar room. The adrenalin surging through him mutated into relief. Instead of regaining consciousness in a South American hospital bed he was at home in his own room in New Zealand.

What the *hell*...?

It had to be at least a couple of years since he'd re-lived the crash. He searched for a trigger that could have summoned the dream but his memory—usually sharply accurate—failed him.

Again.

Six years should have accustomed him to the blank space in his head after the crash, yet although he'd given up on futile attempts to remember, he still resented those forty-eight vanished hours.

The bedside clock informed him that sunrise was too close to try for any more sleep—not that he'd manage it now. He needed space and fresh air.

Outside on the terrace he inhaled deeply, relishing the mingled scent of salt and flowers and newly mown grass, and the quiet hush of the waves. His heart rate slowed and the memories receded into the past where they belonged. Light from a fading moon surrounded the house with mysterious shadows, enhanced by the bright disc of Venus hanging above a bar of pure gold along the horizon where the sea met the sky.

The Mariposan pilot had died on impact, but miraculously both he and the wife of his estancia manager had survived with minor injures—the blow to the head for him, and apparently nothing more serious than a few bruises for her.

With some difficulty he conjured a picture of the woman—a drab nonentity, hardly more than a girl. Although he'd spent the night before the crash at the estancia, she'd kept very much in the background while he and her husband talked business. All he could recall were those amazingly green eyes in her otherwise forgettable face. Apart from them, she had been a plain woman.

With a plain name—Mary Brown.

He couldn't recall seeing her smile—not that that was surprising. A week or so before he'd arrived at the estancia she'd received news of her mother's sudden stroke and resultant paralysis. As soon as Rafe heard about it he'd offered to take her back with him to Mariposa's capital and organise a flight to New Zealand.

Rafe frowned. What the hell was her husband's name?

He recalled it with an odd sense of relief. David Brown—another plain name, and the reason for Rafe's trip to Mariposa. He'd broken his flight home from London to see for himself if he agreed with the Mariposan agent's warnings that David Brown was not a good fit for the situation.

Certainly Brown's response to his offer to escort his wife back to New Zealand had been surprising.

"That won't be necessary," David Brown had told him brusquely. "She's been ill—she doesn't need the extra stress of looking after a cripple."

However, by the next morning the man had changed his mind, presumably at his wife's insistence, and that evening she'd accompanied Rafe on the first stage of the trip.

An hour after take-off they'd been caught by a wind of startling ferocity, and with it came rain so cold the woman beside him had been shivering within minutes. And the plane's engines had cut out for the first time.

If it hadn't been for the skill of the doomed pilot they'd probably all have died.

Of course! There was the stimulus—the trigger that had hurled his dreaming mind back six years.

Rafe inhaled sharply, recalling the email that had arrived just before he'd gone to bed last night. Sent from his office in London, for the first time in recorded history his efficient personal assistant had slipped up. No message, just a forwarded photograph of a dark young man wearing a look of conscious pride and a mortarboard, a graduation shot. Amused by his PA's omission, Rafe had sent back one question mark.

Last night he hadn't made the connection, but the kid looked very much like the pilot.

He swung around and headed for his office, switched on the computer, waited impatiently for it to boot up and smiled ironically when he saw another email.

His PA had written, *Sorry about the stuff-up. I've just had a letter from the widow of the pilot in Mariposa. Apparently you promised their oldest boy an interview with the organisation there when he graduated from university. Photo of good-looking kid in mortarboard attached. OK to organise?*

So that explained the dream. Rafe's subconscious had made the connection for him in a very forthright fashion. He'd felt a certain obligation to the family of the dead pilot and made it his business to help them.

He replied with a succinct agreement to London, then headed back to his bedroom to dress.

After a gruelling trip to several African countries, it

was great to be home, and apart from good sex and the exhilaration of business there was little he liked better than a ride along the beach on his big bay gelding in a Northland summer dawn.

Perhaps it might give him some inspiration for the gift he needed to buy that day, a birthday present for his foster-sister. His mouth curved. Gina had forthright views on appropriate gifts for a modern young woman.

"You might be a plutocrat," she'd told him the day before, "but don't you dare get your secretary to buy me something flashy and glittering. I don't do glitter."

He'd pointed out that his middle-aged PA would have been insulted to hear herself described as a secretary, and added that any presents he bought were his own choice, no one else's.

Gina grinned and gave him a sisterly punch in the arm. "Oh, yeah? So why did you get me to check the kiss-off present you gave your last girlfriend?"

"It was her birthday gift," he contradicted. "And if I remember correctly, you insisted on seeing it."

She arched an eyebrow. "Of course I did. So it was just a coincidence you broke off the affair a week later?"

"It was a mutual decision," Rafe told her, the touch of frost in his tone a warning.

His private life was his own. Because he had no desire to cause grief he chose his lovers for sophistication as well as their appeal to his mind and his senses. Eventually he intended to marry.

One day.

"Well, I suppose the diamonds salvaged a bit of pride for her," Gina had observed cynically, hugging him before getting into her car for the trip back to Auckland. She'd turned on the engine, then said casually through the open window, "If you're looking for something a bit different, the gift shop in Tewaka has a new owner. It's got some really good stuff in it now."

Recognising a hint when he heard one, several hours later Rafe headed for the small seaside town twenty kilometres from the homestead.

Inside the gift shop he looked around. Gina was right—the place had been fitted out with taste and style. His appreciative gaze took in demure yet sexy lingerie displayed with discretion, frivolous sandals perfect for any four-year-old girl who yearned to be a princess, some very good New Zealand art glass. As well as clothes there were ornaments and jewellery, even some books. And art, ranging in style from brightly coloured coastal scenes to moody, dramatic oils.

"Can I help you?"

Rafe swivelled around, met the shop assistant's eyes and felt the ground shift beneath his feet. Boldly green and cat-tilted, set between lashes thick enough to tangle any heart, they sent him spinning back to his dream.

"Mary?" he asked without thinking.

But of course she wasn't Mary Brown.

This woman was far from plain and an involuntary glance showed no ring on those long fingers. Although her eyes were an identical green, they were bright and challenging, not dully unaware.

Her lashes drooped and he sensed her subtle—but very definite—withdrawal.

"I'm sorry—have we met before?" she asked in an assured, crisp voice completely unlike Mary Brown's hesitant tone. She added with a smile, "But my name isn't Mary. It's Marisa—Marisa Somerville."

Indeed, the assured, beautifully groomed Ms Somerville was a bird of paradise compared to drab Mrs Brown. Apart from the coincidences of eye colour and shape, and first names beginning with the same letter, this woman bore no resemblance to the woman he'd seen in Mariposa.

Rafe held out his hand. "Sorry, but for a moment I thought you were someone else. I'm Rafe Peveril."

Although her lashes flickered, her handshake was as confident as her voice. "How do you do, Mr Peveril."

"Most people here call me Rafe," he told her.

She didn't pretend not to know who he was. Had there been a glimmer of some other emotion in the sultry green depths of her eyes, almost immediately hidden by those dark lashes?

If so, he could hear no sign of it in her voice when she went on, "Would you rather look around by yourself, or can I help you in any way?"

She hadn't granted him permission to use her first name. Intrigued, and wryly amused at his reaction to her unspoken refusal, Rafe said, "My sister is having a birthday soon, and from the way she spoke of your shop I gathered she'd seen something here she liked. Do you know Gina Smythe?"

"Everyone in Tewaka knows Gina." Smiling, she turned towards one of the side walls. "And, yes, I can tell you what she liked."

"Gina isn't noted for subtlety," he said drily, appreciating the gentle feminine sway of slender hips, the graceful smoothness of her gait. His body stirred in a swift, sensually charged response that was purely masculine.

She stopped in front of an abstract oil. "This is the one."

Rafe dragged his mind back to his reason for being there. Odd that Gina, so practical and matter-of-fact, couldn't resist art that appealed directly to the darker, more stormy emotions.

"Who's the artist?" he asked after a silent moment.

The woman beside him gave a soft laugh. "I am," she admitted.

The hot tug of lust in Rafe's gut intensified, startling him. Was she as passionate as the painting before him? Perhaps he'd find out some day…

"I'll take it," he said briskly. "Can you gift-wrap it for me? I'll call back in half an hour."

"Yes, of course."

"Thanks."

Out of the shop, away from temptation, he reminded himself curtly that he'd long ago got over the adolescent desire to bed every desirable woman he met. Yet primitive hunger still quickened his blood.

Soon he'd invite Marisa Somerville to dinner.

If she was unattached, which seemed unlikely in spite of her ringless fingers. Women who looked like her—especially ones who exuded that subtle sexuality—usually had a man in the not-very-distant background.

Probably, he thought cynically, stopping to speak to a middle-aged woman he'd known from childhood, he'd responded to her so swiftly because it was several months since he'd made love.

From behind the flimsy barrier of the sales counter Marisa watched him, her pulse still hammering so loudly in her ears she hardly heard the rising shriek of the siren at the local fire-brigade headquarters.

She resisted the impulse to go and wash Rafe Peveril's grip from her skin. A handshake was meant to be impersonal, an unthreatening gesture…

Yet when he'd taken her outstretched hand in his strong, tempered fingers an erotic shiver had sizzled through every cell. Rafe Peveril's touch had been unbearably stimulating, as dangerous as a siren's song.

If a simple, unemotional handshake could do that, what would happen if he kissed her—?

Whoa! Outraged, she ordered her wayward mind to shut down that train of thought.

For two months she'd been bracing herself for this—ever since she'd been appalled to discover Rafe Peveril lived not far from Tewaka. Yet when she'd looked up to see him pace into the shop, more than six foot of intimidating authority and leashed male force, she'd had to stop herself from bolting out the back door.

Of all the rotten coincidences... It hadn't occurred to her to check the names of the local bigwigs before signing the contract that locked her into a year's lease of the shop.

She should have followed her first impulse after her father's death and crossed the Tasman Sea to take refuge in Australia.

At least her luck had held—Rafe hadn't recognised her. It was difficult to read the brilliant mind behind his arrogantly autocratic features, but she'd be prepared to bet that after a jolt of what might have been recognition he'd completely accepted her new persona and identity.

She swallowed hard as the fire engine raced past, siren screaming. Please God it was just a grass fire, not a motor accident, or someone's house.

Her gaze fell to the picture she'd just sold. Forcing herself to breathe carefully and steadily, she took it off the wall and carried it across to the counter.

Gina Smythe was the sort of woman Marisa aspired to be—self-assured, decisive, charming. But of course

Rafe Peveril's sister would have been born with the same effortless, almost ruthless self-confidence that made him so intimidating.

Whereas it had taken her years—and much effort—to manufacture the façade she now hid behind. Only she knew that deep inside her lurked the naive, foolish kid filled with simple-minded hope and fairytale fantasies who'd married David Brown and gone with him to Mariposa, expecting an exotic tropical paradise and the romance of a lifetime.

Her mouth curved in a cynical, unamused line as she expertly cut a length of gift-wrapping paper.

How wrong she'd been.

However, that was behind her now. And as she couldn't get out of her lease agreement, she'd just have to make sure everyone—especially Rafe Peveril—saw her as the woman who owned the best gift shop in Northland.

She had to make a success of this venture and squirrel away every cent she could. Once the year was up she'd leave Tewaka for somewhere safer—a place where her past didn't intrude and she could live without fear, a place where she could at last settle.

The sort of place she thought she'd found in Tewaka…

Half an hour later she was keeping a wary eye on the entrance while dealing with a diffident middle-aged woman who couldn't make up her mind. Every suggestion was met with a vague comment that implied rejection.

Once, Marisa thought compassionately, she'd been like that. Perhaps this woman too was stuck in a situation with no escape. Curbing her tension, she walked her around the shop, discussing the recipient of the proposed gift, a fourteen-year-old girl who seemed to terrify her grandmother.

A movement from the door made her suck in an involuntary breath as Rafe Peveril strode in, his size and air of cool authority reducing the shop and its contents to insignificance.

Black-haired, tanned and arrogantly handsome, his broad-shouldered, narrow-hipped body moving in a lithe predator's gait on long, heavily muscled legs, he was a man who commanded instant attention.

Naked, he was even more magnificent...

Appalled by the swift memory from a past she'd tried very hard to forget, she murmured, "If you don't mind, I'll give Mr Peveril his parcel."

"Oh, yes—do." The customer looked across the shop, turning faintly pink when she received a smile that sizzled with male charisma.

Deliberately relaxing her taut muscles, Marisa set off towards him. He knew the effect that smile had on women.

It set female hearts throbbing—as hers was right now.

Not, however, solely with appreciation.

In Mariposa his height had struck her first. Only when he'd been close had she noticed that his eyes were grey, so dark they were the colour of iron.

But in Mariposa his gaze had been coolly aloof.

Now he made no attempt to hide his appreciation. Heat licked through her, warring with a primitive sense of approaching danger. She forced a smile, hoping he'd take the mechanical curve of her lips for genuine pleasure.

"Hello, Mr Peveril, here's your parcel," she said, lowering her lashes as she placed it carefully on the counter.

"Thank you." After a quick look he asked, "Do you give lessons in parcel wrapping and decoration?"

Startled, she looked up, parrying his direct, keen survey with a mildly enquiring lift of her brows. "I hadn't thought of it."

A long finger tapped the parcel. "This is beautifully done. With Christmas not too far away you'd probably have plenty of takers."

Easy chitchat was not his style. He'd been pleasant enough in Mariposa, but very much the boss—

Don't think of Mariposa.

It was stupid to feel that somehow her wayward thoughts might show in her face and trigger a vagrant memory in him.

Stupid and oddly scary. It took a lot of will to look him in the eye and say in a steady voice, "Thank you. I might put a notice in the window and see what happens."

As though he'd read her mind, he said in an idle tone at variance with his cool, keen scrutiny, "I have this odd feeling we've met before, but I'm certain I'd remember if we had."

Oh, God! Calling on every ounce of self-preservation, she said brightly, "So would I, Mr Peveril—"

"Rafe."

She swallowed. Her countrymen were famously casual, so it was stupid to feel that using his first name forged some sort of link. "Rafe," she repeated, adding with another meaningless smile, "I'd have remembered too, I'm sure." Oh, hell, did that sound like an attempt at flirtation? Hastily she added, "I do hope your sister enjoys the painting."

"I'm sure she will. Thank you." He nodded, picked up the parcel and left.

Almost giddy with relief, Marisa had to take a couple of deep breaths before she returned to her customer. It took another ten minutes before the woman finally made up her mind, and while Marisa was wrapping the gift, she leaned forwards and confided in a low voice, "Gina Smythe's not really Rafe's sister, you know."

"No, I didn't know." Marisa disliked gossip, so she tried to make her tone brisk and dismissive even though curiosity assailed her.

"Poor girl, she was in a foster home not far from here—one she didn't like—so she ran away when she was about six and hid in a cave on Manuwai."

At Marisa's uncomprehending glance she elaborated, "Manuwai is the Peveril station, out on the coast north of here. The family settled there in the very early days. It's one of the few land grants still intact—an enormous place. Rafe found Gina and took her home with him, and his parents more or less adopted her. Rafe's an only child."

"Ah, I see." No wonder Gina and Rafe didn't share a surname.

And she'd been so sure the woman's sense of confidence had been born in her...

The woman leaned closer. "When I say his parents, it was his stepmother, really. His *birth* mother left him and his father when Rafe was about six. It was a great scandal—she divorced him and married a film star, then divorced him and married someone else—and it was rumoured the elder Mr Peveril paid millions of dollars to get rid of her."

Shocked, Marisa tried to cut her off, only to have the woman drop her voice even further. "She was very beautiful—always dashing off to Auckland and Australia and going on cruises and trips to Bali." Her tone made that exotic island paradise sound like one of the nether regions of hell.

Hoping to put an end to this, Marisa handed over the purchase in one of her specially designed bags. "Thank you," she said firmly.

But the woman was not to be deterred. "She didn't even look after Rafe—he had a nanny from the time he was born. His stepmother—the second Mrs Peveril—was very nice, but she couldn't have children, so Rafe is an only child. Such a shame…"

Her voice trailed away when another customer entered the shop. Intensely relieved, Marisa grabbed the opportunity. "I'm pretty certain your granddaughter will love this, but if she doesn't, come back with her and we'll find something she does like."

"That's very kind of you," the woman fluttered. "Thank you very much, my dear."

The rest of the day was too busy for Marisa to think about what she'd heard, and once she'd closed the shop she walked along the street to the local after-school centre. She'd chosen Tewaka to settle in for various reasons, but that excellent care centre had been the clincher.

Her heart swelled at the grin from her son. "Hello, darling. How's your day been?"

"Good," he told her, beaming as he always did. To five-year-old Keir every day was good. How had Rafe Peveril's days been after his mother had left?

Keir asked, "Did you have a good day too?"

She nodded. "Yes, a cruise ship—a really big one—came into the Bay of Islands, so I had plenty of customers." And most had bought something.

Fishing around in his bag, Keir asked, "Can I go to Andy's birthday party? Please," he added conscientiously. "He gave me this today." He handed over a somewhat crumpled envelope.

Taking it, she thought wryly that in a way it was a pity he'd settled so well. A sunny, confident boy, he'd made friends instantly and he was going to miss them when they left. "I'll read it when we get home, but I don't see any reason why not."

He beamed again, chattering almost nonstop while they shopped in the supermarket. Marisa's heart swelled, then contracted into a hard ball in her chest. Keir was her reason for living, the pivot of her life. His welfare was behind every decision she'd made since the day she'd realised she was pregnant.

No matter what it took, she'd make sure he had everything he needed to make him happy.

And that, she thought later after a tussle of wills had seen him into bed, included discipline.

Whatever else he missed out on, he had a mother who loved him. Which, if local gossip was anything to go by, was more than Rafe Peveril had had. He'd only been a year older than Keir when his mother had left.

She felt a huge compassion for the child he'd been. Had that first great desertion made him the tough, ruthless man he was now?

More than likely. But although the sad story gave her a whole new perspective on him, she'd be wise to remember she was dealing with the man he was now, not the small deserted boy he'd once been.

That night memories of his hard, speculative survey kept her awake. She hated to think of the way she'd been when she'd first met him—ground down into a grey shadow of a woman—and she'd been hugely re-lieved when he didn't recognise her.

Images sharpened by a primitive fear flooded back, clear and savagely painful. Two years of marriage to David had almost crushed her.

If it hadn't been for Rafe Peveril she'd probably still be on that lonely estancia in Mariposa, unable to sum-mon the strength—or the courage, she thought with an involuntary tightening of her stomach muscles—to get away.

It had taken several years and a lot of effort to emerge from that dark world of depression and insecurity. Now she had the responsibility of her son, she'd never again trust herself to a man with an urge to dominate.

Twisting in her bed, she knew she wasn't going to sleep. She had no camomile tea, but a cup of the pep-permint variety might soothe her enough.

Even as she stood in the darkened kitchen of the little, elderly cottage she rented, a mug of peppermint tea in hand, she knew it wasn't going to work. She grimaced as she gazed out into the summer night—one made for lovers, an evocation of all that was romantic, the moon's silver glamour spreading a shimmering veil of magic over the countryside.

Bewildered by an inchoate longing for something un-known, something *more*—something primal and con-suming and intense—she was almost relieved when hot liquid sloshed on to her fingers, jerking her back into real life.

Hastily she set the mug on the bench and ran cold water over her hand until the mild stinging stopped.

"That's what you get for staring at the moon," she muttered and, picking up her mug again, turned away from the window.

Seeing Rafe Peveril again had set off a reckless energy, as though her body had sprung to life after a long sleep.

She should have expected it.

Her first sight of him at the estancia, climbing down from the old Jeep, had awakened a determination she'd thought she'd lost. His raw male vitality—forceful yet disciplined—had broken through her grey apathy.

From somewhere she'd summoned the initiative to tell him of her mother's illness and that she wasn't expected to live.

Then, when David had refused Rafe's offer to take her home, she'd gathered every ounce of courage and defied him.

She shivered. Thank heavens she was no longer that frail, damaged woman. Now, it seemed incredible she'd let herself get into such a state.

Instead of standing in the dark recalling the crash, she should be exulting, joyously relieved because the meeting she'd been dreading for the past two months had happened without disaster.

Oh, Rafe had noticed her, all right—but only with masculine interest.

So she'd passed the first big hurdle. *If only she could get rid of the nagging instinct that told her to run. Now—while she still could.*

What if he eventually worked out that she and Mary Brown were the same woman?

What if David was still working for him, and he told her ex-husband where she and Keir were?

What if he found out about the lie she'd told David— the lie that had finally and for ever freed her and her son?

Marisa took another deep breath and drained the mug

of lukewarm tea. That wasn't going to happen because her ex-husband didn't care about Keir.

Anyway, worrying was a waste of time and nervous energy. All she had to do was avoid Rafe Peveril, which shouldn't be difficult, even in a place as small as Tewaka—his vast empire kept him away for much of the time.

Closing the curtains on the sultry enchantment of the moon, she tried to feel reassured. While she kept out of his way she'd make plans for a future a long way from Tewaka.

Somewhere safe—where she could start again.

Start again...

She'd believed—hoped—she'd done that for the last time when she'd arrived in Tewaka. A soul-deep loneliness ached through her. Her life had been nothing but new starts.

Sternly she ordered herself not to wallow in self-pity. Before she decided to put down roots again, she'd check out the locals carefully.

Also, she thought ruefully, if she could manage it she'd buy some dull-brown contact lenses.

CHAPTER TWO

To save money, Keir stayed at the shop after school two days each week. He enjoyed chatting to customers and playing with toys in the tiny office at the back.

Which was where he was when Marisa heard a deep, hard voice. Her heart thudded painfully in her chest.

Rafe Peveril. It had been almost a week since he'd bought the gift for his sister, and she'd just started to relax. *Please*, let him buy another one and then go away and never come back, she begged the universe.

In vain. Without preamble he asked, "Do you, by any chance, have a relative named Mary Brown?"

Panic froze her breath. Desperately she said the first thing that wasn't a lie, hoping he didn't recognise it for an evasion. "As far as I know I have no female relatives. Certainly not one called Mary Brown. Why?"

And allowed her gaze to drift enquiringly upwards from the stock she was checking. Something very close to terror hollowed out her stomach. He was watching her far too closely, the striking framework of his face very prominent, his gaze narrowed and unreadable.

From the corner of her eye she saw the office door slide open. Her heart stopped in her chest.

Keir, stay there, she begged silently.

But her son wandered out, his expression alert yet a

little wary as he stared up at the man beside his mother. "Mummy…" he began, not quite tentatively.

"Not now, darling." Marisa struggled to keep her voice steady and serene. "I'll be with you in a minute."

He sent her a resigned look, but turned to go back, stopping only when Rafe Peveril said in a voice edged by some emotion she couldn't discern, "I can wait." He looked down at Keir. "Hello, I'm Rafe Peveril. What's your name?"

"Keir," her son told him, always ready to talk to adults.

"Keir who?"

Keir's face crinkled into laughter. "Not Keir Who— I'm Keir Somerville—"

Abruptly, Marisa broke in. "Off you go, Keir."

But Rafe said, "He's all right. How old are you, Keir?"

"I'm five," Keir told him importantly. "I go to school now."

"Who is your teacher?"

"Mrs Harcourt," Keir said. "She's got a dog and a kitten, and yesterday she brought the kitty to school." He shot a glance at Marisa before fixing his gaze back on the compellingly handsome face of the man who watched him. "I want a puppy but Mum says not yet 'cause we'd have to leave him by himself and he'd be lonely all day, but another lady has a shop too, and she's got a little dog and her dog sleeps on a cushion in the shop with her and it's happy all day."

And then, thank heavens, another customer came in and Marisa said evenly, "Off you go, Keir."

With obvious reluctance Keir headed away, but not before giving Rafe a swift smile and saying, "Goodbye, Mr Pev'ril."

Rafe watched until he was out of hearing before transferring his gaze to Marisa's face. "A pleasant child."

"Thank you," she said automatically, still spooked by the speculation in his hard scrutiny. "Can I help you at all?"

"No, I just came in to tell you I'm now very high in my sister's favour. When I told her you had painted the picture she was surprised and wondered why you hadn't signed it. We could only make out your initials."

She couldn't tell him the last thing she wanted was her name where someone who knew her—or David— might see it. So she smiled and shrugged. "I don't really know—I just never have."

He appeared to take that at face value. "She asked me to tell you that she loves it and is over the moon."

Marisa relaxed a little. "That's great," she said. "Thank your sister from me, please."

"She'll probably come in and enthuse about it herself when she's next up, so I'll leave that to you." His matter-of-fact tone dismissed her, reinforced by his rapid glance at the clock at the back of the shop. "I have to go, but we'll meet again."

Not if I see you first, Marisa thought uneasily, but managed to say, "I'm sure we will."

Parrying another hard glance with her most limpid smile, she tried to ignore her jumping nerve-ends as she moved away to deal with another customer, who'd decided to begin Christmas shopping.

Surprisingly for an afternoon, a steady stream of shoppers kept her so busy she had no time to mull over Rafe's unexpected visit or the even more unexpected attention he'd paid to her son.

Or her reckless—and most unusual—response to

him. It had absolutely nothing to do with the fact that she'd slept entwined in his arms, heart to heart, her legs tangled in his, her skin warming him…

Get out of my head, she ordered the intrusive memories.

Later, after they'd got home, she hung out a load of washing, trying to convince herself that her apprehension was without foundation. A wistful pain jagged through her as she watched Keir tear around on the bicycle that had been her father's final gift to him.

It was foolish to be so alarmed by Rafe Peveril. He was no threat to her or—more important—to Keir.

Because even if her ex-husband was still working for the Peveril organisation, she no longer needed to fear David. Not for herself, anyway… She was a different woman from the green girl who'd married him. She'd suffered and been lost, and eventually realised that the only way she'd survive was to rescue herself.

And she'd done it. Now she had a life and the future she'd crafted for herself and her son. She'd let no one—certainly not Rafe Peveril—take that from her.

Yet for the rest of the day darkness clouded her thoughts, dragging with it old fear, old pain and memories of will-sapping despair at being trapped in a situation she'd been unable to escape.

Because there was the ugly matter of the lie—the one that had won her freedom and Keir's safety.

Unseeingly, Rafe frowned at the glorious view from his office window, remembering black-lashed eyes and silky skin—skin that had paled that afternoon when Marisa Somerville had looked up and seen him. Her hands, elegant, capable and undecorated by rings had stiffened for a few seconds, and then trembled slightly.

A nagging sense of familiarity taunted him, refusing to be dismissed. Yet it had to be just the random coincidence of eye colour and shape. Apart from those eyes, nothing connected Marisa Somerville to the drab nonentity who had been married to David Brown.

Marisa was everything poor Mary Brown wasn't.

He let his memory range from glossy hair the colour of dark honey to satiny skin with a subtle sheen, and a mouth that beckoned with generous sensuality.

A sleeping hunger stirred, one so fiercely male and sharply focused it refused to be dismissed.

So, Marisa Somerville was very attractive.

Hell, how inadequate was that? he thought with a cynical smile. His recollection of a body that even her restrained clothes hadn't been able to subdue prompted him to add *sexy* to *attractive*.

It hadn't been simple recognition that had shadowed that tilted, siren's gaze. His frown deepened. He considered himself an astute judge of reactions and in any other situation he'd have guessed Marisa's had come very close to fear…

Only for a second. She'd recovered fast, although a hint of tension had reappeared when her son had entered the shop.

Possibly what he'd seen in Marisa Somerville's face was nothing more than a feminine resistance to the basic, sexual pull between a fertile woman and a virile man—a matter of genes recognising a possible mate— a pull he'd also felt.

Still did, he realised, drily amused by his hardening body.

That certainly hadn't happened in Mariposa, when

he'd met Mary Brown. She'd looked at him with no expression, shaken his hand as though forced to and immediately faded into the background. What *had* lodged in his mind had been the dislocating contrast between fascinating eyes and the rest of her—thin, listless, her dragging voice, sallow skin and the lank hair of pure mouse scraped back from her face into a ponytail.

Rafe looked around his office, letting the warmth and practicality of the room soak into him.

This room represented the essence of his life; five generations of Peveril men and women had sat behind the huge kauri desk and worked to create the superbly productive empire that had expanded from a wilderness to encompass the world.

He hoped one day a son or daughter of his would occupy the same chair behind the same desk, with the same aim—to feed as many people as he could.

His father had set up an organisation to help the Mariposan government introduce modern farming practices, but after his death Rafe had discovered a chaotic state of affairs. That first, fact-finding trip to Mariposa had been the impetus to impose a proper chain of control, a process that involved total restructuring as well as hiring a workforce he could trust.

He made an impatient gesture and turned to the computer. He had more important things to think about than a possible—if unlikely—link between Marisa Somerville and the wife of one of his farm managers.

Yet he couldn't dislodge the memory of that flash of recognition and the fleeting, almost haunted expression in Marisa's eyes.

Although Rafe rarely had hunches, preferring to follow his logical brain, when they did occur he'd learned to stick with them. A self-derisive smile curving his mouth, he checked the time in Mariposa, then picked up the telephone.

His agent there was surprised at his question, but answered readily enough, "I was not part of this organisation then, you remember, but of course I do recall the circumstances. It was in the newspapers. Señor Brown burned down the machinery shed on that estancia. One of the farmhands almost died in the fire. I understand he was given the chance to leave or be handed over to the police. He left."

Brows drawing even closer together, Rafe demanded, "Why was I not told of this?"

"I do not know."

In fact, it was just another example of the previous agent's inefficiency. Mouth compressing into a thin line, Rafe said, "Of course you don't. Sorry. When did this sabotage happen?"

There was a pause, then the manager said a little stiffly, "I will need to check the exact date, you understand, but it was a few weeks after you and Mrs Brown left for New Zealand."

Rafe's gaze narrowed. The phrase probably indicated only that English wasn't his agent's first language. Technically true, but not in the way it seemed to indicate.

But if David Brown had thought...?

With a sardonic smile Rafe dismissed the idea.

However, it kept recurring during the following week as he hosted an overseas delegation, wining and dining them before intensive discussions that ended very satisfactorily.

He celebrated by taking an old flame out to dinner, tactfully declining her oblique suggestion they spend the night together. Although he was fond of her and they'd enjoyed a satisfying affair some years previously, he was no longer interested. And was irritated when a roving photographer snapped them together as they left the reception. New Zealand had nothing like the paparazzi overseas, but the photograph appeared in the social news of one of the Sunday papers the next day.

Back at Manuwai he found himself reaching for the telephone, only to realise that it was the weekend and he didn't know Marisa Somerville's number. It wasn't in the telephone book either.

And why did he want to ring her? Because she reminded him of another woman?

Grimly, he recalled what he could of the day he and Mary Brown had left the estancia, little more than irritating flashes and fragments—more sensation than sight—of the storm that had brought the plane down. Even after he'd woken in the hospital bed, fully aware once more, he'd remembered nothing of the aftermath.

He'd been told that Mary Brown had brought him to the hut, that she'd probably saved his life…

And without warning a flash of memory returned—a quiet voice, his gratitude at the warmth of arms around him…

That was all. Rafe swore and got to his feet, pacing across the room to stand at the window. He took a few deliberate breaths, willing his racing thoughts to slow. Why hadn't he remembered that before?

Had the sight of a pair of black-lashed green eyes prodded this elusive fragment from his reluctant brain?

After he'd been released from hospital both he and Mary Brown had travelled to New Zealand in a private jet with a nurse in attendance—a flight he barely remembered, though obviously it had set the gossips in Mariposa buzzing.

Well, let them think what they liked. He never pursued committed women, no matter how alluring.

Ignoring the flame of anticipation that licked through him, Rafe shrugged. He'd find out whether Marisa Somerville was in a relationship soon enough. Tewaka also had gossips, and information inevitably found its way to him.

Keir said fretfully, "Mummy, I don't want you to go out." He thought a moment before adding, "I might feel sick if you do."

At his mother's look he grinned. "Well, I *might*."

"You won't, my darling. I'll be here when you wake up tomorrow morning and you'll be fine with Tracey. And tomorrow is Saturday, so you can come into the shop with me."

Keir knew when persistence could—occasionally—be rewarded and also when to give up. The sigh he heaved was heartfelt, but the prospect of an ice cream muted its full force. "I like Tracey."

"I know. And here she comes now."

But Marisa couldn't repress a few motherly qualms as she drove away. Although her landlord's daughter—a seventeen-year-old with two younger brothers—was both competent and practical, with her mother available only a couple of hundred metres along the road, Marisa had never before gone out and left Keir to be put to bed.

However, taking part in this weekly get-together of local business people was something she'd been promising herself. If nothing else it would expand her circle of contacts and she needed to take every opportunity to make her shop a success.

Nevertheless, she felt a little tense when she walked into the room, and even more so when the bustling, middle-aged convener confided, "We're honoured tonight—normally we don't have speakers, but this afternoon I talked Rafe Peveril into giving us his ideas about how he sees the future of Northland and Tewaka."

"Oh, that should be interesting," Marisa said with a bright, false smile that hid, she hoped, her sudden urge to get out of there.

Ten days should have given her time to get over the impact of meeting him again, but it hadn't. Five minutes later she was producing that same smile as the convener began to introduce Rafe to her.

Smoothly he cut in, "Ms Somerville and I have already met."

"Oh, good," the convener said, not without an interested note in her voice.

Somehow Marisa found herself beside Rafe with her hard-won poise rapidly leaking away.

"I believe you're living in the Tanners' farm cottage," he said.

Of course anyone who was interested—and quite a few who weren't—would know. Marisa said briskly, "Yes, it's very convenient." And cheap.

"So who's looking after your son tonight?"

Slightly startled, she looked up, brows raised. "That's part of the convenience. Tracey—the Tanners' daughter—is more than happy to babysit. She and Keir get on well together."

He nodded, dark head inclining slightly towards her, grey eyes cool and assessing. A rebel response—heady and heated in the pit of her stomach—caught her by surprise.

"I hadn't realised this is the first time you've come to one of these meetings," he said.

"I've been intending to, but..." Shrugging, she let the words trail away.

"Point out the people you don't know."

Surprised again, she did so, wondering if he was using this method to politely move away. However, although he introduced her to everyone she indicated, he stayed beside her until it was time for him to speak.

Good manners, she thought stoutly, nothing more. Dragging her mind back to what he was saying, she realised that the quality of Rafe Peveril's mind shone through his incisive words and she liked the flashes of humour that added to both his talk and his answers to questions afterwards.

Reluctantly, she was impressed. Although his family had an assured position in the district, it was a long climb from New Zealand to Rafe's rarefied heights—a climb into the world arena that would have taken more than intelligence and a sense of humour to achieve. To get as far as he had he'd need uncompromising determination and a formidable ruthlessness.

In short, someone to be respected—and to avoid. Only too well did she understand the havoc a dominating man could cause.

The media lately had been full of him, from headlines about the signing of an important takeover to a photograph of him with a very beautiful woman in the gossip pages, but he'd soon be leaving Tewaka.

Hopefully to be away for another two months... That should give her time to stiffen her backbone and get over her disturbing awareness of the man.

* * *

When the meeting broke up—a little later than she expected—he caught up with her outside the library where the meeting had been held and asked, "Where's your car?"

Ignoring a suspicious warmth in the pit of her stomach, she indicated her elderly vehicle. "Right here. Goodnight." It was too abrupt, but she hid her expression by bending to open the door.

Their hands collided on the handle. The curbed strength Marisa sensed when his fingers closed momentarily over hers blitzed her with adrenalin. Before she could stop herself, she snatched her hand away as though she'd been stung.

And then it took every bit of composure she possessed to meet his focused, steel-sheened scrutiny without flinching.

Eyes narrowed, he pulled the door open and said coolly, "I rarely bite. Goodnight."

"Thank you." The words stumbled off her tongue and she hastily slid behind the wheel.

He closed the door on her and stood back.

Fingers shaking, she dumped her bag and the folder on the seat beside her and fumbled for the car keys. Why didn't he go away instead of standing on the pavement watching? Of course it took a while to find the key, but at last she finally stuffed it into the starter and turned.

Instead of the comforting purr of the engine, there was an ominous click, followed by an even more ominous silence.

CHAPTER THREE

"OH, NO." Swamped by a sickening feeling of impotence, Marisa jumped when the car door opened.

Rafe's voice, level and infuriatingly decisive, further fractured her composure. "Either your battery is flat or the starter motor's dead."

She fought an unnecessary panic, barely holding back the unladylike words that threatened to tumble out. Although she knew it to be useless, she couldn't stop herself from turning the key again, gritting her teeth when she was met with the same dead click.

"That's not going to help," Rafe told her, sounding almost amused. "It's the starter motor. If it had been the battery we'd have heard it try to fire."

Rebellion sparking a hot, barely contained resentment, she hauled the key out. It was all very well for him—*he* didn't have to worry about getting to and from work, or the cost of repairs. *He* could probably write out a cheque for whatever car he wanted, no matter how much it cost, and not even notice...

Rafe's voice broke into her tumbling, resentful thoughts. "This is an automatic, right?"

"Yes," she said numbly.

"So it's no use trying to push-start it. I'll ring someone to come and collect it and then I'll give you a lift home."

Marisa's lips parted, only for her to clamp them shut again before her protest made it out.

Wearing her one pair of high heels, it would take an hour—possibly longer—to walk back to the house. And she'd promised Tracey's mother the girl would be home at a reasonable time.

Then she had to get to work tomorrow. Marisa couldn't yet afford any help in the shop and weekend child care cost more than she could afford, so on Saturday mornings Keir came with her.

Rafe's voice brought her head up and indignantly she realised that while she'd been working through her options, Rafe had taken her assent for granted. He already had his cell phone out and was talking as though to an old friend.

"Patrick? Can you come to the library and pick up a car? Starter motor's gone. No, not mine." Without looking, he gave the name and model of Marisa's elderly vehicle. "OK, thanks, see you soon."

He cut the connection and said to Marisa, "He'll be here in a few minutes so you'd better clear anything you want from the car. I'll take out your son's car seat."

Marisa scotched her first foolish urge to tell him she could do it. Frostily, she said, "Thank you", and groped for her bag.

She'd vowed she would never let another man run her life.

So did she wear some subliminal sign on her forehead that said *Order me around—I'm good at obeying?*

Not any more.

Oh, lighten up, she told herself wryly as she got out. She was overreacting. Rafe was a local; he knew the right person to contact. Allowing him to organise this didn't put her in an inferior position.

But that clutch of cold foreboding, the dark taint of powerlessness, lingered through her while she waited.

Fortunately the mechanic arrived within minutes, a cheerful man around Rafe's age who clearly knew him well.

He checked the starter motor, nodded and said, "Yep, it's dead. We'll take it to the garage."

Surprised, Marisa watched Rafe help. He was an odd mixture—a sophisticated plutocrat on terms of friendship with a mechanic in a small town in New Zealand.

But what did she know of the man, really? He'd revealed impressive endurance and grim determination during their interminable trek through the Mariposan night and the rain. He'd made his mark in the cut-throat world of international business. Extremely popular with women, he'd been linked to some of the loveliest in the world.

It was oddly—dangerously—warming to see that he still held to his roots in this small town in the northern extremity of a small country on the edge of the world...

Once in Rafe's car and heading home, she broke what was developing into an uncomfortable silence. "Thank you very much for your help."

His sideways glance branded her face. "What's the matter?"

"Nothing," she said automatically, then tried for a smile. "Well, nothing except for major irritation at being let down by my car!"

Rafe asked, "How will you manage without it?"

"It won't be a problem." She hoped her briskness indicated her ability to deal with any situation. "As your friend Patrick seems fairly sure the car will be ready on Tuesday, I'll ring the taxi service when I get home and organise a pick-up for tomorrow and Monday."

It would be an added expense on top of the repairs, one she could ill afford, but she'd manage.

Rafe broke into her thoughts. "Can you drive with manual gears?"

Startled, she nodded. "Yes."

She'd learned to drive the tiny car her parents towed behind their house bus. And in Mariposa the only vehicle available to drive had been an ancient Jeep.

Although David had taken it out most days on to the estancia, and even when he didn't, the keys were never in evidence.

At first she'd believed he was concerned for her safety; Mariposan drivers could be pretty manic. Eventually she'd realised it was another way of exerting control.

Dismissing that bitter memory, she asked bluntly, "Why?"

"There's a spare car at home that might suit you." Rafe's tone was casual. Clearly he saw nothing odd in offering a replacement vehicle.

She gave him a startled look. The lights of an oncoming car revealed the austere framework of his face, a study in angles and planes. Even the curve of his mouth—disturbingly sexy with its full lower lip— didn't soften the overwhelming impression of force and power.

He looked exactly what he was—a ruler, born to authority...

A man to avoid. Yet every time she saw him—or thought of him—a forbidden, dangerous sensation darted through her. Fixing her eyes on the dark road ahead, she said firmly, "That's a kind offer, but it's not necessary."

"Think it over before you refuse. I know you open the shop tomorrow morning. Nine o'clock?"

"Yes."

"I'm coming into Tewaka just before then, so I could pick you up on the way. Then in the afternoon we could go out to my place and you can try the car."

"That's very kind of you…" she said warily, her voice trailing away as every instinct shouted a warning.

Dominant he might be, but it was ridiculous to think his offer meant he was trying to control her.

Ridiculous. Silently she said it again, with much more emphasis, while she searched for a valid reason to refuse.

"I can hear your *but* echoing around the car." The note of cool amusement in his voice brought colour to her skin. "Independence is a good thing, but reluctance to accept help is taking it a bit too far."

Crisply she returned, "Thank you, but there's no need for you to put yourself out at all."

His broad shoulders lifted in a negligent shrug. "If you're ready on time tomorrow morning, calling for you will add less than five minutes to my journey."

Marisa opened her mouth, but he cut in before she could speak, saying, "Small country towns—even tourist places like Tewaka—build strong communities where people can rely on each other when they need support. The car I'm offering used to belong to my grandmother. No one drives it now, but it's in good shape."

She rallied to say calmly, "I'll accept your lift tomorrow, but I really won't need to borrow a car. I can manage for a couple of days. And you don't even know if I'm a good driver."

Heat flared in the pit of her stomach when her eyes clashed with his sideways glance. There was altogether too much irony in the iron-grey depths—irony backed by a sensuous appreciation that appealed to some treacherous part of her.

She should be able to resist without even thinking about it.

Well, she *was* resisting—resisting like crazy.

Only she didn't want to.

And that was truly scary. Rafe Peveril was really bad news—danger wrapped in muscled elegance, in powerful grace, in unexpected kindness...

"How good *are* you?" he asked almost idly, his tone subtly challenging.

Marisa took a short, fortifying breath to steady her voice. "I think I'm a reasonably proficient driver, but everyone believes they're competent, don't they? It's very kind of you to offer the car—"

His mouth curved in a hard smile. "No more buts, please. And to set the record straight, I'm not particularly kind."

That made sense. Men who made it to the top of whatever field they entered usually didn't suffer from foolish generosity.

Remember that, she ordered the weak part of her that tempted her to—to what? Surrender? Accept being told what to do?

So stop that right now, she commanded abruptly, and squared her shoulders. She'd vowed never to allow herself to feel useless again and wasn't going to renege on that promise just because this formidable man was offering her the use of a car.

So she said, "If I needed the help I'd accept it with gratitude, but it's not necessary." She might not buy food for a couple of days, but the pantry held enough to tide them over and independence was worth it.

"Right." His tone changed, became brisk and businesslike as he turned the wheel to go up the short drive to the cottage. "However, the offer's still open."

Tracey met them at the door, her beam turning to blushing confusion when she saw who accompanied Marisa. Rafe knew how to deal with dazzled adolescents; his smile friendly, he offered the girl a ride back to the homestead.

Marisa watched the car go out of the gate and stood for a moment as another car came around the corner, slowed and then sped by. Shivering a little, she closed the door on the darkness, her thoughts tumbling and erratic.

Clearly Rafe Peveril was accustomed to getting his own way. And perhaps having grown up as son of the local big family, he felt some sort of feudal responsibility for the locals.

Well, he didn't need to. This new local was capable of looking after herself and her son.

She walked into Keir's room to check him. In the dim light of the hall lamp he looked angelic snuggled into the pillow, his face relaxed in sleep.

Her heart cramped. Whatever she did, she had to keep him safe.

But she stood watching him and wondered at the source of her unease. Rafe hadn't recognised her.

And even if he did remember who she was and where they'd met, would it matter so much…?

Pretending she'd never seen him before now seemed to be taking caution too far, her response based on a fear she thought she'd overcome. Thanks to the strength she'd developed, David was no longer a threat to her and no threat to Keir either.

But only while he still believed that lie…

She drew in a deep breath, wondering if the room was too hot. But Keir hadn't kicked off his bedclothes and a hand on his forehead revealed a normal temperature. Stooping, she dropped a light kiss on her son's cheek, waited as he stirred and half-smiled and then relapsed back into sleep, then left.

Back in her bedroom, she walked across to the dressing table and opened a drawer, looking down at a photo taken by her father a few days after she'd arrived back home. Reluctant even to touch it, she shivered again.

Never again, she swore with an intensity that reverberated through her. That pale wraith of a woman—hopeless, helpless—was gone for ever. Wiser and much stronger now, she'd allow no arrogant male to get close to her.

So although Rafe Peveril was gorgeous and exciting and far too sexy in a powerfully male way, she'd take care to avoid him.

She closed the drawer and turned away to get ready for bed. All she had to do was inform him she could deal with the situation and keep saying it until he got the message.

And avoid him as much she could.

But once she was in bed, thoughts of him kept intruding, until in the end she banished the disturbing effect he had on her by retracing the path that had turned her from a normal young woman to the wreck she'd been when she'd first seen him.

Loneliness, early pregnancy—and a husband who'd callously greeted that news by saying he didn't ever want children—had plunged her into a lethargy she couldn't shake off. A subsequent miscarriage had stripped her of any ability to cope. The shock of her mother's illness and David's flat refusal to let her go back to New Zealand had piled on more anguish than she could bear.

And then Rafe had arrived, tall and lithe and sinfully attractive, his intimidating authority somehow subtly diminishing David, and made his casual offer to take her home with him. By then she'd suspected she might be pregnant again and it was this, as well as her mother's illness, that had given her the courage to stand up to her husband.

Back in New Zealand and caring for her mother and a father whose grief-stricken bewilderment had rendered him almost helpless, she'd discovered that her pregnancy was a fact.

It had been another shock but a good one, giving her a glimpse of a future. With that responsibility to face, she'd contacted a counsellor.

Who'd told her not to be so harsh on herself. "A miscarriage, with the resultant grief and hormonal imbalance, can be traumatic enough to send some women into deep depression," she'd said firmly. "Stop blaming yourself. You needed help and you didn't get it. Now you're getting it and you'll be fine."

And during the years spent with her parents and looking after her son, she'd clawed her way back to the person she'd been before David. Her fierce determination to make sure Keir had everything he needed for a happy life had kept her going.

For him she had turned herself around. And because of him she would never marry again...

* * *

The next morning was busy, which was just as well. She'd been wound tightly, waiting for Rafe to call for her and Keir, but his pleasant aloofness almost convinced her that she had no reason to fear him. He might find her attractive, but a small-time shopkeeper was not his sort of woman. They tended to be tall and beautiful and well-connected, wear designer clothes and exquisite jewels, and be seen at the best parties all over the world.

In the afternoon she and Keir worked in the cottage garden; by the time she went to bed she was tired enough to fall asleep after only a few thoughts about Rafe Peveril.

She woke to Keir's call and a raw taint of smoke that brought her to her feet. Coughing, she shot into Keir's room and hauled him from bed, rushing him to the window and jerking back the bolt that held it in place.

Only to feel the old sash window resist her frantic upwards pressure. A jolt of visceral panic kicking her in the stomach, she struggled desperately, but it obstinately refused to move. Ignoring Keir's alarmed whimpers, she turned and grabbed the lamp from the table beside his bed, holding it high so she could smash one of the panes.

And then the window went up with a rush, hauled up by someone from outside.

Rafe, she realised on a great gulp of relief and wonder and fresh air.

He barked, "Keir, jump into my arms."

Gasping, her heart hammering in her ears, she thrust her son at him and turned, only to be stopped by another harsh command. "Get out, now! The verandah is already alight. The house will go any minute."

She scrambled over the sill and almost fell on to the grass beneath. A strong hand hauled her to her feet.

"Run," Rafe commanded and set off across the lawn and on to the drive, Keir safely held in his arms.

Half-sobbing, she watched as Keir was bundled into the back seat, then crawled in beside him as Rafe opened the driver's door and got in.

She had time only for a quick, hard hug before Rafe commanded abruptly, "Seat belts on. I need to get this car out of the way of the fire brigade."

So he must have called them. By the time Marisa had fastened the belts Rafe had the car purring quietly down the drive.

Rafe glanced briefly over his shoulder, his words cutting through the darkness. "All right?"

"Yes, thank you." Her voice sounded thin and wavery, and in spite of the warm summer night she was trying to stop herself from shivering in case it frightened Keir further.

"I've just come from the Tanners' place, so they'll still be up. I'll take you there."

Desperate to get Keir away from the sight of the burning building, she nodded. A few hundred metres down the road the fire engine tore past, siren wailing, lights flashing, followed by a stream of volunteers' cars.

Keir stared, fascinated. "Can we go back?" he asked eagerly. "I want to see them."

"No." She choked back a laugh that felt suspiciously like a sob. "The firemen need room to work and we'd only be in the way, darling."

"When I grow up," he told her importantly, "I'm going to be a fireman."

Her hand tightened around his. "When you grow up you can be anything you want to be."

The big car slowed, drew into the Tanners' gateway. All the house lights were on and Sandy Tanner came hurtling through the front door. He stopped, looked hard, then peered into the back as Rafe eased the car to a stop.

"Oh, thank God," he said hoarsely, wrenching the door open. "Come on, all of you, get into the house. Jo's got the kettle on."

Obeying, Keir and Marisa scrambled out and into the comfortable homestead, Keir with a wistful glance over his shoulder at the belt of trees that hid the cottage. "Our house is all smoky," he informed Jo Tanner, who gave him a swift hug.

"But you're here now and quite safe." She straightened and looked at Marisa.

Who asked steadily, "Could we put him down on a sofa somewhere under a blanket?"

"Of course we can. Come with me and we'll settle him."

Keir's hand clutched in hers, Marisa followed Jo into the big family room.

Briskly the older woman said, "You'll find the sleeping bags in that cupboard, with the sheets folded beside them. You'll want something else to wear too—I'll get Tracey's dressing gown. You and she are about the same size."

Still numb with shock, Marisa moved as if in a dream, spreading the sleeping bag on to the sofa and thanking the heavens that Keir still clutched his teddy bear. Like small boys the world over, Keir adored playing with his train and bulldozer, but Buster Bear went to sleep with him.

By the time Jo arrived with a summery, striped dressing gown she'd calmed Keir down enough to tuck him in and promise him she wouldn't go away. It was only when she pulled on Tracey's gown that she realised she was still wearing pyjamas.

OK, so the thin singlet top and boy-leg shorts would have revealed every line and curve of her body. Big deal, she thought trenchantly.

She had a lot more than that to worry about.

Everything she had was in the cottage, every precious memento—Keir's baby photographs, his wide grin showing his first tooth, her parents' wedding photo and the small silver-leaf brooch she'd loved to see her mother wear when she was a child...

Swallowing, she forced down the nausea that gripped her. She couldn't afford to break down. She had to be strong.

Nevertheless, when Keir dropped off to sleep, she had to force herself to get up and walk out of the room.

To her intense relief, the only person in the sitting room was Jo. She looked up and asked, "Has he dropped off?"

"Yes, it didn't take long. He rarely stirs, but I've left the door open and the light on just in case..."

Her voice trailed away and she blinked back stupid tears.

"He'll be fine," Jo said firmly. "Kids are surprisingly resilient. You're the one in shock, not him. I'll put the jug on—what would you like, tea or coffee?"

"It had better be coffee." She smiled weakly. "Jo, thanks so much—"

"Nonsense," Jo cut in firmly. "Don't worry, we've got everything organised. Rafe wanted you to go home with him, but I managed to convince him that Keir would be happier here for the night, where he knows us. The men are over at the cottage checking up, but they should be back soon, and then we'll know how badly the cottage has been damaged." She glanced at the clock and added more water to the electric jug.

Five minutes later a car pulled up outside. Nerves jumping, and acutely aware of the flimsiness of her clothes, Marisa leapt to her feet, bracing herself to meet Rafe's iron-grey gaze when he walked in. "What's happening? Is the cottage…?"

She couldn't finish, couldn't force herself to put it into words.

"Uninhabitable," Rafe said, not trying to soften it.

Marisa closed her eyes against his watchful scrutiny and dragged a painful breath into her lungs. "Did… Was it anything I'd done? I've been trying to work out whether I left anything on—the iron or…"

"Relax, it had nothing to do with you." Still in that level, dispassionate voice he went on, "It looks as though it was caused by someone flicking a cigarette butt out of a car window. The grass on the verge caught fire and the wind carried it up to the verandah. Once the balustrade caught it was pretty much all over."

"Was anything saved?"

This time Sandy answered, his voice sympathetic. "A good part of your stuff is all right, thanks to Rafe calling the brigade as soon as he saw the line of fire towards the house. The brigade killed the flames and Rafe and I helped them carry what was salvageable into the old garage there. It's smoke and water-stained, but it should be OK."

She dragged in a painful breath. "I'm so sorry, Sandy. Can you repair the place?"

"Not worth it," he told her bluntly. "It's an old house and once the fire got in it went up like a bomb. Bloody lucky Rafe happened to be passing and got you and young Keir out."

With an ironic smile Rafe said, "I had nothing to do with it, beyond yanking up the sash and catching the boy as Marisa pushed him through the window."

Foolishly, she wondered if meeting Rafe again had somehow set off some sort of tornado in her life, hurling all her careful plans into chaos...

She locked her fingers together to stop them shaking. Struggling to master her weakness, she blinked again, perilously close to collapsing into undignified tears as she recalled her frenzied terror when the window refused to open.

Rafe dropped one lean, strong hand over hers and squeezed. In a rock-steady voice he said, "Calm down. You saved yourself and your son, that's the most important thing right now. Everything else we can deal with."

We? Forget about that, she thought, and then felt surly, because he was being unexpectedly kind. "I haven't thanked you for opening the window," she said. "I was panicking, and Keir—"

He let her hand go and stepped back, waiting until she sank on to the sofa before continuing, "You were carrying something to break it—you'd have managed. Don't worry, Marisa, everything will be all right."

Conventional words, yet strangely they were of some comfort. When Rafe spoke in that coolly purposeful tone she couldn't imagine any power on earth gainsaying him.

Lifting her chin, she straightened her spine and asked with irony, "Is that a promise?"

Rafe smiled. "Only if you do as you're told."

And watched with interest as her delicate black

brows shot up at his blatant challenge. He was beginning to get some idea of her quality and admired that quick recovery and the strength it showed. Shocked and desperately worried, she was no weakling and her independence was bone-deep, as fierce and strong as the maternal devotion that had seen her get the boy out.

Sure enough she said sweetly, "I gave that up years ago."

He looked across at the two interested spectators and asked, "Jo, is that coffee I can smell?"

"Oh—yes, of course it is!" Jo went into the kitchen.

Rafe left half an hour later, farewelling Marisa with an order. "Make sure you've got the all clear from the fire brigade before you go over to the cottage."

"Yes, sir," Marisa said, clearly too tired to think of anything else. In her borrowed dressing gown she didn't look much older than its owner.

He regarded her with a lurking smile, a smile she returned. But before she turned away she said seriously, "Thanks, Rafe. You're right, I'd have got him out, but— I'm glad you arrived when you did."

Rafe almost managed to repress an image of her clad in pyjamas so closely fitting they revealed every curve of her delectable body and softly sheened skin. His heartrate had careered off the chart.

The memory brought his body to full attention, so much so that he knew it was time to leave. Laconically he said, "If you're going to thank anyone, thank Jo and Sandy. I'll see you tomorrow. Goodnight."

CHAPTER FOUR

MARISA'S decision to get up early and go over to the cottage by herself was stymied when she didn't wake until almost nine in the morning.

Through the door, she could hear voices and laughter, and a glance at the sofa revealed nothing but an empty sleeping bag and Buster Bear. After an incredulous look at her watch she leapt off the inflatable mattress on the floor.

At the door she hesitated, then went back and put on Tracey's dressing gown. For some reason she had to brace herself before opening the door.

But Rafe wasn't in the big living area of the farmhouse. Relief and a strange loneliness hit her as she saw Jo and her daughter washing dishes.

Jo looked around and smiled. "Well, you look as though you've had a good night's sleep! Keir's out the front, playing with the boys. Tracey and I are just working out what clothes she can lend you until we get some of yours washed and ready to wear."

"Do you mind if it's jeans and T-shirts?" Tracey asked a little worriedly.

Marisa hesitated, then said with a wry smile, "Of course I don't mind. I'm just finding it a bit odd being a refugee. If it's all right with you, I'll wear them over to the cottage to see what I can find in the garage that Keir and I can wear straight away." A thought struck her. "What's Keir got on now?"

"I fished out some of the twins' old clothes and I put him in them. They're a bit too big but he doesn't seem to mind." Jo said firmly, "And you're not going over there until you've had some breakfast and a cup of tea or coffee, whichever you like."

"Thank you," Marisa said a little starkly. "You've been absolutely wonderful."

But Jo brushed her thanks away. "Tracey will bring some clothes along to the room you slept in and you can see if they're decent on you."

They were a little tight, but they would do until she managed to wash some of her own—always providing, she thought wearily as she walked along the road to the cottage, she had any left. Jo had offered to go with her, but she'd refused. She needed to be alone.

But the sight of the cottage stopped her, and for a horrifying moment she had to fight an urge to turn and run, snatch Keir up and run away from it all...

She dragged in a slow, painful breath and blinked back tears. Although the flame-blackened walls still stood, the whole place stank of smoke. Her heart clamped painfully when she saw the charred sticks of what had been hibiscus bushes against the verandah balustrade, their wonderful silken blooms gone for ever.

Some members of the fire team were back, checking the place and damping down any hot spots. She gave her eyes a quick surreptitious dab as the fire chief came out to meet her.

He said, "I wish we could have done more for you. Don't go anywhere near the house—it's not entirely safe yet. The garage is OK, though. You might like to go and check on things." He paused before saying a little diffidently, "We couldn't save all your boy's toys and only a few of his books."

Regaining control, she said, "Thank you so much. Some is better than nothing."

She'd find some tangible way to thank them, but right then she could only stand in the doorway of the garage, nostrils wrinkling at the stench of smoke, and fight for composure.

Someone had hauled out the drawers from the dressing table and dumped them and their contents on the floor, along with what looked like clothes from the wardrobes, Keir's toy box and a handful of his books. A few pots and pans had made it, but nothing much else from the kitchen.

The pathetic remnants of her life made her swallow hard, but mourning could come later. Right now she needed to be strong.

After a deep breath she walked in, only to flinch when the first thing she saw was the photograph on the ground—the one she loathed yet couldn't bring herself to throw away.

Unmarked by smoke and free from water damage, that pale wraith of a woman haunted her. Never again, she vowed silently, and snatched it up, only just stopping herself from furtively glancing over her shoulder.

"Are you all right?"

Rafe's voice—too close—brought her heart into her throat, blocking her breathing and setting her pulse rate soaring. Her fingers shook as she crumpled the betraying paper, the tiny sound it made echoing in her ears like a small, suspicious explosion.

Had he seen it—that betraying photograph?

In a thin voice she lied, "I'm fine, thank you."

Don't break down, she commanded, her composure cracking. *Don't even think of it. You've coped with worse than this—you can deal with anything...*

Clearly he didn't believe her, but he said only, "I brought some plastic sacks. Do you want me to help you?"

After a swift desperate struggle to subdue her rioting apprehension, she forced herself to turn, hoping her face didn't show anything more than mild interest.

Rafe's trademark vitality was as potent as ever and he examined her face in a searching survey that sent shivers the length of her spine.

All she could trust herself to say was a quiet, "That was thoughtful of you. Thank you."

"It's not the end of the world," he said calmly and reached out his hand.

She stepped back, saw the infinitesimal narrowing of his eyes and said swiftly, harshly, "If you—anyone— touches me now I'll start to cry."

His mouth hardened. "Would that be so bad? It might be a good idea to release some emotion."

"Later, perhaps," she said bluntly, trying for a smile and failing badly. "There's enough water around without me adding to it."

Her breath huffed out in a long, silent sigh when he turned and walked out.

Like the lord of all creation, she thought ironically, watching the way the smoky sunlight kindled a lick of flame across his black head.

If he'd touched her she'd have crumbled, sagging into a humiliating heap of misery.

After another deep breath she hid the crushed photo in her handbag. She'd never be able to throw it away. It reminded her of how far she'd come and how strongly she refused to allow herself to revert.

So do something practical right now, she told herself, and after opening the big plastic sack, began to sort swiftly through the piles, grabbing the first clothes to hand. They stank of smoke and were damp, but a good wash would see them back in a wearable state.

Where could she go? At the most, she and Keir couldn't stay more than a couple of nights with the Tanners—it would be a total imposition after their kindness to her. So, even though she couldn't afford it, she'd have to book into a motel. Tewaka had several; at least one must have accommodation until she found somewhere more permanent.

Scarcely had the thought formed in her mind when she felt Rafe's presence behind her again and stood up, turning to face him.

He said, "All right?"

Jerkily she nodded.

He waited a moment, before saying calmly, "Where do you plan to stay?"

"I don't know yet," she said flatly, hating him for bringing her unspoken fears out into the open. Head held high, she tried to read his expression and failed.

Calmly he said, "Then I suggest you and young Keir move into my house until you find somewhere else to live."

Unable to believe he'd actually said what she'd heard, she stared at him, a swift rush of adrenalin surging through her.

One black brow climbed and his mouth quirked. "I'm pretty certain I haven't suddenly developed horns. It makes sense. Manuwai has enough bedrooms to billet a small army. If you think Keir needs reassurance at night, you could share the nursery suite, which has two bedrooms."

OK, so he didn't mean…what she thought he *might* have meant. Hot-cheeked yet relieved, Marisa recovered enough composure to say a little stiffly, "It's very kind of you, but I'm sure I can find somewhere—a motel, perhaps."

Amusement vanishing, he elaborated, "It's summer, this is a tourist area and the schools will be closing within weeks. Any chance of finding a motel unit— let alone a place to rent—is remote, possibly until the end of the holidays. Actually, you're not likely to get anything until after February because that's when people without schoolchildren take their holidays. I'm assuming you want a house within driving distance of Tewaka."

Numbly she nodded. "Yes."

Keir was very happy at school and she would *not* put him through the sort of upheaval she'd endured as a child. Nevertheless, the prospect of sharing a house with Rafe Peveril set every instinct jittering protectively.

Rafe went on, "Once summer is over you'll have a much better chance of finding a place."

His cool, reasonable tone grated her nerves. She blurted, "The end of summer is three months away."

The sound of her voice, sharp and almost accusing, stopped any further words. She drew a rapid breath and struggled for composure.

It took a lot of energy to steady herself and say with more than a hint of formality, "I'm grateful for the offer, but Keir and I can't possibly live in your house for that long."

"I knew there'd be a *but* in there somewhere," Rafe

said ironically. "So what will you do? Camp in the back of the shop?" He finished with a biting undernote, "Hardly a suitable place for a child."

Rallying, Marisa called on all her hard-won assurance to say briskly, "Please don't be offended. And, no, the shop is no solution. As my car appears to be unreliable, I'll see if I can find somewhere closer to town—preferably within walking distance—before I give you a definite answer."

There, that sounded sensible and practical and—her thoughts skidded to a noisy hum as Rafe nodded, a micro-flash of emotion in his eyes intensifying her unease.

"I'm not offended," he said coolly. "I'll ask around myself. Just don't be alarmed if nothing turns up." He gave a narrow smile. "And while you're looking around, the homestead is there. I'm heading overseas in a few days, so if me being there is a problem it needn't be."

The temptation to surrender to his calm assumption of authority was potent enough for her to pause before answering. Yet it fretted at something fragile and hard-won in her to accept Rafe's hospitality.

However, if she and Keir could find no other place to go, she'd grit her teeth and accept it for Keir's sake.

"I— No, of course it wouldn't be a problem. Thank you," she added lamely.

"Then I suggest you think seriously about it. Jo and Sandy will offer you beds, but it's not particularly convenient for them, or for you."

"No," she said swiftly. "I wouldn't dream of it…" Her voice trailed away as she desperately tried for some solution, only to realise she had no other options. That hard knot in her chest expanded, and she surrendered.

"Then—all right, I'll accept your very kind offer for a few days while I try to find a more permanent place."

Any place!

He didn't look pleased, merely nodded. "Fine. Thanks bore me, so let's have no more of them."

The urgent summons of her cell phone stopped him. She grabbed it and heard Tracey Tanner's agitated voice, and a background sound she recognised immediately. Keir—heartbroken.

"Can you come, please?" Tracey implored. "I've made him cry and he needs to see you're all right."

Marisa said, "We'll be there in a few moments", and switched off. Heading for Rafe's car, she told him over her shoulder what the girl had said.

At the Tanners' house a sobbing Keir ran into Marisa's arms and clung, while she looked her questions above his head.

Mrs Tanner frowned at her daughter. "I'm afraid he overheard Tracey talking to a friend about the fire and got it into his head that it was happening still, with you in danger."

Flushing, Tracey chimed in guiltily, "I'm really sorry—I should have checked to make sure he wasn't listening."

"Keir, it's all right. Stop crying now—Mummy's fine," Marisa soothed, aware of Rafe's hard face.

But his voice was cool, almost detached. "He'll get over it. Marisa is Keir's home base; now he knows she's safe he'll be fine. Won't you, Keir?"

Muffling his sobs in Marisa's breast, Keir nodded, but although he was manfully trying to control them, great half-choked sobs still shook his body.

Rafe went on, "And most of his toys are all right."

Acutely aware of an undercurrent of curiosity from the two Tanners, Marisa said briskly, "Keir, Mr Peveril helped me collect your clothes and your toys. What do you say to him?"

After a hiccup or two Keir emerged from her embrace to say, "Thank you. And my bulldozer?"

"Yes." Before he could run through a catalogue of his toys, she prompted, "And what do you say to Mr and Mrs Tanner and Tracy and the boys?"

Keir made his thanks, adding a codicil, "And thank you for the yummy chocolate, Tracey."

"Any time," Tracey said and ruffled his hair before exchanging a high five that dried the last of his tears and left him smiling. "See you later, alligator."

As they turned to go, Mrs Tanner asked in a worried voice, "Marisa, what are your plans? Is there anything I can do for you?"

Before Marisa had time to answer Rafe said smoothly, "She and Keir are free to stay at Manuwai until she finds somewhere else to live."

At Mrs Tanner's surprised look, Marisa inserted herself into the conversation. "Rafe has been very kind in offering us temporary refuge, but if you know of anyone who has a unit or a small place to rent, I'd be so grateful if you'd tell me."

"I'll ask around," Mrs Tanner said. She exchanged glances with Rafe and grimaced. "I'm afraid it won't be easy."

"Rafe's already warned me of that."

But the more people she had looking out for a place to rent, the more likely she was to find one. Tomorrow— no, as soon as they got to Manuwai—she'd call every estate agent in town to see if anything was available.

Once in the car Rafe glanced at Keir and said, "Straight home?"

Marisa nodded. "You took the words from my mouth. He's over-tired and overwrought. I'll do something about the rest of my stuff tomorrow."

Rafe nodded and started the engine and Marisa tried to relax, deliberately tightening and loosening muscles. It didn't seem to work. Every sense was alert and quivering, as though she felt an unknown danger.

In his car seat in the back, Keir was silent, but after several silent minutes he'd recovered enough to sing a song he'd learned at school, something about a car, only to stop halfway through with a cry that made her twist sharply.

"Look, Mummy! Camels!"

The car slowed and Marisa shook her head. "Not camels, although they're related. These are alpacas."

"Alpacas." He said the word with pleasure, then asked, "What does *related* mean?"

"Part of the same family," she said easily, aware of Rafe listening. "You're related to me."

"Like Nana and Poppa?"

"Yes."

"And like uncles and aunties like Tracey's Auntie Rose?"

"Just like that. Camels are cousins to alpacas."

While Keir digested this Rafe said, "They come from South America and they're bred for their wool."

From the back her son demanded, "Why don't I have any uncles or aunties or cousins, Mummy?"

Marisa said steadily, "Sometimes that happens in families, darling. The alpacas have wool that people use to make jerseys. I might go and see the people who own them to see if they make anything from them that we could sell in the shop."

As she'd hoped, that gave Keir something else to think about.

"Can I come too and pat the alpacas?" he asked.

"You can come, but they might not be tame enough to pat. Mr Peveril might know more about that than I do."

Rafe said, "I'm afraid I don't, but I can find out."

"No need," Marisa was quick to answer. "I'll do it."

Fortunately her words satisfied Keir and he settled back, humming to himself as he gazed out of the windows. Once more trying to relax, Marisa too looked out of the side window, her gaze skimming the hills and deep valleys of this part of Northland. On the very edge of her vision she could just discern a plume of smoke and had to swallow again.

Rafe asked, "Did you live in a city before you came here?"

Woodenly she answered, "Yes." Having to settle in one place had been a blow to her parents, but they'd needed to be close to the services available for her mother.

And she was being foolish to worry about the direction the conversation was taking. Rafe was merely making small talk, something to fill in the silence.

"In Auckland?"

"In the South Island," she said without elaboration. Right down in Invercargill, New Zealand's southernmost city, and about as far away from Auckland as you could get. Coolly she said, "I believe your property's on the coast."

Surely that was safe enough.

He inclined his head. "The house is almost on a beach."

An understatement, she realised when they arrived at Manuwai station. The homestead was a couple of kilometres from the road across paddocks that bore every sign of good farming. A thick, sheltering belt of kanuka trees separated the house from the working part of the station, the evocative, spicy perfume of their foliage permeating the warm air as the car moved into their shadow. From the feathery branches cicadas sent their high, shrill calls into the quivering sky.

A subtle, surprising delight filled Marisa and she leaned back in the seat. Ahead the drive bisected a large grassy paddock to head towards a far-from-modern house set in gardens that covered what seemed to be a peninsula.

She turned her head. Through the sheltering trees a basin-shaped inlet glittered blue against low, bush-clad cliffs. The point on which the homestead stood was its northern headland. In the opposite direction she glimpsed the long, silvery-pink sweep of a beach curving northwards.

"You're looking north to Ocean Beach and south to the cove," Rafe told her. "It's the only safe haven for about thirty miles and served as a refuge in bad weather for the scows that brought goods up and down the coast until the roads were developed."

"It's beautiful," Marisa responded inadequately.

A glitter caught her eye; she turned her head and glimpsed a helicopter parked just outside a hangar.

Well, *naturally*, she thought, mocking herself for her surprise. Of course Rafe Peveril would have a chopper on call. Did he fly the thing too?

Probably...

The big, orange-tiled house sprawled gracefully, its surrounding gardens melding imperceptibly into pohutukawa trees, their sombre foliage and twisted, heavy branches lightened by the silver reverse of each small leaf. Soon each ancient tree would glow scarlet and crimson and ruby, carpeting the beaches with brilliant blossoms like exploding Catherine wheels.

"This is the third house on the site—built in the 1920s," Rafe told her. "The family then had several very pretty daughters, so their father commissioned a house for entertaining. It's been modernised and added to down the years, but basically it's the same as it was then."

He spoke so matter-of-factly Marisa wondered if he took the house and its wonderful position for granted. A little wistfully, she tried to imagine what it must be like to know that your forefathers lived here, that for you there was always a base, a place you could call home...

The gates suited the mature opulence of the house, but were opened electronically, much to Keir's interest, and revealed a paved forecourt. Looking around, Marisa decided that the parking space was big enough to satisfy the social urges of a whole school of girls.

Rafe stopped outside the wide, welcoming front door and killed the engine. "You must both be hungry. I know I am."

"I am too," Keir piped up.

"I thought you probably would be," Rafe said, "so I phoned ahead to the housekeeper and warned her to have something ready that would please a boy." He lowered his voice. "And I wondered if you might like to go down to the beach afterwards."

But Keir's sharp ears picked up his words. Explosively

he said, "Yes, we do like to go to the beach!" and added, "Please, Mr Peveril, and thank you."

Tonelessly Marisa said, "That's very kind of you."

Rafe was too astute not to guess how she was feeling, but nothing of that knowledge showed in his face until they were out of the car and Keir had wandered a few steps away to gaze around.

Rafe looked quizzically down at her. "Sorry, I hadn't bargained for such good hearing on his part. It's been a while since I had anything to do with children. If today's not suitable, another day will be fine."

She tried for a casual smile. "We'd love to go to the beach today, wouldn't we, Keir?"

"Yes, please," he said with heartfelt fervour.

Rafe glanced at the opening door. "Ah, here's Nadine, who rules Manuwai with a rod of iron."

The housekeeper, a slim, brisk woman in her forties, smiled at both Marisa and Keir. "There's only one boss here and it isn't me. Lunch is ready if you'd like it now. I hope there are no allergies I should have taken into consideration."

"Not a one, thank you," Marisa told her. Keir enjoyed rude good health. She glanced down at him, sighed when she saw his hands and said ruefully, "But first we need to wash our hands."

CHAPTER FIVE

LUNCH was served in a sunny, pleasantly casual room where wide glass doors opened out on to a terrace over-looking lawns and the sea. Although Keir ate with his usual enthusiasm, his conversation revealed that his mind was bent on the beach rather than food.

After his second assertion that he wasn't hungry, Rafe pre-empted Marisa's response with a crisp, "We'll go to the beach when we've finished eating and after I've made a phone call, so it won't be for a little while yet."

Keir accepted this without protest. Uncomfortably—and not for the first time—Marisa wondered if she was depriving him of something vital by cutting his father out of his life.

Since her own father's death the previous year there had been no masculine influence on her son; watching him with Rafe now made her very conscious of Keir's simple pleasure in his presence.

As the years went by, that gap was likely to become a problem.

"Stop worrying," Rafe said.

Startled, she looked up, met a speculative gaze and felt her heart give a sudden leap. "I'm not," she told him, not quite truthfully.

"There's no need. Things will settle down."

His astuteness made her jumpy. It would be too easy to fall into the habit of relying on his strength.

On the way down a paved track to the curved stretch of sand at the base of the cliff, Rafe broke into her thoughts. "We've always called this the children's beach. It's very safe."

"And utterly beautiful." Mentally picturing the children who'd played here over the years, she looked around.

This exquisite boundary between land and sea—the brilliant sky, low red cliffs held together by the tenacious roots of the trees, salt and sand and the shrill calls of seabirds, a limitless ocean—this was the stuff of memories that made expatriate New Zealanders homesick.

And the unwavering self-sufficiency she sensed in Rafe, that deep inner confidence, was what she wanted—no, what she was *determined* to achieve for her son.

After some enthusiastic stamping and splashing in the tiny wavelets, Keir settled to build a large sandcastle, discussing the best way to construct it with Rafe in a very matey, man-to-man way that increased Marisa's tension.

If only there'd been an alternative to coming here. Not only was she far too aware of Rafe, but she didn't want Keir forming any sort of bond with him. Although he was surprisingly relaxed and easy with her son, there was no place for him in their lives.

And that was *not* maternal jealousy. As much as she could, she'd protect her child from any chance of future pain.

But she had to admit that Rafe was good with children. Possibly he'd had experience with them, although it didn't seem likely. What she'd read about him in the media indicated that most of the women who'd been linked to him were gorgeous creatures who flitted from party to party at all the "in" spots around the world. If any had children, no doubt nannies kept them well out of sight.

His world was very different from hers... Although Rafe might be attracted to her, she'd bet permanence was not his intention.

When he married he'd choose someone who'd fit into his world, not a nobody without a family.

Marriage? Stunned, she pushed the word away.

If—and it was an *if* so remote she couldn't ever see it happening—but if she ever again trusted a man sufficiently to consider marrying him, for Keir's sake any decision would have to be the right one, made with great care.

A decision that concentrated on good solid qualities rather than the impact of a glinting iron-grey gaze and seriously muscled elegance!

Rafe straightened up from a close examination of part of the sand fortification and glanced across to where she perched on a convenient rock. Her nerves tightened when he said something to Keir, who nodded and smiled and went back to his work as Rafe walked towards her.

Even in the casual shirt and trousers that had clearly been made for him, he looked like a model out of a photo shoot, one selling something magnificently masculine and expensive and powerful.

His first comment widened her eyes in shock.

"I gather Keir's father plays no part in his life."

Was he thinking of the mother who'd played no part in his?

"None," she said, her briefness making it clear she didn't want to discuss this.

His gaze narrowed slightly, but he nodded. "Or in yours."

"No."

After another level, penetrating look, he transferred his survey to the child. "Of the man's choice, or yours?"

Afraid to reveal too much of her nervous guilt, she monitored both her face and her tone. "Both."

"And you're happy with that?"

"Very." Her direct glance emphasised that he was trespassing.

But he was still watching Keir, his head turned to give her an excellent view of his profile. Her wary gaze skimmed arrogant nose and cheekbones and a jaw that epitomised formidable strength.

Handsome was too smooth a word to describe Rafe Peveril. *Commanding* sprang to mind, but even it didn't convey the essence of the man beside her.

It just didn't seem fair that any man should have everything. Except a mother, she reminded herself, and found herself hoping his stepmother had loved him.

Rafe turned his head, catching her eye. His gaze sharpened, darkened, ratcheting up her heart rate. "So is Keir the only man in your life?"

Very blunt. Why did he want to know?

Oh, don't be an idiot. You know the reason...

Her breath stopped in her throat. His open indication that he was as aware of her as she was of him fired a leaping, spontaneous excitement that took her by surprise.

Yet a cowardly impulse urged her to look him in

the eye and lie—or at least imply that she was in a relationship.

She couldn't do it. The lie that already involved him in her life without his knowledge still tasted bitter on her tongue.

And attraction—that heated, exciting tug at the senses, the disturbing, instinctive recognition of desire—meant very little. Perhaps Rafe was bored, looking for a diversion. He was free, and she was a novelty...

Whatever, he was dangerous.

"He's the only man in my life for the foreseeable future." Trying to ignore the odd husky note to the words, she added quickly, "He's heading for the water. I'll just go—"

"He's perfectly safe. Can he swim?"

"Not yet."

Rafe kept his gaze on the boy, the brilliant yellow plastic bucket Nadine had found clutched in his hand.

Marisa was being evasive. Her answers were straight enough and delivered with conviction, but a note of strain convinced him something was amiss.

He glanced at her. Face rigid, her posture tense, she was watching her son as though his life depended on it. Rafe felt a stab of compunction. She'd endured a gruelling twenty-four hours and he'd pushed her enough for the moment.

Quite apart from the possible mystery of her identity, she intrigued him. His initial flash of recognition had been accompanied by a primal, tantalisingly physical hunger, but that first mainly carnal awareness had been tempered by her stoic independence and her strength, and her love for the boy.

She'd come out to Manuwai only because she had no other option. He still didn't know how she felt about him—and that, he thought sardonically, made a rather refreshing change from most of the other women he met, who let him know they were very interested indeed, either in him, or his assets.

Crouching, Keir had proceeded to fill his bucket with sand. Rafe commented, "He's already worked out that wet sand holds its shape better than dry. He seems very grounded."

His shrewd gaze noted the silent, small signs of relaxation in Marisa before she said, "I hope so. He has his moments, of course, but he's mostly pretty placid."

"He doesn't mention any lack of a father?"

Tensing again, she kept her gaze fixed on her son and answered in a coolly dismissive voice, "Not so far, but I know it's inevitable."

"How do you plan to deal with it?"

Rafe watched her get gracefully to her feet, turning away to tuck the shirt into the borrowed, slightly tight trousers, and perhaps by accident giving him an excellent view of a swathe of taut, golden skin at her waist. Deep inside him a feral anticipation woke and refused to be leashed.

Dark lashes shuttered her green eyes and her voice was remote when she answered, "I don't know. I'm hoping it won't be for a while yet."

Her tone made it clear that was all she intended to say. And because he wasn't ready to take this any further right now he let her get away with it.

For the moment.

Always, he waited to move until he had every available scrap of information. The photograph he'd glimpsed in the garage had been enough to convince him she was Mary Brown.

What he needed to know was her reason for refusing to admit it.

The Mariposan agent's tone and words came back to him...*a few weeks after you and Mrs Brown left for New Zealand...*

In the hospital he'd been told they'd made it to a herder's hut, spent the night there and been found the next morning. He could—just—recall seeing the hut from the plane. After that there was a blank until he woke some days later in a hospital bed in the capital city.

How had they spent that lost night? Why had he never thought to ask? Because he had been too busy dealing with the mess that was the Mariposan agency, he decided mordantly.

He accepted that his cynicism had its roots in the knowledge that his mother had literally sold him to his father. It had been reinforced by the years he'd been a target for fortune-hunters. Was Marisa/Mary trying to set him up, and, if so, why?

You know, he thought sardonically, it would be for the usual reason—money.

She interrupted his thoughts, her gaze steady and unreadable. "I think Keir's been in the sun long enough." Her smile was set, her tone brisk and without emotion. "Besides, I need to wash the clothes I salvaged. We can't go on wearing the Tanner children's gear."

Rafe got to his feet. "Nadine will deal with them."

She glanced across at her son. Frowning, she pitched her voice too low for the boy to hear and said firmly, "Nadine is your housekeeper, not mine. I'm sure she's got enough to do looking after your lovely place without washing smoky clothes. I'll do it."

He said easily, "OK. Keir can stay here with me."

Brows lifting, she met his gaze, those cool green eyes unreadable, although her expression made it clear that he was, as his foster-sister would have told him, over-stepping the mark.

"I wouldn't dream of it," she said cheerfully. "He doesn't know you well enough." She gave him a glimmering smile. "And I'm sure you've better things to do with your time than babysit."

He shrugged, matching irony with irony. "One of which is to make sure you try out my grandmother's car," he agreed smoothly.

She hesitated, then gave another smile, this one with wry but genuine humour. "OK, you win," she conceded. "But clothes first."

Keir's disappointment at being taken away from his construction work was plain, but he submitted with reasonably good grace to being brushed down and chatted cheerfully as they walked back up to the house.

As he'd expected, Nadine was instantly sympathetic. "Of course you'll want to deal with your own clothes. Just call out if you need any help."

Rafe said casually, "I'll bring in the sack." He looked at Keir. "Coming with me? You can help carry in the toys we found."

Keir was only too ready to go. Marisa said, "I'll come too. There are quite a few things to be brought in."

On the way out Rafe stopped outside a garage door and said, "You might as well check out that car now."

He opened the door and stood back to let Marisa look in, waiting with interest for her response.

After a moment of stunned silence, she laughed with genuine amusement. "*This* is your grandmother's car?"

"Indeed it is," he said drily, ignoring the swift stab of some unrecognisable emotion.

She sent him a flustered, half-accusing look. "I'd imagined a solid, sedate, *grandmotherly* car. This—" she indicated the sleek, low sports car in racing green "—is about as suitable for me as a motorbike would be. Keir's car seat won't fit into that tiny back seat, and where on earth would I put the groceries?"

"In the boot—it's very roomy," he told her laconically. "And if you look harder, you'll realise his car seat would fit."

After examining the space more closely, she gave a reluctant nod. "Well—yes, I suppose it would." She glanced down at her son who was inspecting the vehicle with absorbed fascination, then sent Rafe a straight, sparkling look. "It's gorgeous, but unfortunately it's just not suitable."

"How do you know? You haven't even sat in it," he pointed out. "It's in excellent condition—my grandmother used to drive very carefully, especially once she reached ninety."

"Kilometres or years?" she shot back, then stopped, a slight tinge of colour heating the skin above her cheekbones.

Rafe laughed. "Years. Keir and I will watch while you familiarise yourself with it."

Her reluctance was palpable, but after another long-lashed look at him she got in, her hands moving gracefully, confidently, over gear lever and wheel, checking the position of various instruments.

Hiding an odd impatience by talking to her son, Rafe waited. Finally she swung out, managing the exit with grace and style.

Smiling, her expression serene, she said, "It's a lovely

car and I wish I'd seen your grandmother in it. But it's really not necessary, and with the run of luck I'm having right now I'd be terrified I might drive it into a ditch. Thanks so much for offering it though."

Had she been composing that formal little speech while she sat in the car?

If his newfound need to know what really happened in those empty hours after the crash led him to a stone wall, he might feel slightly foolish, but at least he'd be free to find out whether the sensual promise of her fascinating eyes held true.

His silence brought Marisa's head up. A chill of foreboding ran through her when she met eyes of ice-grey.

That arctic survey heated when he smiled, a smile like an arrow to her heart, piercing and melting the armour she'd built around herself with such bleak determination.

That smile stayed with her, lodging in her brain like an alluring, far-too-dangerous irritant while she and Keir washed their clothes, hung them out in the fresh, flower-scented air and were shown into the nursery suite.

It was charming, with two bedrooms and a bathroom as well as a playroom that opened out on to a terrace and a garden. Closer inspection revealed that the garden was walled with timber slats and the only gate had a lock on it.

"Apparently I liked to explore," Rafe told her when he noticed her examining it. "The fence went up the day my mother found me down on the beach by myself." He glanced down at Keir, happily re-acquainting himself with his toys. "I was about half his age."

At her sharp breath he smiled without humour. "Exactly." He glanced at his watch. "I need to make a few calls but if you need anything, Nadine will help. I should be finished in an hour, so get settled in. You'll want Keir to eat when?"

"Six o'clock."

"Nadine can bring along a tray for him to eat here. When does he go to bed?"

"Seven o'clock." She knew she sounded abrupt, but a sudden wave of exhaustion was sweeping through her—not physical tiredness, more a soul-weariness that sapped her energy.

Too much had happened in too short a time; she felt her life slipping out of her control and didn't know how to regain it.

Rafe nodded. "Dinner is at seven-thirty. I'll come and collect you then."

She'd much rather have a tray on the small table in the nursery, but before she could say so, he continued coolly, "There's a monitor in the bedroom, so if he wakes or stirs someone will hear him."

After a slight pause she nodded. "Yes, fine. Th—" and stopped, warned by his sardonic expression to go no further with her thanks.

But over this at least she had some control. With her most dazzling smile she said, "I almost managed to hold back that time. I'll see you at seven-thirty."

Once he'd gone she stared around the room as though in a prison, before collecting herself. She couldn't crumple now. Yet Rafe's absence left behind an emptiness that startled her. He was...overwhelming, she thought, watching her son check out the bookshelf.

Idiot that she was, she'd not thought to bring his pathetic pile of books from the garage. Were his favourites a pile of ashes—the much-read tractor book and his favourite bedtime story about a cheeky dog, the bear tale she must have read a thousand times…?

Right then she could do nothing about them. And she didn't want to think of Rafe Peveril's disturbing impact, either. If his absence could make her feel this worrying emptiness, it was only because he was such a commanding presence, not because whenever she saw him her breath came faster and excitement sang through every cell.

Oh, she was fooling herself. His effect on her wasn't due to his height, nor the breadth of his shoulders or the lean strength that proclaimed his fitness. Or even to his harshly handsome face, its angles and bold features set off by a mouth hinting at a dynamic male sexuality.

It came from within the man, based on character and the formidable, concentrated self-discipline, along with his uncanny knack for reading the world's markets. Add a brilliant brain and he was a man to take very seriously.

She knew little about his rise to the top and not much more about his business empire, but she'd read an article in the business section of a newspaper praising his skilful governance for steering the organisation his father had left to its present prominence. The writer had also admired his firm control of it.

That had made her shiver. It still did. Control was something she understood only too well.

She banished him from her mind. "Keir, why don't you choose one of those books for me to read you later, then we can walk around the garden just to see what's there."

She had a son to settle in spite of a future that had developed a snarl of setbacks. Far better to bend her brain to ways of dealing with them, instead of mooning over a man who'd been surprisingly kind.

* * *

Although it took Keir a while to get off to sleep, Buster Bear eventually worked his nocturnal magic, allowing Marisa to scramble into the one respectable outfit she'd grabbed from the crumpled pile saved by the firemen.

It looked tragic—exactly what you'd expect from something rescued from a fire. Tomorrow night, when she had clean dry clothes, she'd feel more human.

But she bit her lip as she examined herself in the long mirror. What on earth was a woman expected to wear to dinner in the home of a mogul?

"Probably not a green fake-silk shirt and tan trousers," she informed her reflection, "but that's all you've got."

In spite of shaking them out and hanging them in the fresh sea-scented breeze from the window, their faint smoky aroma summoned alarming memories and not just of the previous night. Occasionally images of her sweaty terror as she dragged their luggage free of the plane wreckage still turned up in her dreams.

Squaring her shoulders, she turned away from the mirror and checked the baby monitor for the third time. Something too close to expectation fluttered in the pit of her stomach.

Of all the coincidences to be faced with, meeting Rafe had been the one she'd dreaded most—even more than seeing David again.

If this situation ever came to David's notice it would only add to Keir's safety. She couldn't—*wouldn't*—allow herself to regret the lie she'd flung at her husband when he'd demanded she return to Mariposa with him.

Marisa took a deep breath. She hadn't *cheated* Rafe—she'd just used his name and his reputation.

A knock on the door tightened every muscle, forcing her to take a couple of deep breaths before she opened it.

"Is he asleep?" Rafe asked.

Still stiff with tension, she nodded. "Yes."

Narrow-eyed, Rafe watched her close the door behind her. She looked tired, her exquisite skin paler than usual, those great eyes filled with shadows and mystery, and her lush mouth disciplined. Even so, erect and graceful, it was difficult to believe she was the woman he'd met in Mariposa.

So why didn't he challenge her directly, ask her what the hell this masquerade meant? He had no answer to that, because for once he preferred not to know.

He asked, "Did you have any problems settling him down?"

"Some," she admitted, "but I expected that, it's been quite a day. Buster Bear won in the end though." Her smile was slightly pinched, as though it was an effort. "He usually sleeps like a log, but I'm a bit concerned that he might have a nightmare."

"Does he have many?"

"Not many, but after hearing Tracey's account of the fire…" Her voice trailed away. She stiffened her shoulders and went on more briskly, "I'm glad there's a baby monitor."

Rafe opened the door into the small parlour. "Sit down and I'll pour you a drink. I remember you like white wine."

Would she realise that had been in Mariposa? She'd refused any of the red wine from the local wineries and her husband had said, "You'll have to excuse Mary—she only likes New Zealand sauvignon blanc."

And he'd given her some fruit concoction.

His words brought a faintly puzzled glance as she

accepted the glass, but he noted the fine tremor across the surface of the liquid.

Perhaps she did remember.

However her voice was light and without nuance. "Along with other wines. Perhaps you're confusing me with someone else?"

So she wasn't going to admit anything. He lifted his own glass, untouched until then. "Possibly. Here's to a pleasant stay for both you and the boy."

"Thank you." She sipped, then glanced down at her wineglass. "Would it be possible for me to have some fruit juice too? I'm rather thirsty and I might drink this too quickly."

A faint colour stained her cheekbones, but she met his eyes steadily.

Surprised by a swift impulse of protectiveness, Rafe told her, "A brandy would probably be the best thing for you, but perhaps not until you're ready for bed."

She gave a slight laugh. "Oh, I'll sleep well enough without it. But juice would be perfect, if you have any."

"Lime or orange?"

Not unexpectedly, she chose lime. At this time of the year juice from the oranges on his trees was almost cloyingly sweet.

He poured some for her and some for himself.

After a startled look at his glass, she said, "This is fresh, isn't it? Do you grow limes here?"

"Along with other citrus trees. We have a large orchard that provides enough fruit for the other houses as well as the homestead. In the early days when fruit and vegetables had to be home-grown in isolated districts, my forebears made sure there was enough to keep everyone on the station going."

"It was the same—" she stopped, an unidentifiable

emotion freezing her expression, and took another sip of the lime juice before continuing "—everywhere, really. I read about the early days on one of the high-country settlers in the Southern Alps—amazing that their wives managed."

She'd made a good recovery, but Rafe would have bet on it not being what she'd intended to say. She'd almost referred to Mariposa.

She walked across to the windows to gaze out into the warm summer garden. Gathering strength? It had been a beast of a day for her, and she'd almost given away the one thing she seemed determined to keep from him.

When she turned it was to say quietly, "This is delicious. Thank you so much for asking us to stay. We need to come to some arrangement about sharing costs."

Whatever he'd been expecting, it wasn't this. He returned brusquely, "I don't expect my guests to pay for any hospitality they receive."

Black lashes drooped over her cool green gaze, screening her thoughts. "Your guests are your friends. Of course they don't expect to pay you—and they can offer you hospitality in return. I can't do that." Her lashes came up and she met his eyes steadily. "Rafe, I don't need charity and I won't accept it."

"This is hospitality, not charity. Jo Tanner would have offered you a bed if I hadn't."

Her body stiffened and her voice was brisk and no-nonsense. "And I'd have paid my way there too if Keir and I couldn't find anywhere else."

Something in her tone told him she'd already spent some time trying to find alternative accommodation. "No luck?" he asked, almost amused by the sharp glance she gave him.

Shrugging, she said in a muted voice, "No luck at all. I didn't realise there were sailing championships this week at the yacht club, and I'd forgotten that next week the whole area has a country-music festival. Every bed-and-breakfast place I rang, every motel and hotel too, are booked out until well after the New Year."

Rafe said curtly, "Then forget about trying anything else—and forget about paying too." In his driest voice he added, "You may not realise this, but I can afford a couple of extra guests." When she looked up sharply he added, "Provided they don't eat too much, of course."

A wry, tantalising smile curved her mouth and quick laughter glimmered in the green depths of her eyes. "I'm not such a big eater," she returned, deadpan, "but Keir will probably amaze you with the amount he gets through."

"He looks as though he might grow into a big man." She'd know he was probing, even though he spoke in his most casual tone. "Is his father tall?"

After a taut moment of hesitation, she nodded. Rafe recalled David Brown—over six feet, and well-built—and felt an odd stab of something that was far too much like jealousy. Although he'd never expected virginity from his lovers, for some exasperating reason the thought of her making love to anyone roused an unsuspected resistance.

Experience told him she felt the same heated attraction he did. Which was possibly why she'd just tried to erect barriers with her suggestion of payment.

Setting boundaries on their relationship.

That stung. Periodically his sister accused him of being spoilt by too much feminine attention. Perhaps she was right, although Rafe hadn't been very old when he'd realised that many of the women who flirted with him were more attracted by his financial assets than his personality.

If he knew Marisa's reason for playing this odd game, he might find her reticence and refusal to cast lures in his path refreshing.

Impatience rode Rafe hard, knotting his gut. Once he had all the facts, he'd be better able to deal with the situation.

Her divorce from David Brown had been finalised just over two years after she'd left Mariposa. His PI had also discovered the boy's date of birth, almost exactly nine months after she'd got on to the plane for New Zealand.

Edgily aware of the saturnine cast to her host's expression, Marisa said, "You're going to get thanked in spades if we don't come to some arrangement about paying board. After all, I would have had to pay you for borrowing your grandmother's car."

"Borrowing doesn't require payment," he pointed out.

She stared at him, then summoned a lopsided smile. "It was a slip of the tongue."

"A Freudian one?" he enquired affably.

Her composure slipped a fraction. Heat warmed the skin across her cheekbones, but she kept her head up. "Freudian or not, it doesn't matter. I can't stay where I'm not allowed to pay my way."

He frowned, then lifted his broad shoulders in a dismissive gesture. "All right," he said crisply. "You'd better find out the going rate for board for one woman and a five-year-old child, plus the rental of a thirty-year-old car."

Suspicious, she stared at him and saw a gleam of amusement in the dense blue of his eyes. "I shall," she said stiffly. "And while Keir and I are staying here we'll keep out of your way as much as possible."

"Fortunately that won't be too difficult," he drawled and drained the rest of his glass. "The house is big enough for us to avoid each other quite successfully, but I expect to see you at dinner each night. Anything else—Keir's routine, for example—you'll have to organise with Nadine."

Privately Marisa considered the housekeeper had more than enough to do caring for this huge house without being bothered by the necessary changes a small child would make.

Staying here would only be a temporary measure. And Rafe was right. Not only was the homestead big enough for them to steer clear of each other, but by the time she left for work and came back again, the day would be gone.

Which left only the evenings…

Long evenings, as Keir was in bed by seven o'clock every night.

In spite of everything, the thought of dining each night with Rafe aroused a sneaky, unbidden sense of anticipation that startled her as much as it shamed her.

CHAPTER SIX

RAFE was a sophisticated, considerate host, making sure Marisa had what she wanted, talking about the district with the affection and insight of a resident, even making her laugh, yet his excellent manners didn't quite mask that subtle aloofness.

Until dinner was almost over, when he asked, "Is something wrong with your dessert?"

A note in his voice told her he knew very well that the poached pears and honey-flavoured crisp biscuits were utterly delicious.

Warning herself to control her expression more carefully, she said, "Absolutely nothing—Nadine is a superb cook. I was just thinking that once we've finished dinner I'll go and check Keir again. I don't want him to wake up in a strange place and not know where I am."

"Nadine would have let us know if he'd stirred. Eat up and we'll have coffee."

She said swiftly, "Would you mind if I didn't tonight? It's been quite a day…"

Rafe's mouth hardened, then relaxed. "Of course you can do what you want. As you say, it's been a difficult day for you." And he was perfectly polite when he escorted her to the nursery suite a few minutes later.

Yet every step she took beside him reinforced

Marisa's feeling of narrowly escaping something she didn't even recognise.

Tension had given her a slight headache. All she craved was a good night's sleep with no dreams about fire and no long, dark hours spent worrying over the future.

Keir of course was blissfully relaxed beneath the covers, with a parade of horse and unicorn posters looking down benignly from the walls. Smiling, Marisa picked up his bear and tucked it in beside him.

Keir was safe. That was all she cared about—all she could afford to care about.

As she always did, she bent and kissed his forehead, and as he always did he stirred and his mouth curved before he drifted off again.

Just as well someone was able to sleep, Marisa thought trenchantly some hours later, staring at the moon from her window. She felt like the only person left on earth. Usually a summer night brought some coolness with it, but not this one, and after discovering no night attire in the pile of clothes she'd scooped up from the garage, she'd gone to bed in a T-shirt and briefs.

Wryly she thought if she'd stripped off completely she might have stayed asleep instead of waking feeling sweaty and enervated. At least the air coming through the open windows was a little cooler than inside the room.

Breathing slowly, she gazed out into the night, a place of enchantment lit by the serene light of the moon. It was so still she could easily hear the soft whisper of wavelets on the sands of the children's beach and the long, lamenting cry of one of the waterbirds Waimanu was named for.

Where did Rafe sleep? Unbidden into her mind stole a picture of his lean, strong body sprawled out across a huge bed. Did he sleep naked? A sinful thrill warmed her. In Mariposa she'd been too exhausted and too worried to do more than accept his nakedness, but now she thought he'd be a brilliant lover...

On the other hand, why on earth should she imagine that just because he was a worldly success and had a very good body he'd be some—some super-Lothario?

Banishing the dangerous image, she left the curtains open, pulled off her T-shirt and went back to bed, where her plans for dealing with what had been saved from the fire were eventually overtaken by sleep.

An abrupt knock on the door brought her out of bed to race across the room, blinking sleep from her eyes.

Keir, she thought, panicking. She must have called his name, because through the door Rafe said urgently, "It's all right—he's fine."

"Then what—?" Marisa jerked the door open, then blinked again, staring at him in the glow of a dim light in the hall.

He'd obviously been in bed too, because all he was wearing was a pair of loose trousers, slung low on narrow hips. The soft hall light gilded bronze shoulders and he looked big and powerful and overwhelmingly masculine.

Marisa's pulse leapt into overdrive. After swallowing to ease a suddenly dry throat, she croaked, "What's going on?"

"I've just been rung by Sandy Tanner," he said, and grabbed her by the upper arms as she staggered. His voice harsh, he said, "It's not good news. The fire flared up again and burnt the garage down."

The words made sense, yet she couldn't process them. Dazedly she stared at him as he went on quietly, "With everything in it. By the time the brigade got back it was all gone."

It felt like a fatal blow to the heart. Every memory of her parents and every carefully preserved memento of Keir's life lost to her for ever...

Marisa sagged, but almost immediately tried to pull herself erect.

And then she was held in a strong embrace and Rafe said abruptly, "You don't have to take everything on the chin. You can allow yourself a tear or two."

"I c-can't...I can't..." she started to say, but got no further. Her eyes flooded.

When she choked on the next word Rafe said, "It's all right, I won't tell anyone," with a wryly amused note that finally broke through her resistance.

She couldn't stop weeping, not even when he picked her up and carried her back into the bedroom. Dimly she expected him to put her down and tried not to feel abandoned. Instead, he sat on the side of the bed and held her while she gave in to the tears she hadn't allowed herself since her father died.

Eventually it had to stop. She fought back the sobs and lifted her head, aware Rafe's broad shoulder was wet from her crying.

And that apart from a pair of briefs, she was naked, her breasts against his chest, one of his hands very close to them.

At a complete disadvantage, she muttered hoarsely, "I've got a handkerchief somewhere," and tried to pull away.

Rafe said, "I'll get some tissues from the box on the bedside table."

When he set her on to the side of the bed she shivered and hauled the sheet around her. His support had
enfolded her, kept her safe and allowed her the luxury
of grief—and threatened the life she was building for
Keir.

She didn't dare let herself rely on any man—but oh,
it had been immensely comforting to feel the steady
driving beat of his heart against her cheek, his powerful arms shielding her from a world that seemed suddenly to have turned on her.

Comforting and—something else...

"Here," he said, handing her the box. He left her for
the bathroom and came back shortly with a warm face
flannel and a towel.

"I'm sorry," she whispered and hid her face in the
warm, wet folds.

"Why are you sorry? For crying?" His voice was
level and cool. "After the day you've had there'd have
been something wrong with you if you hadn't released
the tension somehow. And crying is a lot safer and better for you than getting drunk."

She shivered again and he said, "Where's your dressing gown?"

"Burnt by now," she said more steadily. "I'll have to
call the insurance company. Again."

He sat down beside her and slung an arm around her
shoulder in another sexless embrace. "Who are you in-
sured with?"

She had to think; her mind seemed woolly and useless. When she told him he said, "Ah, yes, I know the
local agent."

"I suppose you went to school with him." She moved
away as far as the sheet would let, evading the too-
confining weight of his arm about her shoulders.

Even in the darkness she could see the white gleam of his teeth as he smiled and got to his feet. In the dimness of the room he loomed like some primeval, godlike being. Every cell in her body quivered with delicious tension and she shivered with a sensuous, terrifying mixture of anticipation and apprehension.

It was the darkness, she thought wildly. If she turned on the bedside lamp everything would return to normal. Except that she was almost naked.

So what? It wasn't the first time she'd been almost naked in his arms. But he'd been unconscious then and they'd both slept heavily in the primitive comfort of their mutual warmth.

Now, standing so close to him, with the feel of his arms imprinted on her skin and the faint masculine scent still in her nostrils, she was seized by a sudden fierce longing for all the things she couldn't have—for support, for excitement, for love…

But most of all for Rafe.

Who had held her without the slightest sign of wanting her.

Keir, she thought desperately. Concentrate on Keir. And dealing with the fire.

"As it happens I didn't go to school with him," Rafe said, his voice amused, "but he's a decent chap and good at his job. I'll ring him tomorrow."

It would have been so easy to say thank you, to let him take over. He'd been kind when she needed it and she was grateful, but right now she had to fight this tantalising weakness that melted her bones and sapped her energy in a slow, smouldering heat.

"Thank you for offering, but I'll do it," she said unevenly.

He didn't object. "Will you be able to get back to sleep?"

What would he do if she said no?

"Yes," she blurted, so suddenly she made herself jump. "Goodnight, Rafe."

"Goodnight," he said, his voice level and uninflected.

She watched him walk out of the room, that reckless yearning she'd never felt before aching through her like sweet, debilitating poison.

Keir woke her the next morning, laughing as he tickled underneath her chin. She grabbed him and hauled him close for a kiss, then released his wriggling body to fling back the sheet and get up. The T-shirt she'd huddled into before she finally got off to sleep hung in loose folds.

And she remembered.

Remembered Rafe's arms around her, the powerful contours of his body against hers and the faint, subtle scent that was his alone—heat and virile male. Strange, but she'd always remembered it from the night after the crash, when she'd slept in his arms while rain hammered down on the grasslands...

Her skin burned and she said swiftly, "We have to get ready for work and school, darling." The previous night Rafe had told her he'd take her in and collect her and in the evening she could try out his grandmother's little car, and she'd agreed.

"Can we go to the beach?" Keir asked eagerly.

She glanced at her watch and blinked. "After work, perhaps."

The table on the terrace had been laid for breakfast and to her intense relief Rafe wasn't there.

"He's taking an overseas call," the housekeeper said

when Keir asked. She winked at Marisa and said, "I thought you might like to come and help me bring out the utensils, Keir." Keir's enthusiasm widened her smile. "If Mum agrees, of course."

Marisa laughed. "Of course I do. I'll come too."

"Stay where you are and enjoy the peace," Nadine advised. "Keir and I can do it."

I could get used to this, Marisa thought when they'd gone back inside, looking around at the garden and the trees, colourful and lush and beautiful.

And definitely not for her...

She bit her lip, forcing her mind away so she could concentrate on all she had to do. Get through the day first and then check to see what—if anything—could be salvaged in the burnt-out shed behind the cottage.

A shattering sense of futility gripped her, clouding her mind as she wrestled with a sense of obligation that was interrupted by a prickle of awareness between her shoulder blades.

After an uneasy moment she turned to look towards the house. Rafe was walking out through the French doors, moving towards her with the lithe silence she still found intimidating.

Colour burned up through her skin, accompanied by a pang of need so fierce it almost made her gasp. He looked at her keenly, but although her stomach knotted he didn't refer to her breakdown in his arms.

Instead, after greeting her, he said, "I've had news that will take me away from home for several days. I'll be leaving tomorrow afternoon, so after I've picked you up from work tonight we'll drop Keir off at the Tanners' and check out the garage at the cottage, then find out if you can drive the sports car."

* * *

"It's just like a toy car!" Bouncing with enthusiasm, Keir beamed at the sports car.

Rafe looked down at him. "It might look like a toy, but it's real enough," he said. "Let's strap your seat into the back and we'll see how your mother feels about driving us down to the road."

I'd feel a lot better if you weren't coming too. The moment the thought popped into her mind, Marisa looked guiltily away. He did seem to have a talent for reading her mind, but right then he was concentrating on getting the car seat into position according to Keir's instructions, delivered importantly and with pride.

She didn't want him to be so—so damned thoughtful. That afternoon he'd realised she was near breaking point when she'd seen the smouldering wreckage of the garage and he'd helped her control her shock and desolation by being coolly practical.

Nothing had been saved; the building and its contents were a twisted, blackened heap. Inwardly Marisa had wept at the loss. Yet after they'd collected Keir and driven home, in some odd, perverse way her grief had given way to a feeling of lightness, as though the fires had burned away the detritus of her past to allow her a freedom she'd never experienced before.

Wistfully, she watched Keir direct the attachment of his car seat, envying her son's confidence, his obvious enjoyment in helping Rafe. They could be father and son—both dark-haired and long-limbed...

Another thought to be firmly squelched. It brought with it an even heavier load of guilt.

"We're ready."

Rafe's voice startled her. She turned to see that the child seat had been fitted into the car and locked into place.

His smile was a little ironic. "Satisfied?"

"Yes." She looked down at her son. "In you get, young man."

He obeyed, but when she went to clip him in he said, "Mr Pev'ril can do it, Mum."

Something twisted in her heart. She said, "OK", and watched an amused Rafe follow more instructions, his hands deft and swift and sure as he slotted in the clip.

"There, that should do it," he said to her son's enthusiastic assent.

Marisa slid behind the wheel, fighting a difficult tangle of emotions. Love for her son mingled with fear that she was depriving him of a formative and necessary relationship by keeping him away from his father.

And then there was the confusing ache that had nothing to do with Keir.

She was so very aware of Rafe. Her body sang a rash, forbidden call whenever he was near, a call she didn't dare heed. If only he weren't so…well, so *nice* in his autocratic way. And Keir's pleasure in being with him was obvious from his confident, happy tone when he was chatting to Rafe.

Unfairly, she didn't want Rafe to be good with her son. Why wasn't he what she imagined a typical tycoon to be—dictatorial, overbearing and intolerant, puffed up with pride and a sense of privilege and entitlement?

Then she wouldn't feel this reckless attraction, this disturbing tangle of emotion and sensation that was changing from the initial strong, physical pull into something much more dangerous, an emotion with the power to change her life…

He lowered his long body into the front seat. Hastily she pretended to be studying the dials on the dashboard.

"Ready?" he asked.

Without looking at him, Marisa nodded and switched on the engine. "As ready as I'm likely to be. It's a good thing there's a long drive to practise on."

Although it had been some years since she'd used a manual gearbox, she soon remembered the technique as they set off slowly towards the road. From the back seat Keir chatted away, seeming not to mind that it was Rafe who answered his questions and pointed out various things he thought might interest her son.

At least concentrating on co-ordinating gear lever and clutch kept her from further obsessing about the man beside her.

And then they met the tractor. Not an ordinary tractor, but a behemoth, garish in colour and noisy.

"Stop here," Rafe ordered.

Marisa brought the car to a halt, smiling as she turned to look at her son when Rafe swung out of the car. Keir adored tractors and his attention was fixed on the vehicle and the man striding towards it.

After a brief discussion with the driver Rafe came back and bent to tell her, "The nearest gate is only about a hundred yards behind us, so back up and go into the paddock to let him past. Would you like me to do it?"

Powerfully tempted to surrender the wheel, Marisa set her jaw. Letting him take over would be a disintegrating reversion to the woman who'd allowed herself to become the wreck he'd seen at their first meeting.

In a clipped voice she said, "No, I'll be fine, thank you."

As though he'd expected her answer, he nodded. "Don't try to back through the gate. Reverse past it, then drive through. Once you're in the paddock you can turn around."

It wasn't exactly an order, but she had to conceal a bristling irritation as he straightened up again.

Go and talk to the tractor driver again, she urged silently.

Instead, he walked towards the gate, formidable and compelling, the sun gleaming red-black on his arrogant head.

A heady rush of adrenalin clamoured through Marisa, setting off tiny fires in every cell. Shocked by its force, she realised her hands were clammy on the wheel. As she dragged in a swift, shaky breath she ordered herself to be sensible, an injunction that did nothing to calm her twanging nerves.

Concentrate, she told herself fiercely. *Reversing is not one of your strongest skills, but for heaven's sake, this is dead flat and perfectly straight—you can do it. Just don't scrape the side of the car as you go through...*

How she hoped the mechanic would have her car fixed on Tuesday! And that she could find a place of her own soon—before Rafe returned from wherever he was going.

Tuning out Keir's chatter, she set the car in motion. Rafe stood beside the opened gate, watching her. Acutely conscious of him, she slowly reversed the car down the drive.

"I like Mr Pev'ril," Keir said from the back, waving at Rafe, who lifted his hand in response. "Do you like him, Mum?"

"Yes," she said colourlessly, because what else could she say?

Like? What a pallid, wishy-washy word. She didn't like Rafe Peveril—she wanted him.

There, she'd admitted it. *She wanted him.* Whenever he was nearby her treacherous body did its best to weaken her will. Even though every instinct whispered that he was a dangerous man with the power to cause her huge grief, she thrilled to the sight of him.

To Keir's enthusiastic commentary, she drove carefully into the paddock and turned the car to face the drive. The tractor thundered by, stopping a few metres beyond the gate and the driver swung down to speak to Rafe. Carefully she eased the car on to the drive again before stopping and glanced in the rear-vision mirror.

Something about Rafe's stance caught her attention. Whatever he was being told had made him angry. He spoke briefly and curtly, then strode towards the car.

"Here he comes!" Keir announced superfluously.

Marisa's hands clenched on the wheel. She took a huge breath and turned her head as Rafe got in, meeting eyes as cold and deadly as the moon.

Her stomach knotted and for a moment she froze in a familiar, dreaded fear. Whenever David had been angry with her he'd go silent, refusing to give her a reason and ignoring her tentative efforts to find out what she'd done wrong. Periodically he'd walked out, sometimes for days, leaving her alone without knowing where he was or whether he was ever coming back.

Involuntarily she asked, "Is something wrong?"

And stopped, angry with herself for reverting so rapidly. Rafe wasn't David and she was no longer a depressed girl rendered helpless by those long silences.

"Possibly." He paused, then continued in a level voice, "The driver's been clearing some gorse along the riverbank and noticed some suspicious plants on the other side."

"Suspicious pl—*oh*!" She stared at him. "Does that mean what I think it means?"

"Yes."

"On your property?"

"Yes." In a lethal tone that sent icy shivers down her spine, he finished deliberately, "Which could indicate that someone from Manuwai put them there."

Marisa blinked, then glanced in the rear-vision mirror. Clearly not listening, Keir had twisted around and was watching the tractor drive away.

She said, "They'd have to be awfully stupid, wouldn't they, because your workers would be the first suspects. Is the plot easily accessible from the sea?"

"In an inflatable it's reasonably easy to get at. And I don't for a moment think it's someone from the station. In fact, I have a pretty good idea who it might be."

Marisa switched on the engine and put the car in gear. Choosing her words with care, she said, "Let's remember there's a third party present."

Frowning, Rafe nodded and Marisa eased the car along the drive, asking, "So what are you going to do?"

"Call the authorities." His icy composure was far more intimidating than David's silences had ever been. "No one does that on my land and gets away with it."

CHAPTER SEVEN

BACK at Manuwai Marisa parked the car carefully in the garage and held out the keys.

"Keep them," Rafe told her negligently. "Use this car until you've got your own back."

"I… Thank you." It was on the tip of her tongue to ask when he'd be returning from his trip, but she restrained herself in time. It would have sounded far too personal—as though she had some right to know.

He said to Keir, "Look after your mum while I'm away, young man. She's had a tough day."

Keir managed the difficult task of registering both pride and dismay. "Yes, but when are you coming home?" he asked.

"Probably after six more sleeps."

Watching Keir struggle with disappointment, Marisa winced. It was one thing to wonder if her son needed more male influence in his life; that he was fast fixing on Rafe as that influence was something else entirely. She didn't want Keir to become attached to him, only to find he had no place in Rafe's life.

She fought back a tide of weariness and put Keir to bed, where he dropped off immediately.

When she found that Nadine had ironed their smoke-stained clothes, weak tears sprang to her eyes as she stammered thanks.

"You're worn out and no wonder," Nadine said briskly. "I'll make you a cup of tea."

Marisa straightened. "I'd love that, but I need a shower more, and then shall we sit down and work out a system? I know our being here is making extra work for you, but I'll make sure it's as little as possible."

The housekeeper smiled. "I enjoy having people around and it's lovely to have a child in the house again. Makes it a home, somehow."

Which warmed Marisa, but once she'd drunk the cup of tea she rang around the various estate agents.

And got the same answer—nothing to rent.

Still she kept trying, spurred on every morning by Keir's eager query, "Is Mr Peveril coming home today?" Rafe had departed in the chopper, which he *did* fly to and from the local airport, to Keir's complete entrancement, but every morning when either Marisa or Nadine said, "No, not today," his face fell.

Marisa understood his feelings. Lovely as Manuwai homestead was, the place seemed empty without its driving force, the man who owned it.

She missed Rafe like an ache for something she'd never attain, a hunger that could never be satisfied.

Yet it was too easy to settle, to relax, to let the big house embrace them. She and Nadine worked out their system and enjoyed each other's company, she met several of the farm workers, and Keir demanded to be allowed to travel in the school bus with his new best friend, the son of one couple.

"No, darling, we can't do that," she said at first.

Thrusting out his lower lip, he produced something

too close to a whine. "Why? Manu said his mum said it was all right and she'd take me with him when she takes him and the other kids on the bus down to the gate."

She thought for a moment. "Here's what we could do. I'll talk to Manu's mother and if she's happy to take you down you could go in the morning, but after school Nadine is too busy to look after you. And it's not her job. So in the afternoon you'd still have to go to the day-care centre and the shop."

He wavered, then gave a reluctant nod.

Manu's mother laughed when she rang. "I've been waiting for your call," she said cheerfully. "My little scamp told me all about this plan he and Keir dreamed up. Of course I'll pick Keir up in the mornings—it'll be no bother."

So the next morning Marisa watched Keir climb into Ngaire Sinclair's car, feeling rather as she had on his first day at school.

On the third day Patrick the mechanic rang to say her own car was fixed.

"But it's going to need more work done soon," he warned her when she arrived to pick it up.

Anxiously Marisa asked, "Expensive work?"

He grimaced. "Yeah, 'fraid so. Rafe told me to give it a good going-over so I took it for a drive and your transmission's slipping."

"What does that mean?"

He answered soberly, "Basically it means you'll be driving it one day and it'll stop. And then it will cost you."

Marisa drew a deep, impeded breath and drove carefully home, anxiously trying to work out how she could afford to pay for any future repairs. Renewed efforts to find somewhere to live close to town still met without

success. That and dealing with her insurance claim kept
her busy, and the Christmas buying frenzy was slowly
starting.

A week after Rafe had left, she tucked Keir into bed,
then walked along to the small parlour where she'd
joined Rafe that first night. She pushed open the door
and took two steps inside before she realised she wasn't
alone. Her heart stopped, then began thudding in an
irregular tattoo as an incredulous, terrifying delight
filled her.

"How— I didn't hear the chopper," she said a little
indignantly.

"I came out by car."

Rafe felt a swift jab of something too close to compunction. She looked tired, and although her face was
impassive, she held herself stiffly, as though ready to
stand her ground and fight.

At their first meeting in Tewaka he'd recognised the
brittleness beneath the bright confidence, but now—
now he knew exactly what caused it.

He should despise her. He did despise her, yet whenever he saw her his body sprang to life, reacting with
hot, sexually charged arousal...

Marisa met his gaze with what could almost have
been defiance, but her voice was unsteady as she went
on, "You're back early."

"I've done what I had to do." He poured a glass of
wine and held it out to her. "You seem startled."

Her smile looked genuine, but no amusement showed
in her eyes and again he sensed that tight control.

"Thank you," she said and sipped an infinitesimal
amount, red lips curved against the glass. "Not startled,

just a bit surprised. I didn't think Nadine was expecting you for another couple of days."

The sensation in his gut expanded into lust, like an arrow from some malicious god. *Not now*, he thought grimly, silently cursing his unruly body.

His voice sounded harsh when he said, "Nadine expects me when she sees me."

After another fleeting glance, she hurried into speech. "I've called social services, so I know how much I should be paying you for board." Her voice was almost challenging as she gave him a figure.

Rafe nodded. The amount meant nothing—he'd already decided to put the money into a bank account for her son. But her immediate mention of it meant she was still trying to set barriers between them, reduce everything to a commercial basis.

And if he was going to see this thing through, he needed to follow her example and ignore the fact that the pulsating awareness between them was not only mutual, but unlike anything he'd ever experienced before. The situation was too complex, muddied by other considerations, other concerns.

They had a lot more to deal with than this unforeseen and extremely disruptive physical reaction.

Although, he thought ironically, it could work in his favour…

And cursed again at the leap of hunger in his blood.

As though she sensed it Marisa took a step back and said jerkily, "What a lovely, serene room this is."

"It was my mother's favourite," he told her. "I think the women of the house have always used it for their refuge."

She seemed to be interested. "It must be very…" she stopped a moment or two, finally producing with a slight grimace "...*grounding*, I suppose is the word I'm looking for—to grow up in a house where your family has lived for generations. Unusual too in New Zealand."

"Not so very unusual—plenty of families still live where their ancestors settled. There have been three houses here, actually. My several-times-great-grandfather and his wife camped in a canvas tent until the local tribe showed them how to make a more permanent structure—a *whare* with a frame of manuka poles thatched with the fronds of nikau palms."

He noticed her face go rigid for a fleeting moment, then the long lashes swept down. When they came up again the green eyes were blank and shallow as glass.

So many damned secrets. Why? And the need to know every last one of them was becoming intolerable.

But her words surprised him. "His wife must have been so lonely here."

"You'd think so, but it wasn't long before she had children to look after, and she was an ardent gardener."

"I suppose she had to be."

He nodded. "She became friends with quite a few of the women of the tribe here. In fact, her oldest son—who took over Manuwai when his father died young—eloped to Australia with the daughter of the chief. She was a great beauty."

Her eyes widened. "Goodness, what happened?"

"The girl's parents were furious," he told her drily. "She'd been promised to a chief from the Waikato region so it caused quite a scandal. But once the babies started to arrive all was forgiven."

Marisa stiffened again, but forced herself to relax. "That usually happens, doesn't it?" she said neutrally. "Children have a habit of winding their way into people's hearts."

Although his gaze was far too keen for comfort, his voice was casual. "Where did you grow up?"

For a second she hesitated, then said smoothly and quickly, "Everywhere."

At his raised brows, she managed to produce a smile. "Quite literally. My parents were gypsies—not real ones, but they travelled all over the country."

"In a caravan?"

"No, a house bus."

"An interesting childhood," he observed noncommittally, his gaze never leaving her face.

It was like being targeted by lasers. Shrugging, Marisa said, "I'm afraid I didn't appreciate it as I probably should have. I wanted to be like other kids and stay in one place."

"Why?"

"Herd instinct, I suppose." Before he could put any more questions she asked, "Did you ever hanker for a different life?"

"There was enough here to keep me happily occupied while I was at primary school. But I spent my secondary years away at boarding school and by the time I left I knew I didn't want to come back here and farm the place as most Peverils before me had. So I went to university and did a couple of degrees before setting off to make my fortune."

There had been problems about that decision, she deduced from the raw undernote to his words.

Rafe went on in a coolly judicious tone, "But Waimanu has always been my home, so your choice of word was apt. Grounded is exactly how the place makes me feel. What did your parents do to earn a living?"

"My mother was a fantastic knitter and embroiderer, and my dad made gorgeous wooden toys. Between them they earned enough for us to keep travelling. They loved the life."

So much that she wondered if the illness that forced her mother to stay in one place had worn away their will to live.

She scotched that thought with a rapid, twisted smile. "I'm afraid I was born without their wanderlust, or their manual skills."

"You can paint," he said crisply. "Gina is a connoisseur and she rates your oil very highly."

His words surprised and warmed her. "I have a small talent, that's all. I'm delighted she likes the picture, but I hope she's not expecting it to increase in value much over the years."

Painting was another thing she'd had to surrender in the mockery that had been her marriage. David had considered it a frivolous waste of time. At first she'd thought he didn't understand the pleasure she got from it, but soon she'd realised he understood too well—he saw it as competition, something that took her attention away from him. Without making a decision to give it up, she'd found it impossible to keep going when somehow her materials had disappeared and new ones never arrived.

Bad memories. She dismissed them and sipped some more wine, trying to think of a way to steer the conversation back to Rafe.

"Perhaps you don't fully appreciate the talents that were developed through your unconventional life with your parents. And surely growing up in that sort of milieu must have given you the knowledge and the skills to choose your stock when you set up the shop?"

Marisa gave him a swift, surprised look. "I suppose it did," she said quietly. "Tell me, how big is Manuwai?"

The acreage he gave startled her. "That's huge," she said involuntarily.

He shrugged. "We don't give up what's ours," he said.

A note in his voice sent an involuntary shiver through her.

He went on, "Have you worked out a schedule with Nadine?"

Marisa's smile probably showed too many teeth. Or perhaps it was the saccharine sweetness of her tone when she said, "Yes, sir", that hardened his gaze.

"Did that sound like an order?"

"Very much," she told him coolly.

His smile was a little taunting. "And you don't respond well to them?"

"I tend not to respond to orders at all."

She hoped her voice was a lot more confident than she felt. Periodically the old Mary Brown emerged from beneath the carefully confident shell she'd built around herself, but no one was ever going to control her again.

Not even a man whose efficiency in running a worldwide organisation earned him general respect and admiration.

"Indeed, why should you?" he said negligently. "However, I didn't intend to bark out commands."

Marisa shrugged. "As it happens, Nadine and I work very well together."

"Good," he said, but absently as he checked his watch. "And if we're to avoid her sternest face, we'd better get ourselves to the table. It's such a pleasant evening we're eating out on the terrace."

Once outside, he said, "I assume Keir's already asleep."

"Well and truly. They had swimming sports at school today."

"How did he do?"

"He told me he came third in the dog paddle. That was clearly a big deal." She smiled a little at the memory of his innocent delight. "He informed me that next year he's going to win."

"You didn't go?"

"No. I had to look after the shop."

He gave her a keen glance but made no comment, possibly guessing that she'd spent quite a bit of the two hours allotted to the sports wishing she could be there.

She said sturdily, "And thanks very much for the loan of your grandmother's car. It's been fun driving it. Your friend Patrick told me that you'd asked him to give my car a good going-over."

"Did he?" He looked amused.

She wanted to tell him to step back from her, keep out of her business, but it seemed churlish. "Thank you," she said woodenly, and looked around. "How lovely it is out here."

The terrace garden always reminded Marisa of photographs she'd seen of tropical resorts, usually in glossy magazines filled with impossibly beautiful people. But tonight everything seemed brighter, more sweetly scented, more—well, just *more*.

Because Rafe was here...

After sitting down she kept her gaze fixed on the circle of lawn bordered by plants with dramatic leaves and bold flowers.

"The light's not too bright?" Rafe asked.

"Not a bit." A canopy sheltered them as the sun sank towards the west and a little breeze sighed past, carrying the fresh, green scent of foliage and flowers, the tang of salt.

Some people, Marisa thought almost enviously, had all the luck.

No, luck was for lottery winners. Rafe's life might be based on the hard work of the generations who'd lived at Waimanu before him, but his own efforts had propelled him further than they had gone.

And he was an excellent host. Over the meal she engaged in a spirited discussion that had her forgetting—almost—her very equivocal situation.

What she couldn't ignore was the swift build of excitement, the intoxication of exchanging views with a man whose incisive brain stimulated hers—and the more subtle stimulation of green eyes meeting grey, the deep timbre of his voice, the way a stray sunbeam lingered across his head, kindling a red-black flame before dying as the sun went down and twilight descended upon them.

He was dynamite, his potent masculinity adding to the impact of his powerful personality.

"Don't you like that wine?" Rafe asked.

"It's lovely, but I've had enough, thank you," she said swiftly.

She didn't need wine. This rare excitement that throbbed through her, exhilarating and heady, came from her heart's response to the man who watched her across the table.

He leaned back in his chair and looked at her, his gaze intent yet oddly chilling. Without preamble, he said in a voice that held no expression at all, "I've just flown back from Mariposa."

Her heart stopped. Literally.

Then it started up again, hammering so loudly she couldn't hear the silken song of the waves as they kissed the beach. She felt the colour drain from her skin, leaving it cold and taut. For a horrifying moment she thought she might faint.

Not now, she thought frantically, her gaze locked on to the cold grey of his. She dragged in a deep breath and forced her spinning, shocked brain into action.

"How interesting," she finally got out.

And closed her mouth against any further words in case her voice broke and she shattered with it into a million pieces.

He didn't move. "Is that all you have to say?"

Her skin tightened in a primitive urge to flee, to grab Keir and run as though the hounds of hell were after them. She resisted the urge to swallow and managed to speak. "What do you think I should say?"

"You might start," he said, his tone so level it sounded like a judge's delivery of a verdict, "by telling me exactly who fathered your son."

CHAPTER EIGHT

MARISA dragged a shaky breath into airless lungs. Silence stretched between them as she desperately searched for something—anything—to say. Her voice sounded limp and strained when she finally said, "I have no idea what business that is of yours. Why do you ask me?"

Rafe was still leaning back in his chair, watching her like a predator about to strike the killing blow. "In Mariposa I discovered that when we were found after the crash both of us were in bed together. Naked." His gaze narrowed into iron-hard intimidation. "Did we make love?"

Colour flooded her skin. "No!"

Too late she realised her explosive denial had betrayed her identity. Dismay and a kind of fear paralysed her.

Not a muscle moved in Rafe's hard, handsome face. Without apparent interest he asked, "So why were we naked?"

Abandoning hope of keeping up the pretence, she summoned every ounce of willpower to keep her voice steady. "You were naked—I was not. We crashed in a rainstorm. By the time we reached the hut we were both drenched and you—you looked like death. You were shivering, and I couldn't—"

Marisa stopped, recalling her helpless terror as she'd tried to work out what to do.

"Go on," he said tonelessly.

She bit her lip, then forced herself to continue in a flat voice. "There was a sort of bed—a hammock, really, made of cowhide nailed to a wooden frame. At first I thought we could use the frame to make a fire, but there were no matches. It was freezing…" She took another breath and finished rapidly, "And the only covering was another cowhide. It had no warmth to it. So I went back to the plane and retrieved our luggage."

He said quietly, "In the rain?"

"It hadn't stopped." Terrified the plane might somehow explode, and ashamed of her primitive, anguished fear of the dead pilot, two things had kept her going— fear Rafe might die if she couldn't warm him and the need to collect her passport, her only hope of freedom.

By the time she returned to the hut she was so tired she'd ached as though she'd been beaten, but worse than her exhaustion was seeing Rafe collapsed on the sorry excuse for a bed, his indomitable will finally conquered by the injury.

For a shattering moment she'd thought he was dead.

All emotion drained from her voice she went on, "When I got back I had to shake you awake, but I could tell you had no idea what was happening. I managed to persuade you out of your wet clothes, but after that you relapsed into unconsciousness again, so I couldn't get you into anything dry."

Not that their clothes had been dry exactly, but damp had been an improvement on sodden.

Something of the cold dismay that had overtaken

her then swept through her now. She steadied her voice and said, "I took all the clothes from both our cases and spread them over you and put the skin over them, but you didn't stop shivering. You were cold—so cold—and I thought you might die before anyone came."

Nothing showed in his face, nothing but harsh control. "And you?"

She stared at him.

He said crisply, "I assume you were wet too, and just as exhausted."

Surprised, she said, "I hadn't been hurt. You probably don't remember, but you pushed my head down just before impact and all I got were a few bruises. I was soaked and cold, so I stripped off everything except my bra and pants and got in beside you and held you, and after a while we both warmed up and went to sleep."

His arms had closed around her as though he was accustomed to holding a woman in his bed. That firm, confident embrace had somehow reassured her that he'd survive until rescuers arrived.

"And that's how they found us," he said, but not as though it were any revelation.

His steady, remorseless gaze searched her face. Marisa forced herself to master her chaotic emotions and the choppy, disconnected thoughts racing through her mind.

"The noise of the chopper woke me. I managed to haul on some clothes, but you...you couldn't." He'd been breathing and he was warm, but that time she hadn't been able to wake him.

"In Mariposa," he said, his voice deliberate, "the general opinion is that we made love."

Head held high, Marisa met his unreadable scrutiny

with a steady one of her own. "We didn't," she said bluntly. "Neither of us was in any fit state, believe me."

"So why does your husband believe I am Keir's father?"

Oh, God, how did he know that? She closed her eyes, then forced them open again to meet his coldly implacable gaze. Tension knotted her nerves, scraped her voice raw, but she owed him an explanation. "Because I told him you were. It was a lie."

Still his expression didn't change, and now—too late—she understood the hard power of the man. The ruthless determination that had got him out of that plane and supported him to the hut was as much a part of him as his brilliance and the splendid bone structure of his face.

Still in that cold, uncompromising tone he asked, "Why?"

Her throat was dry. This must be how a person on trial felt. "Because it was the only thing I could think of that would keep my child safe."

"What do you mean—safe?" The question came hard and fast as he straightened. "Did he beat you?"

She shook her head. "He never hit me." And couldn't say anything more.

Because in spite of David's rigid self-control, the threat of his leashed violence had been ever present, eventually dominating her life. Strangely, Rafe's anger didn't frighten her; he was truly formidable, but she couldn't imagine him ever losing that iron discipline.

Not even now, when he had every reason to be both disgusted and furious.

An inner caution taunted her, *How do you know that? How can you be so sure?*

She'd been so wrong before—could she be equally wrong about Rafe?

His regard for her and Keir had almost convinced her that he had no taint of her ex-husband's desire to control. Yet it could be because he'd wondered if Keir might be his own...

Rafe stayed silent, waiting. She took a deep breath and tried to explain. "David wants—*needs* to control. I think it must be a compulsion. That's why he took the job in Mariposa, away from everyone we knew. The people there were lovely—so hospitable—but David wouldn't join in the district's social life. And he didn't want me to, either."

"You can drive," Rafe said, frowning. "What stopped you from going out on your own?"

"We didn't have a car."

His brows rose. "There was one on the estancia—a Jeep."

"It was usually needed—David took it with him."

Rafe's frown deepened. "And when it wasn't?"

She flushed, angry with herself for being so embarrassed after all this time. "When he didn't need it he read the odometer before he left the house and again after he came home." Once, early on and feeling mutinous, she'd driven into the nearest town, a mere village, but the resultant inquisition had been such a fraught experience she'd never repeated it.

She glanced at Rafe's hard face and said flatly, "It happened. It will *never* happen to me again."

"You're implying that he kept you a prisoner on the estancia."

"Yes," she said, unsurprised by his attitude.

Rafe said, "The contrast between you now, and the

woman I saw in Mariposa, is almost unbelievable. I'm trying to understand how it happened."

"I was barely nineteen when I married and we went straight to Mariposa after the wedding," she returned in her crispest tone. "Apart from David, I knew no one for thousands of miles and I didn't speak Spanish."

David had had some small knowledge of the language—enough, she discovered later, to turn down all invitations from the warmly hospitable Mariposans in the district.

She went on doggedly, "I couldn't walk anywhere—the distances are too great."

"Your parents? The estancia has a computer. Were you in contact with them?"

"They didn't have a computer and I couldn't ring—the telephone system was chancy at the best."

And what could her parents have done? Even if she'd appealed to them they didn't have the money to pay for her to go home.

Her upwards glance clashed with Rafe's burnished, metallic survey. In that cool, judicial voice he stated, "And I don't suppose you had any money."

Words froze on her tongue and she had to swallow to ease her parched throat. "No," she admitted. "I was far too young—too unsophisticated—to deal with it. My parents adored each other—and David said he loved me and wanted to keep me safe. I knew something was wrong, but I had no weapons to fight him."

"What were your parents thinking of to let you get married so young?"

She shrugged. "They married young and it worked for them. But I was the one who insisted on it. I wanted a home, somewhere to call my own, where I could make a place for myself. Each year my parents chose a place to stay over the winter, so I had time to make friends and enjoy going to school instead of doing correspondence lessons. Then in the spring we'd leave. My friends and I would promise to keep in touch, but eventually the letters would stop and I'd have to start all over again. So I married the first man who offered me a settled life."

"Did you love him?"

Her smile was wry. "I was sure I did. My parents really liked David and they thought Mariposa was a wonderful idea, that at last I was showing some adventurous spirit. And it seemed so romantic." She allowed herself a small, cynical smile. "For the right man and the right woman, it could be. For me the estancia was literally a prison. I was so lonely. When I made him angry David would disappear for days and days, and I'd be left in silence and isolation. I didn't know how to deal with it."

A cool breath from the sea made her shiver. Rafe said abruptly, "We'll go inside."

"No, I'd rather stay here." Where she could breathe. After a few seconds' pause, she resumed quietly, "Then I got pregnant. David didn't want the baby. I lost it in the first trimester, and he said it was a relief—he was happy with the way things were. He didn't ever want children."

For a moment she thought Rafe was going to speak, but when she glanced at him his face was carved in stone.

Marisa stiffened her spine, squared her shoulders. Her voice was sombre and harsh with memories. "That was when I realised that I'd never have anyone to love—no child to love me. It was the last straw. I slid into depression and when he made it impossible for me to go home after my mother became ill I was too numb to even fight any longer. I just wanted to die."

Silence, heavy with unspoken thoughts, stretched between them. She looked down at her hands, so tightly clasped together that the knuckles were white, and forced herself to drop them into her lap. "But then you came and I saw an opportunity."

His arrival had cut through the stifling oblivion of her days, offering a tantalising, life-saving chance of freedom. "Besides, I thought I might be pregnant again, so I knew I had to take any chance I could to get away."

"You said David wasn't violent, so why do you believe he'd have harmed his own child?"

"He wouldn't have hurt him physically," she said quickly, then paused. She met his gaze without flinching. "At least, I don't think so. But there are different ways to hurt. Children don't flourish in a dictatorship."

"So you told him we'd slept together and the child was mine."

His voice was neutral, but the icy depths of his eyes told her he was holding himself on a tight rein.

"I couldn't think of anything else to do," she admitted bleakly. "About a month after I'd got back to New Zealand he rang and demanded I go back to him. By then I knew for certain I was pregnant. I was— desperate. My parents needed me and the thought of returning to Mariposa filled me with a kind of terror. I did the only thing I could think of to make sure David would never want to claim my baby. I used you and it worked."

She hesitated, then confessed on a spurt of raw honesty, "I wish I could say I regret it, but I don't. I'd do it again in a blink to keep Keir safe."

Rafe's face remained emotionless—an arrogant study carved in granite.

Nerves jumping, she finished, "Rafe, I am so sorry I involved you. But it shouldn't be a problem—no one else knows…"

Her voice trailed away as she recalled his statement that in Mariposa people assumed she had slept with him.

He said without inflection, "No one else is sure, but it seems to be accepted that he left Mariposa because you and I had an affair."

"He's left Mariposa?" Her voice shook and she jumped to her feet, staring at him in shock. "When?"

"About six months after you did." He stood too, a formidable silhouette in the dimness of the terrace. Relentlessly he demanded, "Why are you so afraid? If he doesn't want children, then surely Keir is safe enough even if Brown does find out the boy is his."

Fear hollowing her stomach, Marisa gathered her thoughts, trying to adjust to the news. A gull cried in the distance, harshly distinctive, and she shivered.

"I think he saw me as some kind of chattel," she said after several silent moments. "Love for him meant— *means*—ownership, not respect. He grew up in a foster home where he had to fight to keep anything. I'm afraid that if he ever finds out that Keir is his he'll want to own him too."

Rafe's survey was keen and hard to bear, but his thoughtful answer made her hope he was beginning to understand. "That seems rather melodramatic."

She shrugged. "I don't pretend to understand him. What I'm certain of is that men like David don't make good husbands or fathers. You know Keir—he's a bright, happy, confident child. You must remember what I was like after just two years spent with David. Although, to be fair," she added with unsparing candour, "that wasn't entirely his fault."

Rafe's brows lifted again. "No?"

"No. When I got back to New Zealand my mother insisted I see her doctor. He sent me off for tests and they finally decided that a mixture of depression and chaotic hormones after the miscarriage had dragged me down. Medication and a good therapist fixed me."

"With some effort from you," he said quietly.

She nodded. "Lots of effort," she agreed.

"Tell me one thing."

The almost casual tone was so much at variance with his hard scrutiny that she tensed. "What?"

"How did Marisa turn into Mary—the name change, I mean, not the emotional disintegration?"

She flushed, but said coolly enough, "David thought Marisa was a silly, pretentious name, so he chose another one." Like renaming a pet...

Rafe nodded, as though the answer had confirmed something for him. He didn't comment, however, but moved on. "Before we finish this, I'd like to know why you came to Tewaka."

It wasn't exactly an order, but she owed him an answer to that too. At least this one was easy, she thought mordantly.

"I've always loved Northland. Having parents who made a living by catering to people's tastes gave me a feeling for what sells and what doesn't, and the shop seemed like a missed opportunity."

"In what way?"

"Poor buying," she explained. "I researched Tewaka and found it has a six-month season of cruise-ship visits as well as a year-long tourist trade, and the district is prosperous. Small shops like mine can't compete with the big chain retailers, so they need to cater for a different market. Which was what my parents did with their handmade stuff." She gave him a taut, glittering smile. "One thing I did *not* learn from my research was that you lived here."

One black brow shot up. "Would that have killed the deal?"

"Yes. I felt—still feel—guilty about using you. When my father died last year I decided to leave the south. It holds bad memories. David is from there, my parents died there and I wanted to find a place where no one would know me. Where I could make a new beginning."

"I can understand that," he said unexpectedly.

Disconcerted, Marisa looked at him and then hastily away again. While they'd been talking dusk had given way to night. Soon the moon would rise, but for now the velvet sky was spangled with stars. Her dark-attuned eyes clearly made out the arrogant bone structure of Rafe's face, the width of his shoulders against the fall of white blooms from a creeper along the wall. Something stirred deep inside her, a slow, sensuous melting, as though a resistance she'd hadn't known existed was being smoothed away.

Steadying her voice, she went on, "I wanted to settle before Keir started school. And once I started the process, everything just fell into place—it was so simple I got the feeling it was meant to be, you know?"

Only to fall spectacularly apart as soon as she'd learned he lived here.

With a twist to his mouth he said, "I'm always suspicious of deals that seem to come together perfectly. Usually it's because someone's manipulating things to their own advantage."

"Not in this case." She gave him a rueful smile. "I'd been here several weeks before I found out you lived here and my first instinct was to get the hell out of town. But Keir loves the school here and the shop is going so well." And she'd been told Rafe was rarely at home. Quickly she went on, "Anyway, I was pretty sure I could carry off my new identity. What made you recognise me? I hope there's very little resemblance between poor Mary Brown and me."

"It seems that the poor Mary Brown you refer to so disparagingly could well have saved my life. For which I'm grateful."

The tone in which he drawled the final sentence jolted her senses to overstretched alertness. Was this the only reason he'd been so helpful towards her?

A pang of disappointment shocked her with its intensity.

If he'd gone to Mariposa to find out what had happened after the crash, something she'd said or done must have aroused his suspicion.

Banishing that entirely inappropriate chagrin, she said on a note of humour, "I'll make a bargain with you. I'll stop thanking you if you stop thanking me."

"Done!" He held out his hand, and she put hers in it, ready for the sizzle of response that ran through her whenever he touched her.

It happened, but this time she didn't jerk away.

As their hands parted he said, "Although offering you a refuge is hardly recompense for saving my life. It never occurred to you to leave me in the wreckage of the plane?"

Amazed, she stared at him. "No. It wasn't an option. You sort of came to while I was checking the pilot and you muttered something about fire, and then I smelt petrol—"

"Avgas," he corrected with a half-smile.

"Whatever. It smelt like an explosion to me. You were set on getting out and it seemed a really good idea. Do you remember any of that?"

"No," he said briefly. "Finding the hut in the storm must have been difficult."

She recalled it only too vividly. "It wasn't easy. I was afraid the effort would be bad for you, but although you were obviously in pain you were so determined to get to the hut I realised you'd set off by yourself if I didn't come with you."

"Apart from the blow to my head I had no injuries," he said shortly.

"I thought the hut would be a better bet than staying in a plane that might explode." She returned to her question. "You barely saw me in Mariposa and most of the time you did you were more or less unconscious. How did you recognise me?"

"Your eyes," he said succinctly. He reached out and traced an eyebrow, his lean forefinger leaving a trail of fire on her skin. His voice deepened. "Such a strong, true green is unusual enough, but the way they tilt—and the way your brows follow that tilt—that's both exotic and unforgettable."

His touch transformed that insidious melting sensation into swift heat that ricocheted from nerve-end to nerve-end right throughout her body, sending signals to every cell.

"I have my grandmother's eyes," she said inanely.

The way he looked at her built that inner, shameless heat into a fire. Desperate to quench it, she blurted, "How did you find out about the lie I told David?"

"You told me."

Bewildered, Marisa stared at him. "But you knew before then, surely?"

His mouth curved in a sardonic smile. "I knew what he—and most of Mariposa, apparently—believes. I was intrigued by your attitude—a mixture of forthrightness and extreme caution and reserve. And I couldn't work out why the hell you'd pretend to be someone else, if that's what you were doing, unless you were afraid or had something to hide."

"So you had me investigated." She tried to sound angry, but her tone was resigned.

Hooded eyes never leaving her face, he nodded. "And discovered you'd given no name for his father on Keir's birth certificate. I wondered why."

She said nothing and after a few seconds he resumed, "Keir was born two weeks short of nine months after the night you and I spent together in the hut, so he could have been the result of one night of amnesiac passion on my part."

"No," she said decisively.

"In Mariposa I found out that we'd been naked—"

Hot-cheeked, she corrected, "*You* were naked."

"The general opinion seems to be that of course we slept together. Such a life-affirming activity is quite natural—even normal—after a fatal crash."

His words were delivered in a silky voice that froze Marisa. But only for a moment. The shock of his knowing had receded and she asked angrily, "What I'd like to know is how everyone—*everyone* meaning everyone in your circle, I assume—knew that."

"The people who rescued us talked, of course," he said caustically. "That's why your ex-husband believed you."

Anger dying, she absorbed that, then said quietly, "Keir is David's son."

"I believe you." He reached out and took her hand again. Frowning, he closed his fingers around hers. "Why didn't you tell me you were cold?"

And to her astonishment he pulled her into his arms and held her against the heat of his powerful body. "It's all right," he said evenly, his voice reverberating against her ear. "I'm sorry to take you through this inquisition, but I needed to know what was going on."

She couldn't think, couldn't tease out a sensible answer. A fierce desire clamoured through her, weakening her so that her words were husky and hesitant when she finally blurted, "I'm not cold—just…shocked, I suppose."

"Too much has happened to you lately."

His arms contracted and she looked up, eyes widening as she met the focused gleam in his. She shivered again.

He bent his head and said against lips that ached for some unknown pressure, "After the crash you risked your life to warm me. I wonder if I can warm you up this time."

The kiss rekindled the fires, setting her alight with the passion she'd been fighting ever since she'd seen him again. Sighing, she surrendered to a sharp excitement, a reckless need that came roaring up out of nowhere, summoned by Rafe's touch, his arms, his lips…

Summoned by Rafe.

Desire burnt through her, his mouth on hers causing a conflagration, a violent force that swept away everything but hunger and the ruthless, wildfire longing. Stunned by its intensity, a flash of insight made Marisa face the truth—this heady clamour was what had broken through her inertia in Mariposa. Involuntarily her body had reacted to Rafe's compelling magnetism, stimulating her into the action that had finally freed her.

She wanted more of it... She opened her mouth beneath his insistent demand and he took immediate advantage of the silent plea. The deep kiss that followed caused a peak of sensation, robbing her of all thought, all emotion, except a voluptuous craving unlike anything she'd ever experienced.

She almost cried out when he lifted his head.

"I'm sorry," he said harshly, and let her go, stepping back several paces as though he needed to put space between them.

"Sorry? *Sorry?*" She said unsteadily, "Why—why did you stop?"

CHAPTER NINE

RAFE bit back an oath. *Way to go, you fool*, he thought grimly, looking down at her, the soft lips trembling, her eyes wide and dazed.

The last thing you should be doing is kissing her like some lust-crazed idiot after she's just relived as nasty a case of emotional abuse as you've ever heard.

His voice harsh, he said, "Now is not the time. You've been through hell—"

Marisa crossed the space between them, reached up and put her hand across his mouth. "You're the first man who's touched me since I left Mariposa." She gave a twisted smile. "I used you, lied about you. I'm not going to lie again. I want you too."

Other women had come on to Rafe, some with disconcerting directness, most with considerably more subtlety, but none had made him feel like this. Marisa's touch, her words, sent desire pouring through him so that he had to grit his teeth to stop himself from losing control.

"Are you sure?" he demanded, his voice low and feral.

She dropped her hand. "Sure that I want you? Completely." Her voice shook and heat swept along her perfect cheekbones, but her gaze was honest.

"Why?" And why the hell was he probing? In his previous affairs all he'd expected was mutual desire. Now he wanted more—without knowing what that *more* would be.

The question shocked Marisa like a bucket of water in the face, jolting her out of her sensuous haze.

Panicked, she thought, *However much I want to, I can't do this.* Whatever Rafe was offering, it wouldn't be permanence... She was not only gambling with her life, she was gambling with Keir's.

Yet a flicker of subversive regret made her wonder if she was going to remain celibate until her son grew up.

Ashamed, colour flaring up through her skin, she said awkwardly, "I wish you hadn't asked that—but I'm glad you did. I don't have just myself to think about. Keir is becoming fond of you and it's going to hurt him when we leave." Desperation tinged her voice. "I have to find somewhere else to live!"

Rafe's intent, probing gaze, colder than an Antarctic sky in winter, seemed to pierce the façade she'd manufactured with such effort and patience. Shaking with the need to surrender, she watched him re-impose control and wished forlornly that it could be as easy for her.

"In that case," he said coolly, "I'll stay away as much as I can while you're here."

She firmed her mouth, knowing it was the best thing he could do. "Yes," she said colourlessly. "Thank you."

She looked up and met his level, iron-grey gaze. Deep inside her something contracted, almost banishing her tiredness in a surge of heat.

"Goodnight," she said and shot through the door, closing it behind her and leaning back against it, her heart pounding so noisily in her chest she could hear nothing else.

Of course Keir's welfare was the most important factor in her life. Yet for a moment she wondered what it would be like to be able to dream of something else, something for herself…

Sleep refused to come. Restlessly she tossed beneath the sheet, turning questions over in her mind.

What did she know about Rafe? Not enough to trust him. Oh, he was not only respected in Tewaka, he was liked—but no man could reach the heights he'd achieved without a strong streak of ruthlessness.

Why was she attracted to dominant men? She'd vowed never to allow that to happen to her again.

Yet she wanted Rafe. And he knew it. The minutes spent responding to his kisses with such passionate abandon had given her away completely.

Wildly successful, magnetic, brilliant, worldly—she could probably spend the rest of what promised to be a long and sleepless night thinking up words to describe him, but they all meant the same thing.

The good fairies around his cradle had showered him with more gifts than necessary. He could have any woman in the world.

Which was probably why he'd pulled back when she'd turned to jelly in his arms.

It was so…so *unlikely* that he'd want someone like her, not only scarred emotionally, but so very ordinary.

Unless he still wondered if Keir might be his son? Perhaps that was why he'd invited them to stay at Manuwai?

That thought made her feel sick, but it had to be faced.

She went over the conversation, testing everything Rafe had said. It was possible he did wonder...

Where was David now? Hot and sticky, she turned her pillow over and kicked off the sheet. Outside the little owl the Maori had named *ruru* was calling from a nearby tree. *Morepork, morepork*—a lonely, familiar sound, one she'd heard all over New Zealand, yet in the pleasant bedroom Marisa shivered.

Tomorrow she'd have plenty to face; right now she needed sleep.

Eventually it came.

Keir woke her, saying urgently, "Mum, it's late. You better get up now. The sun has got his smiley face on."

She bolted upright, checked the clock and said something under her breath, then huffed out a sigh and relaxed. "Today's Sunday, you horrible boy," she said affectionately. "It's a holiday. No shop and no school."

He grinned. "We can go down to the beach and swim all day," he suggested eagerly. "After we have pancakes for breakfast with lemon juice and brown sugar?"

Laughing, she threw back the sheet and swung out of bed, ruffling his hair as she went past him. "First I have to shower and get dressed."

At least, she thought a few minutes later, she didn't have to worry too much about what she would wear to face Rafe again. Jeans and a well-worn T-shirt that echoed the colour of her eyes would have to do.

Not too long afterwards she and Keir walked into the kitchen. Rafe looked around from the counter, where he was setting up the coffee machine.

"Good morning," he said, that perceptive gaze going from Marisa's guarded face to Keir's delighted one.

Keir ran across the room, his pleasure so patent it wrung Marisa's heart.

"I didn't know you were here," he said exuberantly. "Did you come home on the helicopter last night? Did you fly it?"

"No and no," Rafe said calmly. "The chopper's having a check-up so I came home by car after you were asleep. How have you been? Has your car arrived back with a new starter motor?"

"Yes, but I liked your grandma's car better, only Mum says we have to drive our own one again."

As she busied herself making pancake batter, Marisa listened to the two of them talking and thought miserably that if only she and Rafe had made love on that wreck of a bed in the hut...

A voluptuous need coiled through her, seductive as the original serpent. *Don't go there*, she thought feverishly.

But if Keir were Rafe's son, his future would be assured.

If only she didn't feel this scary, primal attraction... Every time she saw Rafe her brain went mushy, tempting her in so many dangerous ways.

She switched on the gas, coated a pan with butter and waited for it to sizzle before ladling in the batter.

"Pancakes?" Rafe said thoughtfully. "They're one of my favourite breakfasts."

Ever helpful, Keir said, "Then Mummy can make some for you."

Marisa looked up, saw a glint in Rafe's eyes and smiled, a dangerous expectation scintillating through her like diamond dust in her blood. "I made enough batter for us all," she told him.

Rafe cocked a sardonic brow, but remained silent.

The faint shadows beneath Marisa's eyes were more than enough evidence of a wakeful night.

His gut tightened as he thought of another way she could have spent those hours of darkness—a much more satisfactory way for both of them. The kisses he'd exchanged with her had left him hungry and frustrated in the most basic way, killing sleep until late.

He was a sophisticated man—not promiscuous, and normal in his appetites. He liked rare steak, a good wine, the refreshment of a cool shower after exertion, the softness and passion of women. He expected to marry—some time. His parents' disastrous marriage had convinced him that a steady, safe, completely reliable affection was the best basis for a lifelong relationship.

What he'd never anticipated was this smouldering hunger that wouldn't leave him alone.

Had the situation been normal, Marisa would have spent last night in his bed, in his arms. His body tightened, but he ignored it. Her revelation about her marriage complicated everything. Rafe killed a primitive urge to make David Brown pay for the emotional pain he'd inflicted.

Any further advance in their mutual attraction would have to be on Marisa's terms, not his. And she'd made it very clear that for her, young Keir's welfare came before everything else.

They ate out on the terrace, the sun beaming down on them like a benediction, and the motionless branches of the pohutukawa trees spangled with blue-green glimpses of the sea behind.

* * *

After breakfast Rafe headed off to his study. Mariposa's time zone was fifteen hours behind New Zealand's—if his luck was in, he'd get an instant answer.

Sure enough, the manager emailed back within ten minutes. Rafe's frown grew darker as he read the answer. *You may remember he lit a fire in the machinery shed. When questioned, he said it was to make a point, but that he didn't intend to harm anyone. The previous agent believed this.*

Rafe could almost feel the agent's curiosity smoking off the screen, but contented himself with a terse note of thanks. An odd sensation of foreboding gripping him, he left the computer and walked across to the huge kauri desk his father had worked at, like his forefathers before him. Making up his mind, he lifted the telephone and punched in a number.

He listened to what his private investigator had to say with a gathering grimness.

After a short conversation he put down the phone and strode across to the window to stare unseeingly out.

His strong sense that something was wrong had stood him in good stead before. He'd learned to pay careful attention to it.

He found Marisa with Keir in the garden. "We need to talk," he told her and switched his gaze to Keir, absorbed in examining a large, jazzily striped Monarch butterfly caterpillar on the swan plant. "I've asked Ngaire Sinclair to come across with young Manu around ten; she's happy to keep the boys down on the beach until midday."

Marisa opened her mouth to object, then closed it again. If they needed to talk, it would have to be without any chance of Keir overhearing. But her stomach clamped at the thought of what lay ahead. She'd desperately wanted a peaceful day to recharge her batteries.

"All right," she agreed.

From the terrace off the small parlour Marisa watched the boys frolic around Ngaire like two puppies across the lawn and disappear down the cliff path to the children's beach. Turning, she tried to relax taut muscles. Colour stung her skin when she realised Rafe was watching her, his grey eyes coolly speculative.

Heart jumping, she said, "Something's happened. What is it?"

"Your ex-husband is somewhere in New Zealand."

She flinched as though struck by a blow. Rafe had to rein in a fierce, intemperate anger. The man might not have hit her, but she was actively afraid of him.

"How—?" She stopped, cleared her throat and firmed her lush mouth into a straight line. "How do you know?" she demanded.

He frowned, "Come inside. You're shivering."

Silently she accompanied him into the house. Once inside one look at her convinced him this was hugely unpleasant news. Her eyes were blank in her white face, but as he watched she gave herself a little shake and some colour came back into her skin.

Tight-lipped, he said, "I thought you knew that. You divorced him a couple of years after he left Mariposa."

"That was done through lawyers," she shot back. "He had a lawyer in Invercargill. I certainly didn't know he was here in New Zealand."

"He went to Australia first," Rafe said, watching her closely.

Her relief was patent, but it didn't last long. She

looked up at him. "When did he come back to New Zealand?"

"When you moved north to Tewaka."

The little colour in her skin leached away and she sent an involuntary glance towards the beach as though she thought her ex-husband might be there, threatening their son.

Once more Rafe watched her get a grip on her fears. "How do you know all this?" she asked in a quiet voice very much at variance with that first moment of panic.

"Sit down," he ordered.

She gave him a speaking glance, but sat down in the chair. "I'll be back in a moment," he said and strode through to the other room.

Marisa was sitting very erect when he came back, but there was an emptiness in the green eyes he recognised, and her soft mouth was held in firm restraint. No woman should ever look like that. He reined in his anger and handed her the glass.

She took it automatically, and sipped, then choked. "Ugh!" she spluttered. "What *is* this?"

"Brandy. Drink at least some of it. You've had a shock and it will help."

"Not to keep a clear head, it won't," she said, and put it down. She fixed him with a determined stare. "You didn't answer my question. How do you know all this?"

"I employ an extremely experienced firm of private investigators to check up on anything I need to know," he said, half-amused by her attempt to wrest control of the situation from him.

Half-amused, impressed—and secretly frustrated as hell.

Because his body still thrummed with a ruthless

need. But that wildfire hunger was backed by a strong urge to protect her and the boy.

She frowned, her lips easing into a faint, humourless smile. "Yes, of course you do. Are they so good you know where David is now?"

"Not that good," he acknowledged drily. "In Australia he was working on a cattle station in the Outback. He flew to New Zealand about a month ago, landing in Christchurch. Since then, nothing."

Which possibly meant he was travelling under an assumed name.

She drew in a sharp breath. "I could try his lawyer."

"Even if they're still in touch, his solicitor isn't likely to tell you unless you can give a damned good reason. Like the fact that Brown is Keir's father..." Deliberately he let the words trail off.

"That's never going to happen," she asserted fiercely.

"In that case, stay away from his solicitor."

Narrow black brows met for a moment and then she agreed, "You're right, I'd be stupid to make any contact."

Her hands clenched together in her lap. She raised her dark green gaze to meet his and said bleakly, "It's all right. I'll work something out."

His voice raw, he said, "Hell! You're not just afraid of him, you're terrified."

Marisa looked away, but he caught her chin in a firm grip and turned her face towards him. The heat faded from her skin. Unable to answer, she nervously swallowed and he let her go.

"Yes," he said, as if somehow she'd confirmed it. "Why? He has no power over you now."

Buffeted by his formidable determination, she couldn't assemble any coherent answer from the disconnected fragments of thought that tumbled and jostled through her mind. When she did find her voice it sounded weak and ineffectual. "If he ever finds out that Keir is his, he'd fight me for him." She glanced up at him, eyes shadowy and troubled. "Rafe, this is not your battle, even though I involved you in it."

"I want to know why you're so afraid of this man," he stated, not giving an inch. "Have you told me everything? You're a strong woman—yet you're terrified of him. Even if he does discover that Keir is his son and gain access, you'd be able to monitor the situation."

Surrendering, she dragged in a breath. "I suppose I'm as much afraid of myself as I am of him," she said, her voice rough. "I married him as a normal nineteen-year-old and within two years I was a wreck. Loneliness was a big part of it. But there were other things—little things…"

Her voice died away.

"Go on," Rafe said steadily.

She summoned her courage. "One of the men brought me a parrot—a little gold-and-blue bird that lives in the trees by the streams and can be taught to talk. It had fallen out of the nest somehow and I nursed it back to health, but almost as soon as it started to repeat the words I was teaching it, it died. He wouldn't let me see the body. He just told me about it and then he buried it. I didn't think anything of it. Then there was a kitten. It was fine one day, playing at my feet, but it died overnight too."

Although she paused, Rafe remained silent, the only sign of any reaction the thinning of his mouth. So she went on, "He promised me a puppy to replace it, but it never arrived…"

She glanced up, saw him frown and went on starkly,

"And painting—he referred to it as a hobby, but as the months went by it became my lifeline. When I ran out of paints he said he'd ordered more, but none ever came. I wish I could explain just how empty I felt with nothing to do except housework, nobody to talk to except him. There were no books and he didn't see any reason for a garden..." Her voice tailed away.

Rafe said, "Go on."

"I wanted to learn Spanish; he thought—or said he thought—it would be a good idea. He was learning quite a bit from the men, but he was always too tired to teach me and he didn't want me talking to the men. He used to read my parents' letters, so I couldn't say anything to them." She made a swift gesture of despair. "It sounds petty and foolish—"

"It sounds like a reign of terror," Rafe said grimly. "What about his parents? Were you in contact with them?"

"Oh, no. David never knew his birth parents—he was given up for adoption as a baby. But something happened when he was seven—I don't know what— and he spent the rest of his childhood in foster homes. Some were good, but he never stayed long enough in one to really find a home."

"Why?"

She shrugged. "I don't know. He didn't like talking about it. He told me he had to be tough; when he was hurt he didn't rest until he'd paid people back, punishing them, because that way they left him alone. And if—if he still feels that way, what better way to punish me than try to take Keir away?"

Recounting this took all of her courage, but she owed Rafe. She finished, "Keir is starting to look more and more like him. If he forced me to allow Keir to be DNA tested he'd discover the truth." She lifted her gaze at Rafe, searching his hard, arrogant face for some sign of understanding. "You called it a reign of terror. That's what I'm afraid of—the damage he might be able to do to Keir's peace of mind, his lovely, sunny personality…" She blinked back tears and said fiercely, "I'll do anything I can to make sure it doesn't happen."

"I see now why you don't want him in Keir's life, but if he did apply, he'd almost certainly get access." Rafe spoke objectively, clearly weighing the information. "Your lies would put you in an unfavourable position."

Bleakly she admitted, "I know. Do you think I don't worry about what I've done? I do. That lie has weighed on my shoulders ever since I told it." She caught her breath and held her head high, meeting his eyes with a defiance based on fear. "But I'd do it again. Is it too much to want Keir to have a serene childhood, one where he can grow up and be happy and not be burdened with adult problems? You know him—does he seem to be missing anything?"

"Not obviously, no." Rafe paced across to the window, big and lithe and predatory. Once there he swung around and surveyed her, his expression closed. "But that could change. Children are said to need a stable male figure in their lives. If it did come to a custody dispute, you'd be in a much stronger position if there was a man in your life, someone Keir liked and respected." He paused, before saying calmly, "The simplest way to ensure that would be for us to get engaged."

Marisa stared at him, his words dancing crazily through her head. It took every ounce of self-control to say, "No, no, that's not necessary."

"It makes sense," he said coolly, his mouth twisting

as he took in her patent shock. "If it does nothing else, it will reinforce the idea that the boy is mine."

"Yes, but there's absolutely no reason for you to be involved—"

"You involved me when you came up with that lie," he told her uncompromisingly.

Colour burned her skin, then faded. She couldn't refute that.

Before she could come up with a reply, he said, "You can't admit to the lie without possibly jeopardising Keir's well-being, so you might as well make use of it again."

Marisa shook her head, swamped by bone-deep exhaustion.

Rafe touched her shoulder, then dropped his hand. "You're exhausted and no wonder. Drink some more brandy." His tone was remote and decisive, as though working out some strategy.

Nerves jumping in a complex mixture of tension and dismay—and something deeper, more basic, that she wasn't prepared to explore—she tried to match his judicial tone. "I don't need brandy, thanks. And I can't believe that being engaged to you would sway a family court."

"You'd be surprised," he said cynically, adding in a gentler voice, "Marisa, try not to worry. We don't know that Brown is interested in establishing contact with Keir. We'll discuss this further when you've had time to think things over."

Not if she could prevent it. All she wanted to do was crawl into some hole, pull the door shut behind her and stay there until this whole thing went away.

If it ever did...

But Rafe's use of *we* comforted her.

The sound of children's voices dragged her gaze towards the garden. Surely it wasn't lunchtime—no, Ngaire was piggybacking young Manu.

Galvanised, she said, "Something's happened to Manu, I think."

"Probably a cut from a shell. I'll get the first-aid kit."

Before he left she said in a muted voice, "Rafe, when you told me David was back in New Zealand I panicked. All this time I'd presumed he was still in Mariposa, you see, which is why I didn't—*couldn't*—tell you who I was."

"I understand that your son's welfare is the most important thing in your life."

He sounded completely in command, as though it was quite ordinary to propose a fake engagement with a woman he barely knew to safeguard a child who wasn't his own.

CHAPTER TEN

THE children were so disappointed by the early cessation of their stay on the beach that Ngaire said, "Look, why don't you let Keir come home with us? Quite frankly, it would be a good thing. Manu's going to have to keep off that heel for the rest of the day, so he and Keir can watch a DVD together. I'll drop Keir off around four?"

At Keir's exuberant little jump, Marisa laughed. "You have your answer. Thanks very much, he'd love to come."

Which left her alone in the house with Rafe. However, he retired to his office, emerging for lunch with an abstracted air and returning immediately afterwards. She told herself she was relieved. Feeling awkward was irritating and she refused to accept that she had any reason for it.

The problem was it wouldn't go away.

When he walked out and found her bringing in a load of washing from the line, he asked, "Surely Nadine can do that?"

"These are our sheets," she said firmly. "And our clothes." She folded one of Keir's small shirts and put it over the top of a lacy bra.

A smile curved Rafe's mouth, but he said, "Have you made up your mind yet? Are we engaged or not?"

At the sardonic note in his voice her stomach went into free fall. "Oh, don't be silly," she blurted, then could have kicked herself for coming up with such an unsophisticated retort. "You know it's not at all necessary."

"I'm beginning to feel it's very necessary," he said curtly, eyes never leaving her face.

Eyes widening, she stared at him, a torrent of thoughts cascading through her mind. "You've heard where he is," she breathed.

He shook his black head. "No." Then paused, as though weighing his words.

His tone was level, perfectly steady, yet when she looked at him an emotion close to fear chilled her.

"But I've just been talking to the chief of the local fire brigade."

"You don't need to tell me—you went to school with him," she said brightly, sensing he was about to tell her something she didn't want to hear.

His smile was brief and unamused. "As it happens, yes, I did. He said the first fire—the cottage—was probably caused by a cigarette thrown from a car. The long grass at the fence line caught and it got to the house. The garage might be arson."

She blinked and felt her muscles sag. When he took a step towards her she stiffened, straightening her spine and warding him off with a rapid, involuntary gesture. He stopped a pace away.

"Kids?" she hazarded tautly. "Bored teenagers?"

"Possibly." He paused, then said, "Your ex-husband was sacked from the estancia because he burned down the machinery shed shortly after you told him I was

Keir's father. He didn't intend to harm anyone, but one of the farmhands had a narrow escape."

Marisa could feel the colour drain from her skin, leaving her cold and shaken. "Who?" she breathed, her mind ranging over the farmhands.

He looked surprised. "I don't know—whoever it was got out just in time. As far as I know he wasn't hurt."

Before she could say anything he continued, "One of the Tanner boys looked out the night the garage burned down and saw a vehicle parked by it. He thought it was another volunteer checking the cottage. However, the brigade had left, convinced there was no further chance of the place catching fire."

"And you think…" Marisa searched for words, but could only shake her head.

His gaze still on her face, Rafe went on, "You told me Brown rang you about a month after you'd come back to New Zealand to be with your parents."

"Yes."

"And that was when you told him you'd slept with me and that the baby you were having was mine?"

His coolly judicial voice steadied her.

"Yes," she repeated numbly.

"He lit the fire five weeks after you'd left him."

Marisa's teeth clamped down on her bottom lip. "Oh, heavens," she whispered. "Rafe, I'm so sorry."

He shrugged. "It's not your fault. I assume he tried to pay me back in the only way he could—by destroying something of mine. If he set the garage alight, he'd be punishing you by destroying something of yours."

"But we don't know… I can't believe…" Her incredulous voice trailed away, because it made a hideous sort of sense.

"I think you do," Rafe said, mercilessly refusing to

offer any sort of comfort. "Why else would you be so afraid he might find out Keir is his child? You sensed he was capable of violence."

"I didn't—" She stopped, met his dispassionate gaze and expelled a long, sobbing breath, facing the truth at last. "Yes. Yes, of course I did. But I can't believe he'd try to *kill* anyone."

"Whoever lit these fires didn't intend to kill," he said crisply. "The danger comes when a fire gets out of control. Or when people aren't where arsonists expect them to be—as happened in Mariposa."

A pause made it obvious he expected a reply, but Marisa remained silent, grappling with the implications of this. From somewhere close by a seagull called, its screech a threat and a warning. She shivered, and hugged herself, rubbing her hands over her suddenly cold arms.

After a few seconds Rafe continued, "Of course this is all supposition. We don't have a single fact to go on beyond that he admitted to lighting a fire in the machine shed in Mariposa. But your instincts are good. You recognised something about him that convinced you he'd never be a good father."

She nodded. "What...what I'm trying to work out is how I can deal with this."

"*We* are going to become engaged," he said deliberately, emphasising the first word. "Then, if it's necessary, I can protect you and Keir."

"That's outrageously noble of you," she fired back, so tempted to surrender it was difficult to get the words out. "But nobody gets engaged for such quixotic reasons."

Rafe's smile curled her toes. "I can be as foolish as

the next man," he drawled and took the shirt she'd just unpegged and tossed it into the clothes basket.

He drew her towards him, but although she longed for his mouth on hers, his arms didn't tighten around her and he said above her head, "If it is arson, and if it is your ex, an engagement to me is likely to be as good a protection for young Keir and you as anything else."

Better, she thought, trying to resist the powerful, honey-and-flame rush of desire she'd been longing for through the night.

And not just last night.

Without realising it, she'd spent the past five years missing the primal security she'd once felt in Rafe's arms. Locked against his lean, strong body while the rain hammered down outside the hut, she'd inhaled the faint, unmistakably masculine perfume of his skin, listened to his regular breathing, been reassured by the steady beat of his heart. And in those long hours, some essential, unknown part of her had surrendered.

Yet it was more than a simple longing for a safe haven...

He'd roused a sleeping hunger in her, an appetite both erotic and emotional—something she'd refused to admit even to herself. Only when she'd seen him again had that forbidden yearning prompted her to wonder what it would be like to share the burden, give her a chance to be more than Keir's mother and protector—to be Rafe's lover.

Now, in this perilous moment, she was given a glimpse of paradise. Rafe's embrace extinguished sanity in a surge of sensual craving, and she barely had time to think, *I mustn't let this happen*, before he tilted her head and examined her face. Heat kindled in his iron-grey eyes and that dangerous, voluptuous yearning overwhelmed her as he took her mouth.

Last night their kisses had been measured, almost experimental. Rafe had explored her lips with assurance and sensuous, erotically charged skill, but she'd been wary, unable to resist, yet not ready to yield to headstrong temptation.

This was different. This time when he kissed her a surge of reckless delight persuaded her to open her lips, to savour his taste as though she'd hungered for it all her life.

His reaction was instantaneous, close to ruthless. With their bodies sealed together as though nothing could ever separate them again, Marisa dug her fingers into the hard muscles of his back with an abandon that felt so good, so completely right.

When at last he lifted his head, her knees buckled and she had to cling desperately.

He held her effortlessly and said on a harsh, raw note, "Marisa."

She looked up into grey eyes, stormy as the clouds that lashed Mariposa in the rainy season. They locked on to hers, probing through to her soul.

Fiercely pleased, she said, "What is it?"

"What you do to me," he muttered and lowered his head again.

She shivered with desperate delight when he kissed her throat and the silky, sensuous spot below her ear, a soft kiss that sent rills of voluptuous anticipation aching through her. Deep in the pit of her stomach a deeper, more primitive sensation tightened into hunger.

His hand slid down to cup her breast. Instantly the rills turned to torrents that drowned her in acute, almost painful anticipation, contracted every pleading muscle with the need to find—to find a place where she could give in to the desire that consumed her with reckless, compelling power.

It would be so easy to stop thinking, to give in to the heady clamour of her body—to make love with Rafe...

Keir, she thought desperately.

Shocked, shamed by her easy surrender, she tried to wrench herself away. Rafe's arms tightened instinctively, but after only a second he let her go. He didn't move; when she took an uncertain, wavering step back his hand shot out to steady her.

"What is it?" he demanded forcefully.

"No," she gabbled, searching the harsh, beautiful contours of his face. "No, we can't do this. It's...it's..." She searched for the correct word, finally blurting, "It's dangerous."

"Not in my book."

His voice was hard and arrogant. It should have frozen her desire, but when she saw her own need echoed in the dark intensity of his gaze she shivered again, fighting herself and the impetuous demands of her body.

"And what is dangerous?" he demanded. "Making love? Or becoming engaged?"

"Both," she flung at him, closing her eyes against his face in case it torpedoed her resolution. "But especially getting engaged. Too many things could go wrong."

"Name one."

She seized on the most painful. "Keir. He's already learning to love you. When we leave I know now he'll be upset, but he knows—I've told him several times— that we're just on holiday here, not going to stay. If he thinks there's a chance we might live here with you all the time, he'll be heartbroken. I don't want him to end up like a child from a broken home."

"He's already from a broken home," he said curtly.

Marisa closed her eyes against this blunt, cruel statement and pulled air into her lungs by sheer force of will. "Until I saw him with you I didn't realise how much he's been missing a father. To find one in you, then to be torn away from you—I couldn't put him through that again."

"Again?" he asked sharply.

She nodded. "He grieved for my mother after her death, but he was heartbroken when Dad went—he'd been Dad's little mate."

He stepped away, leaving her suddenly cold, his expression closed against her. Quickly, before he could say anything, she blurted, "And you could meet someone and fall in love with her."

Only to have him dismiss it with quick, cold assurance. "I keep my promises."

Shocked by a lightning flash of insight, Marisa clenched her teeth on something too close to a sob. If Rafe ever loved another woman it would hurt—so much.

But it would be even worse to be engaged to him and know it was only his unsparing integrity that kept him beside her.

An acute, panicky sense of vulnerability stopped her from speaking. She'd already endured one barren relationship; she was not going to let herself be seduced into another.

Was this love...?

No. She didn't even know what love was. Whatever she'd felt for David had been false, based on her need for security. This too might be the same...

She gave him a hunted look. "Do you think I—any

woman—would be happy knowing only a promise was keeping a man beside her?"

Rafe's brows rose. "I hope that your complete lack of sense is due to raging passion," he murmured lazily, "rather than a sudden loss of brain cells. Relax—it's not going to happen. If it makes you feel any better, I'm not at all sure that I'm capable of the sort of love poets celebrate. But I can assure you I don't deliberately hurt people...and I think we have more than enough going to enjoy a very satisfactory relationship."

And he ran a forefinger from her chin down the slender column of her throat to the far-from-sexy neckline of her polo shirt.

Shivering, stunned by her body's sensuous response to that sure, sensitively judged caress, she concentrated on marshalling her thoughts into a coherent argument. "R-Rafe, this is serious. We can't play with lives like that—not Keir's, not our own. And we don't even know if getting engaged will keep David away."

His finger stilled before he lifted it to tilt her chin so that he could search her face. "I am not in the habit of playing with lives." Each word was clipped and decisive, as though her words had touched a nerve. "And if an engagement isn't likely to keep your ex-husband away, a marriage certainly would."

Marisa had to lock her knees to keep herself upright. Eyes widening, she stared at him as though he'd threatened her with a gun.

"Are you mad?" she asked faintly, managing to take one wobbly step away from him.

"I suspect I am," he said, something like humour glinting in his eyes. It disappeared quickly and in a crisp, judicial voice he said, "You have two options. You can run again and hope Brown never finds you and

Keir, or you can stay and fight this out once and for all. Hiding in New Zealand is pretty near impossible. It's too small, with too few people. Even in huge countries with large populations, it's difficult to stay hidden. If you meet him face to face, you'll feel safer with some protection. I can give you that."

"Why?" she asked starkly. "You don't really want to marry me—you don't even *know* me…"

"I know you saved my life," he said austerely. "I can imagine how hard it was for you to get me out of that plane, then support me to the hut."

He waited, but her quick brain let her down and a more primitive part adjured her to remain silent.

Crisply Rafe said, "I know you'd gladly sacrifice your life for your son. I also know loyalty like that is hard to earn and probably even harder to keep."

"Any mother would do the same," she returned with stubborn determination.

"Not all. My mother took a pay-off of ten million dollars and left without a backwards glance," he told her with savage emphasis. "I was six. I stood in the gateway and watched her drive away, knowing she'd never come back."

Mutely she nodded.

He didn't reach out to her, but his intention was as palpable as though he'd stroked her. "*I* know I want you and that the wanting grows every time I see you."

"Yes, but is that enough?" she asked impulsively, then stopped, dismayed. Her skin heated again when she met his glinting scrutiny.

Damn, she thought urgently. Oh, damn and double damn—she'd just admitted she was every bit as hungry for him as he was for her.

Not that it mattered. Rafe was a sophisticated man

and according to the media he'd enjoyed the charms of some very sophisticated women. He'd have recognised the drumming heat of carnality between them the first time they'd kissed.

"For me, yes." He shrugged. "My father fell in love with my mother and married her out of hand. It was a disaster. His second wife he chose more carefully. They built a very strong marriage and were happy."

Marisa tried to ignore the treacherous inner part of her that was ignoring all the caveats and cautions to whisper seductively *Why not...?*

Swiftly she said, "I've already made one really bad decision when I married David. Now I have to think of Keir. If things fall to pieces one day it's he who will really suffer."

Rafe said calmly, "I agree. I'm not proposing an immediate marriage. An engagement will give us time to know each other better. It will also give you time to discover whether or not you'll be happy here." Clearly he discerned her fears, because he added, "And to find out whether you've made the same mistake with me as you did before."

"I don't think so," she admitted quietly. Rafe was even more dangerous to her than David—in an entirely different way. "But what's in it for you?"

And saw with wry amusement that her directness startled him.

But only for a second. It was soon chased away by a smile that held both amusement and a certain irony. "Apart from anything else, the pleasure of knowing that no matter how much I learn about you, you're always able to surprise me."

She blinked. "I don't set out to."

"I know. That's why I enjoy it. As for the other—"

He reached for her, letting his hands rest lightly on her shoulders before pulling her slowly into his arms, giving her time to step away. "I foresee that I would enjoy being married to you very much."

Her heart thudded to a stop, then lurched into uneven overdrive.

Eyes darkening, she froze. She couldn't say anything, nor did she struggle when he turned her face up towards him.

"And I intend for you to enjoy it very much too," he said with a narrowed, dangerous look that dared her to object.

And kissed her. Lost in the magic of his touch, his mouth, she spun out completely, but a tiny shred of self-control lingered, enough for her to say shakily when he lifted his head, "I d-don't think this is a good idea."

"Why?" he said, his mouth curving.

She dragged a breath into starving lungs, compelling her dazed, dreamy mind to concentrate. Soon, she thought hazily, soon she'd pull away, free herself from the heady exhilaration that drugged her.

"Because," she breathed helplessly.

Rafe's laughter was underlined by a raw note that emphasised the hardening of his body against her. He closed her eyes with quick kisses, then lowered his head and dropped more kisses on her throat.

A sensuous groan tore through Marisa, partly protest but caused by the most intense pleasure—like nothing she'd ever felt before.

It was enough to make her jerk backwards. For a heartbeat he resisted, then let her go, his expression hardening when he inspected her clouding face.

She burst into speech, trying to clear that sensuous haze from her mind. "You're not the sort of man to

marry just to help someone out. And don't give me that
guff about saving your life, either—you're rich enough
to give me a million dollars and not even notice it had
gone. That way you could salve any feelings of gratitude without tying yourself to me and another man's
child. So what's in it for you?"

"Is that what you'd rather have—a million dollars?"
he asked with a mirthless, cynical smile.

"If you gave me a million dollars," she told him, parrying his hooded gaze, "I'd hand the lot to a refuge for
battered women."

He flung his head back and laughed. "I suspect you
would and without a second thought."

"Count on it," she told him, adding with a twisted
smile, "although I can't guarantee not to give it a second thought, or even a third one. But I've learned how
to live without relying on anyone else and I plan to keep
on doing that. I don't want your money."

"Good, because I don't plan to give it to you. I learned
the lesson my father had to learn the hard way—don't
pay people off." He added on a deeper, more harsh note,
"As for what's in it for me…"

He reached out for her.

Marisa's heart began to pound again. He didn't try to
kiss her—he didn't even hold her tightly, yet her body
ached with sweet delight at his nearness and she had to
stop herself from sinking against him.

"I think you know what's in it for me," he said quietly. "And whatever it is, you feel it too."

"Lust," she said, the word stark with an obscure disappointment. What had she expected—a protestation
of undying love?

It would never come from Rafe. Dared she accept his

proposition—follow this fierce longing down whatever path it led her? Dared she risk Keir's happiness?

Stupid questions. Common sense and everything she'd learned told her to refuse his proposition and walk away before she got hurt again.

Yet still she hesitated, so tempted to take a rash chance without putting her son first that she had to clench her jaw to stop the impetuous words tumbling out.

Was it too selfish to want something for herself?

Because she wanted Rafe with an intensity that made her dizzy, setting her body alight and scrambling her brain—and threatening her principles.

At least there would be honesty. Rafe had laid down his terms and she knew exactly what sort of marriage they'd have. One that was convenient for both of them. One that would provide a safe haven for Keir.

"What are you thinking?" Rafe asked.

She said, "That I need something—"

His brows rose. "What?"

Was there a hint of cynicism in his tone? Marisa thought furiously for a few seconds, then snapped her head up. "I want to make a condition. Two, actually."

CHAPTER ELEVEN

RAFE released her. Something in his expression chilled Marisa, but she went on, "I'll understand if you refuse them. I want a promise—a *written* promise—that if you fall in love with anyone else our engagement will finish. And I want you to promise me that when we part, you'll keep in touch with Keir. Seeing him with you has taught me that he needs a man in his life. One he can rely on. I know it's asking a lot—"

He said nothing, and she made a gesture of negation. "Forget about it. It's not worth the risk. We shouldn't let this— I can't let this...this—"

"The word *written* made me wonder if you've learned anything about me at all," he said on an odd note.

His mouth crushed her answer to nothingness and the words fled from her mind. Desire was a primal need in her, a longing that brooked no restraint, a potent force that grew as their lips clung and his body hardened against her.

When he lifted his head, he said harshly, "Lust, desire, passion, hunger—who cares what name we give it?" He released her, dark eyes narrowing as he scanned her face. "It's there and we both feel it."

"Yes," she said, the word a husky sigh.

It was surrender and he knew it. His gaze hardened,

heated, sending erotic shivers through her. "I agree to your conditions. So we'll go ahead with an engagement."

Bemused, her heart hammering so loudly in her chest she was sure he had to hear it, she nodded. A strange mixture of emotions coursed through her as she waited for him to pull her into his arms again with an expectancy that was as much foreboding as hope, as much fear as love.

But he made no move towards her and the heat from his kisses faded, leaving her cold from her heart out.

Rafe didn't ask for love, nor did he promise it. She honoured him for that. Perhaps this fake engagement would enable them to trust each other. They might even forge a bond—a relationship something like his father's second marriage, solid and long-lasting, only without the commitment or the sex...

And Keir would be as safe as she could make him.

In a muted voice she said, "Thank you."

Rafe's gaze narrowed. "I don't ever want to hear that again. If I do, I'll have to thank you in return for saving my life. It could get boring."

Feeling oddly disconnected, Marisa forced a smile and retreated into the new Marisa, the one who could deal with anything. "We can't have that. Anyway, it's untrue. You were utterly determined to get out of that plane."

Her world had suddenly been shaken vigorously and turned upside down. The irony of it, she realised later in the day, was that David might not be anywhere near Tewaka so there was no need for her to put her heart in such jeopardy...

She spent the rest of the afternoon making lists of

things to do, things to buy—the most important and necessary being clothes for Keir and herself. The pile she'd brought home before the garage burned down was pathetically small.

She was also called by the insurance agent, presumably on Rafe's instructions. It was a relief to talk to him of practicalities, although the loss of her small store of treasures and mementoes was still too painful to face.

And she ironed the clothes she'd brought in, the domestic routine almost soothing her. Nadine had the day off but she always made sure there was food prepared, so after organising dinner Marisa put Keir to bed, and then, heart thumping erratically, surveyed her scanty wardrobe. In the end she chose a light shirt in a bittersweet red that somehow gave her skin a honey-coloured sheen, teeming it with a narrow pair of trousers.

"You look like a sunset," she said aloud.

For a few moments she hesitated in front of the mirror, nerves taut, then swung around and headed for the small parlour. Rafe was standing at the window, looking out over the lawn, still spring-green and lush. He turned and the banked fires in her blazed up when he smiled.

"All well?"

"Yes, he's sound asleep." She covered her strange nervousness by glancing at her watch. "Dinner should be ready in half an hour."

He indicated a tray. "Champagne is definitely appropriate for tonight. Do you like it?"

"Of course." Watching him ease the cork free, she found herself wondering dismally how often he'd done this—and for how many women.

The thought alarmed her. She'd never indulged in jealousy and she wasn't going to start now.

And the champagne was delicious.

"It comes from a vineyard I own in the South Island," he said. "Now, I have a toast."

She didn't know what to expect, smiling when he said, "To us—you, Keir and me."

Moved by the simplicity of his words, she repeated them.

Once again they ate dinner out on the terrace. Dusk fell silently and the Southern Cross emerged, diamonds on black velvet. Rafe told her more about Manuwai's fascinating history, indulging her curiosity about the place.

Marisa wondered if he knew that as each minute passed a delicious tension was building inside her.

Eventually they came inside where Rafe said calmly, "You need a ring. There's family jewellery if you'd like that, but I'll also get a jeweller to come up with a selection. I doubt if it's necessary to announce it in any newspapers—"

"Oh, no!" She went a little pale. "No, that hadn't occurred to me."

"It's possibly going to finish up in the media, just the same." Observing her dismay, he said a little tersely, "Expect some interest—and speculation—from the gossip writers, though I'll do what I can to dampen it down."

Slightly relieved, she nodded. David wouldn't read gossip columns. But when she said, "I don't need a ring", Rafe frowned.

"You do."

A note in his voice told her that need it or not, she was going to get one. After a wavering second, she decided this wasn't worth drawing a line in the sand, but she directed a challenging look at him. "Why?"

"An engagement ring means it's serious, not just a case of living together. To satisfy everyone, including your ex-husband, we need all the trimmings. And we need to do some entertaining. My friends will expect to meet you."

She tensed. "Do you think that's necessary?"

"Yes." He observed her a moment. "I hope you like them. Have you met Hani and Kelt Crysander-Gillen?"

The sudden change of subject threw her for a moment, but she shook her head. "I know of them," she said cautiously. "He's some sort of royal, isn't he, from an island in the Mediterranean?"

"No, *she*'s some sort of royal from an island in the Indian Ocean," he said with a glimmer of a smile. "Kelt's some sort of royal from a country in the Balkans, but he doesn't use his title. They live down the coast here on Kelt's station. I've known him since I was a kid. They're both extremely good company, and perfectly normal."

"Except for being royal," she said with a slight snap.

"Don't worry, they won't expect you to curtsy." When she gave a strained smile he said crisply, "You didn't have any such fears about my friend Patrick, the garage owner who fixed your car. I choose my friends for their own sakes, not because they happen to have titles. I've been called plenty of things in my time, but never a snob."

"I know you're not," she said immediately, feeling rather small. She couldn't tell him she was fighting a private battle against becoming too entrenched in his life, and that meeting his friends somehow made their agreement too personal.

His hard gaze warmed. "I'll give them a call and see if they'll come up to dinner shortly."

Marisa said politely, "That would be lovely. Do you want me to be hostess?"

Her refusal to take anything for granted irked him, but she was skittish enough without calling her on it. "Of course." He examined her face, his body tightening when his gaze skimmed the softly full contours of her mouth.

Soon he'd take her to bed and scotch any chance of second thoughts by making her his in the most basic and simple way of all.

She might have agreed to this engagement to protect young Keir, but she'd made no attempt to deny that the attraction between them was mutual.

Rafe sometimes thought he'd been born a cynic. If he had, it had been reinforced by his mother's abandonment. Certainly he doubted that love—the romantic, transcendent passion poets eulogised—really existed. He suspected it was a temporary madness and one he'd long ago accepted he wasn't likely to succumb to.

Desire he understood, and friendship. He felt both for Marisa and, as well, he recognised and respected her protectiveness towards her son—perhaps because of the mother who'd sold him for ten million dollars.

Marisa's kisses told him she'd be a willing and responsive lover. As well, she was a stimulating companion and she'd settled easily into life at Tewaka.

She broke into his thoughts with a coolly delivered statement. "You look like a lion eyeing up an antelope—anticipatory yet satisfied, because the lion knows its prey hasn't got a hope of getting away. And that makes me nervous."

Rafe threw back his head and laughed. He wasn't going to tell her she'd nailed exactly how he was feeling.

"I wasn't thinking in terms of predator and prey,"

he said, "and certainly not of killing anything. On the contrary, my thoughts and emotions are bordering on the lustful."

A surge of colour burned through Marisa's skin, and with it, a bold impulse. "Then why don't—?" Mortified at what she'd almost said, she clamped down on the rest.

But she couldn't pull her gaze away. Fascinated, she watched his gaze kindle as it swept her face, echoing the heat that flamed into life inside her, surging through her like a forest fire...

Fires destroy, she reminded herself and tried to breathe. But forest fires allow new life to flourish in their aftermath.

A little roughly he asked, "Are you indicating I'm being too noble by giving you time?"

Lips clamped tightly together in case she made an even greater fool of herself, she hesitated. He didn't move. Marisa's breath locked in her throat as she wavered on the brink of a momentous decision, one she couldn't take back or flee from.

If she made the wrong decision she'd regret it for the rest of her life.

If only she knew which *was* the wrong decision...

This was one thing she had to decide for herself, yet it took all her courage to follow her heart and give a swift, shy nod.

Rafe covered the distance between them in one rapid stride. He looked down and this time she met his gaze with no hint of challenge.

"Marisa?" He said it steadily, still not reaching out to her.

Why didn't he touch her? She dragged a breath into starving lungs. "What?"

"Say yes," he commanded almost harshly. At her nod, he tipped her chin. "*Say* it—but only if you feel it."

And suddenly it was all right. He did want her—as much as she wanted him.

Yet, like him, she needed the words. "I feel it. Do you?"

"Hell, *yes*," he said fiercely and at last caught her to him and held her there, burying his face in her hair as his grip strengthened and his body became hard against her.

She made a muffled noise in her throat and turned her face up in invitation—one he had no hesitation in accepting.

This time there was no holding back. Rafe kissed her as though he'd been starving for her since they'd first met. The thought flashed across Marisa's mind, only to be immediately banished by the force of his passion, powerful and demanding and everything she wanted.

His arms tightened around her, bringing her against his hips. Responding instantly to their blatant thrust, she gasped his name as he lifted his head and looked down at her, his narrowed gaze intent and gleaming.

"I know how to shut that quick mouth of yours now," he said on a raw note.

"Don't you dare—"

Rafe laughed so deeply she felt it reverberate through her and realised with shock that nothing like this had happened before to her.

"I like to see those green eyes light up like smouldering emeralds," he murmured, his sensuous mouth an inch from hers. "What am I not to dare?"

She had to think, reassemble her thoughts from passionate confusion. "Kissing me might stop me talking, but only while it lasts," she said clumsily, pursuing this because something told her it was important.

His eyes narrowed even further. "I know that," he said quietly. "I am not your ex-husband, Marisa. I value you for the person you are."

Value. A cold, unemotional word compared to love, yet to have Rafe value her was precious. She stiffened.

Love? Stunned, she realised what she wanted.

Rafe's love...for ever.

Because somewhere, sometime, she'd fallen in love with him. How had it happened so quickly, sneaking up on her like a silent-footed predator?

Ambushed by love, she thought half-hysterically. And this was no fly-by-night passion.

Yes, she wanted Rafe, but she loved him for other things—his surprising kindness, the unyielding determination that had got them to the hut, even his intimidating authority.

Her newfound love burned deep inside her, a steady flame that would stay alive for the rest of her life. And one day, perhaps, Rafe might learn to love her. If he didn't...

For a moment she quailed, but forced herself to face the chance of a future without Rafe.

"Get that damned man out of your head," he commanded, the words hard and short.

Marisa rallied. If he didn't learn to love her, she'd cope.

But it would hurt some secret, essential part of her for the rest of her life.

Her uplifted glance told her he expected an answer. Revealing her love for him would be a humiliation she didn't think she could bear, yet she had to bite back the words. They were going into this as equals and she wanted it to stay that way. Confessing to a hopeless love might well wreck their relationship; certainly it would alter the balance of power and put her in an inferior position.

See, you don't really trust him, something cowardly and treacherous whispered at the back of her mind.

"He's not there. I value you too," she said helplessly.

He nodded, but she sensed a subtle withdrawal, an aloofness that fled when he kissed her again and that rapturous fire took her over, mind and body.

Looking around, he said, "We can't make love here. I refuse to make love to you on a sofa."

Marisa laughed huskily and tried to cover her total surrender by muttering, "I feel like a secondary-school kid in a car."

"Not my style, even then."

She wavered, feeling uncommonly like a guilty schoolgirl. He looked down at her and laughed again, and she relaxed and smiled at him. "Nor mine," she said.

"My room."

Rafe's bedroom was huge. And beautiful.

Even living amidst the gracious beauty that was Manuwai, she hadn't expected this. The house was filled with delightful things chosen over the years by people whose wealth was restrained by discernment and taste. There was no striving to impress, no overt opulence or display emphasising wealth and power.

Rafe's room was different, although she couldn't quite put a finger on it. It breathed sophistication from the huge French sleigh bed on a shallow dais, its frame glowing with the polish and loving care of at least a century, to the massive armoire on one wall and the opulent curtains and silk bedcover.

Yet it was oddly impersonal and so far from her experience she hesitated, then stopped.

"It's overwhelming, I know."

She flinched at Rafe's accurate deduction.

He continued, "Apart from the bed, my mother—my birth mother, that is—had it redecorated when she married my father. When she left he moved out, but I like the outlook so I took it over when I was eighteen or so."

Marisa swallowed. "It's very lovely."

His hand light on her arm, he turned her around so the huge bed no longer dominated her field of vision and surveyed her with an expression she couldn't read, his boldly chiselled features impassive. "I hear another *but* coming and you're right. It's expensive and over the top—like my mother, I believe."

"I love that bed," she said swiftly. "And the armoire."

"Are you having second thoughts?"

"Not about you," she said, then stopped, furious with herself. She'd vowed never to be vulnerable to another man, yet here she was, blushing like a virgin.

She swallowed and started again, trying hard to be cool and confident. "Are you and your mother in contact?"

His face could have won him a fortune at poker. "I haven't seen her since she walked out," he said distantly. "A few years ago she got in touch through a lawyer; she'd run through the money she sold me for and needed more."

Marisa opened her mouth, then cut short the impulsive words.

He answered her unspoken question. "I made her an allowance." His mouth twisted. "As much as she needs, not as much as she wanted."

Marisa thought of the boy—barely older then Keir—whose mother had walked away from him and turned into his arms, impulsively hugging him. "Do you hate her?"

"In a way it's worse—I feel nothing for her," he said levelly, pulling her closer. "I saw very little of her even when she lived here. When my father remarried several years later Jane was far more of a mother to me than the one who actually bore me." He shrugged. "You won't have to worry about a mother-in-law. Believe me, she isn't ever likely to want to establish contact."

The last word was a caress against her lips and then his mouth took hers, warmly seductive and very persuasive. Marisa went under—lost in pleasure, in excitement, in the security and sensuality of his powerful body against her.

On fire, she luxuriated in her own response as he explored her mouth and then the warm length of her throat, one hand deftly flicking open the buttons of her shirt to cup a breast. Her heart thundered in her ears, each drumbeat marking another step in her surrender.

Delight shot through her at the sinuous stroke of his fingers across the alerted tips of her breast. Like honey-eyed lightning, pleasure crackled across every cell in her body, mingling crazily with an erotic frustration that urged her to tug his shirt free.

More than anything she wanted to feel his skin against her palms, but the shirt refused to move.

Rafe kissed her again, a snatched, urgent kiss that was cut short when he straightened and in one smooth movement pulled the garment over his head.

He was magnificent—skin sheened coppery-gold over corded muscles as he tossed the shirt on to a chair and turned to face her again. Silken scrolls of hair joined in the middle of his chest, forming a line that plunged downwards. Dumbstruck, Marisa devoured the sight of him, then reached out a tentative finger and followed that line to the waistline of his trousers.

Mouth compressed, he froze. Clumsily, Marisa wrenched off her shirt and tossed it after his. Rafe's eyes narrowed and the ache in her became a demand, an insistence.

And then cold caution forced her to shut her eyes against him. She dragged in a breath too close to a sob and opened them again. "Rafe, we can't. I'm sorry—I didn't think. I'm not protected."

"I have protection," he said curtly. "Do you trust me to use it?"

"Yes." Her voice shook, but she held his eyes steadily.

"You make me feel a hundred metres tall."

Startled, she asked, "Why?"

"You forgot about it until now," he said and gave her a wry smile, "and although it might be arrogant of me, I can only assume you forgot it for the same reason I did."

Because she was too absorbed in the erotic enchantment of his love-making...

Nodding, she waited impatiently, but he didn't take the small step that separated them.

He was waiting for her to make the first move.

What should she do? Colour burned up through her skin, heated her face. She just didn't have what it took to stand there and strip off in front of him.

Silently he turned her with a light touch. She shivered at the feel of his fingers against her skin while he made short work of the clip before twisting her to face him again.

When she met his eyes it was all she could do to hide

a gasp. They blazed, fiercely hungry in a face that was all harshness, its bold planes and angles in high relief.

In a voice that told her how much restraint he was using, he said, "You are beautiful."

"I have stretch marks," she blurted.

He flung back his head and laughed, and before she had a chance to do more than bitterly regret her inane remark he swept her close to him and held her tight, one hand sweeping down to hold her against his aroused loins.

Headstrong hunger took her over. She shuddered at the power of it and even more when he slid his other hand between them, taking with it the zip on her trousers.

"I don't care about stretch marks," he said and kissed her again.

Sinking into pleasure she'd never before experienced, Marisa believed him.

He lifted her and carried her across to that huge bed, easing her down on to it and somehow managing to rid her of her last garments so that she lay naked on the silken cover. Still embarrassed, feeling far too much like some harem girl brought in for her master's pleasure, she closed her eyes under his scorching survey.

Until Rafe's voice caused them to fly open again.

"Look at me," he commanded. "There's no one else in this room but you and me, and I want you." He dropped his trousers and stood straight, splendid as a bronze statue of some ancient athlete. "Do you want me?"

"Yes," she said instantly, her voice sure and direct.

"Then there's no reason for you to worry about anything else," he said and came down beside her and kissed her, one clever, experienced hand slipping the length of her body to show her just how erotically disturbing this potent hunger could be.

Later she'd allow herself the voluptuous luxury of remembering how skilfully he'd coaxed her into wildness, caressing her skin and then covering it with kisses until an agony of need brought a muffled cry from her lips.

But while she experienced his lovemaking, she had no words to use, could only surrender to a raw passion that met and matched his until he said something short and terse beneath his breath and slid over her and into her, and then stopped, every muscle locked while she convulsed beneath and around him, her body in thrall to such transcendent ecstasy she almost sobbed as each wave took her further and further into satiation.

Until finally it shattered and she came down in the safety of his arms, gasping as she dragged air into her lungs.

When she looked up she whispered, "I'm so sorry..."

He frowned. "Why?"

"Because you haven't... I..." She exhaled and said, "I didn't know it could happen so fast." Or at all...

Not to her, anyway.

"Now I feel two hundred metres tall," he said and kissed her, this time with something like tenderness.

To Marisa's stunned astonishment his kiss summoned fire from the embers. She welcomed the slow backwards-and-forwards friction that gently, sensuously, stirred her into life once more. And this time she soared even higher, drowning in a tide of bliss, and almost immediately he followed her, his proud head flung up, skin gleaming as he took his pleasure in her.

When it was finished he held her close as she sank down to something approaching normalcy, her whole being lulled by a kind of radiance that almost made her weep, while their heartbeats slowed and synchronised.

Eventually Rafe said, "I wish you didn't have to leave, but I suppose sharing a bed with me is something we'll have to introduce Keir to slowly."

"Yes," she said, a little jolted at being recalled to real life again.

Would Rafe get tired of always having to consider her son? It should be reassuring to know that although love didn't come into this equation, he enjoyed sex with her.

The question nagged sufficiently for her to ask him.

He didn't hand her an automatic reply, but said after a moment's pause, "I've always had to consider other people—my sister, and the workers here and at the various interests I have around the world. I'm growing fond of Keir—he's a good kid." He moved slightly so he could see her face. "I won't resent him—because that's really what you're asking."

His perception was brutal but accurate. "Yes, I suppose so," she said with a rueful smile. "I'm glad."

"I'll be spending far more time at home than I have in the past," he said, still watching her.

Rafe rather prided himself on his ability to read faces, but Marisa's hid far more than it revealed.

However, he was sure of one thing. She'd enjoyed their lovemaking. Neither orgasm had been faked, not even the second one. His body stirred at the memory and he pushed back the tumble of honey-gold hair from her face and kissed her again.

She responded with gratifying enthusiasm, but he curbed his instinctive urge to take things further. Her shocked delight at her own capacity for passion hadn't escaped him, but he wasn't prepared to jeopardise her fragile trust by exhausting her.

Soon the news would get around and that could well flush David Brown out of whatever rat hole he was hiding in. Tomorrow he'd ginger up his investigator.

CHAPTER TWELVE

THE next day Marisa and Rafe told Keir that he was going to live at Waimanu for a while. Warily, Marisa watched her son absorb this, dark eyes going from one to the other.

Eventually he asked a little tentatively, "Will you be my dad then?"

"I'll always be your friend if you want me to be," Rafe said.

His words and the calm tone were perfect. Marisa let out a silent breath of relief when Keir flushed and beamed.

"Yes," he said exuberantly, adding with automatic politeness, "Please."

He gave another huge grin and high-fived—something he'd learned from his schoolmates. As Rafe bent to clap palms with him, relief gave Marisa's smile a buoyancy she hadn't felt for a long time.

"Yes, I do want to be your friend," Keir said positively. "Like Manu. He gave me half his banana the other day at school and he said I could come and play with him after school one day." He looked at his mother.

Marisa said, "One day, certainly." She didn't expect everything to be so simple, but his acceptance of the situation delighted her—overwhelming for a few minutes her fear that Keir would be hurt.

When he'd gone off to tell an already informed Nadine, Rafe looked at her. "Don't worry about him. Or his father. Even if he turns up, you and Keir will both be perfectly safe."

"How are you going to manage that?" she asked starkly.

"I have ways. By the way, I've warned the school," he said.

Marisa's head came up, and she stared indignantly at him. "I saw the principal in the street today."

"I see. I wish you had discussed it with me first."

"I should have," he agreed urbanely. "It won't happen again."

He reached for her, holding her in a grip that was firm and infinitely exciting.

"Relax," he said. "I know how independent you are—I admire you for that immensely—but let me deal with this, all right?"

Trying to relax, she said, "I'll let you get away with that this time, but don't think it will work every time."

He laughed and kissed her, and for a few precious moments she could forget everything.

Until Keir's voice intruded. "Manu said his parents kiss all the time," he announced from behind them. "Are you going to too?"

Marisa jerked, but Rafe held her in a firm grip. "Quite a lot," he said. "Why?"

Wrinkling his nose, Keir said, "'Cause it looks funny." He switched his gaze to Rafe. "Manu said you can ride like the best jockey in the world. Can you show me so I can ride too? Manu said you still have the horse that showed you how to ride."

"I have," Rafe said, releasing an intensely relieved Marisa.

Clearly her son was going to use Manu's parents as an exemplar for their relationship. Nothing of possessiveness had showed in his voice and her spirits soared.

"Sammy is too old for anyone to ride now," Rafe continued. "I'll put you up on another horse. Then if you still want to learn to ride, we can see about finding a pony for you."

While Marisa was warily digesting this, Keir bounced with excitement. "Now?"

The telephone rang and Rafe said easily, "No, not now. This is an important call and I'll take this in my office."

As he left the room Keir grumbled, "I don't like that telephone. I want to ride."

"You heard Rafe. He'll take you for a ride when he can. Let's go and see if any birds have found the feeder we made yesterday yet."

But as they went out Marisa felt a cold finger of foreboding down her spine.

It took three days for Rafe to be able to fulfil his promise, and neither he nor Marisa had been allowed to forget it.

Marisa was surprised at how well it went. That afternoon Keir had been allowed to come home on the school bus with Manu and play at his house. She'd collected him after shutting up the shop and he was still buzzing about it. However, he obeyed instantly when Rafe warned him to speak quietly because it might spook the little brown mare.

Watching a little anxiously, Marisa was impressed by Rafe's patience and expertise.

"I should know what I'm doing," he said coolly when she commented on it. "My father put me up on a horse before I could walk and I watched him teach Gina to ride."

"I have to say the horse is extremely patient." They had made love the previous night and she had not been patient at all during the two other nights. Although she tried to convince herself she was imagining things, that odd sense of disconnection was still between them, as though he was building a wall against her.

"That's why I chose her," he said. "She's very sweet-tempered."

Keir was clearly enjoying himself, frowning with concentration as he listened, and instantly obeying each of Rafe's instructions.

"He has good balance and no fear," Rafe observed when the ten minutes he'd allotted for the first lesson was over. He looked at Marisa. "Do you ride?"

"This is probably the closest I've ever been to a horse."

Rafe asked, "Are you afraid of them?"

"Only in as much as they're a lot bigger than I am and I have no idea how they think."

"If you like," he said casually, "I'll take you on as a pupil too."

It was said lightly enough, but something in his tone alerted her, adding to her creeping apprehension.

Something had definitely changed. It was too subtle for her to put a finger on, but every sense was on full alert, stretched so tight she felt light-headed. He seemed to have withdrawn, revealing nothing but the most superficial of feelings and making polite chitchat as though she were a visitor, not the woman with whom he'd made wild and uninhibited love the previous night.

Her cheeks grew warm at the memory. Now she knew just how reckless she could be, how her body could sing under his skilful hands and turn to fire...

"Marisa?"

"Oh," she said, startled. Her colour deepened and she said swiftly, "Yes, I think I would like it, thank you."

When she looked up his gaze kindled, was shielded by thick black lashes, but he said merely, "Fine. But if Keir's to have his dinner on time, it's time to go."

Later, when Keir had been put to bed, she walked along to the terrace where they normally had dinner. Rafe wasn't there, and that elusive apprehension abraded her nerves once more.

The housekeeper came in. "Ah, there you are. Rafe said to tell you he's riding and he'll be later than usual tonight. Shall I get you a drink?"

"No, thanks." Marisa paused before asking, "Where does he ride?"

"He's gone along the beach. Usually that means he needs to think through something. If you walk out to the summerhouse you'll probably see him coming back." Nadine smiled affectionately. "I think he misses playing polo. He had to give it up after his father died because he was so busy."

The summerhouse was placed to take in a view of the long sweep of the ocean beach. Cicadas shrilled their high-pitched wooing calls—like miniature buzz-saws, Marisa thought as she took up the binoculars kept there and focused them on the horse and rider in the distance. Her heart thudded when she noted great clumps of wet sand flying from the big gelding's hooves.

It couldn't be as dangerous as it looked.

And Rafe was obviously a superb horseman, moving as one with the animal. When they came closer she could see his face, purposeful and set as though he'd made a difficult decision.

She waited until horse and rider left the beach, then ambled back to the house, enjoying the scents and sounds of summer. A stray bee buzzed around her head before zooming off like a golden bullet in the sunlight towards a bush humming with other nectar-seekers.

She loved this garden. *Face it, you love everything about Manuwai—the house, the beaches, even the workers you've met so far...*

And she'd give it all up if the man who owned it decided he no longer wanted to live here.

She'd been told love was all-encompassing, and during the short time since Rafe had entered her life again, she'd learned that it was true, there were no limits to it.

How long she walked in the muted light of early evening she didn't know. Questions—most of them unanswerable—beat her bluntly like physical blows.

Was Rafe regretting their engagement? Pierced by pain, she faltered. Whatever happened, she'd deal with it. But she'd never be the same again.

And coping seemed a dreary way to spend the rest of her life.

You'd have Keir...

It hurt to admit it, but her son was no longer enough. She was a woman and Rafe had woken her to her full potential.

She stopped beside the vivid flowers of a tropical rhododendron, so blazingly golden they were incandescent in the soft light. They dazzled her eyes and brought tears to them.

Was that all it was? Sex?

No, she loved Rafe for what he was, not just because he made her feel a rapturous certainty in his arms.

And she'd had this conversation with herself before. She had to stop going obsessively over and over the same worries, the same concerns.

A sixth sense lifted the hair on the back of her neck. She swivelled and saw him watching her. Something she saw in his face brought an icy wave of fear.

"You'd better tell me," she said harshly.

If anything, his face hardened even more. "Walk with me to the summerhouse."

Once there, she met unreadable eyes, burnished and brutal as the barrel of a gun. Voice shaking, she demanded, "What is it?"

"David Brown is dead."

The words fell like bombs into the still, salt-fragrant air. *"W-what?"* she stammered, her legs shaking so much he caught her.

Only for a moment. As though he no longer wanted to touch her, he lowered her into one of the chairs and stepped back, turning slightly to look out to sea before he spoke.

"He died this afternoon on the road here." No emotion was evident in his cool, judicial tone. "You know that steep patch through bush just before you come out on to the coast? He was driving too fast to take the corner. He drove straight over the edge on to the rocks below. He'd have died instantly."

She flinched, imagining the fall—the terror and the pain. And then oblivion…

Tears burned behind her eyes. Whatever she had feared, she had never wanted this. "Thank heaven for that at least," she said unevenly. "I'm glad he didn't suffer. It's horrible to be so—so relieved, but I d-didn't want him to die. But—he was coming here?"

"No, speeding away. It looks as though he was waiting for Keir to come home in the school bus with Manu." He paused as she dragged in a sharp breath and turned blindly towards the house. Roughly he said, "It's all right, Marisa. He's still in bed, still asleep. I've just checked."

That stopped her. After a short hesitation she turned back to him and said harshly, "How do you know this?"

"I had someone keeping an eye on both you and Keir." He saw her blink at that, but she said nothing, and he went on, "Yesterday she noticed a man in a car who seemed very interested in the children leaving school. When she phoned the details through she found the vehicle had been bought by Brown in Auckland a month ago."

Struggling to control her distress, she asked, "But how did David know Keir would be on the bus today?"

Rafe quelled an instinctive desire to comfort her. Better to get the ugly truth done with first. "He was there again today, watching Keir get on to the bus with Manu. He left then and my investigator stayed with the bus, following it. When they reached Waimanu he was waiting, but as soon as he saw her drive up he took off. She followed and he took the corner too fast and went over on to the rocks."

He restrained himself from telling her that his investigator had unearthed enough information for him to be very concerned about the reappearance of David Brown.

White-faced, she stared at him, absorbing the implications. "No, that won't fit. He didn't know Keir was his son. Even if he had been, he wouldn't have been interested…" Her voice trailed away and her gaze narrowed, became accusing. "You know more than you're telling me."

She had to know sooner or later. It might as well be sooner. "The garage at the Tanners' place *was* deliberately set on fire and his car was seen on the road close by that night."

"But if he was following Keir, he must have had plans for him too," she said thinly.

"We'll never know. Possibly he was finding out where I lived so he could set fire to something else."

She refused to accept his false comfort. "But you don't believe that."

He shook his head. "I don't know. Nobody will ever know. Leave it at that."

Visibly gathering strength, Marisa straightened her shoulders. Sombrely she said, "I suppose when he found out I'd moved to Tewaka, he'd have thought I'd chosen it because you live here."

"Almost certainly." When she shivered, he said brusquely, "You realise that his death has freed you from any need to be concerned about Keir's future?"

She stared at him, her eyes too darkly shadowed for him to guess at her thoughts.

So that was it.

Marisa tried to speak but her throat was too dry. He was telling her she could go. She had to swallow before she could say, "Yes, I do." Moving carefully, like an old woman, she got to her feet. "Then I have to thank you for…for everything. Keir and I will move out as soon as I can organise it."

Stone-faced, he said, "You don't have to." He paused, then added curtly, "I'd like you to stay. But if you want to go, then of course you must."

Marisa looked away, pride fighting a losing battle with need. *Tell him,* she urged herself. *Tell him you don't want to go—then at least you'll know...*

But cowardice kept her silent.

Almost aggressively Rafe asked, "Do you want to go, Marisa?"

She stiffened her spine and looked directly at him, and took the biggest gamble of her life. "No, I do not. I want to stay here and marry you and have your children—if—"

Her voice broke on a sob.

After one short, explicit word under his breath, he grabbed her—*grabbed* her, her cool Rafe, always so self-sufficient, so confident—and hauled her against him as though he would never let her go.

"I knew I loved you when you made those conditions for our engagement," he said unsteadily.

Joy burst through her, a nova of delight and relief and pleasure. Trembling, she asked, "Why? I thought they'd put you off."

He didn't kiss her. Instead his arms clamped around her and he said unsteadily in a raw, formidable voice, "You were prepared to set me free without any recriminations if I met someone I could love and I thought, *I've already met her.* Before that I wanted you—your eyes caught my attention in Mariposa and when I saw you again I got a shock of recognition, as though I've been marking time since then, waiting for you."

"I know," she whispered, filled with a joy so palpable she felt she could fly. "Oh, yes, I know exactly how you felt—it was just like that for me too."

Eyes kindling, he looked down into her face. "But I had no idea how *much* I loved you until I heard of Brown's death. I've been through hell, afraid you'd leave once you knew any danger to Keir was over." He took in a sharp, impeded breath. "Damn it, Marisa, how do you feel about me? I need the words."

"I love you, of course. Surely you must know that?" she cried. "I think I must have started to love you when we met in Mariposa—before then I'd been that drab, miserable shell of a woman, but you arrived like a storm—like rain after drought. I'd been so passive, so—so *useless*—and somehow—by just being *you*— you forced me to realise that if I wanted to get away, I had to fight for it. And I did. I told David that I was going home whether he wanted me to or not."

"And you did," he said with immense satisfaction and at long last bent his head and kissed her.

Later that night, lying in Rafe's arms, she thought dreamily that she was where she belonged. Her parents had loved her, but they'd wanted a daughter like them, a gypsy at heart, and David had tried to force her to become whatever he'd wanted...

She hoped he'd found peace at last.

As she had. Along with passion and laughter and the sweet torment of love, she had found a home. Rafe was everything she'd wanted without even realising it and he accepted her as she was; with him she could be her true self.

"Going to sleep?" His voice was rough and tender at the same time. "When are you going to marry me?"

She yawned and turned over and kissed his shoulder. "How soon can we get married?" she murmured.

Rafe laughed, the low, triumphant laugh of a lover. "We can probably get married within a month." He paused, and then said in a voice she'd never heard before, "I've been so sure I could never lose my head over a woman, that I simply didn't have it in me to fall in love, and then you moved in and I fell before I understood what the hell had hit me."

"You and me both," she told him with love and a sense of utter commitment, and ran her hand down his chest.

"I love you," he said deeply. "I'll love you for the rest of my life."

"And I love you and always will."

Their wedding would come in time, but both knew those words marked their pledge to each other.

Rafe kissed her, murmuring against her mouth, "Tired?"

"I thought I was," she purred, running her hand across his chest, "but I seem to have new lease of life…"

He smiled. "Me too."

And together, confidently, they embarked on their future.

* * * * *

MILLS & BOON®

Why shop at millsandboon.co.uk?

Each year, thousands of romance readers find their perfect read at millsandboon.co.uk. That's because we're passionate about bringing you the very best romantic fiction. Here are some of the advantages of shopping at www.millsandboon.co.uk:

* **Get new books first**—you'll be able to buy your favourite books one month before they hit the shops

* **Get exclusive discounts**—you'll also be able to buy our specially created monthly collections, with up to 50% off the RRP

* **Find your favourite authors**—latest news, interviews and new releases for all your favourite authors and series on our website, plus ideas for what to try next

* **Join in**—once you've bought your favourite books, don't forget to register with us to rate, review and join in the discussions

Visit **www.millsandboon.co.uk**
for all this and more today!

MILLS & BOON®

Why not subscribe?

Never miss a title and save money too!

Here's what's available to you if you join the exclusive **Mills & Boon® Book Club** today:

✦ *Titles up to a month ahead of the shops*
✦ *Amazing discounts*
✦ *Free P&P*
✦ *Earn Bonus Book points that can be redeemed against other titles and gifts*
✦ *Choose from monthly or pre-paid plans*

Still want more?

Well, if you join today, we'll even give you
50% OFF your first parcel!

So visit **www.millsandboon.co.uk/subs**
to be a part of this exclusive Book Club!

MILLS & BOON®
By Request

RELIVE THE ROMANCE WITH THE BEST OF THE BEST

A sneak peek at next month's titles...

In stores from 7th April 2016:

- **His Most Exquisite Conquest** – Elizabeth Power, Cathy Williams & Robyn Donald

- **Stop The Wedding!** – Lori Wilde

In stores from 21st April 2016:

- **Bedded by the Boss** – Jennifer Lewis, Yvonne Lindsay & Joan Hohl

- **Love Story Next Door!** – Rebecca Winters, Barbara Wallace & Soraya Lane

Available at WHSmith, Tesco, Asda, Eason, Amazon and Apple

Just can't wait?
Buy our books online a month before they hit the shops!
visit www.millsandboon.co.uk

These books are also available in eBook format!